D0422496

BILLY SURE

· KID ENTREPRENEUR ·

4 BOOKS IN 1!

INVENTED BY **LUKE SHARPE**

DRAWINGS BY **GRAHAM ROSS**

Simon Spotlight

New York London Toronto Sydney New Delhi

This book is a work of fiction. Any references to historical events, real people, or real places are used fictitiously. Other names, characters, places, and events are products of the author's imagination, and any resemblance to actual events or places or persons, living or dead, is entirely coincidental.

SIMON SPOTLIGHT

An imprint of Simon & Schuster Children's Publishing Division

1230 Avenue of the Americas, New York, New York 10020

This Simon Spotlight bind-up edition December 2016

Billy Sure Kid Entrepreneur, Billy Sure Kid Entrepreneur and the Stink Spectacular,
Billy Sure Kid Entrepreneur and the Cat-Dog Translator, Billy Sure Kid Entrepreneur and
the Best Test © 2015 by Simon & Schuster, Inc.

Text by David Lewman and Michael Teitelbaum. Illustrations by Graham Ross.

All rights reserved, including the right of reproduction in whole or in part in any form. SIMON SPOTLIGHT and colophon are registered trademarks of Simon & Schuster, Inc. For information about special discounts for bulk purchases, please contact Simon & Schuster Special Sales at 1-866-506-1949 or business@simonandschuster.com.

Series designed by Jay Colvin. The text of this book was set in Minya Nouvelle.

Manufactured in the United States of America 1116 FFG

10 9 8 7 6 5 4 3 2

Library of Congress Control Number is available from the Library of Congress.

ISBN 978-1-4814-9691-9

ISBN 978-1-4814-3949-7 (*Billy Sure Kid Entrepreneur* eBook)

ISBN 978-1-4814-3952-7 (*Billy Sure Kid Entrepreneur and the Stink Spectacular* eBook)

ISBN 978-1-4814-4763-8 (*Billy Sure Kid Entrepreneur and the Cat-Dog Translator* eBook)

ISBN 978-1-4814-4766-9 (*Billy Sure Kid Entrepreneur and the Best Test* eBook)

These titles were previously published individually by Simon Spotlight.

Contents

AND THE STINK SPECTACULAR

AND THE CAT-DOG TRANSLATOR

AND THE BEST TEST

Chapter One

Backstage at Better Than Sleeping!

I'M BILLY SURE. YOU'VE PROBABLY HEARD OF ME.
Wait, that sounds weird, like "Who is this kid and why does he think I've heard of him?" But it's not like that. I mean, I'm not like that. And you probably weren't thinking that anyway because . . . well, like I said, you've probably heard of me. Because I'm *that* Billy Sure, the famous kid entrepreneur, inventor, and CEO of **SURE THINGS, INC.** At the moment I am also the kid who is sitting on a blue couch in a plain little room backstage at the **Better Than Sleeping!** show.

Maybe you will see me on the show tonight, if your parents let you stay up that late on a school night. (If not, maybe you can watch it in your room with the sound turned way down. Just don't get caught—I don't want to be the kid who gets your TV taken away!)

"You're bouncing your legs," Manny tells me. Manny Reyes is my best friend. He is also the chief financial officer of Sure Things, Inc., which is just a fancy way of saying he likes crunching numbers and has a really smart head for business.

I didn't even realize I was doing it. I look at my legs. Reason #35 why Manny is the greatest CFO: He is always right. My knees are definitely bouncing like Ping-Pong balls on a trampoline.

"Don't do that when you're onstage," Manny continues. "It makes you look nervous. Don't pick your nose, either. Or burp. Or throw up. Definitely don't throw up."

"But I *am* nervous. I might throw up," I say.

Manny gets a puzzled look on his face. "Why? You've been on TV before."

"Just the local news. This is national TV. Millions of people will be watching!"

Manny grins. "Exactly. This is a fantastic marketing opportunity. So don't blow it!"

"Way to make me less nervous," I reply, grabbing my knees in an attempt to stop my bouncing legs.

My dad leans forward. He's sitting at the other end of the blue couch. "You'll do great, Billy. We're proud of you. I just wish your mother could be here."

My mom travels a ton, as a scientist doing research for the government. I don't know much more than that. She's been on assignment for a while now, but she knows all about what's been going on with me because we e-mail a lot.

"Why do *I* have to be here?" my sister, Emily, moans. She hasn't looked up from her cell phone in three hours. "I'm bored, hungry, and thirsty."

"I couldn't just leave you at home while we

came to New York, Emily. That'd be illegal," replies my dad.

"I'm fourteen!" she argues, keeping her eyes on her phone. "And very mature for my age. I'm perfectly capable of taking care of myself!"

"Sure you are, Ninja Spider," I taunt her. Lately Emily wears only black. Black shirts, black pants, black shoes, black everything. That's why I've nicknamed her Ninja Spider.

Emily finally looks up from her phone to glare at me. She wipes her blond bangs out of her face. Everyone says we look alike, which is weird because she's a girl. She notices my legs are bouncing again, despite my best efforts to stop them.

"A kangaroo called. He wants his legs back," she says.

Before I can think of a comeback, a can of soda appears in front of Emily's face. "Soda?" someone asks. "I heard you say you were

THE SODA

thirsty. In the room across the hall there's a fridge full of free drinks. Stuff to eat, too. Chips. Candy. Fruit, if you're feeling healthy."

Emily, being in a classic Emily mood, takes in a deep breath. I know her well enough to know that when she exhales, she'll snap that she doesn't want a soda; she wants to go home. But before she speaks, she looks up and sees who is holding the can in front of her.

DUSTIN PEELER!

I'm sure you know who Dustin Peeler is too. (See? I don't just say that about myself. Not that I think I'm as famous as Dustin Peeler.) In case you don't know, Dustin Peeler is the most popular teen musician on the planet at the

moment. He can sing. He can dance. He can walk on his hands. He can play guitar, piano, drums, English horn, and didgeridoo—upside down. And according to Emily, he is the most gorgeous human being who ever graced the earth with his presence.

Dustin Peeler smiles his perfect smile, teeth glistening like ocean waves on a sunny day. Emily's mouth drops open, her jaw practically scraping the floor. "Thank you," she manages to squeak out as she takes the can of soda. Her knees begin to shake.

"No problem," he replies.

"Now who's part kangaroo?" I whisper, pointing discreetly to Emily's shaking knees.

But Emily ignores me. She still can't take her eyes off Dustin.

I try again. My sister is seriously making a fool of herself, and I feel like it's my duty to let her know. "Emily," I whisper a little louder this time. "You look really dumb with your mouth hanging open like that!"

And then Dustin Peeler notices me for the

first time. "Hey, you're the All Ball dude! That thing is awesome!"

"Thanks," I say.

An assistant sticks her head in. "Dustin, we're ready to do your hair."

"But his hair is already perfect," Emily says like she's in a trance.

"Oh, they're just doing their jobs," Dustin says, smiling another dazzling smile. "Have fun out there!" He gives us a double thumbs-up and leaves. Emily resumes breathing.

"Who was that?" Dad asks.

Emily sighs.

"He said the All Ball was awesome," Manny says. "Maybe we could get him to do an endorsement of some kind. Or even write us a jingle!" Quietly singing, "All Ball, All Ball . . . the only ball you'll ever need," Manny pulls out his phone and taps a note to himself.

I told you Manny has a great head for business. He has a ton of brilliant ideas about how to sell Sure Things, Inc.'s products. Without Manny, I wouldn't have a business, just a bedroom full of inventions. And dirty laundry. And a few hidden candy bars (okay, maybe dozens).

Emily pulls out her phone again and immediately starts texting all her friends that Dustin Peeler just handed her a can of soda. She even texts a picture of the can. "I'm keeping this can forever," she announces.

"Be sure to rinse it out," Dad says.

I guess it was cool to meet Dustin Peeler. I've never bought any of his songs, but I've certainly heard them. But I am much more excited about the other guest on **Better Than Sleeping!** tonight. Manny spots him first, standing out in the hallway.

"Hey," he says. "Isn't that the baseball player you like? Carl Somebody? The shortstop?"

"Like" is a slight understatement.

Carl Bourette has been my favorite athlete since I was in kindergarten. I have every Carl Bourette baseball card. Carl Bourette bobbleheads. A nearly life-size poster of Carl

Bourette, hanging on my door. I know all his stats. His favorite kind of bat. What he puts on his burgers.

My brain is screaming, "CARL BOURETTE!"

But my mouth is saying nothing. My jaw is hanging open, but no words are coming out. Possibly a little drool, but no words.

"Might want to lift your jaw off the floor, genius," Emily suggests.

Then Carl Bourette notices me staring at him. Instead of getting as far away as possible from the weird kid with the staring problem, he smiles and starts walking over to me.

"Hi," he says, shaking my hand. "I'm Carl Bourette."

"Billy Sure," I manage to murmur.

Carl nods. "That's what I thought. You invented the All Ball, right?"

Now it's my turn to nod. "Yes," I say. "I did."
I seem to be limited to one-syllable words and
two-word sentences.

"I agreed to do the show tonight because
they told me you were going to be on it," he
says, chuckling.

WHAT?!

"Man, that All Ball is great!" Carl continues enthusiastically. "My kids love it! Heck,
my *teammates* love it! We've got one in the locker
room!"

DOUBLE WHAT?!

I can practically see Manny's eyes turn into
dollar signs. He whips out his phone and taps
another note to himself.

"Thank you," I croak, keeping to my one-
syllable, two-word rule for talking to Carl
Bourette.

Carl reaches into his jacket pocket and
pulls out a pen and notepad. "I'm sorry to do
this, but would you mind signing an autograph
for my kids? They'll be so excited I met you!"

Carl Bourette just asked *me* for *my* autograph?

What kind of bizarre, backward world am I living in? What next? Emily asking for my opinion on her outfit?

"Sure," I reply. "You got it." Three words in one sentence! A new record for talking to Carl Bourette!

I sign a shaky autograph on the notepad and hand it back to him. "Thanks!" he says. "I really appreciate it."

Before my head can explode, the assistant hurries back into the room. "Billy, we're ready to do your hair."

Carl laughs. "Bet you thought you knew how to do your own hair. Welcome to being famous!"

Chapter Two

Catch!

NOW I'M STANDING NEXT TO THE CURTAIN, WAITING to walk out onto the set of *Better Than Sleeping!*, where I will be interviewed by the host, Chris Fernell.

In my hands I am holding a carrying case. Make that "in my very sweaty hands." I'm really nervous. I can't help it.

Behind me another assistant places his hand on my shoulder. I have no idea why. All I know is that I'm supposed to enter when Chris Fernell says my name.

"Please give a warm welcome to Billy Sure,

APPLAUSE

kid entrepreneur!" I hear from onstage.

As the studio audience applauds, the assistant gives me a little shove to start me walking. Maybe some people get so nervous they freeze.

I walk out onto the set, remembering to smile. I don't know if you've ever been on a television set before, but it's *bright*. Also, the furniture seems smaller than it looks on TV. In fact, the whole set seems kind of small. And there are big cameras pointing right at me. *Now would be a really terrible time to trip,* I tell my feet.

Chris Fernell shakes my hand and motions for me to sit in the chair next to his desk. I have never understood why TV hosts need desks. Do they have homework they need to work on during the commercials?

"So you invented the All Ball, and now this

thing is huge!" Chris begins. "How old are you, Billy?"

"Twelve," I say. "Thirteen next March."

"Twelve years old!" Chris marvels. "When I was twelve, I was just playing video games. And not complicated video games. Simple games. You know, like, 'click on the door to open it.'"

The audience laughs. I don't think what he said was very funny, but it seems weird not to laugh, so I do. *You need to work on your fake laugh,* I tell my mouth. *That didn't sound very good.*

"When did you invent the All Ball, Billy?" Chris asks. He seems genuinely interested. Of course, that is his job.

I explain that I actually came up with the idea for the All Ball last year in sixth grade, but I had trouble figuring out exactly how to make it work. But then at the very beginning of the summer, the trouble all went away and it came together. (At least, that's what I tell him. The real story is much more complicated than that. But I won't be telling any of that to

Chris Fernell.) Instead I talk about how Manny started a company with me called Sure Things, Inc., and we found a manufacturing company to make the product.

"The product," Chris repeats, smiling. "I love that! You're twelve years old and you've got a product! Can we see it?"

The audience applauds again. I open my case. "Here it is," I say, bringing out two All Balls. "It comes in two sizes: large and small. Wanna play?"

The only ball you'll
ever need.

The audience whoops and cheers. They want to see Chris play. "Sure!" he says. "Let's do it!"

"Great. Let's start with soccer," I say. Then without anyone seeing, I press a button on a remote and the All Ball turns into a soccer ball.

We walk over to the side of the stage, toward the band, where two goals have been set up. I set the small ball aside and toss the larger All Ball to Chris. "How does it feel?"

"Like a perfectly normal soccer ball," he says. Then he drops it on the ground and kicks it toward me. I kick it back. Chris works the ball with his feet a little, but lets me steal the ball and kick it into the net. "GOAL!" Chris shouts. More applause.

"Okay, now what if you wanted to play volleyball?" I say.

"I love volleyball," Chris says. "But we need a different ball."

"No, we don't," I say, taking a small remote control out of my pocket. "That's the beauty of the All Ball."

I press a button on the remote. And the ball changes from a soccer ball to a volleyball. Just like that.

"That is amazing!" Chris yells. We hit the ball back and forth. "Incredible! It's exactly like a volleyball! How did you do that?"

"I'm afraid the ball-morphing technology is patented, proprietary, and top secret," I say, using all the terms that Manny has coached me on. I gesture toward the basketball hoop set up on the stage. "I see you've got a basketball hoop."

"Why, yes we do!" Chris says, hamming it up. "If *only* we had a basketball!"

I press a different button on the remote, and the volleyball in Chris's hands starts turning into a basketball. It grows. The seams move. The surface changes. And the ball turns orange.

The audience loves it. Chris dribbles the ball and shoots a layup, which he makes. The crowd *really* goes wild at that one.

"Okay," Chris says. "This All Ball is, like,

the most amazing thing I've ever seen. Soccer ball to volleyball to basketball, unbelievable. But I've got to ask, what if I want to play football? No way, right?"

"Actually, way," I say, pressing another button on the remote control unit. With a kind of **ZZZWOOP** sound, the basketball shapes itself into a football.

Chris stares at the football. "Okay, now you're freaking me out. How? Huh? *What?*"

As Chris tosses the football to the drummer in his band, I remember another one of the things Manny told me to say. "The large All Ball eliminates the need to buy and haul around five different balls. Now you just have to buy one."

The drummer tosses the football back to Chris. Tossing it from one hand to the other, he turns back to me. "Hold it," he says. "I'm no mathematician, but I'm pretty sure you've only shown us four balls—soccer ball, volleyball, basketball, and football. What's the fifth ball?"

I aim the remote control. I don't mean to time it this way, but I hit the button just as Chris tosses the football into the air, ready to catch it in his other hand. **Zzzwoop!** In midair, the large All Ball morphs from a football into a bowling ball. "Catch!" I call out.

Naturally, Chris isn't prepared to catch a sixteen-pound bowling ball, and drops it. **Clonk!** Luckily, the bowling ball doesn't land on his foot.

I let out a sigh of relief. I totally don't want to be that guy who goes on TV and injures the host. Chris looks up at me in surprise and then starts cracking up. The audience roars with

1+1+1+1+1=5?

laughter, and then breaks into a long round of applause.

It is cool. No, it is awesome. I look around and have trouble believing that this is really my life.

"Can I try one of those? Maybe the small one?" someone asks.

It's Carl Bourette! He appeared on the show earlier, but now he's walking back onstage! The audience starts cheering even louder!

"Hey, Billy," he calls. "Toss me that other All Ball!"

Carl Bourette remembered my name! He just said it out loud! On television!

I run back to my seat, grab the small All Ball, turn it into a baseball, and toss it to Carl. I'm no pitcher, but luckily it goes right to him. "Nice!" he says, tossing the ball up with one hand and catching it in the other.

"Get out your remote," he continues. "And zap it just as I toss this to Chris. Ready, Chris?"

"It's not going to change into another bowling ball, is it?" Chris asks, pretending to be nervous.

"Here it comes!" Carl says, throwing the ball at Chris.

I hit the remote. **Zwoink!** The baseball turns into a hockey puck midair! Chris catches it and holds it up over his head in triumph.

"Looks like I'm missing all the fun," someone else says. The audience starts going nuts. I look to see Dustin Peeler strolling onto the stage.

So I, Chris Fernell, Carl Bourette, and Dustin Peeler play catch, changing the small All Ball from baseball to hockey puck to tennis ball to golf ball to Ping-Pong ball.

When Chris gets a signal that we are out of time, he puts his arm around me and shouts, "Billy Sure and the All Ball!" As the audience applauds, my dad, Emily, and Manny come out onstage to join me. Chris introduces them as my family, so everyone probably thinks Manny is my brother, which is fine with me.

On the plane ride home, everybody tells me what a great job I did on **Better Than Sleeping!** and how well it went, and how we are going to sell a zillion more All Balls. I feel happy, but I'm also nervous.

Does that ever happen to you, where you feel two emotions at once? It's very complicated. How can you be happy and nervous at the same time? I don't know the answer to that, but I guess it's better than feeling happy and nauseated at the same time. Nervous and nauseated would be really terrible. I'm not so nervous that I feel nauseated, but I'm pretty close.

Why am I so nervous, you might be wondering? Tomorrow I start seventh grade. I'm a tiny bit nervous about that. But that's not it.

I have a secret about the All Ball that nobody knows, not even Manny.

And that secret has me feeling *really* nervous.

Chapter Three

Seventh Grade Begins

ALL SUMMER I FIGURED THAT THINGS WOULD BE A LITTLE different when school started, but as soon as I walk into the building, I realize just how different.

Some kids stare at me. Some point. Some act like they aren't looking at me, but their eyes dart in my direction. I hear kids whispering, "That's him!"

One tall guy I don't know yells, "Hey, Sure! Can I borrow a million dollars?" His friends laugh.

It is really weird. In sixth grade, Manny

and I were just regular kids, floating under the radar, trying not to get stuffed into lockers by the older kids. But now under the radar is totally over.

I find my locker and spin the lock, when a group of girls comes up to me. "You're Billy Sure?" one of them asks. I know her name. It's Allison. She was in my math class last year.

I nod my head.

"We saw you on that show," Allison says.

"Oh, great," I respond, not knowing what else to say.

"What's he like?" another girl asks a little breathlessly.

"Who?" I ask. "Chris Fernell? He's really nice."

The girl rolls her eyes. "No, not him. Dustin."

"Um, he seemed nice," I say, trying to remember something interesting about Dustin Peeler. "He gave my sister a soda."

The girls squeal with delight. "That is so Dustin!" Allison shrieks. "He cares so much!"

"If Dustin Peeler gave me a soda, I think I'd just die right on the spot," another girl says.

"And I'd never drink it," another adds. "I'd just keep it forever."

"It'd go flat," I say. "And it might get moldy."

The girls laugh like this is the funniest thing they've ever heard.

"He's cute," one of the girls whispers to her friends. "Almost as cute as Dustin." Then all the girls erupt into giggles.

Well, that's a first for me. I've never been called cute by a girl before. Except my mom, and she doesn't really count. I can feel my cheeks tingling and I know I'm blushing.

Lucky for me, the bell rings. **Brrrring!** The girls hurry off. "See you, Billy!" they call back to me as they go.

I round the corner to my homeroom before the second bell rings. It isn't hard to find, because there is a colorful banner hanging over the door that reads WELCOME, BILLY SURE!

Have you ever wished that the floor could

open up and swallow you, because you're so embarrassed? Yeah, that's exactly how I feel.

But the floor is not cooperating today, so I have no choice but to go to homeroom. It seems like everyone had been waiting for me to get here. When I walk in, a kid shouts, "He's here!" And then everyone starts clapping. I even hear someone whistle. I think it's Peter MacHale. He has a huge space between his two front teeth that he always tries to use to his advantage. You should see what he can do with bendy straws. My homeroom teacher, Mrs. Welch, smiles. "Congratulations on all your success over the summer, Billy! And welcome to my class!"

"Um, thanks," I mumble, and then I find a seat in the back of the room, wishing the whole time that Manny was in my homeroom. He would know how to handle this. But unfortunately we're in different homerooms this year. We don't even have any classes together. At least I have lunch to look forward to.

"Before we get started," Mrs. Welch says after I sit down, "I know we're all curious about the incredible summer Billy has had. Perhaps he'd like to tell us a little bit about his adventures as an inventor and a businessperson."

She smiles again and raises her eyebrows. Kids twist around in their seats, waiting for me to say something.

"Um, it's been pretty amazing," I say, because I can tell she wouldn't be happy if I said what I was thinking, which is, *No, thanks, I'm good just sitting here.* Mrs. Welch bobs her head up and down, and I realize I'm expected to say more. "Um, it's all kind of a jumble in my head. Maybe I could think about it and tell you some stuff later. Like, in a week or two. Or maybe a month."

Mrs. Welch looks a little disappointed, but she doesn't lose the smile. "That sounds fine, Billy." Not wanting to miss a potential teaching moment, she adds, "Preparation is a vital part of public speaking."

I hope that Mrs. Welch will be the only teacher who knows about the All Ball. Or at least the only teacher who makes a big deal out of it.

If only I could be that lucky. My first period is science, and it becomes clear pretty quickly that the teacher, Mr. Palnacchio, wants to talk about the All Ball too. We're barely settled into our seats when he tells us that we're going to start off the year with a unit on inventions. At first I think, *Cool, I should do really well on this unit.* And then as he talks more, I realize exactly what that means. "The very essence of science is curiosity. Discovery. Invention. But it's challenging. It takes a lot of hard work. So

it's not often that you get to meet a successful inventor face to face," Mr. Palnacchio says
dramatically, beaming at me.

UH-OH.

"But we're lucky today, class, because we
have an extremely successful inventor right
here in our own little science lab—Billy Sure!"
He gestures toward me with an open palm, and
I realize that, once again, I am expected to say
something. But this time my mind goes completely blank. So I do the only thing I can think
of: I duck my head down and pretend to be
really interested in some graffiti on my desk.
After a few awkward moments of silence, Mr.
Palnacchio seems to take the hint. "Well, more
on that later, right, Billy?" he booms. "I have
an idea I'll discuss with you right after class."

When the bell rings at the end of the period,
I jump up to hurry to my next class, hoping
Mr. Palnacchio forgot that he said he wanted
to talk to me. But no such luck. He intercepts
me at the door. "I was thinking we could plan
the semester around an investigation of the

All Ball and how it works. We could cover mechanics, physics, even the chemistry of the materials and how they change! The students would love it! And for coteaching the class with me, you'd get lots of extra credit! What do you think, Billy?"

Think of a nice way to say no, I tell my brain. "It's an interesting idea, Mr. Palnacchio," I say slowly. "And you're right; there's some cool science behind the invention of the All Ball. . . ."

I take a breath. Mr. Palnacchio seems to be hanging on my every word, and the look on his face reminds me of the look my dog, Philo, gets on his face when he sees me reach into his treats jar. *You need to get to the "no" part,* I remind my brain.

". . . But I'm afraid the ball-morphing technology is patented, proprietary, and top secret," I say, thankful once again for Manny and his great ideas. "If I teach the class how it works, I'd get in a lot of trouble with the lawyers. And my business partner."

Mr. Palnacchio's face falls, and he nods. "Yes, that makes sense. I understand that you can't reveal your secrets." Then he brightens. "But think about it! I'm sure there's a way you could teach some of the general principles you've mastered without giving any secrets away!"

"Okay, Mr. Palnacchio. I will think about it," I promise, but not because I really want to. Right now I just want to leave. "Can I get to my next class now?"

As I jog down the hallway, I see a kid at the other end of the hall coming straight toward me. He locks eyes with me.

He's a big kid. A really big kid.

I think about turning around and going the other way, but the huge guy is already right in front of me. With those long legs, the entire hallway is only about three steps for him.

"You Billy Sure?" he snarls.

I consider making up a fake name on the spot, like McCallister Snifferton.

I look around for help. The hall is empty. Where is everyone?

"Yeah," I admit. "I'm Billy Sure."

"The guy that invented the All Ball?" he growls in his low, bearlike voice.

I nod, wondering if I will be able to block his punches with my backpack.

Maybe this bully is a mind reader, because right then he reaches into *his* backpack. What is he going to pull out? A rock? A club? Nunchucks?

No. He pulls out an All Ball.

"Would you mind signing this for me?" he asks.

A wave of relief washes over me. "Of course not!" I squeak as I pull a pen out of my pocket. "Who should I make it out to?"

"Dudley. Dudley Dillworthy," he says.

He takes his signed All Ball and runs off to class.

By the time I get to lunch, I am wishing I'd asked Dudley to be my bodyguard. In the cafeteria, kids mob around me and Manny, asking us to sit with them. The table we end up at is so crowded, there is barely any room to sit. I have never felt so much pressure eating before. With everyone staring at me, I have to be careful with every bite. I'm usually the last one to know when I have mustard on my nose or poppy seeds in my teeth. As a best friend, it's Manny's job to tell me these things, but he never notices. Right now he's huddled over his phone, probably making some new business deal for the All Ball.

"Hey, Sure," one of the boys at my table blurts out. His name is Jeff. I look down at my shirt, thinking that Jeff is going to tell me that I'm wearing some applesauce.

"How much money do you have?" Jeff asks.

A hush comes over the cafeteria as everyone waits for my answer, even the cafeteria ladies. I see one of them pause with a big ladle in her hand, waiting until after I speak to finish slopping soup in a bowl.

"I don't really know," I admit. "For now, most of the money goes right back into the company. When a company's new, there are lots of expenses. My parents are handling any money that comes to me, putting it in a bank account for college."

I hear sighs. I see frowns. Nobody likes this answer. It's boring, but it's the truth.

"But I heard you carry, like, a thousand bucks in your wallet," Jeff claims.

"I heard ten thousand," shouts someone else.

I shake my head. "I don't think a thousand bucks would fit in my wallet. I don't really know. I've never seen a thousand dollars."

Then everyone in the cafeteria starts arguing about whether a thousand dollars would fit in a wallet, and whether there is a one-thousand-dollar bill. A sixth grader boasts that she held one in her hands, and then her friends tell her that she's a big liar. Which is good, because it takes the attention away from me for a couple of minutes.

I finish my lunch as fast as I can and get out of there.

In English the teacher assigns an essay on "WHAT I INVENTED THIS SUMMER." In social studies the teacher suggests we discuss "the economics of sports, especially new sports technologies." In gym the teacher pulls me aside and asks if Sure Things, Inc. could donate a bunch of All Balls to the school. "It'd really help us out," he pleads. "The budget cuts have been brutal! When we need new nets for the basketball hoops, my wife has to knit them!"

Late that afternoon there's an announcement. "Will Billy Sure please report to the principal's office?"

Why do they always summon you to the principal's office in the form of a question? Are you allowed to say no? *Sorry, but I really can't come to the principal's office right now. Or ever.*

I reluctantly trudge down to the office. I wonder what I did wrong. Am I going to be suspended for disrupting classes with my fame? Given detention for inspiring the teachers to give us crazy assignments?

When I walk in, the secretary behind the counter smiles at me and says, "Hi, Billy. Mr. Gilamon is waiting for you."

It seems like a good sign that the secretary smiled at me, right? I mean, would she smile at a kid who was about to get detention? Unless that's part of her job. Maybe they tell her she has to smile at everyone who comes in, even the kids who are in REALLY BIG TROUBLE.

But when I enter Mr. Gilamon's office, he shoots up out of his chair, steps around his desk, and shakes my hand, smiling broadly. "Billy Sure! Congratulations on your success! Well done!"

"Thanks," I mumble. "Um, am I in trouble?"

Mr. Gilamon gives a big hearty laugh. "No! Just the opposite! From what I hear, you're in the catbird's seat!"

I have no idea what that means, but as long as it doesn't mean "detention," I'm okay with it.

Motioning for me to have a seat (not a catbird's, just a regular seat), the principal sits back down in his big chair. "Billy, I think what you've done, inventing the, uh . . . what's it called?"

"The All Ball."

"Right! The All Ball! Inventing the All Ball, and starting your own company, and having so much success, is incredibly inspirational. It's just the kind of thing we need here at Fillmore Middle School to inspire our students. And future students! Just think, someday students will say, 'Billy Sure went to my school!'"

I hadn't thought of that. That is pretty cool.

Mr. Gilamon makes a little tent with his fingers. "I want to make sure every student in this school is aware of your inspiring achievement. It could spark a tidal wave of excellence!"

I'm not sure how a tidal wave could start with a spark, but I don't point that out to the principal.

"Now, Billy, let me ask you something," he continues. "When's your birthday?"

I didn't see that coming. Does he want to buy me a present?

"March twenty-eighth," I reply. "Why?" I suddenly think of something horrible. "You're not going to make me skip a grade, are you? Because I really don't want to."

He laughs his booming laugh again. "No, no! I just had an idea that we'd make your birthday a special holiday here at Fillmore Middle School."

"You mean we'd get the day off?" I ask. That'd be pretty sweet. Everyone would love me for that.

"Uh, no, not that kind of holiday," he says quickly.

What's the point of having a holiday if you can't get a day off from school for it?

"This would be a celebration of your birthday, honoring your achievement and inspiring other kids to reach for their own dreams!" he says enthusiastically. He looks up at the calendar on his wall, which has a picture of a guy climbing a mountain, and adds "Do what you've always dreamed of doing." That makes me think of swinging so high that I loop around the swing set. I've dreamed of doing that since kindergarten. I've never even gotten close. It

might not be possible, but I'll keep trying until I'm too big to sit on a swing.

I look up at Mr. Gilamon. He's still talking. "But March is a long way off. I was hoping we could inspire the students right at the beginning of the school year. You wouldn't consider changing your birthday, would you?"

I don't know what to say, so I open my mouth. Maybe something will come out and surprise me. I make an "uh" sound. Principal Gilamon laughs as though I'd made the most hilarious joke he'd ever heard.

"Well, maybe we could have a celebration

that wasn't actually on your birthday," he says. "BILLY SURE DAY!"

I don't think I really needed *more* attention at school. "How about just calling it Invention Day?" I suggest. "Or Achievement Day? Or Reach For Your Dreams Day?"

Mr. Gilamon grabs a pad and a pen and starts writing furiously. "Those are all great suggestions!" he says. "Billy, you're full of ideas! No wonder you're so successful!"

When the last bell of the day rings, I launch out of my seat so fast that my math teacher gives me a look. I smile apologetically as I bolt out the door. The first day of seventh grade has been really strange, but at least it's over.

"So, how was the rest of your day?" Manny asks as we head out the door together.

I shrug. Where do I even start?

Manny smiles. "You can tell me all about it at the office."

Chapter Four

The Office

THE OFFICE OF SURE THINGS, INC. ISN'T IN SOME TALL building downtown. It's the garage at Manny's house. His parents generously let us take it over to use as the headquarters of Sure Things, Inc.

Maybe Manny's parents are willing to park their cars on the street because Manny's an only child. He gets away with a lot more than I do. Plus he doesn't have to deal with Emily. On some days, I really envy him. Make that most days.

It used to be just a regular garage—car smell,

oil stains on the floor, dark—but since the All Ball took off, we've made a lot of changes. Sure, there's normal office stuff, which is kinda boring, but I think Manny really likes what he picked out for chairs, lamps, and computers. But what I love about the office are the extras. It's the kind of hideout I always dreamed of having, and now I have it, which is pretty cool.

There's a state-of-the-art soda machine with a digital display that lets you mix custom flavors. Manny once calculated how many possible flavors there are. I forget the exact total he came up with, but I'm pretty sure it was in the millions. Although most of the combinations are things you'd probably never want to drink, like PICKLE-GRAPE-BANANA-COLA. Actually, now that I think about it, I kind of want to taste that flavor. *Remember to try that flavor sometime,* I tell my brain. The machine even has a mystery flavor. We still haven't figured out what it is.

Then, to go with your soda, there's pizza. We have this machine that dispenses hot slices.

Enter the toppings you want, press a button, and a perfectly cooked slice of hot pizza comes sliding out. And like our soda machine, Manny and I made sure there are some crazy flavor combos. You can put chocolate chips on your pizza or use peanut butter instead of tomato sauce. The craziest slice we've come up with so far had graham cracker crust, soy sauce, shredded coconut instead of cheese, and jalapeño peppers on top. Neither of us was brave enough to actually try it, but it was fun to create.

It's really great having so many food options at the office, because my father thinks he's a gourmet cook, but he's completely wrong about that. Lately he's been trying to master something he calls beets à l'orange. Emily calls it BLECH À LA YUCK.

We can't always work nonstop in the office, so we've also got a pitching machine for batting practice, a basketball hoop, and a punching bag. (We tell people those are for testing out the All Ball. Well, not the punching bag. That's for punching.) Oh, and every video game console ever made, going back to the eight-bit systems that my dad used to play. Thank you, Internet!

And a pinball machine. And foosball. And air hockey.

Actually, we're thinking about getting rid of the desks.

Oh, and probably the most important feature of the office is Philo (named after Philo T. Farnsworth, the inventor who helped make TV possible). Philo has shaggy brown hair and big brown eyes. He's technically my family's dog, but I think of him as *my* dog because I'm pretty sure I'm his favorite person. I think Emily's mood swings are a bit much for him, and he learned the hard way to steer clear of my dad when he's in the kitchen. Philo loves hanging out in the office with me and Manny. He even has his own doggy bed in the corner. Philo's

the unofficial mascot of Sure Things, Inc.

The first thing I do when Manny and I arrive at the office today after school is dispense myself a slice and a raspberry-ginger root beer while I tell Manny about the rest of my day.

"My day was pretty strange too," Manny says when I'm done. "Everyone kept asking about you, and how much money you have now, and whether you were interested in giving some to them."

"What did you say?"

"I told them we were broke," he says, laughing. As we talk, Manny tosses a small All Ball from one hand to the other. I hold the unit's remote, hitting a button every time the ball reaches the top of its arc, changing it before it falls into Manny's hand. From tennis ball to baseball to golf ball to hockey puck to Ping-Pong ball and back to tennis ball . . .

Manny never drops the ball.

"Hey!" he says suddenly. "I haven't checked All Ball sales in over three hours!" He sets down the small All Ball and turns to his laptop. Manny loves to review sales figures and see them going up. But it isn't about the money for him. He hardly ever *spends* any money, other than what we spent decking out the office. He just loves big numbers and setting records. It's like he has a collection he's obsessed with, only his collection isn't stamps or pencil toppers, but sales figures.

I decide to check my e-mail. Once Manny starts looking at sales figures, there's no talking to him until he's done.

There's an e-mail from my mom:

Hi, Billy,

How are you doing? How's business? And school, of course? What new inventions are you working on? I'm super busy just now, so I can't write a long e-mail, but I wanted you to know I'm thinking about you and I love you.

Love,

Mom

P.S. Please note my new e-mail address. The old one got hacked, so I had to change it.

I hit reply right away.

Hi, Mom!

Today was the first day of school. It was crazy. Everyone wanted to talk to me about the All Ball, even Principal Gilamon! The Hyenas are doing great. Well, not really, but Carl Bourette hit an in-the-park home run during the last game. I was shouting so loud that Emily threatened to duct-tape my mouth shut.

That reminds me. I had a great idea for a new invention that you can eat when your mouth isn't covered in tape. It's Mud Pie Seasoning, and it'll turn regular mud pies into delicious desserts. What do you think?

Write back soon.

Love,

Billy

After I send the e-mail, I think about how much I miss my mom. It's not the same watching Hyena games without her. Dad and

Emily aren't interested in baseball, but Mom loves it. She says that watching the games with me helps her relax. Since my mom left at the beginning of July, she's missed a lot of games this year.

Eventually, Manny stops looking at his laptop and turns back to me. "So," he asks. "What's next?"

"Another slice of pizza?" I suggest. "I'm thinking of adding jelly beans to this one, but I'm not sure."

"No," Manny says, getting up and wandering over to the foosball table to give one of the rods a spin. "I mean what's next for Sure Things, Inc.? The All Ball's doing great, but we don't want to be a one-product company."

That's Manny. Always thinking about the business stuff. It's a good thing he likes the business side, because it doesn't interest me all that much. I'm much more interested in inventions. I have been since I was a little kid. My mom says that when I was a baby, I invented a new use for diapers (throwing them), but I don't think that counts.

"You mean like a new invention?" I ask.

"Exactly," Manny says.

"How about MUD PIE SEASONING?" I suggest. "Mud pies can finally taste like pie pies."

Manny thinks about it and then frowns. "But who would want to eat dirt?" he says. "No, we need something bigger. And less disgusting."

We both sit there thinking. I start messing with the air hockey table, spinning a puck on its edge. Manny wanders over to a chess set, stares at it a minute, and moves the black knight. He's playing a match against himself, which I don't get at all. I mean, how can you play chess when black knows exactly what white's going to do, and vice versa?

"What about the CANDY BRUSH?" Manny asks as he sits down behind his desk.

Ah, the Candy Brush! The first invention I ever told Manny about. It was the first day of first grade. I'd thought of the Candy Brush that morning when my mom forced me to brush my teeth before school, and I couldn't wait to tell someone about it. At recess I spotted Manny standing by himself, so I blurted out my idea and he liked it. We've been friends ever since.

"I still haven't really cracked that one yet," I admit. The idea for the Candy Brush is that it would make ordinary toothpaste taste like candy. It'd make kids run into the bathroom to brush their teeth after every meal!

"The sweet and sour angle is key," Manny says, drumming his fingers on the desk. Manny thinks we should sell two different kinds of Candy Brush. One would make toothpaste taste like sweet candy, while the other would make toothpaste taste like sour candy. Manny figures kids would want to have both, so we'd double our sales.

With another product Manny would have a whole new set of sales figures to obsess over. He'd be so happy.

We talk about the Candy Brush some more,

but I remind him again that I haven't figured out exactly how to make it work. Manny looks disappointed, so I suggest that we should keep thinking about what our next product will be. Maybe there's an even better idea out there. Manny reluctantly agrees. He really loves the Candy Brush idea. I think he wants one for himself. He hates toothpaste.

When Philo and I get home, I can smell Dad's cooking. Yeech. "I'm adding a new ingredient to my beets à l'orange!" he calls from the kitchen. "Kale!"

Emily sticks her finger in her mouth, making a gagging gesture. Then she sees me, and her eyes narrow. "Thanks for ruining my life."

"How did I ruin your life? I thought you were taking care of that yourself."

"My very first day of high school and all anyone asks me about is you and your stupid All Ball," she says. "Everyone wants to know how much money you have, and if my family is rich now, and if we're going to buy a summer house, and if they can come to our summer house and spend the night. Or the summer."

I shrug. "That doesn't sound so bad. At least people are talking to you. And you didn't seem to think the All Ball was so stupid when Dustin Peeler was playing with it."

She snorts. "Dustin Peeler. I'm totally over him."

"How can you be over him?" I ask, amazed. "You were completely in love with him, like, thirty-six hours ago! Did he do something?"

"Yes," she says. "He played with your stupid All Ball!"

She stomps off to her room.

I manage to eat a little bit of Dad's dinner, watch some TV, and do my homework. (I can't believe we already have homework on the very first day!) Philo gets into his bed in my room, and I get into mine. "Good night, Philo," I say. He sighs, snuggles down, and quickly falls asleep.

I lie there staring at the framed blueprints on my wall.

They're the original blueprints for the All

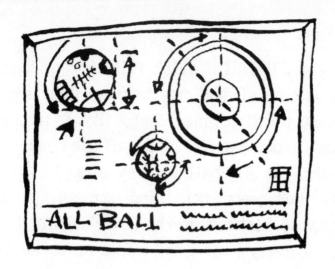

Ball—the diagram showing how to make my amazing invention.

I didn't really want the blueprints hanging on my bedroom wall, but my parents were so proud of me that they gave the framed blueprints to me as a surprise. My dad even made the frame (he's an artist, so he knows all about frames). What could I do? Take them down and slide them under the bed?

So now I find myself staring at them every night before I fall asleep. And I'm always thinking the same thing . . .

Where did they come from?

That's my secret. I didn't draw the blueprints

for the All Ball. I didn't fully invent it, but I'm getting all the credit. Every time someone congratulates me, I feel guilty. In fact, my secret makes me feel guilty all the time.

Yes, the All Ball was my idea. I thought of it last year. But I was struggling with a way to make it work. I worked on it all spring, every time I had a free moment. But I just couldn't crack it. I was getting close, but there were still a few crucial details I was stuck on.

Then one morning in June I woke up and found the blueprints on my desk. They were perfect. They solved every problem I'd been wrestling with. I was so excited, I ran to Manny's house with the blueprints and we got to work right away.

I never told him that the blueprints just appeared on my desk. He was so excited, and I didn't want to let him down. I thought whoever left the blueprints would fess up soon, but it's been months now and I still don't know who put them there.

Dad? He's an artist, so he could draw a really good set of blueprints. But he's never invented anything in his life, as far as I know.

Mom? She's a researcher, and really smart, so maybe she could figure it out. But why wouldn't she tell me?

Emily? No way. She'd definitely want to take credit for figuring out how to make the All Ball.

A ghost?

I thought about asking my family members, but it sounded so weird in my head. "Hey, did you figure out how to make the All Ball and draw up blueprints and put them on my desk but then forget to tell me you did it?" It sounds crazy.

But how did they get there?

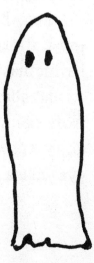

Chapter Five

The Flying Phone

WHEN I WAKE UP THE NEXT MORNING, I HOPE THAT ON the second day of seventh grade things will be a little more normal and everyone will be over staring at me and making such a big deal out of everything. But that's not what happens.

"Hey, Billy!" I hear from behind a tree on my walk to school. At first I think I must be hallucinating. Trees are trying to talk to me?

But then a boy from my homeroom pops out from behind it. His name is Steve Stallings. I don't know Steve well, but I do know that in gym class last year Steve fell during a game of kickball and dislocated his knee. His kneecap was on his thigh. It was weird and scary and cool at the same time.

"What's up?" I reply to Steve. I notice that Steve's kneecap has made it back to its correct position.

"Not much," he says. We walk almost a block in silence.

"So," he says, "you're an inventor."

"Yeah."

"So am I."

"Cool," I say. We walk a little farther.

"Don't you want to know what I invented?" he asks, sounding a little annoyed.

"Um, sure. What did you invent?"

Steve smiles. Then he looks around, checking to see if anyone is eavesdropping on us, before he tells me about his invention.

"THE FLYING PHONE," he whispers.

"Oh," I say. "What's a flying phone?"

"Not so loud!" he says in a loud whisper. He looks around again, and then I guess he feels satisfied that no one can hear us so he speaks

in a normal voice. "It's a phone that flies!"

"Yeah, I kinda figured that. But why?"

"Why what?"

I stop walking and face him. He stops too. "Why would you want a flying phone? What would you do with it?"

"Well," he says. "Let's say your phone is ringing, but you're on the other side of the room. After a few rings, these wings pop out on the side of the phone. Then the phone flies over to you."

"Huh," I say, walking again. "It seems like you could just walk across the room and get your phone."

Steve frowns and I suddenly feel bad. I don't want to dash Steve's dreams. It's just that inventors have to really ask themselves why people would want their invention—that's the first thing I do when I come up with an idea. The second thing I do is try to come up with a cool name for my invention. Steve had come up with a cool name for his invention, at least. "Can I see it?" I ask.

"Oh, I haven't made one," Steve replies. "That's where you come in."

"What's a flying phone got to do with me?"

"You'll figure out how to make it, and then your company will produce it. Since it was my idea, I'll get ninety percent of the money we make," Steve explains.

"Or possibly eighty percent," he says after a minute of my silence. "It's negotiable. To a certain extent."

"I'll think about it," I tell Steve as we walk into homeroom. Steve huffs off to his seat.

At least the WELCOME, BILLY SURE! banner has been taken down. That's a relief.

But before I can get to my seat, Mrs. Welch waves me over. "So," she asks quietly, "have you started working on your speech?"

I don't know what she's talking about. "Speech?"

"About your adventures over the summer!" she

explains. "As an inventor! And a businessperson!"

Oh, right. I completely forgot about that. "I'm thinking about it," I say. "Getting my thoughts organized."

She smiles and nods, as though we're sharing a secret. "Very good! Well, I look forward to it. And I'm sure your fellow students do too."

In science class Mr. Palnacchio takes me aside too, wanting to talk more about which lessons I might be willing to teach. "Now, I know you can't reveal any secrets about the All Ball, but based on the way it changes color, I was thinking you might like to teach the Science of Color unit," he suggests. "After all, I thought I understood color science, but I have *no idea* how you get the ball to change from white to brown to orange. Fascinating!"

I love science, but I can't teach a class in it. What if some of my classmates started goofing around? How would I get them to stop? I'd rather be goofing around myself. I tell Mr. Palnacchio I'm not really sure about helping him teach the class, but I'll keep thinking about it.

It seems as though the teachers are determined to give me lots of things to think about. As if I don't already have plenty to think about.

At lunch more kids come up to me with their ideas for inventions, all of them hoping to make millions of dollars. Here are some of their ideas:

- A knife that comes prepackaged with peanut butter and jelly in the handle.
- Shoes that can change from sneakers to flip-flops to dress shoes with the touch of a button. (I think maybe the All Ball inspired that one.)
- Flying skateboards. (Pretty sure they saw that one in a movie.)
- A device you can hide in your mouth that turns you into a great singer.

No one other than Manny ever used to be interested in talking with me about inventions. But now that I've had a successful one, *everyone* wants to talk to me about inventions! I can't get them to talk about anything else! I like talking about inventions, but not all the time.

By the end of the day I feel lousy, like the time Manny dared me to ride the MegaCoaster seventeen times in a row. My guilt over not really inventing the All Ball is making me feel even worse than the MegaCoaster did. (By the way, I was only able to ride it thirteen times before I threw up. And after that they wouldn't let me back on the ride.)

I can't take it anymore. I need to talk to Manny.

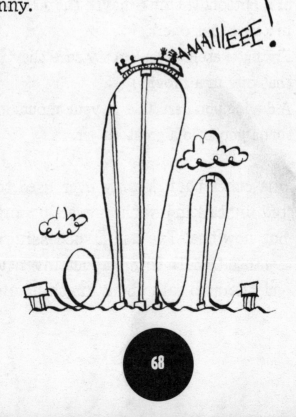

Chapter Six

The Next Big Thing

WHEN PHILO AND I GET TO THE OFFICE, MANNY'S ALREADY there. I smell pizza. Manny is eating a slice.

"Sales figures look good," Manny says, staring at his computer. "Especially South America. Which is a little surprising, since I thought they only loved to play soccer down there."

Philo sniffs around, then settles into his bed in the corner. I hit the punching bag. **Whap!** "Manny, we need to talk."

"I'm pretty sure that's what we're doing right now," he says, still staring at his computer.

I sit down next to him. "No, we need to

really talk. About something important."

Manny finally looks up from his screen, surprised. "What could possibly be more important than sales figures?"

"The whole thing," I say, spreading my arms open. "I want to talk about the whole thing."

He's confused. "What whole thing?" Then he looks excited. "Is that your next invention? THE HOLE THING? Does it fix holes, like in pants? Or buckets? What about holes in hoses? There are so many possibilities!"

I shake my head. "No, it's not my next invention. I mean this whole business thing. Sure Things, Inc."

Manny looks worried. "What about it?"

I take a deep breath. "I'm not sure I can handle all this. It was okay over the summer, but now with school and people coming up to me all the time, it's too much."

Manny looks relieved. He picks up a small All Ball and starts tossing it up, letting it fall, and catching it. He tosses it almost all the way up to the ceiling of the garage. I'm tempted to secretly change the ball with the remote, but we're having a serious conversation.

"You probably just need a few days to adjust," Manny says. "Today was only the second day of school. It'll get better."

"Will it?" I ask, getting up and pacing around. "I thought *today* would be better. That everyone would've gotten over it and start obsessing over something else. Like how Mr. Frankenwald shaved the shape of a chicken into his buzz cut over the summer."

Manny laughs, thinking about the sixth-grade art teacher's new haircut. "Yeah, not sure what he's going for there."

"But today even *more* kids asked me questions!" I continue. "Everyone wants to talk to

me about their ideas for inventions. It never stops. I don't know if I want to do this anymore. Can't we just do it later, when we're older?"

Manny looks alarmed. He obviously doesn't want to just put the business on hold. "Billy, lots of people are depending on Sure Things now. They're working for the company, and it's their job. You can't just take their jobs away! And who knows if people will still buy the All Ball later. Things change! Fast!"

"Yeah, I noticed," I say, thinking of how my life has changed over the summer.

Manny thinks for a minute.

"You know, people telling you their ideas, that part doesn't really sound all that bad."

I think about it. "I guess you're right. It's fun hearing other people's ideas, but I just don't want them interrupting me all the time."

Manny nods. "That makes sense. I can see how that could start to drive you crazy. Maybe next time someone starts bugging you, you can think of a way to let them down easy. It never hurts to stand up for yourself."

He walks over to his chessboard and moves a white bishop. He smiles. Then he walks around to the other side of the board and frowns. I guess it was a good move for white and a bad move for black.

He looks up. "Let me think about it. Maybe there's something we can do to make things better for you. In the meantime, don't give up on Sure Things just yet. And keep thinking about a way to make the Candy Brush work! I still think that's a great idea."

He sits back down at his computer, so I wake up mine and check my e-mail. There's one from my mom:

Hi, Billy,

Wow. Mud Pie Seasoning. Cool idea. What other inventions are you working on? I'd love to hear more about how your business is going. Tell me all about it! When you do, send me lots of details. That way it doesn't seem as though we're so far apart.

Love,
Mom
P.S. Go, Hyenas!

I reply right away, telling her about how I'm working on the Candy Brush. Then I write about the Hyenas' chances of making the playoffs, even though their chances are pretty much zilch minus zero. Same as every other year.

By lunchtime the next day I'm beginning to think that things are getting a little better. I only got five loan requests this morning. Other than the kid who followed me into the bathroom to beg me to invent jet packs, it's been a pretty normal day.

Then I hear the announcement over the loudspeaker. "Will Billy Sure please report to the principal's office?"

"Ooh!" say all the kids around me, assuming I'm in big trouble, especially because this is the second time I've been called down there in three

o-o=definitely o

days. Maybe this time I really am in trouble.

As I walk as slowly as possible through the halls, I think about the announcement: "Will Billy Sure please report to the principal's office?" Why do they always say "report"? Am I supposed to walk in with pages in a binder? Ready to give a speech on *Huckleberry Finn* or the Greek gods? You never "report" to anything good. *"Please report to the carnival." "Please report to the water park." "Please report to your birthday party."*

When I sit down in Principal Gilamon's office, it's pretty obvious I'm not in trouble, because he's got a huge smile on his face. "Billy!" he says. "Just the man I want to see!" He says this as though I just dropped into his office to surprise him, not because I was summoned over a loudspeaker.

"I want to show you something," he says. "I think you're going to like it."

He reaches behind his desk and holds up a poster. Across the top it says, *You'd better believe you're gonna achieve!* There are lots of stars and rainbows and fireworks. And the bottom two-thirds of

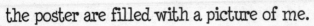

the poster are filled with a picture of me.

As if that's not bad enough, it's not even a good picture of me. It's my school picture from sixth grade. The photographer was trying to make me smile, so he stuck his tongue out. But instead of smiling, I look weirded out.

So even though the poster says, *You'd better believe you're gonna achieve!,* in the picture I look like I don't believe it for a second.

I'm not sure what to say.

"Well," Principal Gilamon says, "what do you think?"

"What's it for?"

"It's our poster for Achievement Day!" he says. "Week after next, we're going to have a day dedicated to achievement. And I was hoping you might be willing to give an inspirational speech to your fellow students."

"What would I say?"

He chuckles. "Well, I was hoping you'd talk about your own achievements with the Everything Ball—"

"All Ball."

"Right, the All Ball, and about some of the qualities it took for you to reach that achievement—drive, discipline, dedication . . . hey! Those all start with *D*! That could be your speech! The Three *D*s! Or you could call it Achieving in 3-D! We could hand out 3-D glasses! Oh, this is great!"

He starts scribbling down ideas on a big pad of paper. He looks so enthusiastic that I hate to burst his bubble.

But I have to. I take a deep breath and then the words just start tumbling out of my mouth.

"Mr. Gilamon, I'm finding all the attention I'm getting really distracting. It makes it hard for me to concentrate on my schoolwork and my . . . work work. I've got a lot on my mind. If I had to write a speech to deliver in front of the whole school, I think I'd go crazy. Achievement

Day sounds like an okay idea, but I don't want my picture on the poster. And I don't want to give a speech. I kind of wish I could just be a normal student that day, instead of the one everyone's staring at and wanting to be like or borrow money from or punch."

I stop speaking and take another breath.

Mr. Gilamon looks concerned. "Has anyone punched you?"

"No," I say. "Actually, everyone's been pretty nice. But I'm afraid giving a speech might make some of them want to punch me."

The principal sits there for a moment, thinking. Then he smiles and nods. "I understand, Billy. Of course I don't want to do anything that'll interfere with your schoolwork—that's the most important thing. And I don't want to make you uncomfortable."

He stands up. So do I.

"Maybe we'll just put Achievement Day on hold for now," he says. "Don't worry about it. It sounds as though you've already got plenty to think about."

Whew. Principal Gilamon is actually a really cool guy.

After school, when I get to the office with Philo, Manny's excited. "I think I've got a solution to your problem."

"Which one?"

"The one where everybody wants to tell you their ideas for new inventions."

"Headphones? Bodyguards? A force field surrounding me at all times?"

Manny actually considers my last suggestion for a second. "Interesting," he says. "Personal force fields. I like it. Maybe it could shoot out of your belt or something. We could call it the AVOID STUFF BELT—"

"But what's your idea?" I interrupt.

"The Internet," he says proudly.

"But, Manny, the Internet already exists."

Manny paces around, moving his hands through his dark hair. He does that when he's excited. Philo follows him, but he doesn't even notice.

"We're not inventing the Internet, but putting something on it. We'll make a website called SURE THINGS' NEXT BIG THING! Kids who have ideas for inventions will be able to upload videos explaining their ideas."

"Okay," I say. "Then what?"

"Then if you and I like any of the ideas, we'll e-mail the inventor and ask if he or she would like Sure Things, Inc. to take the idea and develop it. We manufacture the product and share the profits with the inventor. And we hope each product will be the next big thing!"

"So, a website for kids' ideas for inventions," I say, thinking about Manny's idea.

"I figure it'll take some of the pressure off you to come up with ideas for more inventions like the All Ball," Manny says.

But I'll still have the pressure of actually *developing* the inventions. And Manny still doesn't know I'm not the one who solved the problem of how to make the All Ball. Every day that I don't confess only makes it worse. But every time I think about it, I chicken out.

I need some bravery serum or something. If I couldn't figure out how to make my own idea work, how will I be able to figure out somebody else's idea?

But I don't tell Manny what I'm thinking. Instead I ask, "And how does this solve my problem of kids coming up to me at school and telling me their ideas for inventions?"

Manny grins and hands me a business card. "If anyone comes up to you and starts explaining their brilliant idea, you just give them one of these."

I look at the card. It says *Sure Things' Next Big Thing!* Underneath there's a web address.

"Well," Manny says impatiently. "What do you think? Genius, huh?"

I'm not totally sure about the idea. I mean, I know it's brilliant, but the pressure of having to figure out a way to develop all of these inventions is a serious problem. But Manny's so enthusiastic about his idea that I say yes. Who knows? Maybe no one will submit any ideas anyway.

Chapter Seven

Motor Beds and Super Sleds

BOY, WAS I WRONG.

Manny gets the website up and running quickly. Then he goes through all the media contacts—television reporters, magazine writers, website editors—that he collected when everyone wanted to do stories about the All Ball. I'm pretty sure he even has celebrities like Dustin Peeler and Carl Bourette on his list of contacts. He sends them a press release about Sure Things' Next Big Thing, and the word spreads.

QUICKLY.

In no time at all, we're getting so many videos from kids all over the world that the website crashes. Even though Manny makes the rules really clear (kids only, original ideas only, useful inventions only), there are still tons of videos.

At the office, sipping multiflavored sodas, Manny and I start watching the videos together, taking notes on our computers.

One of the first videos that arrives on the website is from a kid in Canada. He's standing in his bedroom, waving at his computer's camera.

"Hello!" he says. "My name is Mark, and I'd like to tell you my idea for Sure Things' Next Big Thing!"

Mark jumps onto his bed. "Has this ever happened to you? You're lying in bed, snuggled under the covers. You're warm. You're cozy. You're happy!"

Mark gets under the covers and pulls them up to his chin, looking very warm and cozy indeed.

"But then your mom yells, 'MARK! HURRY UP! YOU HAVE TO GO TO YOUR PIANO LESSON!'" Mark screams this part in a high-pitched voice. Then he speaks in his normal voice again. "Now you have to get out of your nice, cozy bed. *Or do you?!*"

Mark gets out of his bed and approaches the camera. "Not if you have a motor for your bed! Just attach a motor to your bed and then you can drive it anywhere. You'll never have to get out of your warm, cozy bed again!"

Mark moves even closer to his computer, reaching to shut it off. I can see up his nostrils. I wish I couldn't. "Thank you for your attention. Please help me make the MOTOR BED Sure Things' Next Big Thing."

Manny turns to me. "Hey! That's not a bad idea."

"Definitely. Is there anyone who loves getting out of bed when you're all snuggled up under the covers?" I say. "But I see one major problem."

"What's that?"

"Doors. How would you get through them? We'd either have to make larger doors or smaller beds. It's too complicated."

"Good point," Manny agrees. "Next."

In the next video a girl holds up a sock. "I present the NO-WASH SOCK! I've come up with a material that's so slick, dirt can't stick to it. So your socks always look nice and clean!"

She moves a little closer to the camera. "But I could use your help with two small problems. One, the socks are so slick, they slide around in your shoes. Two, even though they *look* clean, these socks still start to smell after not being washed for a week or two."

Manny and I laugh. "So they're clean, but they're hard to wear and they stink!" he says.

"I think we'll put that in the 'no' pile," I say.

"Or the dirty laundry pile," Manny adds.

He clicks on another video. This one's from a kid all the way in Finland.

"Hello!" he says, standing outdoors and waving. "My name is Franz. Tired of your plain

85

old sled? Then why not try **FRANZ'S SUPER SLED**! Like a regular sled, Franz's Super Sled slides down snowy hills. But it slides super fast!"

Then the video cuts to a shot of Franz at the top of a hill. He waves, pulls goggles down over his eyes, gets on the sled, and pushes off. *Zoom! Crash!*

Manny and I grimace as we watch the sled zoom down the hill as fast as a cheetah flying a jet plane and then crash into the snowbank at the bottom of the hill.

"I'm okay!" Franz calls as he climbs out of the snow.

"*Snow* way on that invention," says Manny, laughing at his little joke. "Too dangerous."

The ideas just keep coming.

A boy submits an idea for a pencil that does all your homework for you, although the prototype keeps going rogue and scribbling all over his walls and even his parents. Too many bugs to work out.

A girl suggests bubble gum that's stretchy enough that you can blow bubbles as big as hot air balloons. But when a bubble pops, it covers the chewer in gum goo. The inventor had to shave all her hair off. Too sticky.

We watch another video about shoes that can take over for your legs, allowing you to run incredibly fast and jump incredibly high. I think that idea sounds really cool, but Manny quickly points out that it's way too dangerous.

Manny and I watch so many videos that I feel like I need a new pair of eyeballs, they hurt so much. We start to see ideas more than

once. It's amazing that even though two kids live on opposite sides of the planet, they both come up with the same idea about pants with springs in them so you can bounce on your butt.

"My 'no' column is a lot longer than my 'maybe' column," I tell Manny.

"Mine too, but that's good," Manny replies. "We don't need thousands of ideas. In fact, we really only need one terrific one."

We keep watching until we feel as though our eyes are going to fall out of our skulls. Many of the videos are too dark, or too light, or out of focus. Sometimes the person steps out of the picture, so you're just staring at a wall. A lot of times the audio is hard to understand. But while we're watching all these videos, more keep arriving. And more. And more. Just keeping track of which ones we've watched is hard enough.

"Help," Manny moans.

"What's the matter?"

"No, I mean we need help," he explains. "We

can't spend all our time watching these videos from the website. I've got other things to do."

"Okay," I say, nodding. "But where are we going to get help? Who can we get to watch all these videos for us? Philo? He has kind of a short attention span."

Hearing his name, Philo looks up from his doggy bed. When he realizes I'm not giving him a treat, he plops his head back down.

"I've got an idea about who we can get," Manny says.

"No way, genius," Emily says, making the kind of face she usually reserves for Dad's stuffed sardines. "I have no interest in hanging out with you and your math whiz buddy in a hot, smelly garage."

I am standing in my sister's bedroom, pleading my case while she lies on her bed putting polish on her toenails. Black polish, of course.

"It's not hot," I protest. "It's air-conditioned. We have to keep it cool for the computers. And it's not smelly, either. I mean, a lot of the time it smells like pizza, but that's not smelly. That's delicious." I wrinkle my nose. "Nail polish is *way* stinkier than our office."

"Forget it," she says. "Close the door as you go."

I have an idea. "You know, you wouldn't have to work in our office. You can watch the videos and take notes on them anywhere. Then you can e-mail us your notes. And who knows? You might be part of a really important new technology! One that changes the world!"

"You mean like stinky, uncomfortable socks?"

I wish I hadn't talked about that at dinner. I decide to try a new tactic.

"You know, Manny is trying to get Dustin

Peeler to sing a jingle for an All Ball commercial. If he does it, maybe we could arrange for you to meet him again."

"I already told you, I'm not interested in Dustin Peeler anymore. Now get out!"

I forgot she is no longer a Dustin Peeler fan. Emily changes her celebrity crushes so often, it's hard to keep up.

"Who do you like now?" I ask. "Maybe we could get him as a spokesperson or something."

"I like whoever picks you up and throws you out of my bedroom," she says, between blowing on her toenails to dry them. (Most people probably can't blow on their toenails, but Emily used to be a gymnast.)

I start to head out of her room. But when I reach the door, I turn back. "Did I mention you'll get paid?"

Emily looks up. "How much?"

I tell her the first hourly wage Manny told me to say. She tries to look unimpressed, but I see her eyebrows flicker. "I don't know," she drawls. "Seems awfully low."

I tell her the second hourly wage Manny told me to say. "Take it or leave it. I'm sure we can find someone else. It's just that we'd rather have a family member, since sometimes we talk about company secrets."

"Fine," she says. "I'll take it. But don't tell anyone. I don't want the word to get out that I'm spending my afternoons working for two geeks."

"That's not a very nice thing to call your boss," I can't help saying.

"Boss?" she says, making her stuffed sardine face again. "Yuck. Hey, what will you call me?"

"Um, Emily?" I say. "Maybe Ninja Spider, although I'm thinking you need a new nickname."

She looks at me like I'm an idiot. "No, I mean, like, what's my role going to be called at Sure Things, Inc.?"

Manny and I didn't discuss this. "I don't know . . . assistant?"

Emily looks even more disgusted. I wish

her face would freeze like that for a few days.

"Assistant in charge of Next Big Thing development?" I suggest, trying to make it sound more important.

She rolls her eyes. "If I'm going to do this, I want to be *vice president* in charge of . . . whatever you said."

"What do you mean *if* you do it? You already said you're doing it!"

"Am I vice president or not?"

I sigh. Manny isn't going to like this. "Fine. You can be vice president. But you still have to do what Manny and I tell you to do."

I dodge the pillow she throws at me.

Emily turns out to be much faster at going through the videos than Manny and I were. We felt like we had to watch the whole video, but Emily has no mercy. If the invention seems like a bad idea to her in the first few seconds, she goes on to the next video.

She uses her own system to classify the videos. She calls it the D.U.M.B. SYSTEM. Each video is given one of four labels:

D for Dumb (obviously),

U for Unoriginal,

M for Maybe (Manny and I watch all the *M*s), or

B for Brilliant. (So far Emily hasn't given a *B*.)

There are way more *D*s than anything else. She must be wearing out the *D* key on her laptop.

One afternoon a few days later Manny and I are in the office watching the videos Emily has tagged *M* for maybe. We've divided them between us to make the work go faster. If either of us finds an idea we think is decent, we share it with the other one.

We have earbuds in, so we can't hear each other's audio. But out of the corner of my eye I see Manny sit up straighter. He starts to smile. Then he takes his earbuds out and says, "I think you should watch this one."

I move over to his computer. He uses his mouse to click on the video's play button.

A girl appears on the screen. "Hello," she says in a very serious voice. "I believe my invention could be Sure Things' Next Big Thing. It is called the SIBLING SILENCER."

I like the sound of that.

The girl holds up something that looks like an oversized remote control. "The Sibling Silencer is a device designed to do exactly what it says: silence your sibling."

Now, there's an invention that could come in very, very handy.

"Unfortunately," the girl continues, "there are still a lot of bugs to work out. Allow me to demonstrate."

A boy walks into view. "This is my brother," the girl says, gesturing toward him. "Alan, please begin speaking."

"Hey," he says, "what are you doing? Can I play? What's that thing you've got? Can I try it? Mom says you have to let me play with you because I'm your little brother and you've got to be nice to me. If you don't I'm going to tell—"

Click! The girl presses a button on the remote control as she aims it at her brother.

"**Rowf! Rowf rowf arf arf arf! Meow! Meow! Moo moo moo moo! Oink! aRF!**" the boy says.

In the corner of the garage, Philo sits up and barks back. "**Woof!**"

"Thank you, Alan," the girl says. She gives him a cookie. Eating it, he steps out of the picture. "As you can see, or hear, the Sibling Silencer currently does not silence siblings. Instead, it reduces their speech to primitive animal sounds. With your help, I'm sure we can take sibling speech all the way down to silence. Thank you."

She takes a little bow, and the video ends.

"What do you think?" Manny asks.

"I liked it when the brother talked like a dog. And a cat. And a cow. And a pig. That was hilarious," I say. "But he could have been faking it. Maybe the remote control didn't really make him talk that way."

Manny nodded. "Yeah, I was thinking that too. We could ask the inventor to ship us the remote control, and we could test it out ourselves."

"True, if she's willing to ship her invention to us."

"She probably is. She trusts us enough to send us the video about her invention. But in a way, it really doesn't matter whether the brother's faking those animal noises or not."

I stand up and stretch. We've been looking at Emily's *M* videos for quite a while. "It doesn't?" I ask. "Why not?"

"Because we can handle the technology," Manny says. "The important thing is the idea. And I think the Sibling Silencer is a great idea."

"How do you know? You don't have any siblings."

"No," Manny admits. "But I've been around our new vice president enough to know that a Sibling Silencer would be pretty handy for you to have."

He's right. A Sibling Silencer would be pretty sweet. Just about anyone with sisters or brothers would want one. Manny starts hitting the keys on his computer.

"What are you doing?" I ask.

"E-mailing the inventor to tell her we're going to help her develop a working Sibling Silencer," he says.

"Wait! Slow down!" I yell. "Shouldn't we talk about this a little more?"

So we talk. But we still end up at the same conclusion: The Sibling Silencer should be Sure Things' Next Big Thing. I'm worried that I won't be able to figure out how to make it work, but Manny waves my worries aside. He's got all the confidence in the world in my inventing abilities.

Too bad I don't.

Because I know the truth about the All Ball.

Still, I can't think of a convincing reason to say no (other than the truth, and once again, I've chickened out on confessing), so Manny e-mails the girl who thought of the Sibling Silencer. Her name is Abby, and she's thrilled. She agrees to send us her prototype right away, along with detailed descriptions of all the work she's done so far.

• • •

Things are moving fast. Too fast.

We've got the prototype and Abby's plans, so I've been studying them. It was fun testing the prototype on Emily.

"WHAT ARE YOU DOING IN MY ROOM? GET OUT OF HERE OR I'LL TELL DAD THAT YOU'RE arf arf arf arf! meow! woof! meow! oink!"

I've made some progress, but I'm still stumped by some details. And I'm really feeling the pressure. Manny's counting on me. Abby's counting on me. Sure Things, Inc. is counting on me. And siblings all over the world are counting on me, even if they don't know it yet.

A few days later Manny and I are working in the office. In the corner I've set up a minilab where I can run tests and do analyses. I'm trying out a few different approaches to certain details of the Sibling Silencer.

"How's it going?" Manny asks, coming over to the lab corner of the garage. He doesn't come to this part of the office all that often. He's usually too busy with his computer.

"Not great," I mumble, concentrating on a new wiring configuration.

"But it'll all come together soon, right? The Sibling Silencer?"

I shrug.

Manny holds up a printout of an e-mail. "Well," he says, "maybe this'll inspire you!"

"What is it?" I ask, taking the e-mail. I read it, and realize it's a letter from a producer of WAKE UP, AMERICA! saying they'd love to have us on their show to announce our Next Big Thing!

"There must be some mistake here," I say as I continue to read. "The date they're confirming is really soon!"

"That's no mistake," Manny says. "It's the perfect time to announce the new product."

"But we don't *have* a new product!" I say, trying not to shout. "We just have an idea. And I have no idea how long it will take me to turn the idea into something real that we can sell!"

Manny pats me on the shoulder. "You're the genius who invented the All Ball, remember? I figured scheduling this announcement on TV would motivate you!"

"I don't need motivation!" I say, much louder than I mean to. I try to speak in my normal voice. "That's a lot of pressure on me, Manny," I tell him.

"I have faith in you!" Manny replies, grinning at me. "Setting a deadline is one of the best ways to motivate a creative genius. I read that in one of my management journals."

Manny starts to walk away, but then he turns back. I'm pretty sure what he's about to say is the reason he came over to the lab in the first place.

"Actually," he says, looking at the floor, "we kind of *have* to have the Sibling Silencer soon."

"Why?" I ask.

Manny runs his fingers though his hair. "Because I kind of poured a lot of what we made on the All Ball into promoting the

Sibling Silencer. Without the Sibling Silencer, the whole company could go under."

"*Promoting* it? Already? But it doesn't exist!"

"You have to buy commercial time in advance," Manny explains. "And the holiday shopping season is crucial to the success of a new product like this. Every business journal says so," he adds before he walks away.

You need to steal Manny's business journals and file them away in the garbage can, I tell my hands.

I know Manny well enough to know he's not that worried. He really believes I can pull this off.

How do you tell your best friend that his best friend is a big fraud?

Chapter Eight

The Inventor Who Became a Zombie

NOW THAT I'VE GOT A DEADLINE, I'M SPENDING EVERY
spare moment I can find working on the
Sibling Silencer. I've got it to the point where
it doesn't make siblings sound like animals,
but they still speak gibberish.

This is what happened the last time I tested
my prototype on Emily:

"YOU'D BETTER NOT BE POINTING THAT
STUPID THING AT ME AGAIN, BECAUSE I'M
GOING TO TELL GLARBLE FWIMBAH SCHNOOZAY
KALAPP WHEEFEE!"

Funny, but not silent. Far from it. Emily

actually seemed to get a little louder after I zapped her with the remote control.

I've been working on the Sibling Silencer late into the night at my desk. My days are all the same: get up early to work on the Sibling Silencer, go to school, go to the office to work on the Sibling Silencer, come home to eat Dad's bad dinner (last night it was ragout of rutabaga), do my homework, work on the Sibling Silencer, and sleep. On the weekends I just leave out the school part. Oh, and walk Philo. I do that, too. But I've been making the walks shorter and shorter to save time.

And our appearance on **WAKE UP, AMERICA!** is getting closer and closer. . . .

At school one day I fall asleep at lunch. I end up facedown in my sloppy joe. Somebody takes a picture and posts it on the Internet with the caption "GENIUS AT WORK." Luckily, with my face in my lunch, you can't really tell if it's me or not. It could be anyone.

It's tough to stay awake in class, too. In science Mr. Palnacchio calls me up to the front to help him explain the Science of Color. I practically fall asleep leaning against the board and get red marker on my face. Jenny Starling raises her hand and asks, "Mr. Palnacchio, what's the science of getting color all over your face?" Everyone laughs.

I walk through the halls like a zombie. Dressing up like a zombie for Halloween is really fun, but actually feeling like a zombie? Not so much fun.

A sixth grader runs up to me. "Hey, Sure!"

I turn to him and mumble, "Yes?"

"I've got this great idea for an invention!" He lowers his voice so no one else can hear. "It's a pop-up changing room. You could use it on the beach, or even in the locker room so you wouldn't have to change right in front of everyone else."

Zombie Me automatically reaches into my pocket and pulls out my wallet.

I take one of Manny's Next Big Thing cards and hand it to the kid.

"What's this?" the kid asks, disappointed.

"Read it," I mutter. "Explains everything."

Then I zombie-walk my way down the hall toward my next class. Unless it features a unit on eating human brains, I'm probably not going to do very well.

But lack of sleep isn't my only problem. Every time I try to work on the Sibling Silencer, I hear this voice inside my head. It says things like this:

You're a fraud.

There's no way you can do this.

You're going to fail.

Your company will go bankrupt.

You'll go to prison.

Naturally, these thoughts don't exactly inspire me to do my best. But I keep on trying. Luckily, I really like the idea of the Sibling Silencer. Every day, Emily makes me like it even more.

Take now, for instance. I'm standing in the kitchen, minding my own business. (Okay, I'm standing here because I'm so tired I can't remember where I am supposed to be. But that's not the point.)

"What are you doing standing in the middle of the kitchen?" Emily demands. "Just standing there like a zombie? You are so *weird*. This town should build a weird museum and put you in it. You could be their main exhibit. If you're just going to stand there with your mouth hanging open, you give me no choice but to take your picture and post it on the Internet."

She pulls out her camera and takes my picture.

I stumble back up the stairs to my room. The plans for the Sibling Silencer are calling to me. And they have a really annoying voice that's not unlike Emily's annoying voice: "INVENT ME! COME ON, HURRY UP AND INVENT ME!"

Most nights, before I get too sleepy, I take a couple of minutes to write a quick e-mail to my mom. Somehow, just typing my troubles to her makes me feel a little better. It's nice to know that somewhere on the planet there's someone who loves you, even if you can't figure out how to invent a Sibling Silencer.

(I know my dad loves me, even if he does seem to be trying to punish me with his awful cooking. And I'm pretty sure Philo loves me no matter what.)

Hi, Mom,

Hope you're doing great, and that all your research is going well. We sure do miss you. Me especially. I don't actually know about Dad and Emily. I can't get inside their brains. (I don't think I'd want to get inside Emily's brain.) But I do know I miss you a lot.

School is fine. Lots of homework—lots more than in sixth grade, and I already thought that was kind of too much. But I'm keeping up with it, barely. (Don't worry, my grades are good.)

The All Ball's still really popular, and selling well. Manny says we expanded to five new countries this week. He calls them "new markets." To me, "market" seems like kind of a small word for a whole country.

Still working on the Next Big Thing. It's tricky. Hope I crack it soon, especially since we're already booked to announce it on a morning news show. That's Manny for you. Oh well. I owe him a lot.

The Hyenas are just about done with their season, unfortunately. There's always next year.

Love,
Billy

I hit send. Then I crawl into bed and fall fast asleep. The last thing I remember thinking is, *You're a fraud.*

The next day, I'm in the office, twirling the rods of the foosball game, knocking the ball back and forth from one end of the table to the other.

Klop! Klop! Klop! Klop!

I guess if Manny can play chess against himself, I can play foosball against myself. Except I'm not really playing. I'm thinking.

When he hears me knocking the ball back and forth, Manny looks up from his sales figures. "Wanna play a game?"

"No, thanks," I say. "I'm thinking."

"What about?"

"The Candy Brush. I had a thought about the flavor conversion unit. I'd like to test it out, but I'll need some new materials . . ."

Manny looked concerned. "That's great, Billy, but what about the Sibling Silencer? We've gotta go on that TV show and introduce it in just—"

"I KNOW!" I shout, surprising Manny and myself. Philo jumps to his feet to see what the matter is.

It's like a balloon of worry and guilt and stress has been getting bigger and bigger inside me until it finally popped. I take a deep breath. "I know," I say more quietly. "I haven't forgotten."

Manny gets up and comes over to the foosball table. "What's wrong? I know you're under a lot of pressure to come up with this Sibling Silencer, but you'll do it. Just like you did the All Ball."

It's time to tell him. I'm sick of this secret. Maybe I'm finally fed up, or maybe I'm just tired, but, either way, it's time to come clean to Manny.

"I didn't."

Manny looks totally confused. "Didn't what?"

"Didn't come up with the All Ball. I'm a complete fraud."

For a second Manny's speechless. "You mean you . . . *stole* the idea for the All Ball?

I shake my head. "No, I didn't steal it. It was . . . given to me."

"By who?"

"I don't know."

Manny sits down on the closest chair. "Okay, I'm totally confused. You didn't invent the All Ball, but you didn't steal it. Someone gave it to you. But you don't know who."

So I tell him everything. About how I was struggling with the plans for the All Ball, trying for the breakthrough that would make it possible. About how I went to bed, and in the morning the blueprints were right there on my desk in my bedroom. And how I was so excited to have the solution to the problem, I just shared it with Manny, forgetting to mention how I got it. And then the whole thing just took off like a rocket, and I was too busy (and guilty) to tell Manny where the plans came from.

I'm afraid Manny's going to be mad at me for holding out on him, but he isn't. He's just confused.

"That's . . . bizarre! Why would someone draw up blueprints and then just give them to you anonymously? And never come forward, even when the All Ball's a huge success? Who would do that?"

We talk about my family, since they were right there in the house. "Emily, no. Doesn't make sense," Manny says emphatically. "Your dad? He's a good artist. I bet he could draw plans."

"That's what I thought. But inventing's not his thing. Or keeping secrets."

"Your mom? Was she home then?"

"Yeah, she was home. I guess it's possible she did it. But I don't get why she wouldn't just say, 'Here. I did this for you.' She knows how guilty this secret would make me feel, and she wouldn't want to do that."

"Guilty?" Manny says, making a face. "Listen, whoever left those blueprints for you *wanted* you to use them! They *wanted* you to make the All Ball! And you did. So you did exactly what they wanted you to do! You have nothing to feel guilty about."

Somehow I'd never thought about it that way. I feel about ten thousand times better. Reason #1001 why Manny is the greatest CFO and best friend: He always makes me feel better when I'm superlow.

"How about a slice?" Manny suggests. We go to the pizza dispenser and pick our toppings.

"Okay," Manny says after he's bitten through a long string of mozzarella cheese, "now I understand why you've been feeling like a fraud. But let me ask you something. Before these mysterious blueprints showed up, had you done some work on the All Ball?"

I chew and swallow. "Yeah, of course. You know I had. Tons of work. I'd been working for weeks."

"And were the blueprints completely different from anything you'd come up with?"

"No. They followed the same lines I'd been following. But they solved a couple of crucial problems that had stumped me."

Manny smiled. "That's what I thought. See, you're not a fraud at all. You're still an inventor. I've known you a long time, and I think you're a genius."

That's really nice to hear. I don't think Manny's ever actually called me that. Emily's called me genius lots of times, but she's always being sarcastic. I can tell that Manny really means it.

Manny finishes his slice. He picks up a small All Ball and starts tossing it up toward the ceiling and catching it. "So it seems to me that you've just lost your confidence. The mystery of where these blueprints came from is eating you up inside."

I pick up the All Ball's remote and aim it at the ball. When it goes up, it's a golf ball. When it comes down, it's a tennis ball. Manny catches it and tosses it like he doesn't even notice the change.

"What we have to do," Manny continues, "is solve that mystery, so you can stop thinking about it and concentrate on the Sibling Silencer."

The ball goes up a tennis ball and comes down a hockey puck.

"How are we going to solve it?" I ask.

"I don't know," Manny admits. "But figuring out a way to solve the blueprint mystery is my new number-one priority. Right now, that is the most important thing!"

The ball goes up a hockey puck and comes down a Ping-Pong ball.

"More important than sales figures?" I ask with a small smile.

Manny's so shocked by that idea he drops the Ping-Pong ball. It bounces across the garage floor and Philo chases it.

"Let's not get crazy!" Manny says.

Chapter Nine

Manny with a Plan

THAT NIGHT I SLEEP BETTER THAN I HAVE IN WEEKS.

At breakfast Emily says, "Not that I really want to, but do you need me to look at more of those stupid videos? I could use the money."

"For what? Did they get a new shipment of clothes at Goths 'R' Us?" I ask as I eat my bowl of cereal. (Luckily, Dad hasn't turned his gourmet ambitions to breakfast. Yet. He likes to paint early in the morning. He says he loves the light.)

"Ha-ha," Emily says. "Hilarious, genius. So do you need your vice president again or what?"

"Not right now," I answer. "We've got more on our plate than we can handle. The last thing we need is another Next Big Thing. But I guess eventually we'll have to get back to the videos. They keep coming in."

She looks disappointed for a second, but her face quickly slides back into *who cares* mode. "Okay, whatever," she says, getting up from the table. "There's always asking Dad for money. I think I'll ask him right now. Here's a little tip from your big sister: When he's painting, Dad'll say yes to just about anything so he can get right back to his work."

Like I don't already know that. How does she think I got permission to get Philo in the first place?

My school day really isn't that bad. Having gotten some decent sleep really helps make the day better! Plus, no one asks me to lend them money, or teach their class, or give an inspirational speech. I hand out a couple of Next Big Thing cards, but by now most of the kids at Fillmore Middle School who have ideas for inventions have already gotten cards.

One of the kids I give a card to is a short sixth grader. His invention idea is "underpants that secretly make you strong, like a superhero." Since I'm not feeling like a zombie today, I actually smile and encourage him to keep working on it.

"Make a video and send it in!" I say.

"I will!" he says, taking the card and running off. When he gets to the end of the hall, he sticks his arms out like he's flying.

When I stop back home before going to the office, I pick up Philo. As usual he's thrilled to see me.

Philo seems to be in a rush to get to the office. Maybe he's hoping for some pizza. He's really pulling on the leash, so we start running. Philo practically drags me all the way to Manny's house.

"Hey!" I say as I enter the office. "How's it going? How are the latest sales figures?"

"Oh, I haven't checked," Manny says.

That's unusual.

"I've been too busy thinking about your problem, the blueprint mystery. And I think I've come up with a way to solve it!"

I take off Philo's leash and hang it on a hook. He does a quick sniff-around and then settles into his bed in the corner. I toss him a treat from a jar we keep at the office.

"Great!" I tell Manny.

Manny dispenses himself an orange-lime cola and takes a drink. Then he says, "Okay, here's what I'm thinking."

He walks over to a dry-erase board mounted to the garage door. He sets his drink on a table and picks up a marker.

"Some nice person left you the blueprints for the All Ball," he says, drawing a smiling face on the whiteboard. "Let's call them X." He writes a big *X* above the face.

"Hi, X," I say.

Manny continues. "Person X obviously wanted to help you. He or she likes you. Maybe even loves you." He draws a heart on the board.

"So I'm guessing that if this person sees you

really worried about another invention, they'll want to help you again," Manny says, drawing a worried face, with a frowning mouth and eyebrows pointing up. "That's just logical."

"Another invention? You mean like the Sibling Silencer?"

"Exactly!" Manny says, writing *Sib Sil* on the board. "Have you been talking to your family about your struggles?"

I think about it and shake my head. "No," I say. "I guess Dad and Emily might have noticed me working late in my room, but I haven't said anything about what I'm working on. I don't want Dad to worry. Emily probably knows we picked the Sibling Silencer, since I've tested it on her a couple of times, but I doubt she knows I'm worried about it. Or cares."

Manny smiles. "I think it's time to lay out the bait and let them know you're worried."

Manny, Philo, and I walk into the house just in time for dinner. "What's that smell?" Manny whispers, looking scared.

Dad's in the kitchen, cooking.

"Don't worry," I reassure Manny. "It'll be okay. Remember, you're doing this for the good of Sure Things, Inc. The company's very existence may depend on your ability to eat my dad's cooking."

Manny still looks scared. "But I don't know if I can."

"If it gets really bad," I whisper, "just suck on the ice cubes in your drink before you take a bite. The cold helps kill the taste."

"Can't I just sneak my food to Philo?" Manny asks. "I thought that's what dogs were for. They're like garbage disposals with legs."

I shake my head. "When Dad's cooking, Philo steers clear of the kitchen."

Manny sniffs the air. "Smart dog."

"Hey, Dad," I say as we walk into the kitchen. "Is it okay if Manny stays for dinner?"

Dad looks up from chopping something that resembles a brain. "Of course! We've got plenty! Manny, you can tell me what you think of my latest creation."

"What are you making?" Manny asks, trying to erase all the fear from his voice.

"MAC AND CHEESE!" says Dad.

Manny breathes a sigh of relief.

"With garlic and cauliflower!" Dad continues.

"Wow, my two favorites," Manny says. "I always ask for them on my birthday instead of cake."

"Well, isn't that lucky!" Dad cries, not picking up on Manny's sarcasm. "I'll have to give you an EXTRA-BIG PORTION!"

The blood drains from Manny's face.

Since Manny's here, we eat in the dining room instead of the breakfast nook. Dad even gets out our nicer plates and the real glasses instead of the plastic ones.

"Are we celebrating something?" Emily asks, puzzled.

"Sure, why not?" Dad says. "Let's celebrate the success of the All Ball and Sure Things, Inc.! We've all been so busy that we haven't really taken the time to celebrate together!"

As we push the food around on our plates,

holding ice cubes in our mouths, Manny and I exchange a look. Dad's just given us a good cue to put our plan into action.

"Thanks, Dad," I say, trying a bite of the mutant mac and cheese and then quickly spitting it into my napkin. "But actually, to tell the truth, things aren't going all that smoothly at Sure Things, Inc."

Dad stops eating to look at me, concerned. "Really? What's the matter? Is one of the big sports equipment companies giving you trouble? They're probably not too happy having five of their products replaced by just one of yours. But that's business! COMPETITIVE!"

As an artist, Dad basically knows one thing about business: It's competitive. He says that's why he never wanted to go into business, but from what I've seen, art is incredibly competitive too. Maybe even more than business.

"No," I say, "it's not that. It's the new product we're working on. Our Next Big Thing."

"I helped them find it," Emily volunteers in a smug voice. "I'm their D.U.M.B. vice president."

Dad gives Emily a look. He doesn't know that Emily uses the D.U.M.B. system. "That's not a very nice thing to call yourself."

Manny says the stuff we decided he'd say. (He actually insisted on writing it down and memorizing it.) "You see, Mr. Sure—"

"Please, Manny," Dad interrupts. "Call me Bryan."

"Okay . . . Bryan," Manny says a little awkwardly. "Anyway, developing a new product is very challenging. Billy's got to solve a lot of problems and get everything just right. And unfortunately, I've put some extra pressure on him."

We explain about the deadline for the Sibling Silencer and how we have to have it ready in time to demonstrate it on the national morning news show.

"I don't care when you have to have it ready," Emily says. "You're not testing it on me again!" She turns to Dad. "Billy tested it on me, Dad. Like I was some kind of . . . lab rat or something."

"Billy, stop using your sister as a lab rat,"

Dad says to me automatically. "So you're worried about inventing this Sibling Silencer thing in time? Meeting your deadline?"

I nod a little too vigorously. "Exactly. So worried. SO VERY WORRIED. SO VERY, VERY WORRIED."

Emily shoots me a look. "And so very, very weird."

I ignore her. "In fact, I'm so worried that I don't think I'll be able to finish my dinner."

Dad looks a little crestfallen. "Oh dear." Then he perks up. "Still, that just means more for you, Manny!" He ladles another big helping onto Manny's plate.

. . .

After dinner Manny comes up to my room.

"How do you think it went?" I ask.

"Eating that dinner made me never want to eat again," Manny groans, clutching his stomach.

"I don't mean the food," I say. "I mean our plan. Do you think they got the message? That I'm worried about inventing the Sibling Silencer?"

Manny nods, smiling a little. "I think so. I think they picked up your subtle hint: 'I'm so worried. So very, very worried.'"

I hold up my hands. "Okay, so I may have overdone it a little bit."

"Or a lot."

"The important thing is, now my dad and Emily both know I'm worried. So if either one of them slipped me the blueprints for the All Ball, they might do it again for the Sibling Silencer."

"What about your mom? Should you send her a worried e-mail?"

I'd been thinking about that. "No, because she's on the other side of the planet, probably, so even if she wanted to help me out, she couldn't just fly home and sneak some blueprints onto my desk. So now what?"

Manny jumps up enthusiastically and walks over to my dry-erase board. He picks up a blue marker. "Okay!" he says. "We've laid out the bait. Now we just have to set the trap!"

For good measure, he writes TRAP on the whiteboard.

"What are we trying to catch, exactly?" I ask. All this talk of bait and traps has got me a little confused.

"For a genius, you can be kind of an idiot," Manny says in a friendly voice. "We're trying to catch whoever put the All Ball blueprints on your desk. Let's call him or her the antithief." He tries to draw a rolled-up set of blueprints on the board, but they end up kind of looking like a burrito. Which I could go for right about now.

"Are we thinking some kind of cage that drops down from the ceiling?" I ask.

Manny thinks for a minute, tapping on the whiteboard with his marker, leaving little blue marks. "As much as I like the idea of a cage, I think it presents several problems. One: How would we hang it in your room so that the antithief wouldn't notice?"

"Unless it was an invisible cage, like a force field of some kind," I suggest.

"We seem to keep coming back to force fields, but we have to admit they don't actually exist yet," Manny points out.

"True. And we don't have time to invent one."

"Right. Let's put force fields on hold for now," Manny agrees. "So when we say 'trap,' we don't necessarily mean a cage. We might just mean some kind of alarm that goes off, waking you so you catch the antithief red-handed."

To indicate the alarm, Manny draws a bell on the board.

"An alarm sounds good to me," I say, getting up and walking over to pet Philo.

"It'd be pretty simple to rig up alarms that get tripped by someone knocking into or stepping on something," I go on. "Like a booby trap. If someone is trying to leave blueprints for the Sibling Silencer on my desk and unknowingly

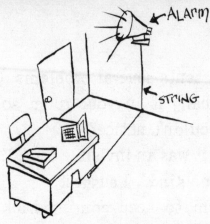

steps on a piece of string, an alarm goes off."

I draw a simple diagram on the dry-erase board. "We'll attach one end of a piece of string to my desk and the other end to an alarm, but make sure it's low enough so that the antithief doesn't trip on the string. But tight enough so if you step on the string, you trip the alarm. We can plant a few of these so that the anti-thief is sure to step on one."

It doesn't take us long to put together an alarm system with stuff I have in my bedroom.

"There," I say, stepping back to admire our work. "If someone tries to put another set of plans on my desk in the middle of the night, I'll know it right away."

"Let's hope they do," Manny says, crossing his fingers. "We really need those plans."

Chapter Ten

an antithief in the Night

I STAY UP LATE, WORKING ON THE SIBLING SILENCER. I want everything to seem normal, so the antithief won't suspect anything.

Finally, I go to bed. I'm thinking so much about the antithief and the alarm system that I can't concentrate on the Sibling Silencer anyway. Philo's already been asleep in his doggy bed for a couple of hours. He seems to be dreaming, because he twitches and makes little snuffling and yipping sounds in his sleep.

I lie in the dark. The house is quiet. I think about the Sibling Silencer and the last couple of snags I've hit. Then my eyes start to droop. They close. I'm breathing more slowly . . .

Brrree-doop! Brrree-doop! Brrree-doop!

The alarm! It's going off! My lights have snapped on!

I see my clock. It's the middle of the night. I must have fallen asleep.

Still groggy, I look around for the anti-thief. But the only other living being in the room is Philo. He's sitting in the middle of the room, staring at me. He lifts a paw, hoping for a treat.

I use a remote control to shut off the alarm. When I set the alarm's volume, I made sure it was loud enough to wake me up, but not so loud that it'd wake up anyone else in the house. I listen for footsteps, but hear nothing except the ticking of a clock downstairs.

I decide to check my desk.

There's something on it!

I can't believe it. Another set of blueprints! When I examine them, it's clear that they're the plans to build a Sibling Silencer.

SIBLING SILENCER

And they look perfect. Brilliant, in fact. The stumbling blocks that I just couldn't get over have been pushed aside. Everything's solved. With these plans, there's nothing standing between me and a working Sibling Silencer. I'm basically holding Sure Things' Next Big Thing in my hands. I can't believe it.

So it's happened again. But we didn't catch anyone!

I spend a few more minutes studying the blueprints, then I put them in a drawer and lock it. I turn off the lights.

Back in bed my mind races. How could someone have come into my room, put blueprints on the desk, tripped the alarm, and then disappeared before I saw them? I'm sure I woke up as soon as the alarm went off.

Philo stands up and scratches his bed, as though he's trying to make it softer, like someone plumping a pillow. He does this every night, even though his bed never gets any softer. He's only managed to rip out the bottom of the bed.

He was the only one in my bedroom when the alarm went off. But a dog couldn't possibly have been the one to figure out the blueprints.

Could he?

I wake up the next morning after a night full of dreams about Philo doing amazingly smart things: going to college, becoming a professor, winning a Nobel Prize made out of bacon.

It's early, and Philo is still sleeping, curled up in his dog bed. He just looks like a normal dog. And that's all he is, right?

I think about when we first got him. I had been begging for a dog for months, and finally Dad said yes one morning when he was painting. We went to the shelter, and Philo stuck his paw out of the cage when I walked by. Like he was choosing me.

It's a Saturday, so I don't have to go to school today. I have all day to solve the mystery of how the blueprints appeared on my desk.

Philo wakes up. He stands, stretches, and looks at me, ready to go outside for his morning bathroom break.

I look at him. In the light of day, I realize that it was pretty ridiculous to wonder if he could have written the blueprints. He almost definitely didn't do it. But maybe he can tell me who did. When I look into Philo's eyes, it sometimes seems like he's thinking. Like he's got something he wants to tell me.

Usually it's *I would like a treat, please.*

But maybe he has more to say today. Secrets that want to spill out of that little doggie brain. And if I'm clever enough, maybe I can figure out a way to communicate with him.

"**Woof!**" Philo says, impatient to go outside. At least, I *think* that's what he's saying. If only I had a DOG TRANSLATOR.

Now that's a great idea! Maybe that should be our *next* Next Big Thing, after the Sibling Silencer, of course.

"Come on, Philo," I say. "Let's go outside." The second I say "go," Philo gets excited. We head downstairs. I grab Philo's leash, clip it to his collar, and head out the back door.

He accomplishes his goal.

But we stay out in the yard. The gate's closed, so I unclip his leash and let him wander around, sniffing the ground.

I pull out my phone and start searching for information about dog intelligence. I read that dogs can understand up to TWO HUNDRED WORDS!

If Philo can understand two hundred human words, then that means he can understand two hundred ideas. And if he can understand two hundred ideas, it seems like one of those ideas could be, *I know who left those blueprints on your desk last night.* If only he could *say* two hundred words.

As we go back inside the house, we run into Dad, headed out to the little art studio he built in our backyard. "Good morning!" he says. As he scratches behind Philo's ears, I want to ask Philo, *Was it him? Did he do it? You can tell me!*

Maybe I can get Dad to admit to it. "How was your night?" I ask innocently.

"What do you mean?" he asks, puzzled. We're both pretty sure this is the first time in my life I've ever asked him how his night was.

"How'd you sleep?"

"Great! Like a rock, all night long! How 'bout you?"

I think about telling him what happened. But not just yet. I'm still trying to figure it all out. If he did leave the blueprints, he's doing an awfully good job of pretending he didn't. And Dad's not much of an actor. When it comes to keeping secrets, my dad is the worst. You can tell he's hiding one because every time he looks at you, his eyes get wide and he purses his lips like he's trying not to say something. It makes him look like a fish.

"I slept okay," I say, checking his face for anything fishy.

"That's good!" he says. "I know you're worried about your next invention, so I'm glad you could sleep. Sleep's important. It's tough to be creative when you're short on sleep."

"How do you know I'm worried about my next invention?" I ask suspiciously.

"Because you said so—repeatedly—at dinner last night!" Dad laughs.

Oh, right.

Philo and I go inside. I feed him and get myself a bowl of cereal and add some blueberries on top. While I'm in the kitchen, Emily stumbles in, rubbing her eyes.

"Why is everyone so loud?" she complains. "It's Saturday. I wanted to sleep in! But you and Philo and Dad are so loud. Ugh."

She opens the refrigerator and stares.

"Sorry," I say. "Did you, um, have trouble sleeping last night?"

"What?" she asks, still staring at the contents of the fridge as though she hopes something delicious will materialize right in front of her eyes.

"Were you awake in the night? Did you get up? Or see anything?"

She finally turns her head and looks at me as if I've lost my mind. "What are you talking about? Did *you* see something?" She closes the fridge without taking anything out. "You didn't see a ghost, did you? I always thought this house was haunted. Remember that time I woke up and there were strange orbs on my walls?"

I remember that night. I don't tell her that I was playing a prank on her with a mirror and a flashlight.

"No, and I don't believe in ghosts," I say.

"You would if you saw one," she insists.

This talk of ghosts is getting us nowhere. I change the subject. "Hey, Em, do you think dogs are smart?"

She opens a cabinet and stares at the boxes of cereal. "As opposed to what?" she asks. "You? Yes, I think dogs are brilliant."

"You think Philo is smart?"

She looks at Philo, walks over to him, leans down, and rubs the sides of his face. "Nope! He's just a big dumb pup!" Philo licks her face. "Kisses!" she squeals. "Kisses!"

"You know, they say dogs can understand up to two hundred words. I wish Philo could tell us what he knows. And what he sees, like, in the night."

I watch her carefully to see if she looks suspicious or guilty because I'm getting too close to her secret. She doesn't. She just looks as though she thinks I'm crazy. I've seen that look many, many times.

I finish my cereal, put the bowl in the dish-washer, and whistle to Philo. "Come on, boy! Come on!" He follows me up to my room. I've got an idea. I want to try something.

I close the bedroom door behind us. I'm used to Emily calling me insane, but there's no need to give her more reason to think so.

After finding the key and unlocking the drawer, I take out the Sibling Silencer blueprints. "Sit!" I say to Philo. He sits. "Sit" is definitely one of the words he knows.

Kneeling down, I show Philo the Sibling Silencer blueprints. "Remember these, boy? From last night?"

Philo licks the blueprints. But just once. Apparently they don't taste all that great.

"Did you see who brought these into my room last night and put them on my desk? Bark once for yes, twice for no."

Philo just sits there, looking like he's grinning, with his tongue flapping out of his mouth.

I look on my bookshelves and find a framed picture of me and my dad. I point to him. "Was it him? Did he bring the blueprints? Bark once for yes and twice for no."

Nothing.

I search through my junkiest drawer in the closet. I must have a picture of Emily somewhere. Oh, wait! My phone! Duh! I slide through the pictures on my phone and find a good one of Emily looking mad, telling me to get out of her room. I show it to Philo.

"Did Emily bring the blueprints? Bark once for yes, twice for no."

Philo licks the phone's screen.

I find a framed picture of my mother. "Was it Mom? Bark once for yes and twice for—"

"Woof!"

He barked! Once! Could it be? Could my mom have somehow found out I was worried, come home, slipped into my room, left the blueprints, and slipped back out before I woke up?

Twick twick twock-a twang twang biddly bong!

My phone's ringing! Is it Mom?

But it's only Manny.

"Billy!" he shouts when I answer. "Meet me at the office right away. I've got to show you something! Bye!"

"Wait!" I say. "Last night the alarm went off! I've got the blueprints for the Sibling Silencer!"

"I know! And I know who the antithief is!"

Chapter Eleven

The antithief, Revealed

AS I RACE OVER TO THE OFFICE ON MY BIKE, MY MIND'S spinning even faster than my wheels. Who gave me the blueprints? Mom? Dad? Emily? Philo? A ghost?

Or does Manny know who did it because he did it *himself*?

I've got the Sibling Silencer blueprints in my backpack, which bounces against my back as I pedal as hard as I can. I arrive at the office and wheel my bike right in through the side door we use as our only entrance and exit. I immediately ask, "Who did it?"

Manny doesn't even look up from his laptop. "Who did what?"

I guess he thinks this is funny. I feel like whacking him over the head with the blueprints until he spills the beans. I hold myself back.

"You know what! Who put the blueprints for the Sibling Silencer on my desk last night, and set off the alarm, and then mysteriously disappeared?"

Manny spins around in his desk chair and pretends he just now remembers what I'm talking about. "Oh, that! Right! Would you like to meet the person who did all that?"

I look around the office wildly. Is my mom here? Or someone else? I don't see anybody, and there aren't really any good hiding places in the office. I guess you could crouch under the pinball machine, but you'd still be easy to spot. And I'm not spotting anyone.

"Yeah," I say, walking quickly over to him. "I would very much like to meet him. Or her. Or it, if it's some kind of robot alien mutant

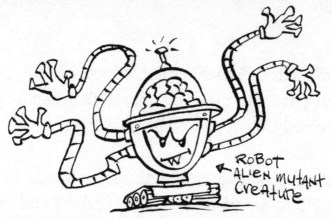

ROBOT ALIEN MUTANT Creature

creature. Just tell me who left the blueprints in my room!"

Manny smiles. "You did."

I just stand there for a few seconds, stunned. "W-what?" I manage to stammer.

"You did it," Manny repeats. "You drew up the Sibling Silencer blueprints and left them on your desk. You drew up the All Ball blueprints too."

"Manny, last night I went to sleep and there were no blueprints. I woke up and there were blueprints. How could it possibly have been me?"

"Here," he says, turning back to his computer. "I'll show you."

He clicks on a video.

"Hey, that's my room!" I say.

It's dark. There's kind of an eerie green glow, but I can make out my desk. Then a figure slowly moves into the shot.

It's me.

As I watch in complete amazement, I see myself sit at my desk, busily writing on blueprint paper.

"I'm using my left hand," I say.

"I know," Manny says. "It seems that when you're awake, you're right-handed. But when you're asleep, you're left-handed. As far as superpowers go, it's not the most exciting."

The video goes on for quite a while with me sitting at my desk, writing blueprints.

"I'm going to fast-forward to the important part," Manny says. He does, and in the video I make little jerky movements as I write in fast motion. Then he puts it back on regular speed. "Watch. Here it comes."

In the video I finish writing. I stand up and walk back to my bed.

"I never tripped the alarm."

"Because you knew where the strings were.

After all, you're the one who set up the trap."

I watch myself get in bed. Philo wakes up. He stands and walks around the room. He passes by my desk. The alarm goes off! The lights snap on!

By the time I sit up in bed, Philo's just sitting in the middle of the room.

Manny shuts off the video.

"I don't get it," I say. "I sleepwalk? And I . . . sleep-invent? Is that even a thing?"

"Apparently it is," Manny says, nodding. "And you do a really good job of it too."

"But where did this video come from?"

"I set up a webcam with night vision in your room and streamed the video to my computer."

"When?"

"When you were setting up the alarm yesterday. You were concentrating so hard, you didn't even notice."

I guess sometimes I really *can* focus. "But why did you do it?"

Manny took a deep breath and let it out. "Well, I've known for a long time that you walk and talk in your sleep. After six years of sleepovers, you tend to pick up on details like that."

"Okay, so I sleepwalk sometimes. But sleep-invent?"

"I was sure you invented the All Ball by yourself. And I knew you were going to crack the Sibling Silencer. But I knew you wouldn't believe it unless I had proof."

The truth starts to sink in. And it feels good. I really did invent the All Ball! By myself! And now I've invented the Sibling Silencer! With Abby!

"Hey, we've got to tell Abby that I cracked the Sibling Silencer! Let's call her right now. We, uh, don't have to mention the part about the sleep-inventing."

Manny grins. "All right. But first let me see those blueprints. I want to admire your latest sleep-work."

Abby's thrilled when she hears that I've figured out how to make the Sibling Silencer work.

(We don't tell her I finished it in my sleep. Some things are trade secrets.) On the phone, she screams, "MY INVENTION! IT'S GOING TO BE A REAL THING!" In the background we hear her brother Alan say, "And I'm going to use it on you!" I can't help but think that parents are also going to love the Sibling Silencer, because bickering kids will end up silencing each other. And Manny loves it because no family will be able to buy just one!

Now that I have the completed blueprints, I get right to work making a prototype. Once I've ordered a few special parts and they've arrived, I'm able to put the Sibling Silencer together quickly, working in the office and the minilab in my bedroom.

As soon as I finish the prototype, I burst into Emily's room, hiding the Sibling Silencer behind my back. "WHAT ARE YOU DOING IN HERE?" she yells. "DIDN'T YOU EVER HEAR OF KNOCKING? YOU CAN'T JUST BARGE INTO MY ROOM WHENEVER YOU FEEL LIKE IT! I'M TELLING DAD!"

I whip the Sibling Silencer out and take aim . . .

"DON'T YOU POINT THAT THING AT ME! I TOLD YOU NOT TO—"

Shhhhhhoop!

Emily's mouth keeps moving, but no sound comes out. EUREKA! IT WORKS!

The device silences her beautifully, but of course it doesn't stop her from jumping up off her bed and running straight at me, giving me a murderous look while still moving her mouth.

I turn and run out of the house.

In a few seconds Emily's able to talk again. Even though I've run all the way down the street, I can still hear her screaming. "I AM

NOT YOUR GUINEA PIG FOR YOUR STUPID EXPERIMENTS! I AM YOUR VICE PRESIDENT! YOU ARE NOT ALLOWED TO EXPERIMENT ON YOUR VICE PRESIDENT!"

Once Emily cools down, I make my way back to our house and cut around through the side yard to Dad's art studio in the back. "Dad?" I ask as I open the door and peek in. "Sorry to interrupt . . ."

"That's okay, Billy! Come on in! I'm done for the day. Just washing my brushes."

He's dunking paintbrushes in various jars of liquid and shaking them.

"I wonder if you'd mind helping me test our latest invention."

"Not at all! What do you need me to do?"

"Just talk."

"What about?"

"Anything. How about . . . cleaning your paintbrushes?"

"You got it. Well, here I have a jar full of turpentine. So I take one of the brushes I used today and . . ."

I aim and hit the button. **Shhhhhhoop!**

". . . if that doesn't work, then I take this stiff metal brush, and I–"

"Thanks, Dad!"

"That's it?"

"That's it!"

I had to make sure that the Sibling Silencer only silenced siblings. It didn't silence Dad, so that was a very good sign. He's a family member, but obviously he's not my sibling.

I keep testing and refining the Sibling Silencer, trying to make it perfect. Manny finds a great manufacturer, and they assure us that we'll have a whole box of the products ready just in time for our appearance on WAKE UP, AMERICA!

My dad even does some artwork for us to use on the boxes and in the ads. His pictures feature happy boys and girls using the Sibling Silencer to silence their noisy sisters and brothers.

Finally, it's time to introduce the Sibling Silencer on WAKE UP, AMERICA! I fly back to New

York, but this time I don't feel so nervous.

Soon I'm standing backstage with another assistant's hand on my shoulder. I hear, "Let's meet Billy Sure, the twelve-year-old inventor of the All Ball!" The assistant gives me a gentle shove, and I walk out onto the set.

It's bright, just like the **Better Than Sleeping!** set. But this time there are two hosts. Bob Roberts and Cassidy Tyson.

After we talk a little about the All Ball, Bob says, "So, Billy, I understand you've got a new invention that you'd like to show us."

"That's right," I say, reaching behind the couch to where I know they've put a few boxes of our new product. "It's called the Sibling Silencer." I pull out a box and show it to them. Dad's artwork looks great. I explain about Sure Things' Next Big Thing contest, the Sibling Silencer, and how Abby came up with the idea and then I helped figure it out.

Bob and Cassidy laugh. "Does the Sibling Silencer do what I think it does?" Cassidy asks.

"Would you like a demonstration?" I ask.

"Absolutely!" she says.

"Emily? Would you come out here, please?"

Emily comes onstage. I realize that she's changed into a blue dress. I guess her all-black phase is over. I wonder what's going to come next. She smiles and gives the camera a little wave.

I stand up and gesture toward Emily. "This is my sister, Emily."

"Nice to meet you, Emily," says Cassidy. "Welcome!"

"Emily," I ask (though we've planned and rehearsed all this ahead of time), "would you yell at me a little, please?"

"Certainly," Emily says politely. I'm not sure, but it almost sounds like she says it in a British accent. Strange. But then again, Emily is strange. She clears her throat, takes a deep breath, and starts doing what she does best, although definitely in a British accent. "BILLY! DID YOU GO INTO MY ROOM TODAY? BECAUSE IF YOU SET ONE STINKING FOOT IN MY ROOM, I'M GOING TO–"

Shhhhhhoop!

Emily's mouth keeps moving, but no sound comes out of it. Not a peep.

"Very impressive!" says Cassidy, laughing and applauding. "I have three older brothers, so I really could have used one of these when I was a kid. As a matter of fact, I could *still* use one!"

"Wait a minute," Bob says. "I don't mean to sound suspicious, but how do we know Emily's not just *pretending* to be unable to speak?"

"I thought you might say that," I say. I call offstage, "Tony, would you come out here, please?"

A man just a little older than Bob walks out smiling. Bob looks completely surprised. "Tony! It's my brother, Tony, everyone! What a wonderful surprise!" He gets up and hugs his brother.

I hand a Sibling Silencer to Tony. Then I ask Bob to start talking. "No problem there. That's what he does best," Cassidy jokes.

"Well, I'm not sure what to say," Bob begins.

"I guess I could tell you about the time Tony's pants ripped right down the middle of his—"

Shhhhhhoop!

Bob goes silent! He keeps trying to speak, but no sound comes out of his mouth.

"Well, *here's* a first!" says Cassidy. "This is the longest I think he's ever gone without talking!"

In a few seconds, Bob's voice returns. "That was unbelievable!" he says.

"How did it feel?" Cassidy asks. "Did it hurt?"

"Not at all," he answers. "I just couldn't make any sound. It was the weirdest thing!" He picks up one of the boxes. "I've got to get one of these things! Payback time, Tony."

"Me too!" says Cassidy. She looks straight into the camera. "Watch out, big brothers! I'm comin' for ya!"

Chapter Twelve

Success!

IN THE OFFICE THE NEXT DAY MANNY AND I RAISE TWO glasses of soda. Mine's black-cherry ginger ale and his is a white-chocolate grape-orange float.

"To the Sibling Silencer!" I toast.

"And its unbelievable sales figures!" Manny adds. "Thanks to Abby and you and your genius inventing ability."

I sip my soda. "But also huge thanks to you, Manny. Not just for your business wizardry, but for showing me that I really did figure out the All Ball and the Sibling Silencer."

"I guess from now on whenever you get

stuck on a new invention, you should just go to bed!"

We laugh. I toss a large All Ball in the air. When it reaches the height of my toss, Manny zaps it with the remote control, changing it before it falls. It goes from football to basketball.

"Be careful not to hit the bowling ball button," I say.

"You know," Manny says, "there was someone who knew all along that you invented the All Ball and the Sibling Silencer in your sleep."

"Who?"

"Philo! He saw the whole thing! Both times!"

"That's true. If only he could have told me, I would've been spared an awful lot of guilt." I set down the All Ball and go over to pet

Philo. "I'm thinking we've got to invent a Dog Translator. Every dog owner in the world will want one!"

Just before I go to bed that night, I check my e-mail one more time. There's one from my mom. But I notice it's from her old e-mail address. Did she switch back to the one that got hacked? Why would she do that?

I click on the e-mail.

Hi, Honey!
I am *so* sorry you haven't heard anything from me for a few weeks.

Huh? I just had an e-mail from her a couple of days ago. What's she talking about? Is this an old e-mail that just now came through for some reason?

I keep reading. . . .

I've been in Antarctica, and terrible storms knocked out the Wi-Fi at the station, so I haven't been able to e-mail you. I feel just terrible about it. I've been thinking about you, wondering how seventh grade is going. Of course, I've also missed the end of the Hyenas' season! I assume they didn't make the play-offs again this year . . .

The e-mail goes on, but I stop reading.

So my mom hasn't had e-mail for weeks.

Which raises a number of very important questions.

Who have I been e-mailing?

Who have I been telling my ideas for inventions?

Who has been pretending to be my mom?

And why?

BILLY SURE

·KID ENTREPRENEUR·

AND THE STINK SPECTACULAR

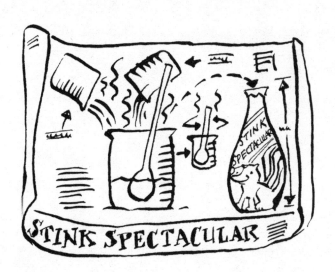

STINK SPECTACULAR

Chapter One

Impostor Mom

I'M SITTING IN MY ROOM STARING AT MY LAPTOP. My brain feels like it's been zapped with a **FREEZE RAY**. I keep thinking the same thing over and over. Maybe my brain has been zapped with a repeat ray. Or a freeze and repeat ray.

How can this be?

How did this happen?

No way. NO WAY!

I read the e-mail from my mom for the twentieth time. Have I misunderstood?

No. There's really only one possible answer here.

My mom's e-mail clearly says that she

hasn't sent me any e-mails in weeks. And that she never switched to a new e-mail address. So for weeks I've been sending e-mails to someone *pretending* to be my mom. Not my real mom. A fake mom. An impostor mom!

And that's not good. It feels crummy. But it's even worse than that. I didn't just e-mail my mom with normal life updates—stuff like how the Hyenas are playing (that's our favorite baseball team, and they've been on a losing streak), or how annoying Emily has been (that's my sister, and for the record, that would be: *very* annoying). None of that would really matter. It'd be okay for Impostor Mom to know about that stuff. Some of it, like the fights with Emily, even our neighbors know about. So it's not exactly private information.

But I also wrote about my ideas for inventions. Which is bad. *Really* bad. Not to mention really private. Because, as you probably know by now, my inventions aren't just things I make up and draw on a piece of paper and then forget about. They're real products manufactured and sold by a real company, **SURE THINGS, INC.** (Named after me, Billy Sure, and run by me and my business partner and best friend, Manny.)

When I say "as you probably know by now," I'm not trying to brag or anything. It's just that our first two products, the ALL BALL ("The Only Ball You'll Ever Need!") and the SIBLING SILENCER ("Like A Mute Button For Your Brothers and Sisters!") are selling like crazy. And there have been lots of stories about Sure Things, Inc. on TV and the Internet. You probably even own an All Ball or a Sibling Silencer. (If your sibling owns a Sibling Silencer . . . um . . . sorry about that. Time to buy one of your own!)

So it's not a good idea for me to share my secret ideas about how to build my inventions with someone pretending to be my mom.

The question is, who is pretending to be my mom?

I've got to figure this out.

It's late at night and I'm sitting at my desk. I do some of my best thinking here . . . that is, when my brain isn't acting like it's been zapped by a freeze and repeat ray. My dog, Philo, is already asleep next to my bed. I can hear him breathing slowly, almost like he's snoring, but not quite. I kind of want to wake him up and tell him about my problem, but I know that won't do any good. It's not like he can tell me what to do.

Who is pretending to be my mom?!

It'd be nice to talk to someone about this. But I don't want to wake up my dad. And I *certainly* don't want to wake up Emily. That could prove fatal—I take my life in my hands walking into her room in broad daylight; I can't imagine that going into her room in the middle of the night would go over very well.

My mom's great to talk to, but she isn't here. She's off in Antarctica doing research for the government. Because of the storms down in Antarctica, the Internet's been down for weeks, so she hasn't been able to e-mail me. But I didn't know that. During those weeks, I was sending e-mails to IMPOSTOR MOM, blabbing about my new inventions like an idiot.

166

But it's not my fault, right? *I thought it was my mom!* Which brings me back to . . .

WHO IS PRETENDING TO BE MY MOM?!

Should I e-mail Manny? Manny is my best friend. He is also Sure Things, Inc.'s CFO (Chief Financial Officer), which means he keeps track of sales and the money. He's probably still up, checking the latest sales figures for the All Ball and the Sibling Silencer. But I'd hate to spoil his good mood. Right now he's really happy with the success of Sure Things, Inc.

And besides, I might get in serious trouble. Revealing secrets must have broken some company rule. Or maybe even the law! By sharing my ideas about new inventions, have I betrayed Sure Things, Inc., dooming our company to failure? Is Impostor Mom going to steal all my ideas and then take away our customers? What if Manny gets so mad at me that he refuses to forgive me? Only twelve years old, and already my life could be ruined.

This is serious.

I decide to lie in bed. I love my bed—it's warm and soft. I guess everyone loves their bed, right? I mean, you spend a lot of time there. It would be terrible to be stuck with a bed you hate. I wonder if you'd just start liking it after a while? Maybe it would become comfortable to you and you would forget that you ever hated it. And then if someone sits on your bed and says, "I hate this bed, it's so uncomfortable!" you'd get really mad and defend your bed because it's yours and you love it. I bet that's what happens.

I stare at the blueprints on my wall, lit up by the light from a streetlight outside my window. My dad framed the blueprints for the All Ball and the Sibling Silencer. Both sets

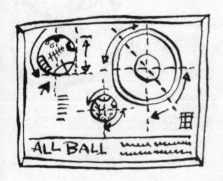

of blueprints were plans I drew up while I was sleep-inventing. I know it sounds weird, but sometimes, when I've been working on a new invention and I've gotten stuck, I get up in the night and finish the invention while I'm still asleep. For someone who loves his bed as much as I do, I still like to sleepwalk apparently. But it's not something I can turn off. I just do it. Plus, it's kind of a good thing because my sleepwalking has turned into sleep-inventing, and let's face it: Where would Sure Things, Inc. be without my inventions?

Speaking of Sure Things, Inc. . . . if it turns out that our company is ruined by my e-mails to Impostor Mom, will looking at those blueprints make me feel sad? If so, I'll definitely take them down and put up some posters. Maybe of Carl Bourette. He's the Hyenas shortstop, and my favorite baseball player.

Sleep is definitely out of the question. I get up and reread the e-mails I sent to Impostor Mom. I make myself read them with a "CRITICAL EYE." (My English teacher, Mrs. Boniface, taught us that term. At first I thought it meant that you could criticize everything you read, which was kind of fun, but what if you like the stuff you're reading? Manny doesn't have Mrs. Boniface, but he told me he thinks it means you're supposed to think really hard about stuff when you read it.) So after rereading my e-mails with a critical eye, I decide that maybe they're really not *that* bad. I didn't write anything all that specific about any new inventions. No details about how stuff works. I wrote more about baseball and school than I did about my inventions or Sure Things, Inc.

Philo twitches in his sleep, making funny sounds, like muffled barks. He must be dreaming. Maybe he's inventing something, like a gadget to let dogs open refrigerators. (There's an invention Sure Things, Inc. will *not* be making.) I get up out of my desk chair, walk over to his bed, kneel down, and pet him. Petting Philo always relaxes me.

I'm still not sure what to do about Impostor Mom, but I also do some of my best thinking when I'm asleep, so I should go back to bed. If I focus on how much I love my bed instead of worrying about Impostor Mom, eventually I will fall asleep. Right?

Maybe in the morning I'll know what to do.

I'm tied up in a chair. I struggle to escape, but the knots are way too tight. I look around for some kind of tool to cut the ropes, but I'm in a small empty room. There's nothing in here but me, the chair, and the ropes. I try to yell "HELP!" but somehow I can't make any sounds.

A tall man dressed all in gray enters. Gray hat. Gray suit. Gray shoes. Gray gloves. And a gray mask hiding his face. He stands still, with his hands hanging at his sides.

"Ready to talk?" he murmurs in a low, threatening voice.

"Talk about what?" I ask.

The man chuckles. "You may call me . . . Impostor Mom."

He walks over to the corner of the room. There's a table I didn't notice before. He picks up a small jar filled with liquid and a brush.

"Unless you talk," he says calmly, "I'm afraid I'm going to have to use more drastic measures."

I swallow hard. "Like what?"

"Like putting this ITCHING POWDER . . . ON YOUR NOSE!"

He dips the brush in the jar and moves toward me. I'm frozen. He begins to paint the itching powder onto my nose. . . .

ITCHING POWDER

LICK. LICK. LICK. . . .

I wake up from the nightmare and realize someone is licking my nose. Philo, of course. You might think that an inventor would invent a really cool alarm to wake himself up in the morning, but I don't need to. I've got a furry alarm that licks me awake every morning. Right on my nose.

"Okay, Philo, okay," I mumble. "Good morning. I'll get up."

I get up, and right away I remember what I was thinking about last night. What should I do about Impostor Mom?

I've got to talk to Manny. Even if it ruins his good mood. And even if what I've done could destroy our business forever. I've still got to tell him. We'll figure this out together. That's what best friends—and business partners—are for.

I get up and go to the bathroom. I'm ready to head downstairs to pour myself a bowl of cereal. Philo trots down the stairs ahead of me. It's Saturday, so I don't have to rush to school. But now that I've decided to tell Manny about Impostor Mom, I can't wait to get it over with. My stomach is growling, though, so I need to eat first.

But then I smell something that makes me lose my appetite. Something . . . AWFUL. I freeze on the second step.

Emily comes out of her bedroom. "Eww. What is that

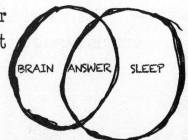
BRAIN ANSWER SLEEP

foul and horrid *smell*? Is it you, genius?"

Emily often calls me genius. But when she says it, it's not a compliment.

And she says it all with a British accent. But she's not British. Despite that little fact, she's been speaking with a British accent for the past few days. I have no idea why. But I have learned from experience with Emily that sometimes it's best not to ask why.

"It's not me," I say, heading downstairs again. "Maybe it's your accent. That stinks pretty bad."

"Wait!" she says. "Stop!"

I stop. I have no idea why she's telling me to stop. Is there a rattlesnake on the stairs? Nah, I think Philo would have noticed.

"I know what the horrid odor is," she says dramatically, as though she's announcing who the murderer is at the end of a mystery.

"What?"

"Dad's cooking breakfast!"

If she's right, this is a terrible development. My dad thinks he's a gourmet chef, but everything he makes is awful. Actually, awful is too kind a word to describe my dad's cooking. Maybe "disgusting beyond belief"? Philo won't even eat food my dad has cooked. And let me tell you, Philo lives for people-food. Just not people-food that's been cooked by my dad.

Luckily, my dad never makes breakfast because he's usually out painting in his studio in the backyard. He says he loves the early morning light.

Philo, Emily, and I cautiously make our way into the kitchen. Sure enough, Dad's at the stove, humming to himself as he turns something in a frying pan. Something **HISSES** and foul-smelling smoke wafts up from the pan.

"Dad?" Emily asks cautiously. "You're . . . making breakfast?" Even in a situation this upsetting, she doesn't lose her new accent.

"Good morning, honey!" he says cheerfully. "I sure am! Hungry?"

"But, Dad," I say, pointing to the window. "You're missing the beautiful morning light."

He salts whatever disgusting thing is in the

pan. "I am. And I still love the light right at sunrise. But for the paintings I'm doing right now, I prefer the light of sunset. So for the next couple of weeks, I can cook you breakfast!"

"Does this mean you won't be able to cook dinner?" Emily asks hopefully.

Dad laughs. "Of course not! Now, who wants turnip turnovers?"

He's holding a big sizzling green blob on the spatula. I'm not a turnip expert, but I'm pretty sure they're not usually green.

Emily and I start talking at the same time, firing off excuses one after the other. Here's what it sounds like in my kitchen:

"Sorry but . . . Ihavetoeatcerealforaspecial homeworkassignment—I'mallergictoturnips— onaturnipfreediet—fastingforworldpeace— Ialreadyatebreakfast . . . I HAVE TO GET TO THE OFFICE!" I finish loudly just as Emily pauses to take a breath.

I run out, knowing I will have to pay later for leaving Emily alone with my dad and his

turnip terrors . . . but when it comes to my dad's cooking, it's every kid for himself.

When I say I have to get to "the office," I'm telling the truth, because I really do have an office. The office of Sure Things, Inc. is in the garage at Manny's house. But it's not like any other office you've ever seen. Sure, there are desks and computers and office stuff like that, but there's much, much more.

We have: A soda machine that can make millions of flavors. A pizza machine that gives you a slice with whatever you want on it. (Now that I am outside in the fresh air, my appetite has miraculously reappeared. For breakfast, I think I'm going to have a slice with bananas and walnuts when I get to the office.) A baseball pitching machine. A foosball table. An air hockey table. Pretty much every video game console ever made. A pinball machine. And, of course, a punching bag.

And a basketball hoop. When I ride in the side door and lean my bike against the wall, Manny's standing at the free throw line he painted on the floor. Lately he's been trying to see how many free throws he can make in a row. He shoots an All Ball. *Swish!*

"Nine," he says, going to get the ball out of the trash can it's fallen into. "You know, I've been thinking about getting one of those chute things that you attach to the hoop so the ball comes right back to you. What do you think?"

"Sounds good," I say.

He walks over to his laptop and starts clicking his mouse through web pages. "Sweet. I'll order one right away."

"Yeah, but first I wanted to talk about something."

"Oh," he says, spinning in his chair to face me. "Okay, cool. What do you want to talk about? A new invention? It's really not too

soon to start thinking about our next product."

"No, it's not that," I say, picking up an All Ball and using the remote control to turn it into a tennis ball. I toss it up over the garage rafters and catch it. I'm not sure how to tell Manny about Impostor Mom. I sort of rehearsed in my head on the bike ride over, but then I started thinking about pizza and now I can't remember what I was going to say. "Um, you know my mom?"

"Of course," Manny says, looking at me strangely. "I've known your mom my entire life, Billy."

"Right," I say, nodding. "Well, while she's gone, in Antarctica, I've been writing her e-mails, you know?"

"Sure."

"But last night I got this e-mail from her saying the Wi-Fi's been down in Antarctica for the last few weeks."

"Probably on account of the storms," Manny says, shaking his head grimly.

Am I the only person in the world who

doesn't follow the weather in Antarctica?

"Yeah. Anyway, the thing is, I thought I was writing to my mom, but it turned out to be some impostor pretending to be my mom."

Manny's grim look gets even grimmer.

"What, you mean, like, a hacker?" he asks.

"I guess so," I say. "Whoever was pretending to be my mom got my e-mail address somehow and then lied and said my mom had a new e-mail address. I wrote back to that address."

Manny sees the problem right away. He looks very worried. The words start tumbling out of his mouth really fast. "What did you write about? Did you talk about your inventions? Did they *ask* about your inventions?"

I nod. Manny looks a little green. In fact, his skin tone reminds me of my dad's breakfast turnips. Now he looks like he's going to be sick . . . like he *ate* one of the breakfast turnips. My best friend is going to throw up and it's all my fault! I have to fix this!

I set the tennis ball down and hold my hands up for emphasis. "They asked a lot of questions, but I didn't talk about inventions that much! I reread all the e-mails last night with a critical eye, and I really don't think it's that bad."

Maybe it's my impressive use of the term "critical eye," but Manny looks calmer. His face goes from bright green to just slightly green. He gets up and starts pacing around. "CORPORATE ESPIONAGE! I suppose it had to happen sooner or later!"

"What do you mean?" I'm watching him pace, trying to figure out if he's going to throw up or not.

"You know, businesses spying on each other! I've read about it in my business journals! It happens all the time! I just didn't think it'd happen to us! At least not so soon. . . ."

He walks quickly over to the door, opens it, and looks around, checking for spies. "I should have seen this coming. I should have beefed up our security. When you're in the invention business, there are bound to be spies and thieves!" He closes the door and starts pacing across the room again, faster and faster.

A moment later he walks over to the pizza machine. "Want a slice?" he asks me, and I suddenly feel a thousand times better. It's not that bad if Manny wants pizza.

"Yeah, a slice with banana and walnuts," I say, grinning.

I walk over to where Manny is standing and watch him press buttons on the pizza maker. "Thanks for not freaking out," I tell him. "I know I messed up, and I'm sorry."

The pizza maker dings and a perfect slice of banana walnut pizza slides out. Manny slips a paper plate under the slice and hands it to me. "This isn't your fault, Billy," he says, and then he presses buttons on the pizza maker to create his own slice. Pepperoni-mushroom-sausage. "Let's eat and then we can figure this out," Manny adds just as his slice comes out. "We both think better on full stomachs."

Chapter Two

Real Mom

AFTER WE FINISH OUR PIZZA, MANNY MOTIONS TO the door leading into his house. I start to ask him why we're leaving the garage, when Manny raises a finger to his lips to **SHUSH** me. I raise my hands and eyebrows and make the universal sign and expression for "What?"

Manny grabs a pad and pen and scrawls a note that he holds up for me to see:

BEWARE OF BUGS!

Bugs? I quickly look around the garage but don't see any bugs.

Once inside the house, Manny drags me

into the kitchen. I'm starting to think he wasn't talking about the CREEPY-CRAWLY kind of bugs.

"Hi, Billy!" Manny's mom says as soon as she sees us. "How are things out in the office? You two need anything?"

"No, thanks, Mrs. Reyes," I say. "We're fine." I give Manny a pointed look. "Unless you want to ask your mom about bug spray?" I ask him.

Manny shakes his head and quickly reassures his mom that they don't have a bug problem in the garage. "What I meant is that we need to make sure the garage isn't bugged. You know, by the spies?" Manny's voice dips down to a whisper for the word "spies," as if maybe there are some hiding in the pantry and he doesn't want them to hear him talking about them.

Manny's mom watches our exchange and seems to decide she has nothing to worry about as long there's not an insect infestation in her garage. "You don't have to call me 'Mrs. Reyes,' Billy," she says. "You can call me DR. REYES!" She laughs. This is her favorite joke.

Manny's parents are always really nice to me. Emily says of course they're nice—their son is super rich because of my inventions. But she's wrong about that. First of all, I've known Manny since first grade, and his parents have *always* been nice to me. One time I threw up all over the fancy blue rug in their living room after Manny and I pigged out on Halloween candy, and Mrs. Reyes—sorry, Dr. Reyes—didn't get mad at all. And second, neither of us is super rich yet. I mean, maybe on paper. But most of the money goes right back into Sure Things, Inc. That's how it is with a new company. Our parents handle the money that comes to us, putting most of it in the bank for college. And then there's the fact that none of my inventions would have ever amounted to anything without Manny. There would be no Sure Things, Inc. without my CFO. So, as usual, Emily has no idea what she's talking about.

After chatting with Manny's mom, we head up to his bedroom. There are three chessboards with the pieces set up on them. Manny loves chess. He says chess is a lot like the business world—strategy and tactics and moves and countermoves. And he's really good at it. I don't know if he's like a grandmaster, but I do know he beats me every time, usually in about five minutes. I don't play chess with Manny anymore.

The nightstand by his bed is covered with a stack of business journals. I don't know how he reads that stuff. I flipped through one of them once and got so bored I actually preferred talking to Emily.

BUSINESS

in case you missed it: it's boring inside

INSIDE: BUSINESS STUFF

more BUSINESS STUFF

VERY BORING STUFF INSIDE

He opens his closet. It's nothing like mine. His is neat and organized, with everything carefully placed on shelves and in bins. Mine is like a pile of clothes and junk with a door to keep it from EXPLODING into my room.

Manny reaches into the closet and pulls out an old beige computer. "The power cord should be here somewhere," he says, opening a plastic box with neatly coiled cords. Each one is labeled to show which device it goes with. I wasn't kidding when I said he was organized.

"Are you sure there's a power cord?" I say. "Maybe we're supposed to crank it. Or maybe it runs on steam."

"You're joking, but a hand-crank computer for people without electricity is actually a pretty good idea," he says, making a quick note on a pad of paper. Manny is always jotting down ideas and then bringing them up to me later. It's a good thing he does that, because I forget half that stuff I say two seconds after the words come out of my mouth.

He plugs the computer in and turns it on.

"So that antique actually works," I say. "But will it even connect to the Internet?"

"It's not *that* old!" Manny insists. "And most importantly, it's perfect for a secure conversation. It's old enough that the new malware programs probably won't even work on it. But video chat should."

Manny sits at his desk. I sit next to him in a chair I've pulled up. We watch the screen slowly light up. "Do you know which research facility your mom is stationed at?" he asks as he drums his fingers next to the keyboard, waiting for the screen to fully come up.

"Um, no, she's never mentioned the name of the facility," I tell him. "Maybe it's a secret."

Manny turns and looks at me. "So your mother travels the world doing research for the government, and her exact location might be a secret. Has it ever occurred to you that she might be a SPY?"

I laugh. "My mom? A spy?"

Manny clicks the mouse and types on the keys, setting up the computer for video chat. "Yeah! Does she ever tell you any of the details of what she's researching?"

I think about it. Sometimes Mom brings me souvenirs from the countries she visits, but I can't really remember her ever telling me anything specific about the work she does. Unless she's told me, and I forgot? It's not that

I don't listen to my mom, but sometimes I tune out boring stuff. It's very possible she told me and it was boring grown-up stuff and I can't remember any of it.

Could Manny be right? Is my mom a spy?

"No," I say. "But maybe that's just normal. Does your mom tell you about the specifics of her work?"

Manny laughs. "My mom's a podiatrist! Dad and I don't *let* her talk about the specifics of her work, especially at dinner! Do you have any idea how many GROSS FOOT DISEASES there are?"

I think about that for a moment and immediately see his point. "I'm guessing *all* foot diseases are gross."

"Exactly."

Manny slides over, and I use the keyboard to e-mail my mom, telling her we need to video chat about something important. I make sure I send this to her real e-mail address, not the fake address Impostor Mom told me to send my e-mails to.

Now we just have to wait for her reply.

"So," Manny says, "while we're waiting, I wanted to talk to you about a suggestion we got for expanding the Sibling Silencer line."

"What is it?"

"A few parents have requested that we make a Son Silencer. You know, a device that parents could use on their sons."

"We can't do that!"

"I agree."

"I guess maybe a Daughter Silencer might be all right . . . ," I say, imagining what it would be like to give each of my parents a Daughter Silencer for Christmas. Best. Gift. Ever.

"Yeah," Manny agrees. "But then if we didn't make a SON SILENCER, people would say we're being unfair."

I think about that for a moment. As usual, Manny is right. "Well, there's no way we're making a Son Silencer!"

"Right," Manny says. "So I guess we'll just leave the Sibling Silencer the way it is, and not expand that line. It's too bad, because the product's doing great."

PING BONG BING! An electronic song plays on the old computer. My mom's calling on video chat! I click on "Answer With Video" and suddenly there she is.

"Hi, honey," she says. "Everything all right?"

"Hi, Mom! Everything's fine. Sort of. I'm here with Manny." I don't want her to say anything too mushy in front of my friend.

"Hi, Carol," Manny says, leaning in so the camera can pick him up. My parents have encouraged Manny to call them by their first names. At first I could tell he felt awkward doing it, but now he seems to have gotten used to it. It still sounds kind of weird to me.

I notice that Mom's dressed all in black, and that she's got some kind of harness attached to her. "Are you . . . busy?" I ask. "Doing something? That requires a harness?"

She glances at the harness and shrugs. "What I was doing can wait," she says. "I want to know what's going on with you."

I start to tell her about Impostor Mom, but Manny interrupts. "Before we start, is this line secure on your end?"

Mom raises her eyebrows and then smiles. "Oh, yes. Very secure."

"For your spy work?" Manny blurts out.

Mom's smile falters for a moment, and then she laughs. "For my research," she says firmly.

See? I knew my mom wasn't a spy!

I bring Mom up to date on what happened with my e-mail. I tell her all about Impostor Mom, and how Manny and I are worried that our office might be bugged. "So *that's* why I didn't get more e-mails from you," she says. "When the Wi-Fi came back on, I thought I'd find all these e-mails from you. But I didn't."

I feel bad about that, even though it wasn't my fault. "I'm sorry, Mom. I was writing e-mails to you. But I was sending them to the wrong address."

She nods. "I understand. Don't worry about that. I just wanted you to know how much I look forward to your e-mails." She smiles a big, warm smile, and I feel better right away.

"Now," she says, getting down to business, "about these e-mails you sent to this Impostor Mom. Did the impostor ask you anything about my work?"

I shake my head. "No, because the impostor was pretending to *be* you, so he or she wouldn't *ask* about you."

"I know," she says. "I just have to make sure. Did the impostor ask about OPERATION TIGER TOOTH?"

Operation Tiger Tooth? I try to ignore the look Manny is shooting me. The one that says, *Why is your mom asking you about Operation Tiger Tooth if she's not a spy?*

"No," I say, trying to act as if this were a perfectly normal thing to talk about with your mom. "They didn't mention Operation Tiger Tooth."

"Or PROJECT CENTAURI?"

I just shake my head. I catch another glimpse of Manny, and his eyes have gotten really big behind his glasses.

Mom looks reassured. "Okay," she says. "Take me through what they *did* ask about."

I tell her about how Impostor Mom asked about my inventions in pretty much every single e-mail.

Mom sighs. "I'm afraid it's clear what's going on here."

"Corporate espionage?" Manny asks.

"Yes," Mom confirms. "A spy from a rival business is definitely trying to learn your secrets. The good news is, I don't think you have to worry about your office being bugged—I think your spy has used e-mail infiltration. The bad news is, I think your spy has used e-mail infiltration!"

WORST-CASE SCENARIO: CONFIRMED!

"I knew it!" Manny says. He actually sounds happy. He loves being right. But this is not a happy piece of news. I've definitely been trading e-mails with a spy. This is so not good.

"So what do we do now?" I ask.

My mom knits her eyebrows together the way she does when she's thinking really hard. "I have some resources at my disposal that might be helpful," she says.

"What kind of resources does a 'researcher' in Antarctica have?" Manny asks.

"You don't need to know the details," my mom replies. She's sounding more like a spy by the minute. "In the meantime, you should keep writing e-mails to the corporate spy."

"*What?* I don't want to ever write to that fake again! I was planning to delete the impostor from my contacts list and block all communications from that e-mail address."

Mom shakes her head. "That's no way to catch a spy. You have to keep the lines of communication going. You can't let the spy know that you know he or she is a spy."

"That makes sense," Manny says, nodding his head. "If you stop writing to spies, they'll know you're onto them."

"So what?" I ask. "Isn't the whole point to stop communicating so the spy can't learn our secrets?"

"Yeah," Manny says. "You want to be sure you don't reveal any secrets. But we also want to find out who the spy is."

"Exactly," Mom says. "You two need to launch your own investigation."

Manny and I look at each other nervously. He knows business, and I know invention, but we're not spies. How do you spy on a spy?

Mom sees our nervous looks. She tries to reassure us. "You can do this, Billy. I'm going to e-mail you a special software program that will provide you with the identity of anyone who e-mails you—their *real* identity, not their fake one!"

"So we'll know the spy's real name?" Manny asks, excited.

"Not just the name," Mom says, leaning forward as if she's getting really into this. "With this program, you get a picture of the person who sent you the e-mail."

"That's amazing!" I cry. "How does it work?"

"I'm afraid I can't tell you," Mom says. "It's top secret."

Manny shoots me another look. I know what he's thinking: *Top secret?! That's spy talk!*

"In fact," Mom continues, "the copy of the software program I'm sending you will only work for five days. Then it will self-destruct."

Another quick look from Manny. *Self-destruct?! That's DEFINITELY spy talk!*

"Got it," I say. "So we've got to get the spy to write back to me within five days."

"Basically, we need to set a trap," Manny says. "An e-mail trap!"

"Exactly!" Mom exclaims, grinning happily that Manny caught on so quickly.

A trap? Well, that does sound interesting. . . .

Chapter Three

To Catch a Spy

AFTER I SAY GOOD-BYE TO MOM, MANNY SHUTS down his antique computer. "Let's go back to the office now that we know we don't have to worry about bugs," he says. "I think better there. Plus, there's pizza."

Back in the office, Manny heads straight to the pizza machine and starts picking his toppings for his second slice of pizza that morning: green pepper, olive, red onion, basil. He actually likes vegetables—it's weird.

When his slice is ready, he takes a bite, but then sets it back down on the paper plate and picks up the large All Ball. It's still in basketball mode. He walks over to the free throw line, bounces the ball a couple of times, and pushes the ball from his chest. **SWISH!**

"One," he counts. "So, we've got the secret software from your mom, the spy. . . ."

"She's not a spy!"

"Oh, she's a spy all right."

"We don't actually know that. Don't jump to conclusions. Research scientists have to keep their work secret too."

He gets the ball out of the trash can, walks back to the free throw line, and shoots again. **SWISH!**

"Two. Why would a research scientist need software that secretly takes a picture of whoever's sending them e-mails?"

"I don't know," I say. "Maybe sometimes scientists try to steal ideas, so they use software to learn who the thieves are."

Manny raises his eyebrows skeptically. I know he's sticking with this spy business because he thinks it's cool, but it's kind of freaking me out. I mean, it's weird to think that your mom might have a secret job. A secret dangerous job.

"Look, can we deal with the real spy, Impostor Mom, first?" I say finally. "One spy in my life is enough right now."

And just like that, Manny drops it. "You're right. Let's think about Impostor Mom and the trap we're going to set." **SWISH!** "Three," he adds a moment later.

Do I have a great best friend or what?

I walk over to the air hockey table and slide a puck across it. "Okay, so let's focus. How are we going to trap this corporate spy?"

Manny tosses up another free throw. **SWISH!** "Well, your mom said you should get Impostor Mom to write back so we can use the spy software to identify him or her."

I nod. "But what should I write?"

"Something that'll definitely get Impostor Mom to write you back."

"How about: Help! I just accidentally fell

into a hole and I don't know what to do! E-mail me back ASAP with advice to save me!"

Manny makes a confused face. "You fell in a hole with your computer?"

"I could be writing on my phone. Impostor Mom would have to write back—I mean, what mom wouldn't want to help her kid if he fell into a hole?"

I'm really liking this plan. Until Manny points out the obvious.

"If you have a phone, why don't you just call your dad? Or nine-one-one?"

Reason #478 why I chose Manny to be my CFO: He has a lot of common sense.

Manny takes another free throw. This one bounces just off the rim. He doesn't seem to notice. "Impostor Mom is a corporate spy, right?" he asks, getting up from his chair.

"Right," I say.

"So what the spy wants to know about is your latest invention."

"Yeah, exactly. But I can't give away our company secrets. That'll ruin everything!"

Manny shoots another basket from behind the air hockey table. It's a shot I've seen him make a million times. **CLUNK!** The ball bounces off the rim again. It almost hits the soda machine, but Manny manages to catch it in time. "But what if you tell Impostor Mom about an invention we're *not* doing? That could be the bait in our trap!"

That sounds good to me. We talk about some of the inventions we've been mulling over recently. A PERSONAL FORCE FIELD BELT: You put on the belt, press a button, and you've got a force field around you that no one can get through. Objects couldn't get through, either. With a Personal Force Field Belt, you could make sure you were never hit with a water balloon again. Guaranteed protection against wedgies, noogies, wet willies, and more.

PERSONAL FORCE FIEL
BELT

Or the DOG TRANSLATOR. It'd be so great to know what your dog was saying every time he barked. I'd love to know exactly what Philo is trying to say. (Most of the time, it's probably "Give me more treats, please!") I'm sure the millions of people who own dogs would all want a Dog Translator. I guess we could try to make a Cat Translator, too, but I'm personally more interested in hearing what dogs have to say. Cats would probably just complain about dogs. And everything. I don't know why, but cats seem like big complainers.

The 3-D CHOCOLATE PRINTER. This would be so great. Not only could you print a three-dimensional object, you could print it in chocolate! Then you could eat it! It'd be like printing your own candy bars. Only they wouldn't have to be bars—they could be lizards or shoes or even little statues of you! (Though I'm not sure why you'd want to eat a chocolate statue of yourself. So you could pretend to be a giant? A giant who is eating you? Why would you possibly want to do that?)

There's nothing I love more than talking about inventions, but there's a problem.

"These are all *good* ideas," I say. "What we need is a *bad* idea."

"We do?" Manny asks, puzzled.

"Sure! We don't want to give away a good idea to Impostor Mom. We want to keep all our good ideas to ourselves. What we need is a bad idea that we don't care about giving away."

Manny nods. "That makes sense. The idea would have to be bad enough that we don't want to invent it, but *interesting* enough for Impostor Mom to write back asking for more details."

Manny quickly walks over to our dry-erase board. He uncaps a purple marker and writes "BAD" and "INTERESTING" on the board.

We both stare at the board, thinking.

"A TURTLE TRANSLATOR?" I suggest.

"Why is that a bad idea?"

"Who cares what turtles think?"

"Other turtles. Turtle owners. Fishermen."

"Why do fishermen care what turtles think?"

"You could send the turtle into the water to find out where the fish are, and then the turtle could report back to you," Manny says. "Turtle Translator is an excellent idea. I'm writing it down." He makes a note on his phone.

I get an idea. "Maybe we should look for ideas on the website! It's full of bad ideas!"

We've got this website called Sure Things' Next Big Thing where kids from all over the world can send in their ideas for inventions. If an idea's really good, we help make the product and share the money with the inventor. That's where the Sibling Silencer came from. A girl named Abby came up with the idea and a rough prototype, and then Sure Things, Inc. turned it into a successful product. (Again, I apologize if your brother or sister has one.)

I turn to my laptop, click on the website, type in my username and password, and scroll through kids' ideas. "Let's see . . . the SOAP SCUM ELIMINATOR, the LEAF-CATCHING TREE SKIRT (so you never have to rake leaves again), the TIME TRAVEL MACHINE-boy,

Manny, we sure do get that one a lot."

"Because it's a great idea," Manny says. "It's just very, very hard to invent."

"Like, maybe, impossible," I say, staring at the screen. Then I spin around in my chair. "This doesn't feel right. Looking at these kids' ideas and using them as Impostor Mom bait. Sure, a lot of these ideas are pretty bad, but the kids like them. It seems mean somehow to use them as bad ideas."

"But you just said they were bad ideas!"

"I know, but there's a difference between just saying, 'Oh, that's a bad idea,' and ignoring it, and saying, 'Oh, that's a bad idea, so I think I'll use it as bait to catch Impostor Mom.'"

"The kids will never even know we did it!"

"Are you sure?" I ask. "What if Impostor Mom *really* takes the bait and runs with the bad idea and manufactures it! Then the kid who came up with the idea would see that we gave it to a mean manufacturer who steals ideas!"

Manny thinks about this and nods. "Yeah,

I see what you mean. It's just not right. We'll have to come up with a bad idea of our own."

"That shouldn't be too hard," I say.

Actually, it is.

We need an original bad idea of our own that the spy will go for. We have to make sure it's not *so* bad that it'll give away the fact that we're onto the spy. If the spy smells a trap, whoever it is might refuse to answer our e-mail and cut off communication. We'll never find out who Impostor Mom is. And never get revenge.

We come up with a few ideas, but none of them seem right. Manny can still see something good about them. He writes them down and refuses to let us tell the spy about them.

Manny and I decide to sleep on it. There's no rush.

Except that Mom's secret software will self-destruct in five days . . .

At school on Monday I'm still thinking about the perfect bad idea. I haven't come up with anything when lunchtime rolls around, so I decide to sit by myself. Manny is cool with it. He knows that I need to concentrate. Maybe I'll think of something while I'm eating.

I chew my sandwich and look around. A small kid named Jacob has a can of Dr. Fizzy soda to drink with his lunch. He must have brought it from home, because the cafeteria definitely doesn't sell Dr. Fizzy. They probably should, though, because it's popular.

Unfortunately, another kid sees Jacob's soda too: Darrell Fliborg. If bullies had a club, Darrell would be president.

"Hey," Darrell says to Jacob. "Where'd you get that?"

"Get what?" Jacob asks nervously. Conversations with Darrell Fliborg rarely end well, and he knows it. Jacob's smart.

"That can of Dr. Fizzy," Darrell grunts.

"Oh," Jacob says, sensing trouble. "I, uh, brought it from home."

Darrell smiles, but it's not a friendly smile. More of a "just what I wanted to hear" kind of smile. "Then I'm afraid I'm gonna have to conjugate it. No outside drinks allowed."

Knowing what's good for him, Jacob doesn't correct Darrell's use of "conjugate" by telling him he means "confiscate." But he does do something interesting.

Though he keeps looking right at Darrell, I see Jacob sneak his hand over to his sandwich. There's a red onion sticking out of the sandwich. Jacob rubs the red onion between his fingers.

"Oh," Jacob says, stalling for time, "I didn't know that. Well, that's okay. I think there might be something wrong with this can of Dr. Fizzy anyway."

Darrell squints suspiciously. "What's wrong with it?"

"I don't know," Jacob says. "It just smells really weird. Here."

Jacob holds the can right under Darrell's nose. What Darrell doesn't realize is that he's also holding his FINGERS right under Darrell's nose—the same fingers he used to rub the onion!

"EW!" Darrell says loudly, pulling his head back. "Gross! Get that away from me!" He leaves to go find someone else to bully. Unfortunately, there's always someone else.

As he leaves, Jacob smiles and wipes his fingers on a napkin. Then he takes a good, long drink from his can of Dr. Fizzy. Even though he wiped his fingers, he holds the can close to its base. Onion smell is hard to remove.

Jacob's little trick is brilliant. And it gives me an idea. . . .

After school I pick up Philo at my house. (He's thrilled to see me, but then he's *always* thrilled to see me—and just about everyone else, too. Maybe not the mail carrier or the veterinarian, but pretty much everyone else.) We head on over to the office together. I'm eager to tell Manny my idea.

When we get there, Manny's standing at the free throw line. Once again, he's holding the large All Ball in its basketball form. Since Manny got on his free throw kick, I don't think it's been changed to any of the other four forms (soccer, foot, volley, or bowling ball).

"Twenty," he says when we walk in.

"Twenty free throws in a row? That's great!"

"No," he explains. "Twenty is my *goal*. So far I've got six in a row."

I unclip Philo from his leash and he goes straight to the water bowl we keep for him in the office. **SHLURP! SHLURP! SHLURP!**

"Why have a goal of twenty?" I ask. "Would you really stop if you made twenty free throws in a row? Why not have a goal of infinity?" ∞

"Because setting realistic goals is one of the secrets to success," Manny says. "All the business books say so."

"Okay," I say, launching a ball in the pinball machine. "Then maybe your goal should be seven. Not twenty."

"Ha-ha," Manny says. He throws the ball. *Clunk!* "That's your fault. You threw me off."

"No, you threw the *ball* off. *Way* off." The pinball rolls straight down between my flippers. I flap the flippers like mad, but it's no use. I turn away from the pinball machine. "I have an idea."

"What is it?" Manny asks. He sits down and looks right at me. When I say I have an idea, he always gives me his full attention.

"It's called the STINK SPECTACULAR," I say.

"Okay . . . ," Manny says doubtfully.

"It's a drink that smells terrible, but tastes great."

Manny still looks confused. "Why?"

"So that you'll want to drink it. You wouldn't want to drink it if it didn't taste good."

"No, I mean why does it smell terrible?"

"I'm glad you asked. The terrible smell

makes the drink bully-proof! Let's say a bully starts to steal your delicious soda. He takes one little whiff, and *zoom!* That bully's out of there! He leaves, and you get to enjoy your delicious Stink Spectacular!"

Manny just sits there for a second, thinking about this. Then he smiles. "Oh! I get it! This is your *bad* idea! To use as bait for the spy!"

This hurts my feelings a little bit. I don't think the Stink Spectacular is a bad idea. I think it's a *great* idea!

"No!" I argue. "This isn't a bad idea! It's a really good idea! I think it should be Sure Things, Inc.'s next product!"

"Seriously?" Manny asks.

"Yes! Seriously!"

"Nobody wants to drink a drink that smells terrible," he argues. "Isn't smell, like, some huge percentage of taste, anyway? How can something smell terrible and taste great?"

"I don't know," I say, picking up a small All Ball and tossing it in the air. "How can one ball change into five balls? I didn't used to know that, either, but I figured it out."

I keep tossing the ball and catching it. Normally Manny would use the remote control to change the ball while it was in the air, but he doesn't do it this time. He just sits there, thinking.

"How often do bullies try to steal your drink?" Manny asks. "Is that really a common problem?"

"I don't know—look it up," I suggest.

"What am I searching for?" he asks. "'Bully steals drinks?'"

"Sure," I say. He hits the keys on his laptop. We're both quiet for a while.

"You know, though," I finally say, "there might be a *version* of the Stink Spectacular that could work as bait for the spy. . . ."

Chapter Four

Stench Quench

WE'RE BACK IN MANNY'S BEDROOM. I'M TYPING ON his antique computer. When I work on this thing, I feel as though I should be wearing a top hat and a black suit. I tell Manny this.

"You mean like you should be dressed formally?" he asks, confused.

"No, I should be dressed like in olden times, because it's an antique."

"I think people still wear top hats and black suits to really formal occasions."

"Like what?"

"Presidential inaugurations?"

I look at what I've written to Impostor Mom.

Dear Mom,

    Hi! How are you doing? I'm fine, and so is Philo. And Emily. And Dad.

"Seems kind of stiff," Manny says. "Is this the way you always write to your mom?"

"Yeah," I lie. Then I admit the truth. "No, not really. But I'm kind of nervous. I mean, I know I'm writing to a corporate spy, not my mom. It's weird. It's also kind of strange writing with you reading over my shoulder."

"Sorry, but this is important Sure Things, Inc. business," Manny says, sitting back a little. "Just pretend you're writing to your mom. But don't give away any of our real secrets."

"Duh," I say, deleting what I've written. I start over.

Hi, Mom,

    Everyone here is great. We sure do miss you. When will you be back home?

"That's better," Manny says. "But you'd better cut that last question."

"Why?" I ask. "That's exactly what I'd say to my mom!"

"Yeah, but it might freak out Impostor Mom, since he or she doesn't know the real answer."

That is actually a pretty good point. I hit the backspace key. Then I resume typing.

School is good. Yesterday I found out I got an A on that math test.

Emily's still speaking in a British accent. She even calls the hood of the car the "bonnet" and the elevator the "lift."

Dad's working on a series of paintings lit by the sunset instead of the sunrise, which means he's been fixing us breakfast. Today he made pancakes with celery, fennel, liver, and lingonberries.

I taught Philo a new trick. It's called Lying Around Doing Nothing. He's—not surprisingly—really good at it.

217

"Okay, now it seems like you're stalling."

"This is exactly the kind of stuff I write to my mom! Isn't that what you want me to do?!"

"I do! But the parts about your family and dog don't have to be long. Impostor Mom's probably going to skip those parts anyway!"

"Okay, fine. Let's bait the trap. . . ."

Things at Sure Things, Inc. are great. The All Ball and the Sibling Silencer are selling really well. Manny's thrilled with our sales.

"You're putting *me* in this?!"

"Yeah, I have to if I'm going to talk about the business! Which is kinda the whole point!"

Manny frowns. "I don't know if I like having a corporate spy know my name."

"Your name is already very well known as part of Sure Things, Inc.! It'd take, like, two seconds to search 'Sure Things' and have your name pop up!"

"Yeah, well, I still don't like it."

218

"Now you know how I feel. You don't like having your name mentioned. *I've* got to write to the spy and pretend it's my mom!"

"Just go ahead and write."

Even though our first two products are doing great, Manny says it's really important to get another product going right away.

"Oh, so now you're going to put my name in every single sentence. Nice."

I laugh.

We've been kicking around ideas, and we've come up with one that we really like.

"That's the fourth time you've used 'really.'"

"It's an e-mail to my mom! Not an English assignment! Do *you* want to write it?"

Manny considers it. Then he shakes his head. "No, you know how you've been writing to the spy? This has to sound like your other e-mails. If all of a sudden this e-mail sounds different, Impostor Mom might get suspicious. Go on."

This is definitely a million-dollar idea! It's called Stench Quench. It's a drink that smells terrible . . . and tastes even worse! Kids are gonna love it. There's nothing kids love more than being grossed out, according to Manny's marketing magazines. I'm working on the formula, trying to get the stench just right. I'm so excited about this idea!

"I was going to put 'really excited,' but I changed it in your honor," I say.
"Thanks. 'Preciate it."

Well, I hope you're doing great. I'd write more, but I want to get back to work on my secret formula for Stench Quench.
Love, Billy

"Do you think maybe 'secret formula' is pushing it a little too much?" Manny asks.

"No, not at all. Everyone wants to know the 'secret formula.' That makes the bait even more . . . baity."

I read over what I've written. I put the cursor over the send button, but I hesitate. "Okay," I say. "Last chance to not communicate with a corporate spy. Are we sure we want to do this?"

Manny takes a big breath and lets it out. "Yeah. Send it."

CLICK!

And off it goes! My first e-mail to a corporate spy! No, wait—that's wrong. I've written a bunch of e-mails to this spy. I just didn't know I was writing to a spy. This is my first e-mail *deliberately* written to a corporate spy.

"I'm not sure about this," Manny says, looking worried.

"Oh, *now* you're not sure about this?! After I've already sent the e-mail? Great!"

"Sorry! I'm just . . . not sure."

"What are you not sure about?"

"STENCH QUENCH."

"What about it?" I get up and wander around

Manny's room. I consider moving some of the pieces on the chessboards without Manny seeing, but that seems mean. Funny, but mean. I'm pretty sure these are games he's playing with people over the Internet or something.

"It's just so . . . weird! A drink that smells and tastes terrible? I'm afraid Impostor Mom may not go for it. Or even worse—the spy may smell the stink of bait and never write to you again."

"It's not *that* weird. Kids do like gross stuff. That part is true. In second grade, Mike Stevenson showed me his booger collection. He had them taped to the pages of a notebook, with labels and everything."

"What did the labels say? 'BIG BOOGER'? 'LITTLE BOOGER'?"

"I don't remember. I think they had dates."

"Of what?"

"I'm not sure. The picking?"

"Okay, well, that's different from Stench Quench. Mike Stevenson wasn't drinking or eating boogers."

"Actually, I'm pretty sure he was."

"Gross!"

I stare at the computer screen. "I wonder how long it'll take for Impostor Mom to write back."

"*If* Impostor Mom writes back," Manny says.

We both sit there, staring at the screen together. "Let's talk about the Stink Spectacular a little bit," I suggest.

"Speaking of gross ideas," Manny replies.

"It's not a gross idea!" I protest. "I mean, yeah, it'll *smell* gross! But it'll taste great! Millions of kids are sure to buy it! Think of the 'gross' profits!"

Manny doesn't laugh at my pun. "I don't know, Billy," he says. "I'm still just not sure about this idea. I think you should keep thinking about what our next product should be.

Maybe take a look at some of the Sure Things'
Next Big Thing ideas."

"I don't need to look at the website! *This* is
our next big thing! I'm sure of it!"

Manny lets out a big breath.

Then . . . **DING!**

A new e-mail!

We both lean forward to see who it's from.
Impostor Mom!

Manny and I both try to grab the mouse to
click on the e-mail. He wins.

Hi, honey,

Now that I know it's some corporate spy
writing to me, I find the "Hi, honey" greeting
really disturbing.

Thanks for writing back to me. You must
be awfully busy with work—I haven't heard
much from you lately! But I understand that
your company and your schoolwork take
most of your time.

"Laying on the guilt," Manny says. "Pretty good at pretending to be a mom."

Speaking of your work, I'm so glad you and Manny are coming up with new ideas!
Not quite sure I understand the idea of Stench Quench, though. Why would kids want to buy a drink that smells terrible?

"I agree with you, Impostor Mom!" Manny yells.

Maybe you can explain the whole thing to me. Feel free to send me details.

"Okay," Manny says, taking a deep breath. "Time for the big question. Did your mom's super-secret spy software work?"

"Let's see," I say. I click on the e-mail and drag it over to the icon for the software my mom sent me. The software goes to work. . . .

"Is there a name?" Manny asks eagerly. "And a picture?"

"There sure is."

"Who is it?"

"Some yucky-looking guy with stringy gray hair and an enormous . . . is that a wart? . . . on his forehead."

"That sounds like Alistair Swiped!" Manny exclaims.

I have no idea who Alistair Swiped is, so Manny explains that he's the head of one of our biggest rival companies, Swiped Stuff, Inc. Manny, of course, knows all about him because, as CFO, it's his job to know stuff like that. He's really good at his job.

"Is he in his underwear?" Manny asks, squinting at the picture.

"No," I say. "But he's picking his nose."

"Maybe he'll send his boogers to Mike Stevenson."

"I think Mike moved on to collecting baseball cards. At least, I *hope* he did."

Manny leans back in his chair, puts his hands behind his head, and looks up at the ceiling of his bedroom. "So the corporate spy

is Alistair Swiped. I guess that makes perfect sense, in light of the EVERY BALL."

That's right! I forgot about the Every Ball! Swiped Stuff, Inc. came out with the Every Ball, an obvious rip-off of our All Ball a few months after our All Ball hit the market. It costs a little less than the All Ball, so some kids bought it thinking they were getting a cheaper version of the All Ball, but then word quickly spread that the Every Ball was just a golf ball zipped inside a baseball. And a crummy golf ball at that. And a lousy zipper. Soon the Every Ball was off the store shelves. We thought that Swiped Stuff, Inc. had gone out of business.

Apparently we were wrong.

When I think about Alistair Swiped pretending to be my mom so he can steal my ideas, I get mad all over again. "That guy is no good!" I yell.

"I agree," Manny says. "And a thief!"

"Someone should put his company out of business once and for all, so he'll stop ripping off other companies! And the poor kids who buy his terrible products!"

"Well, we're someone. Maybe *we* should put Swiped out of business!"

"Yeah!" I agree. Then I stop and think. "How?"

Manny thinks for a minute too. "Well," he says, "we've already gotten the ball rolling. He seems interested in Stench Quench."

I smile. "Yeah. Stench Quench may be the perfect way to stop Swiped. We just have to keep him interested. . . ."

Chapter Five

Turning a Nibble into a Bite

I WANT TO WRITE BACK TO ALISTAIR SWIPED RIGHT away, but Manny doesn't think that's a good idea. "Do you often write back quickly?"

"I don't know. Sometimes. But probably not. I write her, like, once or twice a day."

"And when you write to her twice in one day, do you write the e-mails back-to-back, or is it more like one e-mail in the morning and another e-mail in the evening?"

"I guess it's more like one morning e-mail and one night e-mail."

"Then we should wait. We don't want to

make Swiped suspicious in any way."

That makes sense, but it's hard to wait. I'd like to get revenge right away. I guess my face shows that I'm feeling impatient. Manny says he can read my face like a spreadsheet.

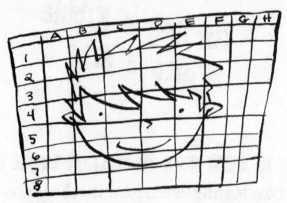

"Look, we got a nibble. But we want a bite, so we can hook this stinking fish," he says.

"Since when do you know anything about fishing?"

"Hey, I've been fishing!"

"How many times?"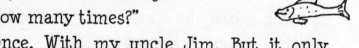

"Once. With my uncle Jim. But it only takes one fishing trip to learn about nibbles and bites and hooks. You learn all that in, like, the first two minutes."

I smile, picturing Manny in a boat, fishing. I see him with a fishing pole in one hand and his phone in the other, checking sales figures while the fish steal all his bait.

"Okay, Mr. Fisherman," I say. "We'll put some really good bait on the hook and get Alistair Swiped to take a huge bite. Then we'll reel him in!"

"Great," Manny says. "We'll write back tomorrow."

The next day after school I head past the office to Manny's back door. His dad lets me in.

"Hi, Billy," he says. "How's business?"

"Good," I say automatically. When people first asked me how my business was doing, I used to give them long, detailed answers until I realized they didn't want long, detailed answers. I was just so excited about our new company that I liked talking about it. Now I mostly just say "good." (I'm still excited about it, though.)

"Not working in the office this afternoon?"

231

he asks. "Is everything okay out there? If there are any leaks, I'll be glad to fix them!"

Mr. Reyes teaches history, and when he's not working he enjoys trying to fix things around the house. Unfortunately, he's about as good a handyman as my dad is a chef. Manny still talks about the Kitchen Sink Disaster from two years ago. His dad tried installing a garbage disposal himself. We're still not sure how he did it, but he made it so when you turned on the faucet, garbage came out instead of water.

"No, everything's fine," I answer. "Manny and I just need to do something on the old computer in his room."

Mr. Reyes smiles. "Yes, I saw you two had set up that antique. I think that was the first computer we got for Manny. He was so excited. We thought he wanted to play computer games, but it turned out he wanted to make a spreadsheet of our household expenses!" He laughs.

I say good-bye to Mr. Reyes and head upstairs. Manny thinks we should keep corresponding with Alistair Swiped from his old computer, just to be safe, since that's the one that has the special spy software on it that my mom sent us.

"Ready to write?" Manny asks. "This baby's all fired up and ready to go!" he adds proudly.

"Ready!" I say, lacing my fingers together and stretching them out in front of me. "Are you sure you don't want to write this time?"

Manny shakes his head. "Definitely not. The e-mails have to stay consistent."

"All right, then," I say, sitting down in front of the computer. "Watch your back, Shakespeare, 'cause here I come." Manny's already opened a new e-mail document. I just have to type. I think for a second and then start writing. . . .

Hi, Mom,
    Had a good day at school today. Even the food in the school cafeteria was good!

"He's not going to believe that!" Manny jokes. "Pretty sure Swiped has never eaten in our cafeteria, so I think it should be okay."

"Let's get right to the stuff about Stench Quench," Manny suggests. "That's all this old thief is really interested in anyway."

"You got it!"

It wasn't easy concentrating on my studies. I'm so excited about Stench Quench! I know this is going to be a million-dollar idea. No, a BILLION-dollar idea!

"Too much?" I ask after I type that.

Manny considers it. "No, I don't think so. Swiped seems really greedy. It's good to tell him Stench Quench is a billion-dollar idea."

"Okay, how about a trillion-dollar idea?"

"Too much."

I know it sounds weird saying that kids will love a really gross drink. But kids love buying gross stuff, and grossing each other out.

"Do you think I should mention Mike Stevenson and his booger collection?" I ask.

"No way. We want to reel Swiped in, not gross him out."

Plus kids love to brag. It's like proving you're brave. "I bought a really gross drink! And I DRANK it! I'm braver than you are!"

"That's really good," Manny says. "Now I think you should put in the stuff about market research that we talked about."

"I'm not sure about this part," I say. "We haven't actually *done* any market research!"

"Yeah, but Swiped doesn't know that!"

"Okay, okay . . ."

Manny and I are doing some market research, and the results are really exciting! They show that kids LOVE the idea of Stench Quench! And they want to buy lots of it right away!

Manny rubs his face, thinking. "Maybe that's enough. We're just trying to bait the hook, not fill the boat with worms."

"Great. I'll wrap it up."

Now that I've told you more about Stench Quench, I can't wait to get back to work on perfecting the formula!
Love, Billy

"When did you fall in love with Swiped?" Manny teases. "And what made you love him? Was it the stealing or the spying? Or both?"

"Ha-ha," I say as I click send. "So what do you think? Do you think he'll go for it?"

Manny shrugs. "Who knows? I hope so. All we can do is wait to hear back from him and see what he says."

We don't have to wait long.

We were starting to leave the room, thinking we had time to go downstairs to the kitchen and grab a snack, when we heard the **DING!** of a new e-mail! We turn around and rush back to our chairs. This time I win the battle for the mouse and click on the new e-mail.

Hi, honey,

"Don't you just hate it when Alistair Swiped calls you 'honey'?" Manny asks, smiling.

"I'm so happy he wrote back that I don't care what he calls me," I say.

My work is going just fine. Glad to hear that you're so excited about your new idea for Stench Quench. And thanks for telling me more about it. I'm really busy, so I'll have to keep this note super short, but I'm curious about your market research.

"Uh-oh . . . ," Manny says.

I'd love to see the results of your research. I'm just so proud of the work you do that I'd love to be able to share it with my fellow employees here at work.

237

"That's pretty lame," I say.

"What is?"

"The 'I'd love to show your stuff to my colleagues' angle," I explain. "My real mom knows we keep our new inventions secret, especially in the early stages, so she'd never ask if she could show some of our research results to the people she works with."

> Gotta go! Love you so much! Love to your father and sister!
> Mom

"Well, it's nice to know that Alistair Swiped loves you back," Manny says, trying to keep the smile out of his voice.

"Yes, that is nice," I say, playing along. "So, what are we going to do about this market research?"

"I don't know," Manny says, getting up and wandering over to one of the chessboards. He moves a piece, and mutters, "Check." Then he looks back at me. "But whatever we do, we'd better do it fast. The longer we take, the more suspicious Swiped will become."

And then, just like that, it comes to me.

"I have an idea," I say.

I stand outside Emily's bedroom. The closed door has a sign on it: PLEASE KNOCK. ESPECIALLY YOU, GENIUS.

I knock. Gently. I've been warned many times about "pounding on the door like some kind of VIKING INVADER." *Knock, knock.*

Nothing.

The problem with knocking gently on Emily's door is that when she's in her bedroom, she almost always wears headphones so she can listen to music. Mostly British pop singers, lately. I don't know if she's listening

to the music to improve her accent, or if the accent came after she started liking British music. It's hard to get inside her brain. And really, who would want to?

I try knocking a little louder. *Knock, knock!*

"WHO IS IT?" Emily yells from inside. From how loud she yells, I'm guessing she's still got her headphones on. She even yells in a British accent.

"It's me!" I say. "Your brother! Billy!"

"GO AWAY, GENIUS!" she shouts.

Silence. I'm guessing she's flopped down on her bed, listening to music and texting her friends and playing a game and reading an article about fashion, all at the same time.

Now I'm getting annoyed. To heck with her sign. I pound on the door. **KNOCK! KNOCK!**

Suddenly the door whips open. I don't even know how she got across her room that fast to open it. "WHAT DID I SAY ABOUT POUNDING ON MY DOOR?" she yells in her best British accent. Her headphones hang around her neck.

I decide to ignore her loud question. "Hi, Em!" I say cheerfully. "Pip-pip! Cheerio! Top o' the mornin' to ya!"

She narrows her eyes. "It's afternoon," she says in a low, murderous voice. "Almost evening. What do you want?"

"I just need a tiny little favor." Before I can explain, she starts to close her door on me.

"Forget it," she says.

I stick my foot in the doorway to stop the door from closing all the way. This is dangerous, since Emily has been known to stomp on my foot, but I really need this favor.

"Actually, it's not for me," I say quickly. "It's for Sure Things, Inc., and as the company's vice president in charge of Next Big Thing development, surely you want to help out."

Not too long ago, Manny and I hired Emily to help wade through all the suggestions for inventions that came in on our Next Big Thing website. She'd insisted on being given a title. I'd actually forgotten what her title was. I had to look it up before I knocked on her door.

When I mention her title, Emily looks slightly less irritated. "Only if I'm paid," she says. Emily likes money.

"Okay," I agree, pretending to think it over, even though I knew she'd ask for money. "You'll be paid. And we need you to get some of your friends to help."

"They'll want to be paid too," she says.

"Fine," I say. "If you could get three or four of your friends to come over and help, that'd be great. Thanks."

I start to leave. Then I remember something and turn back. "Oh, and for this job, you'll have to lose the accent."

"What accent?" Emily asks in her British accent.

A couple days later I'm in the kitchen, pouring fruit juice into the blender. I'm following my mom's old recipe for fruit punch. (*Not* my dad's recipe. When he saw that I was mixing up fruit punch in the blender, he offered to show me how to make one of his kale and cabbage smoothies, "chock-full of vitamins and anti-oxidants!")

I punch the button. **WHIRRRR!** I pour a little of the punch in a glass and taste it. It's really good. Now I just have to make it look awful.

On the counter there's a bag with food coloring in it. I pull out yellow, green, and blue. I pull off the tops and squeeze drops of food coloring into the fruit punch, combining the different colors until the punch looks like brownish, greenish sludge. Perfect.

My dad walks back into the kitchen. "How's the punch coming along?" he asks cheerfully. Then he sees what I've made. "Hey, you decided to use my recipe after all!"

A little later I'm in the backyard with the repulsive-looking punch, a video camera, Emily, and five of her friends—Maggie, Emma, Willa, Lauren, and Jody. (When word got out that they'd be paid for this, Emily had no trouble at all getting five friends to participate, even though I'd only asked for three or four.)

"Okay," I say. "It's really simple. All you have to do is drink this punch and pretend you love it." I gesture toward the muck in the pitcher I've placed on our picnic table.

"Drink that?!" Lauren says. "No way!"

"What is this? Some kind of stupid prank?" Willa asks, folding her arms across her chest.

"It tastes good," I explain. "It just *looks* bad because I put food coloring in it. Here, I'll show you." I pour myself a little glass and drink it. "See? It's fine."

Jody steps forward. "I'll try it," she says bravely. "How bad can it be?" I pour her a glass. She takes a tiny sip, then smiles. "It's good! Like fruit punch!"

"That's because it *is* fruit punch," I say. "But for the video, you're going to pretend it's something called Stench Quench. You're also going to pretend it smells and tastes terrible, but that you love how gross it is."

"Let me get this straight," Maggie says. "That's actually fruit punch. It looks horrible, but it tastes good. We're going to pretend it smells awful and tastes awful. And we love that because we love gross things."

"Exactly!" I say, delighted that Maggie's got it all figured out. I think I remember Emily saying that Maggie is her smartest friend.

"So we're pretending to be crazy people?" Willa asks.

"No, you're just normal kids who like gross stuff," I explain.

"You were right," I overhear Emma whisper to Emily. "Your brother's really weird."

"Just think about all the nail polish we can buy after we get paid," Emily reassures her.

I shoot several takes, and the girls get more and more into pretending that they love Stench Quench. "IT'S SO GROSS, IT'S GOOD!" Maggie says right into the camera.

In a couple of takes, Emily forgets that she's not supposed to use her British accent. When I say we have to do those over, she says "Why? Couldn't this be an international group?"

"Ooh, I want to be French!" Emma says. "Zis ees zee grossest zing I ever tasted!"

I convince them to just talk like them-selves without any accents, and we do another take. I'm starting to worry that I didn't make enough Stench Quench.

In one take, Emily takes a sip and pretends the Stench Quench is so great that she faints. She lies in the grass for a second. "You can get up," I tell her. "I'm not sure we can use a version where the drink makes you pass out."

"The problem with you," Emily says, "is that you've got no imagination."

We finish with a shot where the girls scream like they've won the lottery. "WHERE CAN WE BUY STENCH QUENCH?"

"That's it!" I say. "Great job! We're done!"

In the office Manny and I use video-editing software to cut the different takes together into a single video. "Not too smooth," I say as Manny trims a few more seconds out of it. "We want this to look like a video of a marketing research test, not a TV commercial."

When the video's ready, we practically run with it up to Manny's bedroom. We can't wait to send it to Alistair Swiped. "I just hope that old computer's capable of sending a video," I say. "We may have to shovel some extra coal into its engine."

"I checked the requirements for sending video," Manny says as we clamber up the stairs. "It should be able to do it . . . slowly."

He's right about the "slowly" part. It seems as though it takes forever for the video to load onto the old computer's hard drive. Then I write an e-mail to go with the video.

Hi, Mom,

Just a quick note to say I'm sending you a recent video of a Stench Quench test-marketing session. It went well, as you'll see! All the sessions have gone great. Just thought you might enjoy seeing this one.

Love, Billy

"Oh no," Manny says, looking worried.

"What's the matter?" I ask. "Did I misspell something?"

"I just thought what if he recognizes Emily?"

"How would he recognize her? It's not like she's famous or anything?"

"She was on *Better Than Sleeping!* with you!"

He's right. I went on the late-night talk show *Better Than Sleeping!* to demonstrate the All Ball. At the end of my part of the show, the host, Chris Fernell, brought Manny, my dad, and Emily out onto the stage.

"That was just at the very end," I protest. "He probably didn't see that."

"*Probably,*" Manny repeats ominously. "She was also with you on *Wake Up, America!*"

He is right about that, too. When I went on the talk show to promote the Sibling Silencer, I demonstrated how it worked on Emily.

"If Swiped went through all the trouble to make up a fake e-mail address for your mom and e-mail you with it," Manny continues, "why wouldn't he make sure he recorded every one of your appearances on national television talking about your inventions?"

It's a really good point. I can't believe

I didn't think of this when I decided to put Emily in the phony test-marketing video. "I don't think we have time to reshoot the video," I say. "Swiped might get suspicious if we take too long to send him any proof that kids like gross stuff."

Manny gets up and starts pacing around. He says it helps him think. I think he's just burning off nervous energy. "Could we re-edit the video to cut out Emily?"

I shake my head. "I don't think so. She's right in the center of just about every shot. Emily likes being on camera."

"Maybe," Manny says, still pacing, "I could put a circle over her face, and we could explain that after we did the testing, one of the participants refused to let us show her face on video."

"Why?"

"Um, because she's in the Witness Protection Program?"

"I don't know. . . ."

Then I get an idea. "How about this?" I say, turning back to the computer keyboard.

P.S. One of the test participants may look a little familiar! Yes, that's Emily. She insisted on taking part in one of our marketing tests. (You know how she loves to be on camera.) That's why I'm sending you this particular video out of the dozens of Stench Quench test videos we've made. I knew you'd love seeing Emily again when you're so far away.

"Okay?" I ask.

Manny thinks a long time. Finally, he says, "Yeah. I think that's okay. It's believable that Emily might do that."

"Totally believable."

"All right," Manny says. "Let's send it."

It takes the computer quite a while, but finally a box pops up saying, "Message sent."

"I just hope Swiped takes the bait," Manny says.

"I bet he will," I say, trying to sound confident. "Taking stuff is his favorite hobby."

Chapter Six

Just Sleep On It

THAT NIGHT IN MY ROOM, AFTER I FINISH MY homework, I check my e-mail to see if there's anything from Alistair Swiped. I know I'm not supposed to *open* his e-mails on my bedroom computer, but I'm pretty sure it's safe to see if there's one in my in-box.

Nothing.

I hope Emily appearing in the video didn't ruin everything. Maybe I shouldn't have sent that video. Maybe I should have taken the time to reshoot the whole thing without Emily in it.

I decide to write an e-mail to my *real* mom.

When I type in the e-mail address, I triple-check to make sure I'm sending it to Mom and not to Alistair Swiped.

Hi, Mom,

We sure do miss you around here. Can't wait till your work lets you come back home. We'll all be so happy to see you. Philo might wag his tail right off.

Thanks again for your help with the corporate spy. We know who he is—he's the head of a rival company. And he's terrible— he steals ideas and then sells crummy products to kids. Manny and I decided that we want to put him out of business for good. So we e-mailed him, telling him we had this idea for something called Stench Quench. He acted interested and asked for more info. We sent him a video of some fake test marketing. We'll see if he takes that bait. . . .

I tell her some more stuff about what's going on at school and home and with Sure Things,

Inc. I think about asking her if she really is a spy, but then I think if she could tell me, she would. So either she isn't a spy, in which case I'll seem silly for suggesting it, or else she is a spy, but she can't tell me, so asking her will just make her feel bad about lying.

I decide not to ask.

Not long after I send the e-mail, my computer makes the chiming noise that tells me I've got a new e-mail.

Alistair Swiped?

No, it's my mom, writing back right away!

Hi, honey,

I'm always happy to hear from you and learn all about how you're doing.

I think you and Manny are doing an excellent job trapping the corporate spy. I'm impressed! I'm proud of you! (Of course, I'm always proud of you.) You and Manny would make great spies! That is, I imagine you would, based on what I see in the movies.

Good night, honey. Go to bed. But first pet Philo for me.

Love, Mom (real one, not impostor)

Smiling, I pet Philo and get ready to go to bed. But before I do, I get an idea.

Ever since I thought of the Stink Spectacular, I've been working on coming up with the formula for it. That is, I've been working on it whenever I could get a free moment from schoolwork, the Stench Quench spy trap, walking Philo, and choking down Dad's meals.

I know Manny's not too enthusiastic about this idea, but I love it, so I've been working on it anyway. Without telling him. That part's weird. I hate keeping secrets from Manny.

I've been able to make some drinks that taste good. And I've been able to make some drinks that smell terrible, like rotten eggs mixed with moldy cucumbers. But I haven't been able to come up with a drink that smells awful but tastes wonderful. I've been getting closer, but I still haven't nailed it.

I look up at the framed blueprints for the All Ball and the Sibling Silencer, which I came up with in my sleep. I have finished all of my big inventions in my sleep. I actually get up out of my bed and work on the inventions without ever waking up. In the morning, I find the finished blueprints on my desk. I know I do this, because Manny videotaped me finishing the Sibling Silencer blueprints in my sleep.

Some people sleepwalk. Some sleep-eat. I sleep-invent.

So far this has always happened when I wasn't expecting it to happen. I didn't even *know* yet that I was a sleep-inventor. It just happened.

But now that I know, can I *make* it happen? Or at least help it along somehow?

I'm getting pretty close on the Stink Spectacular formula. When I'm close is when I sleep-invent.

I open a drawer and dig out some blueprint paper. I lay it out neatly on my desk. On the left side of the paper, I carefully place a pen and a pencil. I'm right-handed, but when I sleep-invent I use my left hand. I know because I saw myself doing it in Manny's video.

MURF! MWURF! MOOF!

The muffled barks are coming from Philo. He's already asleep in his doggy bed next to my bed. He doesn't sleep-invent, but maybe he sleep-chases rabbits. Or cats. Or maybe even dragons—who knows what dogs dream about?

I look at the stuff laid out on my desk, satisfied. But is there something else I can do

to nudge my brain into a little sleep-inventing?

I open another desk drawer and find an index card. With a marker, I write "STINK SPECTACULAR" on the card. And even though this seems kind of silly, I put it under my pillow. I guess instead of leaving a tooth for the tooth fairy, I'm leaving a suggestion for my own brain.

Once all that's done, I lie down and fall asleep quickly.

I'm tied to a chair again. In an empty room. The walls go up so high that I can't see the ceiling.

The man dressed in gray enters the room. He stands in front of me, completely still, with his arms hanging at his sides. He's got his gray mask on, but there's a hole for his mouth.

He smiles, but it's not friendly. "Did you really think you could fool me?"

"Did you think you could fool *me*?" I ask defiantly. "I know who you are!"

"Stench Quench," he says slowly, as though it was a ridiculous combination of words.

"Absurd. You expected me to believe that?"

"Let me go," I say.

"Oh, I'll let you go," he says. "Up."

I'm confused. "Up?"

He nods slowly. "Up. Way up."

The man in gray walks over to the wall and flips a switch. Then he seems to get smaller.

But that's because I'm rising. He must have turned off the gravity in this room. Still tied to the chair, I'm floating.

Up.

Higher and higher and higher, until the man in gray is just a speck far below me. His quiet, mocking laughter floats up.

And then someone is licking my nose. . . .

The someone is Philo, naturally. Time to get up. Groggy, I roll out of bed and pull on some clothes, getting ready to take Philo outside.

But then I notice something.

The blueprint paper and the pencil and pen I put on my desk have moved. Suddenly I remember the card I put under my pillow! I pull it out. The word "DONE!" is scrawled across it. I try a quick experiment: I write "Done!" on the card with my left hand. It matches.

I hurry over to my desk and look at the blueprint paper. It's been written on!

I snatch up the papers and stare at them, a big grin spreading over my face. It's definitely a formula for the Stink Spectacular!

"The Stink Spectacular? I thought we agreed that was a bad idea," Manny says.

"Uh, no. *You* thought it was a bad idea. I thought it was a great idea."

We're in the office, playing foosball.

"So you went ahead and worked on it without telling me?" Manny says, twirling a line of miniature players.

"I don't have to tell you every time I'm working on inventing something! Sometimes I'm just thinking about an invention in my head. Do I have to tell you every time I start thinking about an invention?"

I realize that I sound like Emily. Not because I'm speaking with a British accent (because I'm not, of course) but because I sound defensive. But I'm getting kind of mad. I'm also feeling a little guilty about going ahead with an idea I knew Manny didn't like. After all, we're partners. I wonder if Emily has such complicated feelings going on all at the same time, and maybe that's why she's so obnoxious?

"We're partners!" Manny says as though he's reading my mind. "When it comes to the business of Sure Things, Inc., we have to tell each other everything!"

"Okay, I'm sorry," I say. And I mean it. "I should have told you. But last night I sleep-invented the formula! I think it's perfect!"

"Perfectly gross," Manny says.

"Yes, exactly! It's a million-dollar idea!"

Manny sighs. "You keep saying that, but I'm not sure I see it. I mean, I guess there might be a niche market for it."

"'Niche market?' Is that French?"

Manny makes his "I can't believe you don't know this" face.

"A niche market is a small, specialized market—a little group of specialized buyers with a particular, unusual taste for something. I think the niche market for Stink Spectacular is kids who are being bullied out of their drinks."

I think about that for a moment. "Okay, well, I think it's bigger than that. I think it's for kids who want to show they're brave enough to drink something that smells awful. Which is, like, almost every kid."

"It still sounds like a niche market to me. It might not have the big, general appeal of the All Ball and the Sibling Silencer. For our next invention, what about the Personal Force Field? Or the Dog Translator? Those are products with appeal for lots of people. I love those ideas!"

THWACK! THWOCK! The ball's really flying back and forth now, with both of us spinning the rods like mad, moving quickly from one end of the table to the other.

"I love those ideas too," I agree. "But I have a really good feeling about the Stink Spectacular. And now that I've sleep-invented the formula, I can't wait to try it out. All I have to do is get the ingredients, mix up a batch, and see if it works!"

Manny's face scrunches up so I can tell he's thinking hard about what I said. I'm hoping I managed to change his mind.

"I'm sorry, Billy," he says, not taking his

eye off the ball. "I just don't think I see it."

For a while we just play foosball. **THWACK!** **THWOCK!** And then, **CLONK!** The ball goes in the goal. On my end. Manny scores! He raises both fists above his head. I pretend to be mad he won, but Manny knows I'm only kidding. He usually beats me at foosball.

"You may have won the great foosball challenge, but I'm still going to make the Stink Spectacular," I say.

Manny just shrugs. He walks over to the free throw line, picks up the ball, and starts shooting free throws.

For the next several minutes, the only talking either of us does is Manny counting free throws. "One . . . two . . . three . . ."

Chapter Seven

The Fish Takes the Bait

LATER THAT DAY MANNY AND I ARE TAKING A BREAK from our Stink Spectacular debate when an e-mail arrives from Impostor Mom!

Manny's working at his computer in the office, checking sales figures. I'm working at my desk. It's almost like we've both been zapped with the Sibling Silencer. It's *that* quiet in the room.

I glance at my e-mail in-box and see there's new mail. "Swiped!" I yell, getting out of my chair.

"What about him?" Manny asks.

"He sent an e-mail!" Manny jumps up out of his chair and heads inside. I'm close behind.

We race through the kitchen. "Hi, Mom!" Manny yells. She gives a little wave, looking slightly confused. "Did you see more bugs out there?" She looks ready to spring into action.

"No!" Manny answers as he sprints up the stairs. "No bugs! Nothing to worry about!"

Unfortunately, the old computer isn't turned on. "It gets really hot if you leave it on," Manny explains. It takes forever to power up. We finally get through to my e-mail. I click on the message to open it.

Hi, honey,

Thanks so much for sending me that video! It was so nice to see Emily. She looked like she was having a great time. And so did the other girls. It's clear that they really do like the idea of the Stench Quench.

"I guess it was okay to have Emily in the video after all," Manny says.

"Looks like it," I say. "That's a relief."

I have to admit that I found it hard to believe kids would really want a drink that smells and tastes horrible. But now that I've seen the video, I guess they really do!

I'm curious about how you're going to make your Stench Quench. I worry a little that it might not be safe to drink. Would you mind sending your worried mother the recipe?

"Swiped wants the recipe!" I yell. My smile is as big as Manny's.

"He took the bait!" Manny says, holding up his hand for a high five. I gladly high-five him. This is great news!

Please promise me you won't try to make any Stench Quench until I've had a chance to run your recipe by some of the other researchers here. Maybe we'll make a test batch, just to be sure it's completely safe.

"He's obviously trying to keep you from making the Stench Quench before he does!" Manny says excitedly. "He wants to be the first one to sell Stench Quench! This is so great!"

Work's a little slow right now, so this would be a great time for us to test out your formula. But we're probably going to get swamped with work soon, so the sooner you send me your formula, the better.

Love to you and your father and Emily and the dog,

Mom

"He's so excited about the formula that he doesn't even bother to look up Philo's name in his records!" I point out. "We've completely got him! He's hooked!"

"Right!" Manny agrees. "Now all we have to do is send him the formula."

"True," I say. "But there's a problem."

"What's that?"

"We don't *have* a formula for Stench Quench! Remember?"

"Oh yeah," Manny says. "Well, we'll just have to come up with one. How hard can it be to make a recipe for a drink that smells and tastes terrible?"

I think about this for a moment. Then I grin. "I just happen to know an *expert* in things that smell and taste terrible!"

"You want me to do what?" Dad asks, not believing what he just heard me say.

"Show me how to make your kale and cabbage smoothie!" I say enthusiastically.

We're in his painting studio. It's a small wooden building he built himself in our backyard. The ceiling has skylights, so he can get lots of sunlight shining in to light up whatever he's painting. I always like coming into the studio. It smells like paint and wooden boards and stretched canvas. But I don't come in here too often, since Dad doesn't like being interrupted when he's painting.

"Well!" Dad says as he sticks his paintbrush into a jar of clear liquid with a bunch of other brushes spattered with paint. "That's great! But I must admit I'm surprised! I didn't know you were interested in cooking, Billy."

"Oh, I am!" I say, trying to sound as enthusiastic as possible. "Well, at least smoothies. I don't mean to interrupt you, though. I know you're busy. . . ."

"No, no! That's all right!" He wipes his hands off on a rag. "Any time's a good time for learning how to cook! I'll be happy to show you right now, if you like!"

"That'd be great!"

We go into the kitchen and Dad immediately opens the fridge and starts rummaging through the vegetable drawer. "Pretty sure I've still got some kale and cabbage in here somewhere. . . ."

He places the leafy green vegetables on the counter, then reaches up into the cabinet above the stove and pulls down a few small bottles. "The secret ingredients," he tells me with a wink, "are the seasonings. I use a special blend of garlic powder, onion powder, and cumin. That's what makes this drink really special!"

As I watch, my dad carefully measures out the stinky spices and mixes them together in a bowl. "Now let's blend us up a couple of smoothies!" he exclaims.

I ask him to wait just a moment while I run up to my room to get my tablet so I can take notes and pictures. Dad is thrilled I'm taking such an interest in cooking, so he happily pauses.

For once, Emily has her bedroom door open. "What are you doing, genius?" she asks.

"Cooking with Dad," I explain.

She makes a face. "You're a loony!" she says in her British accent. I have to admit, her accent's getting better. I think maybe she's watching British TV shows online.

I'm back downstairs in no time. I make sure to carefully take note of all the ingredients Dad uses, and the exact measurements. Dad turns on the blender, and within moments we have a fresh batch of his kale and cabbage smoothies. It's a disgusting green color. He pours me a glass and one for himself. Then he raises his glass in a toast. "To your health!"

I take a sip, pretending to gulp down more than I'm actually drinking. "Delicious!" I manage to croak out.

"Glad you like it!" he says, beaming. "Any more questions on how it's made?"

I shake my head. "Nope. I think I've got it."

"Good! If you don't mind, I think I'll take my smoothie out to the studio. I'd like to get some more done while the light's still right."

"Sure!" I say. "Thanks, Dad!"

"Anytime! Maybe next you'd like to learn how to make my tuna-guava-lima-bean casserole!"

"Maybe!" I say. "I'm not sure my cooking skills are quite up to that yet, though."

Once he's gone, I add some more ingredients to the drink. Sure it's disgusting, but I think it could be worse. Both the smell and the taste could be even more repulsive. I only use things I find in the fridge, like red onions, stinky cheese, and maple syrup. The more I add, the harder it gets to try tasting it. I consider calling Emily down to the kitchen, but I don't think any amount of money would make her drink this sickening slop. Even she's not *that* greedy.

I keep careful notes on everything I add to the Stench Quench. I think it's ready, but I'm not absolutely sure. . . .

"WHAT IS THAT HORRIBLE SMELL?" Emily suddenly yells from her room, completely dropping her British accent.

That's it. I've got it!

I jump on my bike and zoom over to Manny's. He's got the ancient computer ready.

Hi, Mom!

Thanks so much for offering to test my Stench Quench recipe! I really appreciate it!

I have to admit that at first, I didn't want to wait for you to do the safety tests on my Stench Quench. I'm excited about the idea, and so is Manny, so we'd like to get our new product on the shelves as soon as possible.

But we do want the Stench Quench to be safe for kids to drink, so we decided to wait until you give us the results of your tests. I'm attaching the recipe to this e-mail. IT'S SUPER-DUPER TOP SECRET AND WE HAVE NOT HAD TIME TO FILE ANY PATENTS ON IT OR ANYTHING LIKE THAT! PLEASE DON'T LET THIS FALL INTO THE WRONG HANDS!

"Like Swiped's hands!" Manny jokes.

"Exactly. Hey, maybe I should say that in the e-mail!"

Manny considers it, then shakes his head. "No, I think that's too risky. We should pretend we've never even heard of Alistair Swiped. We don't want him to suspect we're onto him."

"Yeah, you're right. It'd be funny, though. We could say something like, 'that obnoxious, ugly, smelly thief, Alistair Swiped.'"

"That dumb, stinking baboon, Alistair Swiped!"

"That nauseating, loud-mouthed loony, Alistair Swiped!"

""LOONY"?"" Manny asks. "Who says 'loony'?"

"My sister."

"Quick piece of advice: Don't pick up vocabulary words from your sister."

Reason #239 Manny is a great CFO: He gives really good advice.

"Let's see," I say. "Where was I? Oh yeah. . . ."

Manny and I will really be looking forward to hearing what your tests say. Hope the results don't take too long to come back.

Miss you and love you,

Billy

I read over the e-mail to see if it's all right. Manny agrees it's good. I click send, and off it goes.

"When do you think Swiped will send us his safety-test results?" I ask jokingly.

"Oh, probably on the twelfth."

"The twelfth? Of what?"

"Of never."

I get up from the desk chair and stretch. "Well, I'm glad we're done with the Stench Quench. It's in Swiped's hands now. I can concentrate on making the Stink Spectacular."

"Or the Personal Force Field Belt. Or the Dog Translator. . . ."

I pretend not to hear him.

Later in the week I realize I actually feel grateful to Emily for her help in making the Stench Quench video. And feeling grateful to Emily is so unusual that I decide to thank her.

Her door's slightly open, so I stick my head in. "Emily, I just wanted to thank you for all your help with the—"

I stop talking when I realize she's not listening. She's crying and punching her pillow. Like many things Emily does, the crying and punching seem a little overdramatic.

"What's wrong, Em?"

"Get lost!"

I turn and start to leave, but she sits up and shoots her arm straight out. "Wait!" she cries. I notice that even though it sounded like she was crying, her face looks dry. "Maybe it would be good for my soul to unburden myself."

She says this in her British accent.

"Okay," I say. "Unburden away."

She starts to speak, but then stops, as though it's too painful for her to say out loud.

"What is it?" I ask. "Is someone trying to kill you? Is it a vampire? Are *you* a vampire?"

She sighs heavily. Then, with her lower lip trembling, she blurts out, "Dad won't let me wear makeup!"

THAT'S ALL?

My brain immediately says, *That's all?* but luckily I've gotten better at not saying everything my brain comes up with. "Really?" I ask. "That's . . . terrible." I'm guessing, based on how she's acting, that Emily thinks it's terrible.

Sniffing, she says, "Yes, it is. All my friends get to wear makeup. I'm fourteen years old! I'm sure Mom would let me wear it if she were here, but she's off doing her stupid research! So I have to live under Dad's tyranny!"

I've never thought of my dad as a tyrant before. Somehow he doesn't seem like much of a tyrant, painting pictures of animals in his studio and cooking meals for us. If he forced us to *eat* the meals, knowing we hated them, I guess that might be kind of tyrannical. But he thinks his food tastes great, so he thinks he's doing something nice for us. But maybe all tyrants believe they are doing the right thing?

"Dad told me that if I sneak wearing makeup one more time, I'll be grounded."

"That's, uh, terrible." I'm having trouble thinking of different words for Emily's makeup tragedy. Or should I say made-up tragedy?

"There's this huge party tomorrow, and if I can't wear makeup like every single one of my friends, I'll just *die!*" She throws herself back down on her bed with her face buried in the pillow. She resumes punching the pillow, even though it doesn't seem like the pillow's done anything wrong at all.

Emily drives me crazy most of the time, but I certainly don't want her to die. And I feel as though I owe her for the Stench Quench video. I mean, not only did *she* act in the video, drinking my gross-looking fruit punch, but she also got a bunch of her friends to be in it.

She starts making crying sounds again. I know this sounds weird, but I'm pretty sure she's crying in a British accent.

"Em," I say. "Em, listen. I've got an idea."

She immediately stops crying and sits up. "What is it? Some kind of FATHER FREEZER?"

"What? No! What's a Father Freezer? You want to put Dad in a freezer?!"

"No, it'd be kind of like the Sibling Silencer, only instead of silencing your sibling, it'd freeze your father. You could go out and do whatever you want, and then when you came back you'd unfreeze your father, and he'd be fine, but he'd never know he was frozen or that you were at a party wearing makeup."

She's clearly given this some thought.

"Um, no, my idea isn't a Father Freezer. It's much less . . . diabolical. I think I could probably make my idea into a real thing for you in a couple of days."

She frowned. "That's no good. The party's tomorrow! If you're going to help me, you'll have to hurry. Go on! Get out of here! I'm sick of looking at you anyway!"

I guess it's nice to help my sister. But she doesn't make it easy.

Chapter Eight

Making Up Makeup

IT'S LATE FRIDAY NIGHT. I'VE SPENT EVERY SECOND since Emily kicked me out of her room learning about makeup. It's like makeup is this whole world I never knew existed. Thank goodness for the Internet.

I've got kind of a minilaboratory in a corner of my bedroom with a lot of chemicals and other stuff I can use for experiments. But I need even more chemicals, and other compounds that go into makeup. Down in the basement, I find old chemistry sets of mine and raid them. I even ride my bike to this

chemical supply store on the edge of town to
pick up a few things. They know me there. "Hi,
Billy!" they call out when I walk in the door.
"How's the invention business?"

So now it's really late. Luckily, since it's
Friday, I don't have to get up early tomorrow.
I've made some progress on my idea, but there's
still a pretty good distance left to go before I
arrive at the thing I have in mind for Emily.

Should I keep working? I yawn so wide I
think my mouth might split open. If I keep
trying to work tonight, I'm probably going to
pass out facedown in a bunch of chemicals.

Maybe I should forget the whole thing. Let
her wait until she's sixteen to start wearing
makeup, or whatever age Dad'll let her.

But she is my sister. And it would be nice.

How? There just isn't enough time.

Then I get an idea. I open one of my desk drawers and get out blueprint paper. I set the paper on top of the desk with pens and pencils. I find an index card and write "DISAPPEARING MAKEUP" on it.

That's my idea. Makeup that disappears after you apply it, only to reappear after you've left the house and passed Dad-inspection.

The question is, am I close enough with the formula to sleep-invent it?

I don't want to overdo it with the index cards under my pillow. It seems like if I stick a card under there every single night, I'll run out of sleep-invention power or something.

But since I really have no idea how my sleep-inventing works, I don't know how often is too often. I decide it's worth a shot.

I stick the card under my pillow, pat Philo on the head, and lie down in bed.

But before I fall asleep, I have another idea. I get up and turn on the little video camera on my computer, aiming it so it records most of my bedroom. I leave a small light on.

Will I be able to fall asleep with this light on? Yes, almost immediately.

I'm back in the empty room. But this time I'm not tied to a chair.

I'm sitting in front of a makeup mirror, staring at my reflection. There are all kinds of makeup on the counter in front of me, things I never knew existed—base, blush, eyeliner, eye shadow, mascara, lipstick, lip liner. . . .

My reflection starts to move. It turns blurry. And then it turns into the man dressed all in gray. This time he isn't wearing a mask. His face is gaunt and unfriendly.

I stare at him. He stares back at me. Then he frowns.

"What is all this?" he asks in his low voice.

"All what?" I ask.

"All this . . . makeup!"

"Just an invention I'm working on."

He looks confused. "What do *you* know about makeup?"

"Oh, I know plenty," I brag.

"Really?" he asks. He reaches out of the mirror and picks up a small container. He holds it up for me to see. "What's this?"

"That," I say confidently, "is lip liner."

"Wrong!" he says as he unscrews the top. He pulls a small brush out of the container. "Everyone knows that this is nose makeup."

"Nose makeup? There's no such thing!"

"There is now!" he says as he starts brushing wet makeup onto the tip of my nose. . . .

"Philo! Enough! Enough licking!"

It's Saturday morning. Too early to get up yet, but Philo doesn't know that, so he's licking my nose, waking me up. I gently push him away and get out of bed.

I feel really sleepy. Really, really tired . . .

But then I see the blueprints on my desk, and suddenly I'm wide-awake!

I hurry over to look at them. They're the formula for making Disappearing Makeup!

Sitting at my desk, I click on my webcam

video. At first I'm just sleeping. But when I fast-forward, I see myself get up out of bed, walk to my desk, sit down, and write with my left hand.

I pause the video and check my minilab desk. I find prototype makeup—everything Emily needs! It's not perfect yet—some of the colors are pretty weird—but it's a good start.

No wonder I felt so tired when I first got up. I must have been working most of the night!

Still, there's a lot more work to be done. I've got to refine this makeup, test it, and have it ready for Emily before her party tonight.

Just before lunch, I'm ready. I gather everything I've made and go down the hall to Emily's room. The door's closed. I knock. Gently.

"Enter!" she commands in her British accent.

I open the door and go in. Emily's lying across her bed on her stomach, looking absolutely miserable. "I have no life," she says. "I can't wear makeup, so I can't go to the party tonight. My social life is over."

I hand her the makeup. "Here. Try this."

She looks disgusted. "I thought you were supposed to be smart. I told you, Dad won't let me wear makeup! I'll be grounded!"

"This isn't ordinary makeup," I explain. "It's Disappearing Makeup."

Emily picks up the lipstick. "Disappearing Makeup? What's the point of that? If it disappears, you might as well not be wearing any makeup at all!"

"It disappears, but it comes back. When you put it on, it's triggered by the heat and energy from your skin. Within five minutes, it disappears. But then five minutes later, it reappears! And it lasts for hours, until it finally disappears from your face for good!"

Emily takes in what I'm saying. She starts to look a little less miserable.

"So," I continue, "here's what you do. About five minutes before you're going to leave for the party, you put on the makeup. Five minutes later, it's disappeared. You go show your face to Dad, who smiles and says, 'That's my beautiful clean-faced girl! Have fun at the party!' You hurry out the door, and within five minutes, you're all made up for the party. You go to the party, dazzle everyone, and come home completely clean-faced for Dad's late-night inspection. Simple!"

Emily gets it. She smiles. In fact, she's so thrilled, she gives me a big hug! "Thank you, Billy! This is wonderful!"

I pull away. Ew!

She opens the eye shadow and inspects it. "Although this isn't exactly the shade I like. Can you make me a soft bronze?"

Chapter Nine

What's Swiped Up To, Anyway?

AFTER CHOKING DOWN SOME OF DAD'S LUNCH, I TAKE
Philo and go over to the office. As we walk in,
Manny sinks a free throw and says, "Eighteen."

"Wow! Eighteen! That's really good," I say.

"Thanks," Manny says modestly. "My cur-
rent goal is twenty-five." The gadget that
automatically returns the ball arrived in the
mail yesterday.

It's still kind of weird between Manny and
me. I'm working on the Stink Spectacular, but
not around Manny because I know he hasn't
warmed up to the idea. I think he knows I'm

working on it, though, because he doesn't ask me anything about when our next product will be coming out. He works on the marketing and sales of the All Ball and the Sibling Silencer. And he shoots free throws.

"I wonder what's going on with Swiped," I say. "Impostor Mom hasn't written me any more e-mails."

"Maybe that's because he got what he wants," Manny suggests. "Once we sent him the recipe, he had what he needed."

"I just wish I knew what he's up to. It *seems* like he took the bait, since he asked us for the Stench Quench recipe, but we don't know what he's doing with it. Once he saw the recipe, he may have rejected the idea. Or he may have figured out that the whole thing was a trap."

Manny sets down the All Ball and goes over to his desk. He sits down and starts typing. "Let's see if there's any news about what Swiped is up to."

He clicks on an article, reads a little, and says, "AHA! JACKPOT!"

"What is it?" I ask.

"Listen to this! 'Alistair Swiped of Swiped Stuff, Inc. to introduce new product on prime-time TV!'"

"*What?* All right!"

Manny keeps reading. "Alistair Swiped, the CEO of Swiped Stuff, Inc. is betting big on his new product. He's bought seriously expensive television time to introduce the mystery product tonight."

"*Tonight?* That was quick!"

Manny turns and faces me. "Yeah, well, once he got the recipe, it wouldn't take him that long to whip up a batch of Stench Quench. You did it in your kitchen in, what, twenty minutes?"

"I don't think it even took that long."

"So if you're Swiped and you have the resources of your whole company behind you, you could probably get a bunch of Stench Quench made really quickly! I'll see if anyone knows what the product is," Manny says, turning back to his computer. He searches, and comes up with tons of articles. Lots of business websites have articles on Swiped's bold move. They say that Swiped has even hired TV personality Chris Fernell, the host of the late-night talk show *Better Than Sleeping!*, to interview celebrities, getting their reactions to his exciting new product. But no one knows what the product is. Alistair Swiped has managed to keep that a secret, despite the best efforts of every business reporter to find out.

"Do you really think his new product is going to be Stench Quench?" I ask. "That would be so incredibly awesome!"

"And sweet revenge! Because the product would be sure to fail. Nobody wants a drink that smells awful," Manny says gleefully.

This seems like a pretty obvious criticism of the Stink Spectacular, but I let it go. "Wanna sleep over at my house tonight and watch Swiped's big show?"

"Sure," Manny says. "I wouldn't miss it."

I'm a little worried that it might be kind of awkward having Manny spend the night while we're disagreeing about the Stink Spectacular. But I have a plan.

After dinner I'm going to offer Manny an early version of the Stink Spectacular to show him how delicious it is. I'm pretty sure he'll love it, and agree that we should produce it. But if he doesn't, we won't. I respect his opinions. That's why he's my chief financial officer.

Once Dad has finished his painting and comes into the kitchen to fix dinner, we wander in there to find out what he's making. I figure it's better to have a little time to get used to the smell of Dad's dinner instead of just having his latest creation sprung on you. Like a deadly tiger.

Dad's at the counter, mixing something in a bowl. "What's for dinner, Dad?" I bravely ask.

"Well, it's pretty warm today, so I thought maybe I'd grill."

That doesn't sound so bad.

"W-what are you grilling?" Manny asks nervously. He's eaten at our house before. Though he usually does his best to avoid it.

"Cheeseburgers."

CHEESEBURGERS?! Something normal? And potentially delicious?

"I thought maybe some simple, old-fashioned cheeseburgers might taste good tonight," he continues. "I don't have to cook gourmet creations *every* night. Besides, I've noticed a fair amount of food being left on plates lately." He winks at me.

Cheeseburgers! Things are looking up!

Emily comes into the kitchen, which is unusual, since she usually avoids the kitchen when Dad's cooking. She's got her sulky face on. If there were contests for sulking, Emily's room would be full of trophies.

"Well, the party tonight is going to be completely humiliating, since I'll be the only one not wearing makeup," she says.

SULKY GIRL
CHAMPIONSHIPS
1ST PLACE

She turns so that I can see her face but my father can't. She shoots me a quick smile. It's all an act. I think she's laying it on a bit thick.

But my father buys it. "Now, honey," he says reassuringly, "we've discussed this. Right now you're too young for makeup. But don't worry. We'll revisit the whole makeup issue. When you're sixteen."

"By then it'll be too late! I'll already be a social outcast!" She stomps out of the room dramatically, flashing me another smile.

Chapter Ten

The Next Big Thing

AMAZINGLY, THE CHEESEBURGERS ARE DELICIOUS.
Dad didn't even put one little shred of kale in
them. For once Philo hangs around while we
eat. I toss him a bite. *Chomp!*

As we leave the dining room, Manny says,
"I think those were the best cheeseburgers I
ever had. Are you sure your dad made them?"

"Let's have something else delicious!" I say,
pretending it just occurred to me.

"Dessert?" Manny asks eagerly.

"Sort of," I say. "Let's go upstairs and try
some Stink Spectacular!"

Manny's face falls. "You've made the Stink Spectacular?"

"An early version," I say. "I'm still refining it, but it's good. Come on, give it a try."

Manny hesitates. Then he nods his head slowly. "Okay," he says. "I'll try it."

We go up to my room and I get a plastic jug out of the minifridge. It's full of red liquid.

"It doesn't *look* bad," Manny says.

"I want the color to be appealing, since the smell is so bad."

As I take the lid off, Manny looks a little nervous. I pour two glasses and hand him one. He makes a face. "Yuck! Man, does this *stink!*"

"That's the idea," I say. "But wait till you taste it."

He lifts the glass to his mouth, squeezes his eyes shut, and takes a tiny sip.

"Well?" I ask.

Before Manny answers, Emily comes in. She's wearing the Disappearing Makeup. I don't know much about makeup, but it looks to me as though she's put on plenty.

"Well, what do you think?" she whispers.

"Is the party you're going to, like, a circus party or something?" Manny asks, puzzled.

"Circus party? No! Why?"

"Because you're wearing clown makeup," Manny says. He still has a long way to go before he's mastered talking to sisters.

"This is *not* clown makeup!" Emily hisses. "You obviously know nothing about makeup!"

"That's true," Manny admits.

"Eww," Emily says, wrinkling her nose. "What's that smell?"

"Stink Spectacular," I answer, raising my glass. "Want some?"

She rolls her eyes and sighs, as though this

is not even remotely worth an answer.

Suddenly Manny points at Emily. "Hey, the makeup looks better! Less clownlike!"

"That's because it's disappearing," I explain. As we watch, Emily's makeup fades away and completely disappears.

Emily looks at herself in the mirror. "Success! Gotta go!" She gives me a quick hug (I'm not sure I like the new hugging Emily) and rushes out to pass Dad's inspection before she goes with her friends to the big party.

"What was *that* all about?" Manny asks, completely baffled.

I feel a little embarrassed to admit that I've been using my inventing skills on makeup. On the other hand, I'm proud that my Disappearing Makeup works.

"Dad won't let Emily wear makeup, so I invented Disappearing Makeup. She puts it on, and after about five minutes it disappears. She shows her face to Dad and leaves for her party. In another five minutes, the makeup reappears and stays on for several hours. At the end of the night it disappears again, so Dad won't see it when she gets home from the party."

Manny just sits there, staring at me.

"It's really no big deal," I say, wondering if he's mad that I spent so much time on something for Emily instead of focusing on inventing something for Sure Things, Inc. "Just a little thing I made for Emily because she helped us out with the Stench Quench video."

"Disappearing Makeup," Manny finally says, nodding slowly. "That . . . is . . . BRILLIANT!"

"It is?"

"Absolutely! Do you have any idea how big the cosmetics industry is?"

"Um . . . no."

"It's huge! A multibillion-dollar business! And I'm pretty sure teenage girls are a big chunk of that business! And your product is revolutionary! There's never been anything like it!"

I shrug. "Thanks. Makeup's not really my thing, so I didn't think it was a big deal."

Manny is so excited he stands up and paces

around my room. "It may not be your thing, but it could be our next big thing! This is the product we've been waiting for!"

I trust Manny's instincts. If he says Disappearing Makeup is a Sure Thing, I believe him. After all, we're partners. We have to work together if Sure Things, Inc. is going to make it. Or keep making it.

I still like my idea for the Stink Spectacular. Actually, I love it. And I think kids would love it. But like I said, I trust Manny's instincts.

"I think we should try to put out Disappearing Makeup as soon as possible," Manny continues. "We're still getting a lot of attention because of the All Ball and the Sibling Silencer, so we should launch another product while people are paying attention to Sure Things, Inc. And we need some huge platform for the launch."

I'm confused. "We're going to build a huge platform? Out of wood? Like a pirate ship?"

Manny laughs. "You never, ever read the business journals I loan you, do you?"

"I tried. Once. Too boring."

"A platform is something you use to show off you new product, like the Internet or TV. Actually, the one good idea Swiped had was introducing his new product live on TV during prime time with lots of celebrities. He'll probably get millions of viewers."

"Speaking of the show, it's time!" I realize. We run downstairs to the living room.

Chapter Eleven

Showtime!

MANNY AND I SETTLE DOWN WITH MY DAD AND PHILO in the family room. "What is this that we're watching, anyway?" Dad asks.

"It's kind of a spy show," Manny says.

"Okay," Dad says. "I like spies."

Enough to marry one? I think. From the look on his face, Manny's thinking the same thing.

On the TV, a band plays some music, and Chris Fernell enters. The live studio audience applauds.

"Hello, everyone, and welcome to this very special television event! Tonight we're going to learn about an exciting new product from world-famous businessman Alistair Swiped!"

"World famous?" my dad asks. "Never heard of him."

"I know we're all waiting to find out what the new mystery product is, so let's bring it on out, okay?" Chris says enthusiastically.

The audience claps and cheers. A pretty woman wheels a cart out with cups, a bucket of ice, and a stack of cans on it.

"Do those cans say what I think they do?" Manny asks, excited.

"I think so!" I say, standing up and getting closer to our TV.

"Stench Quench!" we both yell at the same time. Philo barks, wanting to join in.

"Stench Quench?" Dad says. "What's that? I thought this was a spy show."

Chris Fernell picks up one of the cans and holds it out so the audience can see it. "Alistair Swiped's exciting new product is . . . STENCH QUENCH!"

There's some quiet, scattered applause, but

mostly the audience seems quite puzzled.

Chris Fernell moves to a couch. "I know, it's kind of a funny name. Let's bring out the inventor to explain it to us. Please welcome . . . ALISTAIR SWIPED!"

A tall, thin man with stringy hair enters from behind a curtain and gives a little wave to the audience. I realize he looks a little bit like the man dressed all in gray in my dreams. And the man in the picture we got from my mom's spy software. Wait, did I just call my mom a spy? I didn't mean that! Anyway, I never realized before now that the guy in my dreams is the same guy from the picture.

Alistair Swiped.

He sits down on the couch next to Chris Fernell. Chris says, "So, Alistair, tell us. What's the deal with Stench Quench?"

Swiped smiles, at least with his mouth. His eyes don't really look like they're smiling. "Well, Chris," he says, "first let me ask you something. Do you have children?"

Chris smiles a real smile. "Yes, I do. Two

beautiful children. Twins. A boy and a girl."

"Do they like gross things?"

Chris laughs. "Yes! They love gross stuff! You should see the things they bring into the house! If we go to the park, it's like they've got some kind of radar for grossness. They zoom right in on it! Next thing I know, it's on our kitchen table!" The audience laughs.

"Well, Stench Quench is perfect for them! Stench Quench is a new drink that tastes even worse than it smells!"

"Okay," Chris says, looking a little puzzled. "Should we try some?"

"I have an idea," Swiped says, trying to act as though this idea just occurred to him, even though it obviously was planned. "Why don't we let Dustin Peeler try some?"

The audience applauds, and Dustin Peeler enters through a curtain. Just last summer, he was the biggest pop star on the planet. But lately he's been getting into trouble, and he's not quite as popular as he was. That's probably why Swiped was able to hire him.

"Dustin Peeler . . . ," Dad says. "Doesn't Emily like him? Too bad she's missing this. Maybe I should record it."

"I don't think Emily really likes Dustin Peeler anymore, Dad," I say.

After greeting Chris Fernell and Alistair Swiped, Dustin pops open a can of Stench Quench. He's obviously repulsed by the smell. "Whew!" he says, waving his hand in front of his nose.

"Isn't that disgusting?" Swiped says. "Kids are gonna love it!"

Dustin holds the can in front of him, hesitating.

"Go ahead," Swiped urges him. "Taste it!"

"Okay," Dustin says. "Here goes."

He lifts the can to his lips and drinks. His eyes bulge. You can see he wants to spit it out immediately, but Swiped glares at him, and he swallows the Stench Quench.

"Well?" Chris Fernell asks.

"Excuse me!" Dustin blurts out. He jumps up from the couch and runs off the stage. From the wings, there's the unmistakable sound of someone throwing up.

Manny and I laugh. Dad's totally confused. "I really don't get this show at all."

But we keep watching, and it just gets better and better. Fernell and Swiped keep bringing out different celebrities and audience members and kids to try drinking the Stench Quench, but they all end up having the same reaction as Dustin Peeler.

Soon the audience is booing. "This is terrible!" one woman yells. "Stop making people drink that horrible stuff!"

Even Chris Fernell can't take it anymore.

"I don't care how much you're paying me, Swiped. This is just wrong. Stench Quench is a DISASTER!"

The audience applauds. Utterly humiliated, Alistair Swiped gets up and runs off the set.

To tell the truth, I feel a little sorry for him. On the other hand, he's a thief and a bad guy, so revenge is sweet.

Chris Fernell watches him go, and then checks his watch. "Well, this is a little awkward, folks. Swiped paid for half an hour of live television, and we've only used up eight minutes." Chris is a professional, so he doesn't look particularly nervous about having to fill twenty-two minutes of live television. "Let's see who else is backstage," he says, consulting a list. "Maybe there's still someone back there who hasn't been sickened by Stench Quench. Oh, here's one of my favorite baseball players, the shortstop for the Hyenas, Carl Bourette!"

I can't believe it. My favorite athlete of all time walks out through the curtain, smiling and waving. The audience goes nuts.

Carl sits on the couch with Chris. "You know," he says, "in all my years playing baseball, I've seen some real disasters, but this one takes the cake."

"You think my career will survive this?" Chris asks.

"Oh, I think so," Carl says. "But I don't know about that Swiped fellow."

"Dad," I say, "are you recording this?"

"Yeah," he says.

"Good, because this is the greatest thing I've ever seen on TV."

Carl's still talking about Alistair Swiped.

"Of course, inventing's a tough business. It might be even more competitive than professional baseball. I sure wouldn't want to try it."

Chris nods. "I agree. I think I'll stick to hosting a talk show. Compared to inventing, that's easy as pie."

"Speaking of inventors," Carl says, "you remember that kid, Billy Sure?"

WHAT?!

"Oh, absolutely," Chris says. "We had him on my show. You were on that night. We tossed around the All Ball."

"What is happening?" I say.

"Whatever it is, it's very, very good," Manny says, his eyes glued to the TV set. He's grinning.

"Now *there's* an inventor!" Carl says. "I wonder what he's up to?"

"Let's find out!" Chris says. He turns to the audience. "Should we call Billy Sure and ask him what he's up to?"

The audience applauds!

"Hey, Sarah!" Chris calls offstage to an assistant. "Do you still have Billy Sure's phone number from when he was on the show? Let's call him right now!"

The assistant walks onstage dialing a cell phone. She hands the phone to Chris.

Our phone rings!

"I can't believe this is happening!" I yell.

"Answer your phone!" Manny shouts.

I answer it. "Hello?"

"Hi, Billy!" Chris Fernell says. "I'm sitting here with an old pal of yours, Carl Bourette, and we were wondering if you've got any new inventions you'd like to tell us about!"

"I know," I manage to say. "I'm watching you on TV."

Chris laughs. "Keeping an eye on the competition, huh? Well, I don't think you have to worry about Alistair Swiped anymore. So, what are you working on?"

I try to tell him about Disappearing Makeup, but I realize I don't know what to say. I'm usually not really nervous when I have to talk about Sure Things, Inc. business, but this time I'm not prepared, and I've never really spent any time talking about makeup before. My mind goes completely blank.

"Ummm . . . Before I tell you about what we're working on, can Carl Bourette maybe tell us who his favorite baseball player is? I'm dying to know."

Carl immediately starts talking, and I figure I have about thirty seconds to come up with something to say about Disappearing Makeup. I try to line up a sales pitch in my head, but all I can think of is how Emily looked like a clown with all her makeup on. I look around the room frantically. Twenty seconds. Still nothing. Philo and my dad stare at me, and it feels like time has stopped. On the television, Carl Bourette wraps up whatever he was saying (I can't believe I missed his answer!) and I know I have about five seconds to come up with something. *Think!* I tell my brain. Then I notice Manny signaling for me to give him the phone. He whispers, "Trust me." And I do, of course. I hand him my phone.

Manny introduces himself and does this

amazing double pitch, perfectly describing Disappearing Makeup *and* Stink Spectacular! He even renames the Disappearing Makeup "DISAPPEARING REAPPEARING MAKEUP," which is a much better name. I'm so blown away by his perfect explanation of it (how does he know so much about the cosmetics industry offhand?) that I almost fall off my chair when he switches gears and starts talking about Stink Spectacular as well. The audience eats up everything he says.

Reason #732 Manny is my CFO: He's brilliant.

The time flies by, and Chris Fernell wraps up the show. "Well, that's all the time we have! Sorry about the start of our show, but wasn't it great hearing about Sure Things, Inc.'s new inventions, Disappearing Reappearing Makeup and Stink Spectacular?"

The audience cheers again.

I can't believe it.

Not only did we get sweet revenge on Alistair Swiped, but we also got to promote our newest product. Products, I should say!

"I can't believe you decided to talk about Stink Spectacular, too!" I say to Manny.

"I realized that right after Stench Quench bombed was the perfect time to introduce Stink Spectacular as a gag gift that tastes delicious."

"You think it's delicious?"

"Definitely! Let's have some more to celebrate!"

My dad just shakes his head. "That was the weirdest spy show I ever saw."

Chapter Twelve

Sure Things

MANNY AND I WORK REALLY HARD TO GET DISAPPEARING Reappearing Makeup and Stink Spectacular ready to sell as quickly as possible.

And after we launch them, sales take off!

I arrive at the office, fully expecting Manny to be glued to his computer, reviewing sales figures. But when I walk in, I'm surprised to see him standing at the free throw line. He launches the ball. *Swish!* He pumps his fist.

"FIFTY!"

"Fifty?" I say. "You just made fifty free throws in a row?!"

Manny nods, grinning.

"That's fantastic! Don't stop. Keep going!"

He shakes his head. "I hit my goal. I'll set a new goal, but for now, I walk away."

"I have something to show you," I say. I take a picture out of my backpack.

"What's this?" Manny asks.

"Disappearing Reappearing Makeup's new model."

"It's Emily! But what about your dad?"

I sit down at my desk and smile. "He talked to my mom, and she said Emily's old enough to wear makeup, so he's cool with it. So Emily gets to be in our ads."

"That's great!" Manny says.

We laugh. My computer goes **PING BONG BING!** It's a video chat request from my mom!

I click on "Answer With Video" and see her smiling face. She's dressed all in black.

"Hi, honey!" she says. "I wanted to congratulate you and Manny again on a great job of counter-espionage! I assume there have been no more e-mails from the spy?"

"Well, there was one," I say.

"Really?" she asks. "What did it say?"

"It said, 'You win. For now!'"

She shrugs. "Well, that doesn't sound too—"

Suddenly there's a commotion behind her. "Oops! Gotta go!" she says.

But before she signs off, I'm pretty sure I see her swing into action, fighting off what looks like a bunch of ninjas!

I sit there, stunned. Then I realize Manny's behind me. He saw the end of the call too.

"I'm telling you, dude," he says. "Your mom's definitely a spy!"

BILLY SURE

• KID ENTREPRENEUR •

AND THE CAT-DOG TRANSLATOR

CAT·DOG TRANSLATOR

Chapter One

a Boy and His Dog

MY NAME IS BILLY SURE. I'M AN INVENTOR. I'm also the CEO of my very own company: **SURE THINGS, INC.** You might have heard of our products. You might even have some of them.

The **ALL BALL** that changes into different sports balls with the touch of a button? That's us. The **SIBLING SILENCER** that, well, silences siblings? Yep, us too. **DISAPPEARING REAPPEARING MAKEUP** and **STINK SPEC-TACULAR**? Well, you get the picture. Sure Things, Inc. has had one success after another.

ALL BALL
small

ALL BALL
large

SIBLING SILENCER

The best *part* of being in business is my business *partner*. Get it? Manny Reyes is my best friend and Chief Financial Officer (CFO for short), which is a fancy way of saying that he takes care of money while I create inventions. Manny's a genius when it comes to marketing, numbers, planning, selling, advertising, computers. . . .

I could go on. But basically, I invent our products and Manny figures out how to make them into hits. It's a bit more complicated than that, but in a nutshell, that's our story.

It's a Tuesday evening. I'm home after a full day at school, followed by a full day at work. It's not easy juggling two lives.

My typical day is: Get up (I suppose you could have guessed that part, right?); shower; go to school; come home and pick up my dog, Philo; then go with Philo to the World Headquarters of Sure Things, Inc. (also known as Manny's garage). Then I come home, eat dinner, do my homework, maybe read a book or watch TV, and then go to sleep.

And you thought you were busy with soccer and school plays and—well, I guess you're busy too. I don't mean to complain—it's just that sometimes all this gets a bit overwhelming. That's when I have to remember how much I enjoy inventing stuff.

At this moment, I'm in the "finished school, finished work, finished dinner, finished homework" portion of my day. I'm hanging out in the living room playing with Philo.

"You want this, boy?" I ask, leaning forward in my seat, waving Philo's favorite chew toy at him. It's a thick rope made up of colored strands all woven together. Or at least they used to be woven together. Months of chewing and pulling have taken their toll.

Philo jumps up from his doggy bed on the

other side of the room, dashes over to where I'm sitting, and grabs one end of the toy in his teeth.

I yank my end back. Philo bares his teeth and growls, a low growl that's as much a moan or a whine as a true growl.

"Who's a FIERCE BEAST?" I ask, moving the toy—and Philo's head along with it—from side to side.

Philo tugs hard, pulling me from my chair. I tumble to the rug and start laughing. Letting go of my end of the toy, I rub Philo's belly. This always makes him go a little crazy.

I roll over, and then Philo jumps on top of me. We tumble across the room, me laughing, Philo growling and barking.

"What's going on down there?!" shouts a voice from upstairs. "Some of us have homework to do, y'know!"

That would be Emily, my sister. Last week, Emily only spoke in a British accent. Before that, she only wore black. Who knows what she'll be into next?

"Just playing with Philo," I call back up the stairs.

"Well, do it quietly!" she screams down.

I pick up Philo's chew toy and hold it over my head.

"Do you want this, boy?" I say in an excited whisper, waving the colorful, floppy rope back and forth.

Philo's head follows the moving rope, as if he were watching a Ping-Pong match.

"Ready?" I ask.

Philo backs up a few steps.

"Go get it!" I shout, tossing the rope over his head.

Philo turns and dashes after the rope. He snatches it up in his mouth, then trots contentedly back toward me, dropping it at my feet.

"Again?" I ask.

"RUUFFF!" he replies.

Sometimes I can almost understand what Philo is saying.

I pick up the rope and waggle it back and forth, then fling it past him.

This time Philo turns his head casually and watches the rope zoom by, then he turns back to look at me.

So much for understanding what Philo says.

"I thought you wanted to play, boy?" I say.

Philo stares at me like he's never seen me before.

"Go get it!" I say again.

Philo continues staring.

Oh well. I walk to the other side of the room, pick up the toy, and come back.

"One more time." I toss the rope back over Philo's head. It bounces a couple of times, then disappears into the dining room.

This time Philo turns and chases after it. He speeds from the living room into the dining room. And then doesn't come back.

"Get the toy, Philo!" I shout.

No Philo. No toy.

"Bring me the toy, Philo!" I yell again.

"Go get the stupid toy yourself!" Emily shouts from upstairs.

She totally does not get the point of this game.

But she may be right. I'm beginning to wonder where Philo went. As I step from the living room into the dining room, I find the chew toy sitting on the floor. Looking up, I see that Philo is all the way on the other side of the room.

"It's right here, boy," I say, pointing down at the toy.

Philo paces back and forth across the floor on the far side of the dining room. He stops, sniffs under some furniture, then turns and walks back to the other side of the room, where he repeats the sniffing, then the pacing, then the sniffing, and on and on.

As he paces and sniffs, Philo lets out a series of low moans and short yelps.

"URRRR . . . YIP-YIP!" he says.

"What is it, boy?" I ask.

"URRRR . . . YIP-YIP!" he repeats.

Now I really wish I could understand what Philo is saying. In fact, there have been many times when I've wished I could understand him. Things would be so much easier. I could just give him what he wants and he'd be happy. And then I wouldn't spend so much time wondering what he's trying to say.

And that's when it hits me. I know what Sure Things, Inc.'s next product should be! I will make a translator for dogs!

This isn't the first time this invention idea has come up. The first time I ever thought of it, I had just discovered the blueprints for the Sibling Silencer on my desk, but I didn't know where they had come from. Let me explain. . . .

You see, I always have trouble figuring out how to make my inventions work . . . at least when I'm awake. When I finally give up and go to sleep, the completed blueprints MAGICALLY appear on my desk the next morning.

You may be wondering who so kindly and

quietly draws the blueprints for me in the middle of the night. I wondered the same thing at first. It turns out that *I* do! In my sleep! Here's how we found out.

My first invention, the All Ball, was a hit, but I didn't know where the working blueprints came from. They had appeared on my desk one morning, and I didn't recognize the handwriting. So when I was struggling to come up with the working blueprints for Sure Things, Inc.'s next invention, the Sibling Silencer, Manny rigged an alarm system so that whoever was sneaking into my room to leave the blueprints would get caught. Except the only one who tripped the alarm was Philo. When he did, I discovered new blueprints on my desk, which meant that Philo saw who put them there.

What I didn't know was that Manny also set up a webcam and watched me work on the blueprints in my sleep. That's right. Some people talk in their sleep; some people walk in their sleep; but me, I invent things in my sleep!

But before I knew that, I remember wishing at that moment for a device that could translate what Philo was saying through his barks. And that's when the idea for the DOG TRANSLATOR first came into my head.

I have to tell Manny about this! The time has arrived for the Dog Translator!

I start to head up to my room to send Manny an e-mail, when I hear Philo scraping his paw against the floor. Turning back, I see him reach under a cabinet and drag out a doggy treat. A dust-covered, stale treat.

That thing must have been under there for weeks! Philo happily munches away.

Yuck! Dogs can be really gross sometimes.

See, if I had a Dog Translator, Philo could have just told me he wanted a treat. Of course, Philo doesn't need a translator for that. Like most dogs, he *always* wants a treat!

I dash up the stairs. I have to pass Emily's room in order to get to mine.

"What? You're done making noise down-stairs, so you decided to come here and make

noise upstairs?" she asks in her usual warm, loving tone.

"The lightbulb just went off!" I say, pointing to my head, hardly able to contain my excitement.

Emily shrugs without looking up from her desk. "So ask Dad to replace it, genius."

"No, I mean I just came up with the idea for my next invention," I say, smiling.

"Uh-huh," she replies, tapping away on her phone, her thumbs blazing. "I'll alert the media."

"Actually, that's Manny's job," I point out.

Emily just shakes her head and rolls her eyes.

"Oh, you were being sarcastic, right?"

With Emily, sometimes it's hard to tell.

I head into my room, flip open my laptop, and shoot off a quick e-mail to Manny.

Hey, Manny.

I just came up with an idea for Sure Things, Inc.'s next invention!

Billy

A few seconds later I get a reply. And this is *so* Manny:

Great! I've got the marketing strategy all planned!

I write back:

But wait, you don't even know what the invention is!

Manny writes back:

Right, right. Whatcha got?

I write back:

The Dog Translator!

I hold my breath waiting for a reply. A few seconds later it comes:

LOVE IT! We'll talk tomorrow.

That's my partner!

Chapter Two

Cats and Dogs

AS IS USUALLY THE CASE WHEN I COME UP WITH AN idea, I sleep poorly that night. I tell myself that I should wait until morning to start thinking this idea through so I can get some sleep.

But, when I'm in the thick of an inventing frenzy, like right now, my brain seems to go on autopilot, tinkering all on its own with the hundreds of tiny details that go into the creation of all of my inventions.

I toss and turn for a few hours, then finally doze off. My dreams are filled with dogs talking to me:

"I'm ready for my walk."
"My bowl is empty! My bowl is empty!"
"Throw the ball. I'm ready! Throw the ball!"

The last image I recall from my dream is Philo saying: *"I love you, Billy,"* then licking my face. I awake to Philo actually licking my face about eleven seconds before my alarm goes off.

"ERRR–RUUFF! RUFF!"

Even without a Dog Translator I know what that means.

"All right, boy, I'll take you out and feed you," I say, dragging my tired bones out of bed.

I shower, get dressed, eat some breakfast, and head off to school—all after taking care of Philo, of course. This whole time I can't get my mind off the Dog Translator. This could be the biggest thing Sure Things, Inc. has ever done. Or could it? I decide to do what Manny would call some INFORMAL, UNOFFICIAL, UNSCIENTIFIC market research. In other words, ask a bunch of kids what they think of my new idea.

As soon as I walk into school, I spot Peter MacHale. When I returned to school after the success of Sure Things, Inc. last summer, Peter was one of the first kids to congratulate me.

"Hi, Peter," I say. "Can I ask you a question?"

"Sure thing, Billy!" he says, a big smile revealing the enormous gap between his two front teeth. "Get it? Sure Thing!"

"Yeah, I get it," I say. "Listen, Peter, you have a dog, right?"

"Sure thing, Billy!" he says again, giggling.

I begin to wonder how many times he's going to make the same joke.

"I have a poodle named Lexi," Peter explains. "Why?"

"How would you like to understand what Lexi is saying every time she barks?" I ask.

"What do you mean?" Peter asks.

"What if there was a device that could translate dog barks into human words?" I ask.

"Cool!" Peter says, seeming genuinely excited. "Do you have one? How much does it cost? Where can I get one?"

"Um, it doesn't exist yet," I explain. "But I am thinking of creating it."

"Sounds like a Sure Thing to me!" says Peter. Then he heads off to class, laughing at his joke a third time.

Well, that's one potential customer.

Next I run into Dudley Dillworthy. Dudley is as tall as a bear standing on the top of Mount Everest. I used to be afraid of him, but it turns out that he's a big fan of the All Ball. Being a famous inventor can have an upside, even in school.

"Hey, Dudley, can I ask you a question?" I

say. I've heard Dudley talk about his dog before.

"What's up, Billy?" he asks. "Invent any-thing good lately?"

"Uh, a couple of things, but I just want to ask you . . . How'd you like to understand what your dog is saying?" I ask.

"What do you mean?" Dudley asks, scratch-ing his head.

"Like when your dog barks or whines or moans. What if you knew exactly what your dog was trying to say?"

Dudley shrugs. "I never thought about that, but it sounds pretty cool to me."

"Great. Thanks," I say. Then I spot Allison Arnolds at her locker. She's in my math class. A few weeks ago, she was totally *in love* with Dustin Peeler, the singer. But Emily doesn't like him anymore, so maybe Allison doesn't either.

Do you want to know a really BIG SECRET? I kinda maybe sorta think Allison is cute, but I have *never* said anything about it to *anyone*, not even Manny. Especially not Manny. He'd

338

probably blurt it out at the worst time. He's almost as bad as my dad when it comes to keeping secrets.

"Hi, Allison," I say meekly.

"Hi, Billy," she replies.

She stands there looking at me, waiting for me to say something else. Then I remember why I started talking to her. "So, you have a dog, right?"

"Yeah. I named him Dustin, but I'm thinking of changing his name. 'Dustin' just seems so sixth grade," she says.

"Okay. Well, how would you like to know what what's-his-name is saying?" I ask.

"Who, Dustin Peeler?" she asks.

"No, I mean your dog," I reply.

"Oh, well, I guess so, sure," she says. Then she heads off down the hall.

"Excuse me," I say to a boy I don't know. I figure Manny would want me to include total strangers in my market research. "Would you like it if I invented something to help you understand what dogs are saying?"

"I'd rather you invented something so that I could understand what my *math teacher* is saying," says the boy.

Uh, right. I'll have to file that one away.

I stop several more kids before homeroom. I ask each of them the same question.

"I have a cat," one says. "And a hamster. And a canary. I don't really like dogs."

"I've been waiting for this my whole life! Where can I get one?" says another.

BRIIIIIING!

The bell rings, signaling the end of my research session. Overall, I'd have to say that the majority of people I asked thought that the Dog Translator was a great idea. I'll put it at 84.3 percent in favor. Manny loves it when I use stats like that!

When the school day ends, I launch into my usual routine. I jump on my bike and speed home. Typically it takes me about fifteen minutes to ride from school to home. But on a day like today, when I can't wait to see Manny and start working

84.3% LOVE THE DOG TRANSLATOR

on our next invention, I make it in twelve.

Hurrying around to our backyard, I poke my head into Dad's art studio. He's a painter, and he spends most of his day out here in what is a former garden shed that he's turned into a pretty nice studio—if your definition of "pretty nice" is a paint-splattered shack filled with easels, brushes, and canvases.

Dad is wearing his painting overalls, which he calls his "inspiration apron." This formerly white garment looks like the result of an explosion in the paint section of a hardware store.

"Hey, Dad. I'm home," I say. "Whatcha working on?"

"It's a portrait of Philo," he replies. "I'm trying to capture a sense of what goes on inside his head."

I look over at the canvas. Dad has drawn a pretty good likeness of Philo. He's now adding colors . . . lots of colors that I've never seen on any dog anywhere.

"Cool," I say.

"Off to work?" he asks.

I nod.

"What are you working on today?"

"Let's just say . . . I think you'll like it. And I think Philo will like it too. See ya later for dinner."

"Okeydokey," says Dad.

I dash into the house. Throwing open the fridge, I spy half a peanut butter sandwich leftover from yesterday. I gobble it up, gulp down some milk, and head off in search of Philo.

I take Philo with me to the office every day. I love having him around, and I know he misses me when I'm at school. Philo loves hanging out at the office with Manny and me. He even has his own doggy bed in the corner. Philo is definitely the UNOFFICIAL MASCOT of Sure Things, Inc.

I let out a long whistle. "Phiii-looo," I call.

Philo comes tearing through the house, skidding to a stop at my feet. I lean down and scratch his head. He licks my cheek, and I laugh.

Back outside I hop onto my bike and speed off. Philo trots happily alongside me.

A few minutes later we arrive at Manny's house. I lean my bike against a tree, and Philo and I head to the garage. I can't wait to talk to Manny about the Dog Translator.

I open the door to our office. As soon as I do, **La! La! Laaah!**, a sound comes blasting out of a speaker hanging just above my head.

It's every ball you'll ever need; the greatest ball you'll own, indeed. No matter what sport you like to play, the All Ball helps you every day. That's all! That's the All Ball!

It's the new jingle for the All Ball! But why is it coming out of this speaker?

Across the room Manny is sitting at his desk. He's having a conversation with someone on his smartphone, messaging someone else on his tablet, and replying to an e-mail on his laptop—all at the same time. Look up the word "MULTITASK" in the dictionary and you'll see Manny's picture.

He turns toward me and puts his hand over his phone.

"You like it?" he calls out. "It's our new doorbell! It'll play every time the door opens. Isn't that great?"

Without waiting for a reply, Manny goes back to his phone call.

Manny loves that jingle. He says he never gets tired of it—maybe that's because he wrote it for our first TV commercial for the All Ball. Me, well, I've heard it plenty of times, and now I have to hear it every time I open the door? We may have to talk about this.

I head inside to my desk, past the soda, pizza, pinball, foosball, and air hockey machines. I squeeze past the basketball hoop and the punching bag. I could go for a custom slice of cherry pie pizza and my very own concoction that I call LIME-PICKLE SODALICIOUS right now, but there's too much work to do. Philo trots over to his doggy bed and curls right up.

"It's simple," Manny says into the phone, "any kid from anywhere in the world can submit any idea to us on our website. The contest is always open and we're always reviewing ideas."

I smile. Manny's talking about Sure Things' Next Big Thing contest. That's how we started manufacturing the Sibling Silencer. It's co-owned with a girl named Abby who came up with the idea. We just helped her create and manufacture it.

But right now the contest will have to be put on hold. The Dog Translator just has to be the next thing we work on.

"Manny, I have to tell you about my idea!" I say. I usually don't like to bother Manny when he's on a call—or three—but I just can't wait to talk about the Dog Translator.

"I'll call you back," Manny says into the smartphone. Then he taps a button on the touch screen. He quickly responds: "Be right back" on his tablet, then hits send on the e-mail he's been writing.

"Yeah, Billy, what's up?" he says, swiveling his chair toward me. "I've just been going through sales figures, and everything is looking up: the All Ball, the Sibling Silencer, the Stink Spectacular, and Disappearing Reappearing Makeup!"

"So what do you think about the Dog Translator for our Next Big Thing?" I ask.

"I love it, but I figured out a way to broaden the scope, as in . . . double the market!" Manny says, smiling. "I did some research. It seems that between 37 and 47 percent of all US households have a dog. That's great. But here comes the broadening-the-scope part—between 30 and 37 percent of all US households have a cat!"

"Yeah," I say cautiously.

"So let's make Sure Things, Inc.'s next great invention . . . the CAT-DOG TRANSLATOR! Whatcha think?"

Before I can answer, Manny continues. "The way I figure it, we can almost double the profits by including cats, allowing us to lower the price and sell more total units."

That's Manny for you, always looking to maximize profits. It's not that Manny cares about money. In fact, the money we make at Sure Things, Inc. usually goes right back into the business . . . or into our college funds. But Manny loves numbers—the bigger, the better. Sometimes I think it's all a game to Manny. And Manny loves games.

Manny is still talking about his big plans. "I figure we start with a stand-alone unit. If that does well, we expand into creating smartphone and tablet apps that can be integrated into—"

"Whoa! Manny, hold on one sec!" I shout.

"What's the matter?" Manny asks, truly puzzled.

"You have failed to take one very important point into consideration," I explain.

"Really?" Manny asks, scratching his head. "What's that?"

"The invention doesn't EXIST yet!" I exclaim.

You know, for a brilliant guy, sometimes Manny misses the most obvious stuff.

"Right, right," Manny says, turning back to his smartphone, tablet, and spreadsheets. "Well, then you better get busy, partner!"

Chapter Three

To the Lab!

I SETTLE INTO MY INVENTOR'S LAB. OKAY, IT'S REALLY a corner of Manny's garage with a workbench, a tool cabinet, a parts cabinet, a bunch of shelves, and a pegboard. Manny calls it the "mad scientist" division of Sure Things, Inc., but that's just because he doesn't understand the type of environment that inventors need to allow our minds to work.

Above my workbench hangs a sign with a quote from my favorite inventor, THOMAS EDISON: "To invent, you need a good imagination and a pile of junk."

I couldn't agree more.

I admit, it's a little messy. I haven't actually seen the surface of the workbench in a few months. And the cables, wires, plugs, and gizmos dangling from hooks on the pegboard could perhaps be a little more organized. And yes, the last time I needed to find the power drill all I had to do was look in the drawer labeled PRINTER CARTRIDGES.

See? I know where everything is. Just because no one else would have a clue where to find anything . . . well, let's just call that my version of a security system.

I start, as I usually do, with a pencil and a blank piece of paper. Sitting on my official inventor's stool, I quickly sketch out a box in which to hold all the electronics necessary to interpret dog and cat sounds. The device will need a microphone to pick up the sounds, and a speaker so we can hear what the animals are actually saying.

Okay, I have point A and point B all set up. Now I just have to connect those dots. Slipping off my stool, I crawl under my workbench. There I have piles of things I started and never quite got anywhere with.

I find a wooden box in decent shape. That's a good enough start for me. Placing the box on the workbench—or more accurately, shoving aside steel pipes, plastic doll heads, and four roller skate wheels (don't ask!), I set the box on the workbench.

Grabbing my drill—from the printer cartridge drawer—I cut out a large hole in the front of the box. I pick up a curved pipe, which I had just knocked onto the floor, and fit it into the hole.

Now I need wires. Did I mention not to try this at home? Well, don't. Standing on my stool, I look up at a high shelf. There I see a row of boxes. I grab a box of green wires and step down off the stool.

I run about two feet of wire through the pipe and into the box.

Next I need a microphone. I open a drawer in my parts cabinet labeled MICROPHONES (you're shocked, I know) and find a large round microphone.

I connect it to the wire running through the pipe. I'm starting to get a good feeling about this. This just may work.

"Hey, Billy, I already have three major stores interested in the Cat-Dog Translator!" Manny calls out.

Okay . . . so much for my good feeling. Now all I'm feeling is pressure to get this thing done . . . and to get it right.

Next I need a speaker. Since cats and dogs use a variety of sounds and tones rather than actual words, I think an old-fashioned speaker would make it easier to understand the translation.

Back under the workbench for me. I take a stack of blueprints off of an old wooden trunk and place them on the floor. Flipping open the trunk's lid, I rummage around.

Let's see . . . knobs—I could use a couple of those to control the volume . . . buttons, nah . . . dials, and . . . AHA! Speakers!

I pull out a large cone-shaped speaker. It looks like a cross between a megaphone that a cheerleader might use and something people used to use to help them hear.

I drill an even larger hole in the top of the box, then fit the smaller end of the speaker into the hole.

Over the next hour I place knobs, meters, dials, a couple of lightbulbs, and what feels like two miles of wire into the box. Screwing the last knob into place, I step back and look at my creation.

It looks kind of primitive, like something out of an old black-and-white horror movie. Still, my inventor's instinct is that the Cat-Dog Translator needs to be simple and kind of old-fashioned. Anything too sophisticated might go beyond the ability to capture what dogs and cats are saying.

"Make that four major stores, Billy!" Manny shouts across the garage. "I'm on a roll!"

Wonderful. Let's hope that I'm on a roll too!

I'm sure this thing will need some tweaks,

but the only way to fine-tune it is to test it. Conveniently, we just happen to have a perfect test subject right on the premises.

"Phiii-looo!" I call out.

Philo lifts his head up from his dog bed and stares at me. He looks puzzled. I'm sure he's thinking, *I haven't had time for a full nap. It can't be time to go home already, can it?*

Of course, if this thing works, I'll know exactly what he is thinking.

"Come here, boy!" I call.

Philo just yawns.

Fortunately, I keep a box of doggy treats in my tool cabinet in a drawer labeled DOGGY TREATS.

I pull out the box and shake it. Philo jumps up and trots across the room. All signs of sleepiness VANISH.

I toss a treat into the air. Philo stands up on his back legs and catches it in his mouth. We repeat the process one more time, and then I pick up my rough model of the Cat-Dog Translator.

I hold the microphone portion of the invention up to Philo's mouth.

"Speak, boy!" I say. "Say something."

But Philo just looks up at me, hoping for another treat, and drools. A huge glob of drool splashes down onto the microphone.

Sparks fly from the box. The lightbulbs flash on and off several times, then the whole thing goes dead, making a sickly fizzing sound. A curl of black smoke rises from the box and drifts up toward the ceiling. Philo takes one sniff and trots back to his bed.

"Did you leave some pizza in the machine?" Manny asks without turning around.

"Funny," I say. "Guess I need to add a DROOL GUARD to the microphone portion of this thing. Just think about how much dogs drool."

"Do I have to?" asks Manny.

"No, but I do."

"That's why you're the inventor and I'm the guy who just got a fifth major store interested in the Cat-Dog Translator!" boasts Manny, firing off a text.

As usual, he's so focused on the big picture that the tiny details that make up any invention are lost on him. That's me. The "tiny details" guy. Speaking of which . . . climbing back onto my stool, I reach up to one of my supremely organized shelves for a plastic box labeled PLASTIC STUFF. I pull down the box.

Rummaging through the box I find a square piece of plastic. I hold it up against the microphone and it seems to fit pretty well. At least well enough for a prototype. Using a special bit, I drill a few holes in the plastic. My hope is that the piece will allow the dog and cat sounds in but keep any extraneous drool out. I secure the plastic drool guard to the microphone.

About fifteen minutes later I've replaced all the burned-out wires, circuits, and bulbs. Screwing the box back together, I'm ready for another test.

Grabbing his box of treats, I lure Philo back out of his doggy bed.

"Okay, boy, speak!" I command. "Speak!"

Nothing. Philo always barks at the wrong time. Why can't he bark at the right time?

I hold a treat over my head. "Want it, boy?" **"RUUFFF! RUUFFF!"** barks Philo.

I manage to move the device over to Philo's mouth, just before the second "Ruufff!" A glob of drool bounces off the plastic guard and spatters on the floor. But the machine's lights start flashing.

"I think it's gonna work!" I shout excitedly. "For the first time in human history, we'll actually know what a dog is saying!"

Manny hits save on his laptop and spins his swivel chair around. "This I have to see," he says.

"Or it would be more accurate to say 'hear.'"

The lights stop blinking, and out of the Cat-Dog Translator comes:

"RUUFFF!"

Philo's original bark. Actually, a static-and-feedback-filled, distorted version of his bark.

Without saying a word—because he knows better, even after only being my business partner for a few months—Manny swivels his chair back around to his desk.

I take a deep breath and grab my electric screwdriver. I've been in this situation before. Nothing ever comes that easy. Nothing I invent ever works on the first try. I've got to just keep at it.

"RUUFF! RUFF!" Philo barks.

"Good boy, but I don't need you to bark right now to test the—"

"RUUFFF!" Philo barks even louder.

It's then I remember the treat in my hand.

"Oops. Sorry, buddy. Here you go." I toss the treat into the air, and he snatches it and gobbles it right up.

I open up the box and get back to work tweaking the wiring and the circuits, adjusting my rough blueprints as I go. Before I know it, it's time to head home for dinner. I didn't expect to bang this thing out in one evening anyway. I gather up the prototype and all my drawings and get ready to leave.

"I'm going to have to work this out using the only tried and true inventing method that's ever worked for me," I say.

"SLEEP-INVENTING," says Manny.

"Yup. Sleep-inventing."

Manny slips his laptop, tablet, phone, and a stack of papers into his briefcase. Manny *loves* his briefcase. Even though he's just walking from the garage to the main house, he always carries it. Makes him feel like a BIG-TIME DEAL MAKER, which I guess he is. He follows me to the door.

Suddenly a terrible thought grips me.

"What if I have trouble sleeping?" I ask, becoming genuinely worried. "I mean, the whole future of Sure Things, Inc. depends on my ability to sleep well, but not well enough that I stay in bed all night."

"Maybe you should invent something that helps you sleep, like a helmet that stimulates sleep patterns in the brain," Manny suggests.

"Sure," I say. "No problem. As long as I can invent it before bedtime tonight, we're golden!"

I hop onto my bike and head home, with Philo trotting alongside me—but not before jotting down "SLEEP HELMET" on a piece of paper, which I shove into my pocket.

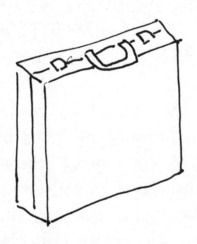

Chapter Four

are You Talking to Me?

THAT NIGHT, FOLLOWING HOMEWORK, DINNER, and watching my favorite reality TV show: GIGANTIC FAILS—INVENTIONS THAT WENT NOWHERE!, a show I hope to never appear on, I go to bed . . .

. . . where I lie on my back, staring at the ceiling, followed by lying on my side and staring at the numbers changing on my clock. I'm usually a pretty good sleeper. It's only been lately, since Manny and I realized that I invent in my sleep, that I have trouble dozing off. Especially when I'm feeling pressure to come up with a new invention.

Finally, after what feels like half the night, I doze off. The next morning I wake with a start, before my alarm even goes off, jump from my bed, and stumble in a sleepy haze over to my desk—where the prototype sits, right next to the rough blueprints I'd brought home the night before. Nothing new. Not even a pencil mark. Clearly I did not get up to sleep-invent last night, and that is not a good thing.

I could use that sleep helmet right about now.

I shower, get dressed, and scramble downstairs for some breakfast, all the time doing my best not to freak out about the fact that I didn't bang out those blueprints in one night.

Emily is waiting at the table. She's wearing glasses. Emily doesn't need glasses. I guess that's her new thing now that she's not talking in a British accent anymore.

"Whatcha workin' on, genius?" she asks, pushing her glasses up on her nose. I can see

that there are no lenses in the frames. "What's the next *brilliant* invention that's going to change the world forever?"

I decide not to say anything about Emily's new accessory. It's best not to engage.

"I'm building a Cat-Dog Translator," I say.

Without changing her expression one bit, between bites of cereal, Emily says: "That's the dumbest thing I've ever heard!"

"Well, thank you for your continued support," I say, shoving an English muffin into my mouth.

Emily just rolls her eyes, which is way more noticeable now that she's got them framed in fake glasses.

I head off to school, where things go about

as well as they've been going everywhere else for the past twenty-four hours, which is to say frustrating.

Peter MacHale stops me in the hall.

"Hi, Billy, seen any talking dogs lately?" he shouts. Then he walks away, laughing.

"Hey, Sure, know what my dog said last night?" asks Dudley Dillworthy.

"No, not really," I reply.

"BOW-WOW, WOOF-WOOF!" says Dudley, bursting into laughter, as if he's just said the funniest thing anyone has ever said. "Pretty smart dog, huh, Sure?"

"Pretty smart, yeah," I reply softly.

After school I zip home, grab my bike and Philo, and speed over to Manny's.

I open the front door, completely forgetting about the new "doorbell" he installed:

It's every ball you'll ever need; the greatest ball you'll own, indeed. No matter what sport you like to play, the All Ball helps you every day. That's all! That's the All Ball!

If that jingle rings every time I walk in, I

think I'm just going to crawl through Philo's doggy door.

"I just can't get enough of it," Manny says, humming the jingle's tune. Then he gets right down to business. It's so Manny. "So at lunch you were really worried about how you didn't sleep-invent last night."

I nod. "I might need to invent that sleep helmet so I can sleep-invent again. But then how am I going to invent the sleep helmet if I can't sleep-invent!"

"Slow down, Billy," Manny tells me. "It's just been one night. You'll get it tonight."

Reason #653 why Manny is my best friend and business partner: He always knows just the right thing to say.

I spend the rest of the afternoon making small adjustments to the device, but I hesitate to test it on Philo until I've managed to finish the blueprints.

That night after dinner, instead of watching another episode of *Gigantic Fails*—which, now that I think about it, is probably not the best show for me to watch on a night before I need to invent something—I get into bed with a book: a biography of Thomas Edison.

Maybe it's because I didn't get much sleep last night, or maybe it's because of Manny's reassurance, but tonight I quickly doze off.

"*Billy . . .*" A soft voice enters my dream. "*Billy, honey, time to get up.*"

It's my mom's voice. Actually, it's a recording of my mom's voice, which I programmed into my alarm clock as a nice way to wake me up. She used to wake me up herself every morning, and I miss that now.

My mom isn't around much. She's a scientist who works on TOP-SECRET projects for the government, and so she's often in some far-flung corner of the world. She's been gone since the summer, right after the All Ball made it big. It's nice to hear her voice every morning, but it also reminds me of how much I miss her. I can't wait until she comes home. Until then, we e-mail a lot. In fact, I should make sure to e-mail her today.

Thinking of e-mailing my mom makes me think of my desk, which makes me think of my blueprints. Did I sleep invent last night? Well, there's only one way to find out! I slip from my bed and scoot over to my desk. There, sitting in the middle of my desk, are fully rendered blueprints for Sure Things, Inc.'s Next Big Thing—the Cat-Dog Translator!

Obviously, my good night's sleep included a very productive sleep-inventing session! Rolling up the blueprints, I breathe a little sigh of relief. Now all I have to do is build a working model of the thing.

I have trouble concentrating at school that day. I'm too excited. I can't wait to get to the office and tell Manny the good news. (Manny was busy at lunch, so we hardly saw each other all day.) Finally the afternoon comes, and with Philo at my side, I race to the office.

I'm so excited about the new blueprints that I don't even mind hearing the All Ball jingle again as I slip through the door.

"How'd you sleep?" Manny asks.

"Terribly," I reply, holding up the completed blueprints.

"WONDERFUL!" Manny says. "I knew you'd do it. You are the best!"

It's at moments like this that I remember why Manny and I were best friends long before we became business partners.

Time to get busy! I happily spread the blueprints out on my workbench right next to the prototype. Opening up the prototype's main box, I compare the wiring and circuits inside with the blueprints I drew up last night. I can see right away where I went wrong.

Switching a few connections and adding a few parts from my vast stash of stuff, I do my best to match the blueprints wire for wire, circuit for circuit—each part fitting precisely with all the others.

Finally, after about an hour, I'm ready to test my invention. I power it up. The two lights on top of the translator start blinking—left, right, left, right. A low whirring sound rumbles from the speaker. It's now or never.

Out come the doggy treats.

"Philo! Treat time!" I shout, shaking the box.

Philo hops out of his doggy bed, trots over to me, and sits down. I hold a treat up over his head.

"Speak, boy! Speak!" I say, holding the treat up with one hand, while holding the translator's microphone down near Philo with the other hand.

"**RUUFFF! RUFFFF!**" he barks. I toss him the treat.

A second later a sound comes out of the

translator's speaker: ". . . ov . . . oo . . ."

Well, it's the closest to a translation that I've gotten to so far, but it's still not precisely right.

I rotate the dials on the front of the device slightly, then repeat the experiment.

"RUUFFF! RUFFFF!" Philo barks again.

This time ". . . love . . . oo . . ." comes out of the speaker.

Closer! Definitely closer!

A few more tweaks on the dials, another doggy treat, and . . .

"RUUFFF! RUFFFF!" Philo is really getting impatient for his treat now.

This time it comes out as: "I LOVE YOU!"

During this whole testing process Manny has been hard at work at his desk with his back to me. He knows enough to leave me alone when I'm in the middle of inventing. But as soon as the "I love you," in a somewhat high, squeaky, yet totally recognizable voice, comes out of the speaker, Manny leaps from his chair, races across the office, and gives me a high five.

"I knew you could do it, Billy!" he cries.

Don't get too excited just yet, I tell my brain. "We still have to make sure it works for cats, too," I point out.

Don't get me wrong. I'm thrilled I've gotten so far, but no invention is complete until everything works the way you want it to. If not, you've just got more work to do.

"Why don't I go get Watson?" says Manny. Watson is Manny's cat. "He usually has to stay in the house, but I can bring him into the garage. Just don't open any doors."

"Great," I reply. "And Philo has always gotten along with cats, so that shouldn't be a problem."

A few minutes later Manny returns carrying a large gray-and-white cat. Watson rests in his arms like a giant furry loaf of bread.

"Okay, kitty, you go say hello to Billy," says Manny, placing Watson on the floor.

Philo is half-asleep in his doggy bed. He lifts his head and sniffs at Watson, who ignores him, walks once around the doggy bed, and then rubs up against Manny's legs.

"Come here, Watson!" I urge the cat.

"Do you have any string?" Manny asks.

Silly question. I pull open a drawer in my parts cabinet labeled jUNK DRAWER #3. I have a total of five junk drawers, plus all my other drawers, which are basically junk drawers too.

Rummaging around among paper clips, rubber bands, and twist ties, I find a length of string. Placing the translator on the floor, I dangle the string near the microphone.

"Come on, Watson, over here!" I call.

Watson spies the bouncing string and darts across the room. As he swats at the string he lets out a loud: **"MWOW! MWOOOOW!"**

The lights flash, the speakers hum, and out comes: **"RUUFFF! RUFFFF!"**

"Uh, that sounds like Philo," says Manny.

I always appreciate it when he points out the obvious.

"Hmmm . . . ," I say, scratching my head. "When we decided to make our invention a

Cat-Dog Translator, this is not what I had in mind."

I adjust the dials and slip a sound filter into a slot I had built into the side of the box.

"Let's try this again," I say.

I dangle the string, making it dance right in front of the microphone. Watson grabs it with both paws, then flops over onto his back and moans: "**BWaaaRRR!**"

From out of the translator's speaker comes: "YOU'RE NOT PETTING ME. IS THERE A PROBLEM?"

you're not petting me!

Manny jumps so high, his head almost hits the ceiling. He gives me another high five and says, "Another home run, partner! Nicely done!"

"Thanks," I say, breathing a sigh of relief. Another Thomas Edison quote comes to mind: "Genius is 1 percent inspiration and 99 percent perspiration." Not that I'm saying I'm a genius or anything like that. But inventing does takes hard work.

"Thanks, Watson," I say, leaning down and rubbing his belly.

Manny picks up Watson to bring him back into the house.

"I'd like to take Philo and the translator to the park," I say. "You know, kind of field test it out in the 'wild,' so to speak."

"Great idea," says Manny. "Stop back here before you go home and let me know how it works."

I snatch up my backpack and carefully slip the translator inside. "Come on, Philo. You wanna go to the park?" I ask.

At the sound of the word "park" Philo is up and racing to the door. I follow him out and we head to the park, with a working prototype of Sure Things, Inc.'s Next Big Thing!

Chapter Five

Panic in the Park

PHILO TROTS a FEW STEPS aHEAD OF ME aS WE HEAD out through the fence in Manny's backyard and into the park that juts right up to Manny's parents' property. Ever since the success of the All Ball changed my life and I've been coming to Manny's garage every day, this park has been a huge help. I can take a break from work when I need it and make sure Philo gets a quick walk.

Philo jumps up on a bench, then jumps back off and races around the trunk of a thick tree. I set my backpack down and pull out the translator. A few seconds later Philo comes scampering back to me. It makes me smile to see him so happy.

"What's up, boy?" I ask, moving the translator close to him.

"GRR–RUFFF!" he barks. Out comes: "I'M HUNGRY!"

"All right, let's get you some food." It's thrilling to be able to understand what it is that Philo wants. Although ninety-nine times out of a hundred, what Philo wants is food.

I toss him a treat, which he catches and gobbles down. Then he happily trots alongside me, sniffing at the ground as he goes. Philo moves closer to me and sniffs near my feet.

"Your feet smell DELICIOUS!" he says through the translator.

Knowing what Philo is saying is both cool and kinda gross at the same time!

We walk a little farther until Philo spots a squirrel dashing through the grass. He stops in his tracks, his tail whipping back and forth, his ears pointing straight up. He begins growling, then barks. What comes out of the translator is: "I'll chase that squirrel . . . NOW!"

Philo bolts after the squirrel, who takes off like a fuzzy gray blur. The squirrel tears through the grass, darting sharply to its left, then cutting back to its right, heading for the edge of the park's large grassy field. Philo matches his moves step for step.

With Philo closing in on him, the squirrel makes for a large tree at the end of the field. Just as Philo is about to catch him, the squirrel reaches the base of the tree and leaps up onto the thick trunk, scrambling up into the high branches, its claws grabbing the craggy bark.

Philo skids to a stop just in time to avoid crashing into the base of the tree. He places his front paws onto the tree and starts barking loudly. I catch up to him in time to use the translator to hear: "PLEASE COME DOWN, SQUIRREL. PLEASE COME DOWN SO I CAN CATCH YOU."

The squirrel probably can't understand what Philo's barks mean, but he certainly gets the point. That squirrel is not budging from its

perch. If the squirrel could, it would probably stick its tongue out at Philo, taunting him. I scratch Philo's head, and he brings his front paws back down to the ground.

"I don't think the squirrel speaks Dog, buddy," I say, realizing, of course, that the Cat-Dog Translator only works one way. I can now understand what Philo is saying, but my words are still just gibberish to him. Now, if I could invent something that would translate human speech into dog language . . . Slow down, Billy. One BRILLIANT INVENTION at a time!

Philo resumes his barking: "I would like to catch that squirrel. Squirrels are fast. Squirrels can climb trees. I also can climb trees."

A strange look comes over Philo's face. As if he has just solved a problem that he's been working on for years, as if a lightbulb has just gone off inside his doggy brain.

"I can climb trees. I can climb trees," he repeats.

Philo looks straight up the tree trunk. But he's too late. The squirrel has disappeared into the highest branches of the tree and is nowhere in sight.

We continue our walk. I decide right then and there to add a long shoulder strap to the Cat-Dog Translator, so that it can hang down near Philo's mouth. That way I won't have to bend down to allow the machine to hear what he's saying.

We pass a garbage can. Philo shoves his nose into the top of the can and sniffs so loudly I can hear it from a few feet away.

"GARBAGE SMELLS DELICIOUS!" he says through the translator. "I'D LIKE SOME GARBAGE, PLEASE."

"Never mind," I say, gently guiding his nose and the rest of him away from the trash can. So far, mostly what I have learned from the Cat-Dog Translator is that Philo thinks just about everything—the more disgusting, the better—smells delicious.

A few minutes later I see someone coming toward us, walking a dog on a leash. Philo spots the dog and starts barking as they pass each other. His barking is loud enough that the translator's microphone picks it up. Out comes: "I WOULD LIKE TO MEET THAT DOG! I WOULD LIKE TO SNIFF THAT DOG'S BUTT!"

The dog walker stops and gives me a pointed look. "Excuse me? What did you just say?"

UH-OH.

"I—um—I didn't say anything," I squeak out and start hurrying away. "I mean . . . Well, it was my . . . well, it's kind of hard to explain, and—um—never mind, have a nice day!"

I think about heading back to the office. The first official field test of the Cat-Dog

Translator has been a great success out in the wild. Except for the whole "causing a stranger to think I was VERY, VERY WEIRD" part. I need to wrap up work for the day and get home with Philo in time for dinner, English homework . . . well, you know the routine.

But at that moment another squirrel darts out right in front of Philo and looks him squarely in the eyes.

Philo cannot resist this obvious challenge. He barks. "I'LL CHASE THIS SQUIRREL— NOW!" comes out of the translator. The squirrel dashes off, sprinting across the lawn, heading for the nearest tree. Philo takes off after it.

"Philo, come back here!" I shout, slapping my thigh. I really don't have time to chase him down. But Philo is on a mission, and even the thigh slap move doesn't stop him.

Oh great. Now I have to chase him.

I start running after Philo, but carrying the big, bulky translator in my hands really slows me down. I stop, kneel on the grass, and slide the device into my backpack, which I then slip over my shoulders. But by now Philo has quite a lead on me.

I see across the field that the squirrel has reached a tree, jumped onto it, and is climbing quickly up its trunk. This time Philo remembers, in a timely manner, that he, too, knows how to climb trees, although not quite as gracefully as the squirrel.

When I get to the tree, Philo has leaped up onto a low branch and is making his way up, paw by paw, branch by branch. At this point, neither of us can see the squirrel, who has obviously scrambled way up into the tree to safety.

"Come down, Philo!" I shout, now barely able to see him through the leaves. "You lost him, and we have to go home!"

Philo starts to make his way down. His steps are uncertain, and I start to get worried. When he reaches a low branch, he can't seem to figure out how to make it from there back down to the ground.

"Hold on, boy. I'll help you," I say, slipping off my backpack. I place the backpack down on

a nearby bench and turn back to the tree.

"Come on," I say, lifting my arms as high as they can go.

Suddenly, Philo starts growling.

"Oh, be quiet and come down," I say. "I'll help you. Here we go." I stand up on my tippy-toes, stretching my arms to reach him, but Philo continues to growl and bark.

What's he growling about? I wonder. *Maybe he's just scared of jumping down from the tree?*

Finally, after I stretch so far that I think I might be a couple of inches taller than I was when I woke up this morning, Philo jumps down into my arms.

"There you go," I say. "Forget about that dumb squirrel. Let's go and get you some dinner."

But as soon I put him down on the ground, Philo starts growling and barking again.

"What are you trying to tell me, boy?" I ask. "What's got you so worked up?" Then I remember that I've just invented something that can help answer my question. And it's right here in my backpack. "Let's just find out what you're trying to tell me."

I turn to the bench and open my backpack, only to discover that it's EMPTY! The Cat-Dog Translator is GONE!

Chapter Six

Where's Philo?

OKAY, I'M PANICKING. I SEARCH ALL AROUND THE bench where I set my pack down—under it, on the grass near it. Nothing.

Where could the translator have gone? It was only out of my sight for a minute. Maybe it fell out of my backpack while I was chasing Philo. If I retrace my steps, maybe I can find it.

With Philo at my side, sniffing everything he passes, I walk slowly back to where I slipped the device into my pack, retracing my steps, scouring every inch of the ground.

No sign of the translator.

Could someone have taken it? But how is that possible?

I look down at Philo. "Did you see someone take it? Huh, boy? Is that why you were growling and barking?"

"RAFF-RAFFF!"

Philo's not much help without the translator.

How could someone have lifted it out of my backpack in such a short amount of time—unless whoever took it had been following me, waiting for an opportunity to snatch the device. But who would do that?

I make my way back to the office with Philo.

A few minutes ago I was thrilled with how well the Cat-Dog Translator worked. Now I not only have to tell Manny that it's gone, but that someone may have stolen it. We'll have to figure out who . . . and why . . . and where it is . . . and how to get it back!

All right, I have to calm down.

I arrive at the garage and throw open the front door, bracing myself for the dreaded All Ball jingle doorbell. It doesn't come. Could Manny have actually taken the fact that I was sick of hearing it to heart? Could he have put aside his pride in having written it? Did he turn it off as a gesture toward harmony in our office?

Nah, must be a short in the audio system.

"No, I don't believe that it will work on hamsters," I hear Manny say as I step into the room. He turns toward me and hits the mute button on his phone.

"It doesn't work on hamsters, right?" he asks me.

I shrug. "Well, I really can't tell without testing it."

Who thought we liked to run around in circles?

Manny nods and hits the mute button again.

"Good news. The hamster setting is in the testing phase," he lies. "What? Fish? Fish don't make any noise. Listen, I'll be in touch when we get the hamster thing up and running."

Manny ends his call. "That was someone from Pet-A-Palooza, the pet store giant. They've got stores in malls all across the country. And they are very, very interested in the Cat-Dog Translator. Hmm . . . we may have to change the name if it works on hamsters, too. CAT-DOG-HAMSTER TRANSLATOR is a bit of a mouthful. Do you think a hamster setting can be integrated into the device?"

"Maybe," I reply. "Of course, that would require us to actually have the device in our possession."

"What do you mean?" Manny asks.

"Someone stole it."

Manny remains calm. In fact, Manny always remain calm. It's reason #207 why he's the best CFO a kid entrepreneur could ask for. It's one of the reasons we became friends, and it is certainly a big reason why Sure Things, Inc. has been such a success. Well, that and the inventions, of course.

"How did that happen?" Manny asks.

"It was only out of my sight for a minute . . . maybe less," I explain. "I think someone was following me and planned to steal it. When Philo got stuck in a tree—"

"Wait? Philo got stuck in a tree?" Manny asks.

"Yeah. That doesn't matter now. What matters is that I put the translator in my backpack, and then I put the backpack down so I could help Philo get out of the tree. When I picked my backpack up again, it was empty."

Manny thinks for a moment, then turns back to his desk. "Hey, I started working on the press release for the Cat-Dog Translator. It's just a rough draft, but tell me what you think:

Wonder what your dog is asking for when he barks at you?

Curious about why your cat paces from one end of the house to the other, moaning?

Well, wonder no more:

Sure Things, Inc., the company that brought you the All Ball, the Sibling Silencer, the Stink Spectacular, and Disappearing Reappearing Makeup, announces their latest, greatest invention:

THE CAT-DOG TRANSLATOR!

Coming soon to a pet store near you!

"We may have to tweak it if the hamster thing works out. Hamsters squeak, right?" asks Manny.

"It's a great press release, Manny, but the device is gone and we have no idea where it is. What are we supposed to do?"

"Build another prototype," Manny says casually, and then he turns his attention back to his press release.

"That's it? Just build another prototype? Just like that?"

"Uh-huh," Manny replies. "Because let's be honest, Billy. You're not the most organized person. I'm sure it'll turn up eventually."

It takes a moment to sink in, but I slowly realize that Manny is right. We have to have a prototype if we're going to demonstrate this thing and make it a hit. And as for what happened to the first prototype, it could have been some kind a prank. Like Manny says, maybe it'll turn up.

"Right!" I announce, as much to get myself psyched as to let Manny know that I agree with his plan. "I'll get on it first thing tomorrow. I have to get home now. See ya."

"Which sounds better: 'LATEST, GREATEST INVENTION' or 'GREATEST, LATEST INVENTION'?"

"Good night, Manny," I say, heading for the door. "Come on, Philo. Let's go home."

That night, as I try to fall asleep, my brain is going a trillion miles a minute. It will take me a couple of days to build a new prototype from scratch. The good news is that I'll be starting with my completed blueprint, so this second model should work even better than the first one. But part of me can't stop worrying that the theft of the first prototype might have been more than just a simple prank.

On Saturday, with Philo at my side, I head to the office. As usual, Manny is hard at work at his desk.

"I definitely like 'latest, greatest invention' better than 'greatest, latest invention.' We should go with that," he says.

Sometimes Manny forgets about stuff like "hello" and "how are you?" But that's okay. He's got bigger things on his mind.

"Did you go to bed last night?" I ask, worried that he will burn himself out. "Have you been here all night fretting over 'latest' and 'greatest'?"

"Nah, I solved that one yesterday," Manny explains, tapping away on his laptop's keyboard. "I just wanted to let you know what I decided."

I slide over to my workbench, unroll the blueprints, and get to work on the Cat-Dog Translator prototype, take two. Philo curls up in his doggy bed.

An hour later I've got the box built. As I go about connecting the wires and circuits, Philo gets up and comes over to me. I don't need a translator to know what that means. He wants to go out for our daily stroll in the park.

I enjoy our walks too, as a short break in my workday. But today I'm trying to get this second prototype built in time for Manny to show it to all the big shots he's lining up.

"Sorry, buddy, no walk today," I say. "But you can go out into the backyard. Come on."

Philo follows me to the door. I open it and he runs out. He'll stay out there for a while, then come scratching at the door so I can let him back in. We've done this before. And with the fence enclosing Manny's backyard, I can send him outside and he's nice and safe.

I dive back into my work. An hour later, with the wiring done and the piping for the microphone and speaker in place, I decide to call it quits for the day. I should be able to wrap this up tomorrow and put Sure Things, Inc. back on track.

That's when I realize that Philo never came scratching at the door.

I get up and step out into the backyard, but there is no sign of him.

"Philo!" I call. Nothing. "Here, boy!" I shout. No Philo.

Where could he have gone?

I walk to the far end of the yard and see doggy paw prints in the dirt. It appears that Philo has jumped the fence! But why would he do that? More importantly . . . where is he?

I stick my head back into the office. "Philo's missing," I tell Manny. "I'm off to search for him. He's probably in the park."

Manny types away furiously. I'm not sure if he even knows I'm in the room.

"Try the park," he says, without breaking his tappity-tappity rhythm on the keyboard. It's like he never even heard me.

"Good idea," I say, then I head back out.

Leaving through the gate at the back of the yard, I walk into the park. As I enter, I look around on the ground, still hoping that I might find the first prototype. No such luck, of course.

"Philo!" I shout. "Here, boy!"

A few seconds later Philo comes bursting out of a clump of nearby bushes.

"**aRRUFFF!**" he barks.

"What's gotten into you?" I say. "How did you get out of Manny's backyard? Did you jump over the fence?"

"**aRRRRRR!**"

Uh-huh, I think. *Where's my prototype when I need it?*

Soon Philo and I are back in the office.

"Found him!" I announce.

By this time Manny has finished what he was doing. "He must have jumped the fence," Manny says. "Good thing the park is fully enclosed with a higher fence. Philo isn't going anywhere farther."

"It's still strange behavior for him, though," I point out. "Anyway, we're heading home. See you tomorrow, Manny."

"Hey, how's this: 'the latest *and* greatest invention'? What do you think? I like the 'and.'"

"Good night, Manny," I say, heading out with Philo by my side.

The next afternoon at the office the same thing happens with Philo. I let him out into the backyard. Making the final connections for the microphone and speaker, I complete the second prototype. Time to test it. And that's when I realize that Philo never came back and scratched at the door to be let in. Just like yesterday.

Again, I head to the park, and again I call out for Philo.

"Here, boy!" I shout.

Philo comes tearing out of the same clump of bushes as the day before.

"What could be so interesting in those

bushes that you jumped the fence and came here two days in a row?" I ask Philo.

He sniffs the ground and remains silent.

I walk over to the bushes and shove the branches aside, not exactly sure what I'm expecting to find there, other than some kind of answer. Maybe the first prototype? But there's nothing interesting about these bushes. There's just dirt and grass and twigs and a startled bird that flies away.

"Come on, Philo. Let's go back," I say.

A few minutes later, back in the office, I decide to test out my new prototype on Philo, hoping to learn why he's been sneaking off to the park.

Powering up the device, I hold it near Philo's mouth.

"Why have you been jumping the fence and going to the park?" I ask.

"GRRRRRR-UFFF!" Philo replies. A few seconds later from the translator's speaker comes: "TREATS ARE DELICIOUS!"

So much for getting the truth out of Philo!

Chapter Seven

Sure Secrets!

ON MONDAY MORNING, I JUMP FROM BED, ENERGIZED by the completion of the second translator prototype. Now we're ready for the testing and marketing phase, something I always enjoy. It helps me grasp the fact that all this is real—the inventions, Sure Things, Inc., this double life I'm leading. The thought of another hit invention is enough to get me through even the toughest day at school—usually. But nothing could prepare me for what happens as soon as I walk through the front door.

As I walk down the hall on the way to

homeroom, it seems as if everyone is pointing at me and smirking, or hiding a giggle, or whispering into the ear of the person standing next to her.

Now, by this time I'm somewhat used to being the center of attention—I don't like it, but I am getting used to it. But today's reaction to me seems just plain weird.

Peter MacHale comes up from behind, taps me on the shoulder, and says: "Hey, Sure, you still wear footie pajamas?"

Uh . . . WHAT? I am so stunned by this out-of-left-field comment that by the time I can pick up what little is left of my wits off the floor, Peter has disappeared down the hallway—though I think I can still hear the nasal snort that passes for his laugh.

And for the record, what's wrong with wearing pajamas with feet? They're way warmer than regular ones, and it's not like I wear them to school or anything. I've never noticed a label on them that that says: "If you are twelve and still wearing these, then you are officially super totally lame."

But here's the main thing. How in the world could Peter MacHale know what I wear at home?

Footie pajamas are warm.

As I ponder this new mystery, Dudley Dillworthy waves at me from across the hall. "Hey, Billy, I heard that you talk in your sleep," he shouts, loud enough for everyone in the entire school to hear him. "What do you talk about? Do you count all the money you make from your inventions instead of counting sheep? One million, two million. Ha-ha-ha!"

And again, mocking laughter trails away down the hall. What Dudley said is just as true as what Peter said. I do talk in my sleep. But why would he know that? And why would he care?

"Jelly beans on pizza, Billy?" says a girl behind me.

I know that voice without even turning around. It's ALLISON ARNOLDS.

"Hi, Allison. What was that?" I ask, hoping that I didn't just hear what I'm sure I just heard.

"I asked if you really put jelly beans on your pizza?" she says. "You are just too weird."

Then she walks away.

Again, what she said is true, but who cares what I like to eat? But that's not the real problem. The only one who's ever seen me eat jelly beans on pizza is Manny, and he's certainly not going around blabbing with anybody about stuff that goes at the office. When it comes to the goings-on at Sure Things, Inc., everything, right down to the jelly beans, is top secret to Manny.

So how can all these people know about stuff that happens when it's only me or when it's just Manny and me at the office?

And I thought this was going to be an okay day!

After school I pick up Philo and head to the office. Manny's math class took a field trip to a museum today, so he missed hearing about all the fun I had to endure.

"You are never going to believe what happened to me at school today," I say to Manny, who is deeply absorbed in some website on his laptop. "Peter MacHale made fun of me for wearing footie pajamas, and then Allison Arnolds told me she thinks I'm weird because I like jelly beans on my pizza."

"Uh-huh," Manny mumbles, still riveted to whatever website he's stuck on.

"How do they know these things about me?" I continue. "I didn't tell them. You certainly didn't tell them."

"No, I didn't," says Manny, finally acknowledging the fact that we are having a conversation. "But someone else did. Look." He points to his laptop's screen.

404

I lean over Manny's shoulder. Pulled up on the screen is a website called SURE SECRETS! EVERYTHING YOU EVER WANTED TO KNOW ABOUT KID INVENTOR BILLY SURE.

I'm stunned. I'm speechless. I don't even know where to begin to start to think about what to say. Fortunately, Manny sees this and picks up the conversation for us both.

"You know I have a bunch of web alerts that let me know anytime Sure Things, Inc. is mentioned?" Manny begins.

I nod weakly, but I am not ready to actually utter a sentence.

"Well, this website popped up in my alerts late last night," he explained. "But I didn't need an alert to find out about it. It's all anyone could talk about during the field trip today."

Words finally return to my frozen lips. "Who would do such a thing?" I ask.

"There's more. Look," says Manny.

Looking past today's three "headlines," which just happened to be about footie pajamas, talking in my sleep, and eating jelly beans on my pizza, Manny finds a longer list of Sure Secrets.

Billy Sure sings in the shower. (Who doesn't?)

Billy Sure turns his socks inside out and wears them two days in a row. (So, they're a little stinky. It saves me from running out of socks.)

Billy Sure won't eat purple candies. (That's true. Not even purple jelly beans.)

Billy Sure hides his spinach under his napkin and then throws it in the garbage when no one is looking.

"I really don't like spinach," I explain

spinach hidden here!

to Manny calmly, as if I were reading these things about someone else. Then the truth that someone is posting these things about me comes crashing down on my brain once again.

"It's a really junky website," says Manny, as if that's supposed to make me feel better. It doesn't.

"Who is doing this? And where is the info coming from? And most importantly, why is someone trying to embarrass me like this?"

"I dug around to see if I could penetrate the site's code," says Manny, "but all I found was a pop-up ad for DON'T-SMELL-LIKE-POO shampoo. I couldn't see who created it. "

"Thanks," I say, back at my workbench.

As I hook up electric meters, voltage measuring devices, and all the other testing tools I use to put every new invention through its paces, I find it hard to concentrate on the work at hand.

Philo gets up and stands at the back door, wagging his tail. Without thinking about it, I get up and let him out.

Time to concentrate, I think. *There's nothing you can do to fix this problem right now.*

The good news of the day is that the

technical testing of the Cat-Dog Translator all goes smoothly. It's time to try it out on other cats and dogs.

When it's time to go home, there is no sign of Philo in the backyard. This is starting to become a pattern. I slip through the gate, walk to the park, and call out.

"Philo! Time to go home!"

Like clockwork, he comes out of the bushes, barking happily and wagging his tail.

When I get home I go right to Emily's room. I knock on her door.

"Yeah!" she calls out.

"Emily, it's me," I say.

"Really?" she says, her sarcastic tone turned up to eleven.

"Can I come in for second?"

"If you must," she replies.

Emily is at her desk, typing furiously on her laptop. She has three history books open and two encyclopedia websites up. She is still wearing her fake glasses.

At that moment I realize that I almost

never see my sister working so hard. She's usually on her phone with three friends at once, fussing with her hair or nails, squealing about the latest bit of gossip. Somehow the sight of EMILY THE SERIOUS STUDENT catches me off guard.

"What?" she snaps.

"Look, I know you're busy, but I need to show you this website," I explain.

She must see how really upset I am, because she saves her work and turns the keyboard over to me.

I bring up the Sure Secrets website, and her mouth drops open.

"What is this?" she asks, scanning the headlines. "Jelly beans? Really? Is that true, because if it is, it's kinda disgusting."

"Yes, it's true, but that's not the point," I say taking a deep breath. "There is all kinds of stuff on this website that is true, but that no one else could possibly know. So I have to ask you, did you do this? Did you tell anyone all this embarrassing stuff about me?"

I brace myself for the confession I am certain will follow, but once again, Emily surprises me.

"No," she says seriously. "I would never do this to you. I mean, I think you're a dork and all, and sometimes I wish you lived in another house, or planet, but I would never do anything like this, Billy."

I know she is telling the truth. Ever since I invented the Disappearing Reappearing Makeup for her, we've been on pretty good terms.

"I know. Thanks. But what about Dad?" I ask.

"Dad?" she repeats. "I don't think Dad has left his studio in a week. The only people he's talked to are me, you, and Philo. And I don't think Philo's talking!"

Not without the Cat-Dog Translator, anyway, I think.

"Thanks, Em," I say.

"Sure. Now get out of my room, genius," Emily snaps, but I can tell that she isn't really annoyed with me. "Can't you see I have mounds of homework to do?"

I head down the hall to my room to begin my own homework, determined to put this website business out of my mind. After all, who cares if everyone knows that I wear footie pajamas or talk in my sleep? So what? Besides, I have more important things to focus on. It's time to move forward with the launch of Sure Things, Inc.'s latest invention!

Chapter Eight

Talking Pets

THE NEXT DAY AS I WALK INTO SCHOOL I BRACE myself for another round of people laughing at me because of stuff they saw on the Sure Secrets website.

I hurry along, keeping my head down, hoping to scoot into class without anyone stopping me in the hallway. No such luck.

"Hey, Sure!" Dudley shouts at me from down the hall.

Here it comes, some embarrassing secret about what I eat or wear or how I sleep. Soon I'm not going to have any secrets left. But much to my shock, Dudley has something else in mind entirely.

"So I heard that you actually invented that dog-talking thing," he says.

"The Cat-Dog Translator, yes, I did actually build one," I say, relieved that the topic of hallway conversation has shifted from my secrets to my work.

"Yeah, whatever, the thing that tells you what your dog is saying," Dudley goes on. "Can I come over and try it on my dog?"

I suppose that's not the worst idea. I do need to test the device. Before I can respond, a crowd forms around me. Some of the kids I know, many I don't.

"You're Billy Sure, right?" says one boy. "Can you try your machine on my cat? I've always wanted to know what he's saying when he yowls at me."

"Well, I think that's possible if I—"

"Billy, I think my dog is really smart," says a girl I don't know. "He always knows what I'm saying, but I'd love to know what *he's* saying."

"We might be able to—"

"My cat never shuts up. What the heck is she saying?" says a sixth grader. I think his name is Tommy.

"Hey, I have a gerbil. Will your toy work on him?" says another sixth grader, also named Tommy.

"Um, it's not a toy, actually, it's an—"

"I have a goldfish!"

"Goldfish can't talk!"

"My dog can talk. He never shuts up!"

This is really getting out of control. I mean, on one hand, I do need test subjects, and it seems as though I've got plenty. On the other hand, I have to be able to walk down the hallway in school without creating a scene.

"Okay!" I shout. "Listen up, everyone. Bring your pets to the offices of Sure Things, Inc. this afternoon, and I can test the Cat-Dog Translator on them."

I turn to try to break away from the crowd—and crash right into PRINCIPAL GILAMON.

"Whoa, easy there, Billy," he says, steadying

me so I don't either fall on the floor or knock him over. Knocking over the principal is never a good idea. "Everything okay here? Am I late for this meeting of the Billy Sure Fan Club?"

"No, sir," I say. "I'm just talking with a few friends, but now I'm on my way to class."

"All right, then," says Principal Gilamon as the crowd breaks up. "And perhaps it's time to start thinking about Billy Sure Day again. You, young man, continue to be an inspiration, a model for hard work, and I want the whole school to celebrate that!"

"Thank you, sir. Maybe we could talk about Billy Sure Day another time. It's just that I've been kinda busy and—"

"Well, when you're ready, you just let me know and we'll arrange it," says Principal Gilamon.

"I will. Thank you," I say, hurrying off in the direction of my first class.

Since the first day of seventh grade, Principal Gilamon has been trying to get me to lead a school assembly. Something about my achievements setting off a tidal wave of excellence throughout the school, or some such thing.

Whatever. At least he got me away from the overenthusiastic crowd of pet lovers who had me trapped in the hall.

The rest of the school day follows a similar pattern as the morning. Apparently word of my invention has spread like Principal Gilamon's TIDAL WAVE, and I am mobbed in the hallway between every class by kids wanting to know what their pets are saying.

Finally, the school day ends, and I make my escape. I head home, grab Philo and a peanut butter sandwich, and bike over to Manny's. The

sight awaiting me there is almost too much for me to take in.

As I roll to a stop on my bike, I see a line of kids and pets stretching around the block. Word has obviously spread, not only about the existence of the prototype, but also of my offer to test it on any pet brought to the office.

I wonder how Manny is dealing with all this! Are his parents going to kick us out of our office?

"Hey, Sure. Fluffy's ready to be tested!"

"No fair. I was here first. He cut the line!"

The crowd is starting to get worked up. I slip into the office.

"Have you seen what's going on outside?" I ask Manny.

He's hunched over his laptop, spreadsheets and pie charts flashing across the monitor.

"What? Is it raining or something?" he asks distractedly. "I've been busy working on the marketing plan for the mass launch of the Cat-Dog Translator. Once the beta testing is done I want to go wide with this one, Billy."

"Raining?!" I cry. "Have you taken a look out the window? There's, like, a hundred kids out there. And they all want me to test the translator on their pets!"

Manny looks up from his laptop. "That's fantastic!" he says. "Sounds to me like you've got the entire beta test lined up right here!"

I hadn't thought of it that way. As usual, Manny has found the silver lining. I only hope his neighbors agree.

I go to the front door and throw it open.

"Okay, everyone, come in one at a time, and we'll test the Sure Things, Inc. Cat-Dog Translator on your pet," I announce.

First in is a girl named Sara with a small white fuzzy dog. She carries the dog in her arms. As she enters, the dog lets out a tiny yelp.

Philo lifts his head from his doggy bed, surveys the situation, and then puts his head back down on his paws.

I power up the translator. The lights on top flash, left, then right. A low hum comes from the speaker.

"This is my dog, Marshmallow," says Sara.

"Okay," I say, "just put your dog's mouth over near the microphone, right here." I point to the square box extending from the front of the device.

The girl extends her arms so that her dog's mouth is now near the microphone.

"YIP-YIP-YIP-YIP!" the little dog squeaks. From out of the speaker comes: **"SARA SMELLS LIKE LIVER . . . YUMMY!"**

"I do not!" Sara shrieks, moving Marshmallow away from the device. "I hate liver!" She leaves.

Next in is Dan, with his cat, Boots, a big black cat with white paws.

"I love you, Boots," says Dan, scratching the cat between the ears.

"ME-OOOOOW!" cries Boots, who then turns around and lifts his tail. From the translator's speaker comes: **"TALK TO THE TAIL!"**

Melissa brings in her dog, Hercules. He's a big bulldog. He looks like a Hercules.

"Go ahead, Hercules. Speak!" Melissa says.

"RaRRRFFFF!" barks Hercules, practically shaking the walls of the garage. Out comes: **"I LOVE YOU . . . AND YOU . . . AND YOU . . ."**

Sometimes the toughest-looking pets are actually the sweetest.

Herman Torosian comes in carrying a tiny cat carrier. I've seen Herman around school. He's on the football team. He's in eighth grade, but I think he's already taller than my dad. I have to stifle a laugh when he takes a tiny kitten out of the carrier. Standing in the palm of Herman's enormous hand, the kitten meows. She's saying: **"SCRATCH MY HEAD. . . . SCRATCH MY HEAD. . . . SCRATCH MY HEAD!"**

Herman obliges, though his thumb is almost bigger than the kitten's entire head.

Mary Jane Murphy brings in Killer, her rather large gray cat. She places Killer on the floor, and the cat immediately rolls over onto her back and starts purring loudly. Out of the translator comes: **"SCRATCH MY BELLY."** Mary Jane starts scratching Killer's belly. "THAT FEELS GOOD. . . . SCRATCH THERE. . . . THAT FEELS GOOD. . . . NOW I HAVE TO BITE YOU!"

Which Killer does . . . but gently.

The PARADE OF PETS continues for hours. In addition to a bunch of dogs and cats, kids also bring in their guinea pigs, birds, hamsters, and turtles. Much to their disappointment—but not mine—the translator doesn't work on any animals other than cats and dogs.

Finally, the last pet comes through and is successfully translated. I'm exhausted. I don't know how Manny can get any work done with the racket in here, but I have to go home.

"Sorry about all the noise," I say.

"Huh, what noise?" Manny asks.

I smile. I have to hand it to Manny. I've never known anyone who can concentrate so completely on what he is doing, no matter what else is going on all around him.

"The good news is that the beta test is a rousing success," I say.

This gets Manny's attention. "Fantastic,"

he says. "I'm putting the final touches on the marketing plan. We are good to go!"

Dinner with Emily and Dad that night is fairly quiet.

"Any progress on figuring out who put up that website?" Emily asks, when Dad heads into the kitchen to get the big bowl of spaghetti he's made. As usual the spaghetti will be mostly inedible. Dad says he added beets, anchovies, and asparagus to the sauce.

"Not yet," I say, realizing that with all the hubbub around testing the translator, I had not thought about the Sure Secrets website once that night.

"Who's hungry for spaghetti?" announces Dad, placing the steaming bowl on the table. "Come and spa-GET-y it!"

Emily rolls her eyes. I actually think it's kinda funny. I'd smile if I wasn't grimacing from the smell of Dad's concoction.

"How's that new invention coming along?" Dad asks.

"It's actually working out really well," I

explain proudly. "Today I tested it at the office, and—"

Suddenly a huge commotion breaks out just outside our window. People are yelling. Cats and dogs are howling.

"What is going on out there?" asks Dad.

Fearing the worst, I jump up from the table and race to the window. Pulling aside the curtain, I see a crowd of kids gathered outside our house. Each one has AT LEAST one pet!

Who can ruin spaghetti? My Dad!

Chapter Nine

More Secrets, More Problems

OBVIOUSLY, WORD ABOUT THE PROTOTYPE HAS GOTTEN out! And it seems that it's gotten out to everyone in the neighborhood.

Staring out the window I see a scene of total pandemonium. Cats scurry up trees. Hamsters dig holes in the lawn. A ferret chases a puppy.

Dad may be a terrible cook, but he's an excellent gardener. He's responsible for how nice our yard always looks. At the moment a very large Saint Bernard has one of Dad's prize-winning rose bushes dangling from its mouth.

Then a horse decides that our driveway is a perfect spot to leave us a present. Guess who's going to have to clean up after him?

"What's going on out there, Billy?" Dad asks. "Does this have something to do with your new invention?"

"It does, and I'll take care of it, Dad!" I say.

I head up to my room to grab the prototype, but not before Emily goes to the window and I hear her say: "Billy, what have you done! There's a CIRCUS on what used to be our front lawn! And in the driveway, there's . . . there's . . . What is that? It's . . . oh no. . . ."

I hurry into my room and throw open the window.

"Hello, everyone," I shout.

I'm greeted by a chorus of overly excited pet owners:

"I wanna know what my pigeon is saying!"

"My dog is really smart. I need to know if he understands me!"

"I just have to know which cat food my Muffy prefers!"

This is nuts. There's no way I can meet with each one of these people and translate what the pets are saying. I'd be out in the front yard all night. I've still got homework to finish, not to mention cleaning up after the horse!

I have an idea. I grab the prototype and quickly adjust the long-range settings on the microphone and the speaker so that they will both work at a distance. I go back to the window.

"Quiet, please, everyone," I shout. "Quiet. In a moment I am going to turn on the Sure Things, Inc. Cat-Dog Translator. It should work for all of you with a cat or a dog, so please listen closely to discover what your pet is saying."

I hold the device up to the open window and power it on.

The cacophony of animal noises drifts into

the microphone and back out the speaker, translated, all at the same time. The symphony of sound is very confusing, but at the same time, pretty awesome:

"Time for a walk. . . . I like walks. . . . Time for a walk. . . . I like walks."

"Treat-treat-treat-treat-treat-treat-treat!"

"Why is there another cat here? I'm the cat! I'm the cat! She knows that I'm the cat!"

"I don't see my ball. Where's my ball? Did you throw the ball? You always throw the ball. Where's my ball?"

This crazy scene goes on for about five minutes. In addition to the pet owners, my poor neighbors have gathered in front of their houses to see what in the world this racket is about. Then I turn off the translator.

"Thank you all for coming," I shout. "The demonstration is now officially over!"

"But Muffy never told me which food she prefers!"

"We will be on the market with the product soon!" I shout. Then I close my window.

Slowly, the crowd breaks up. I venture downstairs. Dad is in the kitchen, obliviously doing the dishes. Emily is in the living room, texting. Everything seems normal.

"Zoo time all done?" she asks without taking her eyes off her phone.

"Yeah, all except for the cleanup," I say, sighing.

I head outside. The crowd is gone, and the neighbors are back in their houses. Grabbing a shovel from the garage, I fill in the holes in the lawn, then replant Dad's rose bush. Unspooling the hose, I head to the driveway to get rid of the evidence of that horse.

The next day at the office I'm exhausted. Between the line-up of people at the office wanting to test out the translator, the mob scene at my house last night, not to mention the Sure Secrets website postings, and Philo's daily journeys to the park, I'm wiped out. Oddly enough, despite his unsupervised running around, Philo has actually been gaining weight lately. Yet one more unexplained piece of this puzzle.

"I don't know, Manny, I know that the Cat-Dog Translator is a good thing, but all this stress is starting to wear me down," I explain. "I had a ton of people show up at my house last night, all with their pets. And not just cats and dogs! There were ferrets and horses, and—"

"Well, here's some good news to help cheer you up," Manny says. "I just completed a deal with YUMMY IN THE TUMMY."

"Yummy in the Tummy? The big pet food company?" I ask. "Really?"

"Really!" Manny says proudly. "They have agreed to endorse and help promote the Cat-Dog Translator. And to show their interest, they have sent us a big fat check to seal the deal. This nice chunk of cash will help fund the manufacturing of the product for the mass market. Now that the prototype is a success, we can move right into the mass-production phase. We could have this PUPPY on the shelves by the end of the year!" Manny laughs at his little joke.

I lean back in my chair. It's at moments like this that all the craziness seems worth it. The hard work, school, the double life, all of it, have come together to create something successful. I feel proud of my work, and of Manny. I feel happier than I have in days.

Which is exactly when I hear Manny say, "Uh-oh."

"Uh-oh" is something that you definitely do *not* want to ever hear Manny say. He is so calm, and not much ever flusters him, so an "uh-oh" from Manny is like a "HOLY COW! WHAT IN THE WORLD IS GOING ON!" from anybody else.

I walk over to Manny's desk, bracing myself for the worst . . . which is exactly what I get. Manny has the Sure Secrets website up on his computer.

"It looks like the posts are getting more

intense. You're not going to like this one," he says.

"Let me see," I say, leaning in close. "'Billy Sure has a crush on Allison Arnolds!'" I read aloud.

I can feel my face start to blush.

Manny turns and looks up at me. "You do?" he asks. "You really have a crush on Allison Arnolds? Why didn't you ever tell me?"

"I never told anyone!" I reply, a bit more loudly than I would like. "I mean, I might have said it when I was alone in my room with Philo, just to see how it sounded, but I never told anyone."

Manny says nothing as he clicks through the site. I'm watching his face rather than the monitor. That's how I see his startled expression.

"What now?" I ask.

"Um, I think that this is the most serious post so far," Manny says softly.

"'Billy's mother has been away from home a lot lately,'" Manny reads. "'Everyone in the house misses her, but no one talks about where she is or what she is doing. What SECRET things could she be up to?'"

I have to step away from the computer for a moment. Manny is right. This is the worst post so far. It's enough to spill *my* secrets, but my mom should be left out of it . . . especially because I've often wondered what she's really up to too. Manny thinks she's a spy, and I'm beginning to wonder about that myself. All the more reason her secrets shouldn't be posted on a website.

I turn back to Manny. "Enough is enough," I pronounce. "This has gone on long enough. Time to put a stop to this!"

Chapter Ten

Pet Peeves

THE NEXT DAY, JUST OUTSIDE THE SCHOOL, MY TWO problems confront me at the same time.

"Hey, Sure!" shouts Douglas Braintree. "Is it true that your mom has been away for a long time and nobody knows what she does?"

"No, actually," I begin, wondering why my family's personal business is anyone else's business too. "She's a scientist."

"Yeah, right," sneers Douglas. "That's a great cover story. What does she really do, Sure? Is she a secret agent? A government spy? Come on, you can tell me."

I have no idea what in the world gives Douglas Braintree—who I've maybe spoken five words to in all the years we've been in the same school—the idea that I could trust him with any important information, much less with details about my family.

"Yeah, Douglas, that's it," I say, really getting tired of all this. "Her real name is JANE BOND."

As soon as I enter the building, I hear laughter coming from a group of girls.

"You have a crush on Allison Arnolds?" asks Petula Brown, giggling behind the stack of books she holds in her arms.

Oh no. This is it. I'm doomed!

"Where'd you hear that?" I ask. "Did she say something to you?"

"No! I don't talk to Allison Arnolds," says Petula, using a tone that suggests that I'm the dumbest thing ever to walk on two legs. "Not after what happened with Peter MacHale at the Spring Dance last year."

"No, of course not," I say, trying to sound

like I have any idea what she is talking about. "So, you saw that website?"

"Who hasn't?" says Petula, rolling her eyes.

"Well, do you know if Allison has seen it?" I ask.

"And how exactly would I know that?" she asks, growing more exasperated with each word she says. "I just told you I don't talk to her. Remember?"

Tossing her long red hair over her shoulder, Petula walks away without waiting for a response, which I was not about to give her anyway.

Manny and I simply have to figure out who put the site up and how we can take it down, or my life is going to be over. I'm embarrassed that the whole world knows that I like Allison, but there could be worse secrets that could be revealed, and that's exactly what I want to avoid.

As I make my way to my locker, Brian Josephs, a kid from my science class, comes up to me.

"So, I heard that lots of people brought their pets to your house last night?" he says, reminding me that he is one of those people who makes everything he says sound like a question, whether it is or isn't.

"Yeah, that's true," I reply.

"And that all the pets talked at once?"

"Uh-huh."

"And then everything they said got translated by your toy?"

"Well, it's actually not a toy, it's an—"

"And that it was REALLY, REALLY LOUD?"

"Yeah," I say, wondering if this conversation is ever going to end.

"Cool. I'll see you tonight. I'll bring my dog."

Then he walks right past me.

"No, Brian. Wait, that's really not a good idea . . ." I begin to say, but I can tell he's not listening.

I don't think I can handle another night like the last one. Are there going to be people camped out at my house again tonight, disturbing my family, not to mention the whole neighborhood? How long is this going to go on? And more importantly, what can I do to stop it?

The rest of the school day is thankfully uneventful. I rush from the building at the end of the day to avoid being confronted by any other pet lovers or website viewers.

Still, I can't shake the creepy feeling in the pit of my stomach that things are only going to get worse in both these areas. And, in a way, they are connected.

It's bad enough having kids come up to me at school, telling me they now know secrets about me and messing with my reputation. But I'm also supposed to be a serious entrepreneur (at least, that's what Manny likes to call me), and I have reputation to think about there, too. I am the "Sure" in "Sure Things, Inc." and if people all over the world are going to trust our products, they're going to have to trust *me*.

At home I grab a snack, round up Philo, and head to the office. I arrive to find ten people standing in line, each one with a dog or cat. I don't recognize any of them.

"Are you the guy who can tell what dogs are saying?" one boy asks.

"Well, not me, precisely, but—"

"Who are you? Dr. Dolittle or someone?" another person asks.

"No, really, this is not the best time," I say, searching my mind to see if I can think of a "best time." I can't.

"Okay, we'll come to your house later tonight," says the first kid. "My friend was there yesterday and told me it was amazing! He never knew his cat liked belly rubs so much."

"No, please don't come to my house," I say as the crowd breaks up, but I can see that no one is in the mood to listen to me.

I slip inside.

Manny looks up from his work, starts to look down, and does a double take.

"Are you okay?" he asks, getting up from his desk, something he rarely does.

I must really look terrible.

"You look terrible!" he says.

Well, there you go.

"I've never seen you looking so stressed and exhausted," he continues.

"This is supposed to be a happy time for me—the launch of new product, Sure Things, Inc. moving forward . . . but I'm really stressed," I explain. "Between the people wanting to use the Cat-Dog Translator and the stuff that's on that website . . ." I can't even finish the thought.

"Okay, have a seat," Manny says, guiding me by the shoulder over to my workbench. "I'm going to get you a slice of pizza—you like jelly beans on your pizza, right?"

"Funny," I say, and actually it is since everyone in the world also knows this about me now. It's nice that one of us, at least, can keep a sense of humor about all this.

Manny returns and hands me a slice of pizza covered in colorful (nonpurple) jelly beans. I take a big bite.

"All right, I have a plan that I think will help solve two of your three big problems," Manny begins.

"*Three* big problems?" I ask through a mouthful of pizza. "I have three big problems? I thought I only had two."

"One's an older problem that we'll take care of by solving one of the newer problems," Manny clarifies. Now I really have no idea what he's talking about.

"You know how Principal Gilamon has been hounding you about Billy Sure Day?" Manny goes on.

"Of course," I say. "He brought it up the other day."

"So here's the plan. What if we set up an assembly where every kid who wants to know what his or her pet is thinking can find out all in one shot? They'll just bring their pets to the assembly and one by one, you can use the translator on them. That would stop a lot of people from coming around to your house at night, and at the same time satisfy

Principal Gilamon's desire for you to star in an assembly—to inspire hard work, creativity, and all that other good stuff he loves so much."

I remain quiet and munch on another bite of my pizza.

"And, of course, it would also serve as a major PROMOTIONAL EVENT for the upcoming launch of the Cat-Dog Translator. So, what do you think?"

"Do you think he'd go for it?" I ask.

"Principal Gilamon? In a heartbeat."

"Okay. See if you can set it up. And thanks, Manny."

"Anything for my partner!"

"Now, what about my third problem, the website?" I ask, not wanting to seem ungrateful, but I was still very worried about all these secrets floating out there.

"That's next up on my list, Billy," says Manny. "I promise. We'll figure that one out too."

I spend the afternoon cleaning up my workbench—or, at least what passes for clean to me. Then it's time to get Philo from the park—same bushes—and head home.

Riding my bike, I round the corner to my house and gasp at the sight of twice as many people lined up on my lawn as yesterday! And they've started showing up earlier!

I don't know what to do. I mean, I know what I'd like to do, which is to tell them to all go away. But I don't want any more bad publicity spreading about me, like how I'm mean and I wouldn't share my invention, and that sort of stuff.

Maybe if I take care of this now, everyone will go away and things will get quiet later on tonight. Standing on my front step, I power up the long range settings on the translator.

"Okay, everyone!" I shout to be heard over the barking, screeching, howling, and meowing. "I can't meet with you individually, but I'm going to turn on the Cat-Dog Translator for all of you. So please listen carefully for what your pet is saying. A reminder—the Cat-Dog Translator will only work on cats and dogs.

That's why it's called the Cat-Dog Translator. So, for those of you I see out there who brought rats, donkeys, snakes, and lizards, thank you for your interest, but I really can't help you."

I turn the power on. In a repeat of last night's noisy mess, the sounds of translated pet talk come pouring out of the speaker, all in a garbled stew of words.

I wait about five minutes, and when I can't take any more of it, I turn off the device, thank the crowd for coming, and head inside.

But throughout my homework and dinnertime I hear another round of pet owners gathering outside. By the time I go to bed, the nose is deafening. Manny's plan for the assembly better work, or I may never get to sleep again!

The next afternoon I walk into the office even more exhausted than before. Fortunately, Manny has some more good news—at least I think it's good news.

"I have a plan to trap the person behind the

website!" he says as soon as I walk through the door. "But it will require two things from you, Billy. Some acting, and A DISGUISE. What are your thoughts on fake mustaches?"

So many fake mustache choices!

Chapter Eleven

Sure Secrets Exposed!

"I DON'T KNOW IF THIS IS GOING TO WORK, MANNY," I say, glancing at myself in a mirror on the office wall. I'm wearing a big bushy fake mustache on my upper lip. It looks like somebody's gerbil jumped up onto my face.

I'm also wearing thick glasses, making it kind of hard to see, and a big floppy hat which droops to one side of my head. I must look ridiculous. Of course, I can hardly see what I look like through these dopey glasses, so I couldn't really tell you.

"You can pull it off," Manny reassures me.

Ridiculous!

"I'm not worried about you in the slightest."

Well, that makes one of us.

I slide the glasses down my nose a bit so I can peer over the top of them and actually get a peek at myself. I repeat: I look ridiculous!

"Manny, I look like a hairy, nearsighted old man!" I cry.

"That's okay," Manny replies calmly. "As long as you don't look like Billy Sure, this plan should work just fine."

"I hope you know what you're doing," I say. "Okay, so explain the plan to me again . . . one more time."

"You are going to go onto the Sure Secrets website and convince whoever is running it that you have the juiciest Billy Sure secrets he or she has ever heard," Manny explains. "Go ahead. It may even be fun!"

If I were to make a list of things I think might be fun, doing what I'm about to do would probably come in at #957 on the list—right below going to the dentist after eating roaches!

Manny hands me a piece of paper with a list of secrets he made up.

I sit next to Manny at his computer and bring up the Sure Secrets website. Just looking at it gives me the CREEPS.

"Okay, there's the contact button," Manny says, pointing to the upper right-hand corner of the screen.

I take a deep breath and click. A blank message box pops open. At the top of the box it says: "Tell us your Sure Secret!"

I look down at the piece of paper that Manny has given me and follow his script. I type: "I have the biggest secrets you'll ever hear about Billy Sure" into the message box.

"I hope you know what you're doing, Manny," I say again. Then I click send.

"Now what?" I say, scratching my nose, which itches terribly from the hairy beast sitting on my upper lip.

"Now we wait for an—"

DING!

The bell rings, indicating that a message has arrived. Just below my message, in another box, someone has written: "Do tell! Do tell!"

I look at Manny, impressed that his plan brought such an immediate reply, and thinking for the first time since he explained it to me that it might actually work.

"Perfect!" says Manny. "They took the bait. Now go ahead, send them the first 'secret.'"

I look at the paper and type what Manny has written there: "For starters . . . Billy Sure sometimes goes days without taking a shower!"

448

I turn to Manny. "That is gross!" I say.

"Just send it," Manny replies. "They're going to love it. It's just the kind of thing they're looking for."

"But it's not true!" I say. "Except for maybe sometimes."

"*They* don't know that," Manny explains, smiling and raising his eyebrows.

Sighing deeply, I hit send.

A few seconds later a reply appears: "I like! I like! Tell me more!"

"Oh, we got 'em now!" Manny says, obviously enjoying this way more than I am. "Go ahead, type the next one, but don't send it right away. Let them sweat for a minute."

I type: "Billy Sure walks around his house talking to himself. Sometimes he even has arguments with himself."

"You know that one's not true either, right?" I say.

"Of course I do, Billy," Manny says. "Okay . . . Wait . . . Wait . . . Send!"

I click send.

449

Instantly, the reply comes back. "Excellent. Go on!"

"Okay," says Manny. "This is it. The trap's been set. The bait's been placed. Now let's reel this big fish in! Go ahead and type the next one."

"For the final and most amazing secret of all to have its full impact, I need to be face-to-face with you. Time for a video chat?" I hit send.

Manny and I stare at the screen. Nothing. A minute goes by, then another.

"They're onto us!" I say, getting nervous that all this has been for nothing.

"Just wait," Manny says. "They're weighing their options, trying to figure out how to turn this to their advantage. They'll reply. We just have to be—"

DING!

"And here we go," says Manny.

"I'd prefer it if you wrote the secret out."

"That's weak," says Manny. "Very weak. Well, now is when we seal the deal."

"Okay," I say. "What does that mean? What do I write back?"

"I got this one," says Manny. "Just make sure your MUSTACHE is on tight."

"If it was on any tighter, it would be up my nose!" I say.

Manny takes over the keyboard: "If you're not interested enough in what I have to say to talk to me face-to-face, I'll just send this huge, earth-shattering secret to the local paper's business section, and they can be the first to embarrass Billy and Sure Things, Inc." He hits send.

This time the reply comes right away.

"Click on the video chat link on the Sure Secrets website, please," comes the reply.

"Okay, partner, you're on!" Manny says.

I position myself directly in front of the screen. I check my mustache, adjust my glasses, and straighten my hat. Here goes.

I click on video chat. A small window pops open within the website. A face fills the entire window. It is the face of none other than

ALISTAIR SWIPED, the CEO of Swiped Stuff, Inc., Sure Things, Inc.'s biggest rival! Alistair Swiped came out with the Every Ball, a rip-off of the All Ball, and he recently pretended to be my mom to rip off our other products.

I have to work hard to hold it together. I can't show my shock at seeing Swiped's face on the screen. I can't even let on for the moment that I even know who he is.

"Well," says Swiped, squinting at what must obviously be a pretty ridiculous-looking face (my face, that is) on his computer's monitor. He sounds slightly annoyed. "What is this great big secret that you will only tell me face-to-face?"

"Are you ready?" I ask, milking the moment for all it's worth.

"I'm ready!" shouts Swiped, now clearly annoyed. "Well?"

This is it . . . time for the big payoff.

I pull off the hat, take off the glasses, and yank the mustache off my face, practically taking my nose with it.

"I am Billy Sure!" I shout. "And you, Alistair Swiped, are *sooooo* busted!"

Swiped, whose face has been filling the entire chat window, stumbles back in shock, startled that he's been caught. With his face no longer taking up the whole window, I can now see Swiped's entire office. Sitting on his desk is the original Cat-Dog Translator prototype!

At that moment, Philo catches sight of Swiped's face. He starts barking wildly at the video chat window. I snatch the second translator prototype out of my bag, switch it on, and hold it up to Philo.

His barking comes out: "NICE MAN, GIVE ME ANOTHER TREAT. ANOTHER TREAT. I LOVE YOUR TREATS!"

Manny and I look at each other as the whole truth becomes clear. It was Alistair Swiped who stole the original prototype. He's been using it on Philo during Philo's long periods of time away from me each day. He's been bribing him with treats—which explains Philo's recent weight gain—and getting him to bark into the translator to reveal secrets about me. That explains why so many of the things that have appeared on the Sure Secrets website were things only Philo could have known.

Manny leans in close to his laptop's monitor.

"All right, Swiped, I'm only going to say this once," he begins. "If you don't return our prototype within the hour, the police are going to hear about your little theft. Not to mention our attorney."

The video chat window instantly closes. A few seconds later the entire Sure Secrets website vanishes, replaced by a message which reads, "This web address is no longer valid."

"All right, so we took care of the website," says Manny. "And by the way, great acting job. I definitely think that once you're old enough, you should grow a real mustache. It looks good on you."

I just smile and shake my head. "So how do we get the original prototype back?" I ask. "You told him to return it within the hour, but you didn't say where or how."

"I have a hunch," says Manny. "Let's just give him an hour, then follow me."

The next hour ticks by excruciatingly slowly. When it's up, Manny says, "Let's go."

He opens the back door, allowing Philo to dash out. We follow in time to see Philo easily hop over the backyard fence. Struggling to keep up, we follow Philo to the park. Not surprisingly, he leads us right to the same patch of bushes where I've been finding him every day for the last week.

Philo dives into the bushes, barking and moaning, obviously looking for the treats he's been getting from Swiped there day after day. Pushing the bushes aside, I spot the original translator prototype sitting on the ground. It has a note pinned to it that reads:

All right, Sure. Here's your stupid invention back. You win this time. But next time . . .

Chapter Twelve

You Can't Win Them all!

BACK AT THE OFFICE, AFTER SOLVING THE MYSTERY of the Sure Secrets website and Philo's disappearances, I feel very relieved.

"This has been weighing on me big time," I say to Manny.

"I know . . . one problem down, two more to go," says Manny. "And just in time, too. Here's an e-mail from Principal Gilamon saying that he thinks an assembly featuring your latest invention would be a great idea."

My relief suddenly turns to panic. I really don't like the idea of standing up in front of a packed assembly. But I know that Manny is right. This assembly will get Principal Gilamon off my back and get some of those pet owners to stop coming to my house at night.

Speaking of which, when I arrive home that evening, the usual crowd of owners and pets has gathered in front of my house. I recognize them as mostly kids from my school. Standing on my front step I announce: "Listen, everyone. I have good news. Next Tuesday morning at eight I will be leading an assembly at Fillmore Middle School. Students will have a chance to bring their cats or dogs up to the stage and find out what their pet is saying, using Sure Things, Inc.'s latest product, the Cat-Dog Translator. So good night, and I will see you next Tuesday."

I slip into the house. The crowd starts to break up. Manny would be so proud.

For the next few nights I sleep better than I have in a while now that the Sure Secrets website is gone. Then Monday night comes and I toss and turn, nervous about the assembly the next morning. I keep telling myself that once this assembly is done, kids will stop coming to my house with their pets, and we can start to move ahead with the mass production of the Cat-Dog Translator.

On Tuesday morning, bright and early, I find myself standing up onstage, holding the Cat-Dog Translator, standing next to Principal Gilamon. The auditorium is packed full of kids and their pets. Every student had to have his or her parents sign a permission slip to attend or bring a pet. Manny is watching from the back of the room, giving me thumbs-up signals. Principal Gilamon steps up to the microphone.

"Welcome, students, to this very special assembly," he begins. "As many of you know, we have a bit of a CELEBRITY attending Fillmore Middle School.

"Our own Billy Sure is an inspiration to us all. At the age of twelve he started his own company, which has grown into a great success. We can all learn from Billy's example of hard work, perseverance, and creative problem solving.

"Well, this morning we have a special treat

for you—even better than a dog treat. Billy has agreed to share his latest invention with us, the Cat-Dog Translator. So, what I'd like you to do is, if you have come with your pet, please line up along the right-hand aisle. Billy will use his invention to translate the barks and meows that your dogs and cats make into words we can all understand. Okay, Billy, take it away!"

Kids race from their seats, jockeying for position, forming a loud, unruly line down the aisle.

"Thanks, everyone, for coming and bringing your pet," I say. "Can we have the first pet up onstage, please?"

A boy steps up onto the stage with his dog.

"What's your name and what's your dog's name?" I ask.

"I'm Wilson, and my dog is Brownie," says the boy.

"Okay," I say. "Now I'm going to put the Cat-Dog Translator near Brownie. Let's see what he has to say."

I power up the device and move the

microphone close to Brownie's mouth.

"**RRRRRIIIIIFFF!**" he barks. Out comes: "WILSON THROWS MY BALL FAR!"

"Wow!" says Wilson. "That's amazing!"

The audience breaks into wild applause. I glance over at Principal Gilamon, who is clapping and smiling broadly. I catch Manny's eye at the back of the auditorium and can see him already counting our profits in his head.

Next up onto the stage is Judy Geralds, with her cat, Flick. Holding the translator up to Flick, we hear him say: "JUDY SCRATCHES UNDER MY CHIN."

Judy proceeds to scratch under Flick's chin. "MORE. . . . KEEP SCRATCHING. . . ."

Again, the entire auditorium cheers loudly.

A steady line of kids and their pets come up, one by one. The Cat-Dog Translator works perfectly. I'm completely convinced now that Sure Things Inc.'s next product is going to be a HUGE HIT.

Principal Gilamon walks over to the microphone. "I have a special surprise for everyone," he says. He turns to the side of stage and calls out: "Come here, Scout!"

A cute little dog comes trotting out onto the stage. A collective "AWWW!" fills the room.

"I brought my own dog, Scout!" Principal Gilamon announces. "I can't wait to hear what he has to say."

The auditorium bursts into applause again.

This should be kind of cool, I think. *I don't know anything about Principal Gilamon, except when it comes to school stuff.*

Principal Gilamon leans down and scratches the top of Scout's head. The little dog looks up lovingly, right into the principal's eyes. I put the translator near Scout's mouth. He barks, and out comes . . .

"YOU FART IN YOUR SLEEP."

The entire auditorium explodes into laughter. Principal Gilamon looks horrified. His face is as red as the beets my dad likes to put in his spaghetti sauce. He scoops up Scout into his arms and hurries offstage, returning without the dog a few seconds later, but still

You fart in your sleep!

looking very flustered, embarrassed, and—oh no—a bit annoyed with me, if I'm reading that look correctly.

Everyone is still laughing, and no one is laughing harder than the kid who comes up onstage next with his own dog.

"I'm Stevie and this is my dog, Paws," says the boy.

Holding the translator up to Paws we hear: **"STEVIE LIKES TO HIDE HIS SISTER'S SHOES!"**

"What!" shrieks a girl sitting in the audience. Everyone, including me, turns toward the voice and sees a girl standing and pointing up at the stage. "That's *you* who's been doing that?" she screams. "Wait until I tell Mom. You are in so much trouble!"

Stevie stops laughing and turns angrily to me. "Thanks a lot!" he snarls, then picks up Paws and hurries from the stage.

The room is still abuzz from the last two translations. Kids are laughing and chattering. Just my luck, next in line is none other than Allison Arnolds!

As she walks up onto the stage with her dog, Dusty, I get very nervous. I really hope she didn't see the Sure Secrets website.

"Hi, Allison," I say.

"Hi, Billy." So far, so good.

"Let's see what Dusty has to say."

Dusty barks. Out comes: "ALLISON SPENDS HOURS LOOKING AT HERSELF IN THE MIRROR EVERY SINGLE NIGHT."

"I do not!" she shouts, looking right at me, as if I was the one who said it. "Not every night."

Allison storms offstage with Dusty.

Great. Now she's mad at me too.

The mood in the auditorium is starting to turn ugly. Some kids are screaming at me, like I did something bad. Others are laughing and making fun of the kids who have had embarrassing stuff revealed about them. I know all too well what that feels like.

Amid the chaos, a girl named Stella comes up onstage with her cat, Loafer. I try to gain control of the unruly crowd, but it's hopeless.

I put the translator in front of Loafer.

"STELLA EATS EXTRA CAKE, AND THEN SHE PUTS THE CRUMBS IN HER BROTHER'S ROOM SO HE GETS IN TROUBLE," says the cat.

"Hey! No fair!" shouts Stella's brother from the audience.

Stella glares at me. "Why don't you turn that stupid thing off!" she yells before storming off the stage.

The chaos in the auditorium gets louder. Principal Gilamon has had enough. He walks to the microphone.

"Billy, I think it's time for you to leave the

stage with your . . . your . . . invention," he says, unable to hide the disdain in his voice. "This assembly is over! Everyone get to class!"

After school that afternoon I meet Manny at the office.

"Well, that was a DISASTER this morning," I say as Philo curls up on his doggy bed.

"Yeah, it could have gone better," Manny agrees.

We both sit in silence for a few seconds, neither of us wanting to say what we are both thinking. I finally break the silence.

"Manny, I don't think the world is ready for the Cat-Dog Translator," I say. It sounds correct coming out of my mouth, but it also makes me sad, thinking about all the work we have both put into this.

"I don't know, Billy," says Manny, but I can tell he has been thinking the same thing.

"Our pets simply know too much about us," I explain. "After what happened at the assembly today, not to mention the trouble with Swiped

and Philo, it's just too dangerous. Think of all the problems it can cause—the secrets that have no right to be revealed. Our pets simply know too much. Principal Gilamon has gone from my number-one fan to the president of the 'Say No to Sure Things' movement."

"That was pretty funny, you have to admit," Manny says, smirking.

"Not for Principal Gilamon, or the other

people who got embarrassed," I say. "Sure, we might sell a lot of these, but what do we do about the backlash? Sure Things' reputation is at stake with every product we put out."

"As much as I hate to admit it, I think you're right," Manny finally replies.

"Yeah, it's too bad, but at least we can keep the prototype so we'll know what Philo is saying."

"Well, it's actually more than just too bad," Manny says. "Without the Cat-Dog Translator, we're in a bit of trouble."

"What do you mean?" I ask, really not liking the sound of this at all. Manny is the most upbeat, optimistic guy I know. If *he* thinks we're in trouble . . .

"Sure Things, Inc. is now going to have to pay back all the money that Yummy in the Tummy pet food company has already invested in the promotion and production of the Cat-Dog Translator," Manny explains. "And, since we've already spent half of that money gearing up to manufacture the translator, we're going to have to dip into the profits from our other inventions."

Manny brings up a spreadsheet on his laptop, stares at it for a few seconds, then frowns.

"You know what this means, don't you, Billy?" he asks, looking up at me.

"I don't have to worry about Allison Arnolds finding out that I like her anymore?" I ask, hoping to lighten the mood a bit.

No such luck.

"No, Billy. It means that we need a new invention—and pronto—or Sure Things, Inc. could go **OUT OF BUSINESS!**"

BILLY SURE

·KID ENTREPRENEUR·

AND THE BEST TEST

Chapter One

Not-So-Sure Things, Inc.

I'M BILLY SURE. I'M TWELVE YEARS OLD AND I WOULD say that generally, I'm a pretty happy kid. I have a great family. I love my mom and dad, though I miss my mom—she's away a lot. My dad is great—a great painter, a great gardener—and a terrible cook. And even though my fourteen-year-old sister Emily can be a real . . . well, a real fourteen-year-old sister, lately we've been getting along pretty well. And then there's my dog, Philo. We're great buds, and he's a really cool dog.

I do all right in school, and I have friends.

My best friend, Manny Reyes, also happens to be my business partner. Okay, I know that having a business partner might sound weird for a twelve-year-old, but here's the deal (uh-oh, I'm starting to sound like Manny).

In addition to being a seventh grader at Fillmore Middle School, I'm an inventor. The company Manny and I run is called **SURE THINGS, INC.** We've had a number of successful inventions ever since we came out with our first product, the **ALL BALL**—a ball that changes into different sports balls with the touch of a button. It comes in two sizes. The large All Ball transforms from soccer ball to football to volleyball to basketball and even a bowling ball. And the small All Ball can change into a baseball, a tennis ball, a golf ball, a Ping-Pong ball, and a hockey puck. As soon as it came out, the All Ball was a **hit**!

At Sure Things, Inc., I do the inventing, and Manny handles the marketing, numbers, planning, selling, advertising, computers . . . basically, everything necessary to take my inventions and make them hits. We are a pretty terrific team. We've made some money, which goes back into the company as well as into our college funds, but mostly I invent things because I love inventing things. I also love working with Manny.

I even get to pick up Philo after school each day and bring him to work with me at Sure Things, Inc. Pretty cool. For me, every day is "Bring Your Dog to Work Day."

So, I repeat, I'm a pretty happy kid.

Except at this particular moment. Let me explain.

Sure Things, Inc. has just had to cancel an invention that we were certain was going to be our Next Big Thing. It was called the CAT-DOG TRANSLATOR, and it did exactly what it sounds like it would do. It took the barks and meows of pets and translated those sounds into human language. Sounds great, right? That's what Manny and I thought. But there was a problem.

The problem was not that the Cat-Dog Translator didn't work. Quite the opposite. The invention worked well. *Too* well.

Think about it. Your cat or dog sees you at your best, but also at your worst. You don't care how you look or how you're dressed or even what you do in front of your pet. Now imagine that your pet could share anything with the whole world, including the things you'd rather nobody ever knew. Get the picture? Well, this is exactly what happened.

This morning I, or rather, the Cat-Dog Translator, was the star of a school assembly during which I demonstrated the invention. At first things went pretty well—that is until Principal Gilamon thought it would be a good idea to bring his own dog in to try out the translator.

BIG MISTAKE! The dog blurted out to the entire school that Principal Gilamon farts in

his sleep—and while this was very funny, it was also *very* bad. Principal Gilamon was pretty angry. Make that very angry.

Other kids' pets revealed stuff about them that they were not too pleased about either. And so, by the end of the assembly, the big problems that came along with this invention were enough to make Manny and me decide not to move forward with it.

Which brings me to the whole "not such a happy kid at the moment" thing. Manny and I put a huge amount of time and work into developing the Cat-Dog Translator. We even got a sponsor to put up money to help with the costs of production and marketing, a big chunk of which we spent, figuring that the invention was a . . . well, a sure thing.

So we had to dip into our savings to give back the money we had spent. Our company, which got so successful so quickly, is now in danger of going out of business. And I'm not sure if I even want to invent anymore.

This afternoon Manny and I are sitting in the world headquarters of Sure Things, Inc., otherwise known as the garage at Manny's house, trying to figure out our next move.

"What about getting some money from a bank?" Manny suggests as he scans four websites at once, checking out short-term loans, interest rates, and a whole bunch of other money-type stuff I really don't understand. "Or, like I said earlier, we could invent something new."

"What if we just went back to being regular kids again?" I ask. "You know, like we were before the All Ball?" I feel a small sense of relief having said this aloud, after testing it out in my head about a hundred times.

Manny stays silent, his focus glued to his computer screen.

"I mean, what about that?" I continue, knowing that if I wait for Manny to speak when he's this locked in to something, I could be waiting all day. "No more double life trying to be both seventh graders and successful inventors and businesspeople. How bad would that be to just be students again? It doesn't mean I can't invent stuff for fun, like I used to do."

I pause, giving Manny another chance to respond. No such luck.

"For me, it would just mean that I wouldn't have to live with the pressure of always coming up with the Next Big Thing, of always having to worry about how much money my inventions are going to make."

Still nothing from Manny.

"You know my routine," I go on. "Get up, go to school, go home to pick up Philo, come here, invent, go home, do homework, go to bed, sleep invent. Then get up the next day and do the whole thing again. I mean, what if I didn't have to do that anymore? Would that be terrible?"

I finish. I have to admit these thoughts have bounced around my brain more than once on stressful nights trying to invent while also trying to complete homework assignments on time.

Just as I wonder if Manny is ever going to speak again, he turns from his screen.

"I'm sorry, did you say something?" he says, straight-faced.

"I—I—" I stammer in disbelief. Did I really just go through all that for nothing? Did I share my deepest doubts and worries with my best friend, when I just as easily could have told them to Philo for all the help I'd get?

Manny cracks up and punches me gently in the arm. "I heard you," he says, smiling. "It's just that things were getting a little too serious around here."

"Well, what do you think?" I ask. I really depend on Manny's advice. He's super smart and almost always knows what to do in a tense situation while remaining perfectly cool and composed. That is reason #744 why Manny is my best friend and business partner.

"You could stop being a professional inventor if you want," Manny begins in his usual calm voice. "But we both know that inventing is what you are best at. It seems to me that for you to be anything other than the WORLD-CLASS INVENTOR you are would be cheating yourself, and the world, of your talent."

Hmm . . . I hadn't really thought about it that way.

But Manny is just getting warmed up. "You're lucky," he continues. "You know what you love to do. You know what makes you happy. You know what you're best at. And you're only twelve. Some people go through their whole lives and never figure out what they are best at."

As usual, what Manny says makes great sense to me. I guess I am pretty lucky that I already know what I'm best at. I start to think about people going through their whole lives and not knowing. It's kinda sad. I feel bad for them. Ideas start to WHIZ around and BUZZ through my brain.

"It would be great if we could help those people," I say.

And then—*Ding! Ding! Ding!*—the light-bulb goes off for both of us. Manny and I look at each other and smile. The worry and indecision about my future dissolves in an instant.

"What if we invented something that would help people, whether they're kids or adults, know what they're best at?" I say, feeling ener-gized by the idea. "I can see it now . . . a helmet or something that you put on your head that tells you what your best talent is. No more wondering what you're going to be when you grow up. With Sure Things, Inc.'s BEST TEST HELMET, you'll know what you should do for the rest of your life, the moment you put the invention on your head!"

Manny frowns.

Uh-oh, he doesn't like the idea.

"Well, the slogan could use some tweaking," he says in a mock-serious tone that instantly tells me he's kidding. "And we can just call it the BEST TEST. But . . . I LOVE IT!"

Leave it to Manny to snap me out of my funk and get me excited about a new invention. Now, of course, all I have to do is invent it!

Chapter Two

a Big Problem

THAT EVENING AT HOME I CAN'T STOP THINKING about the Best Test. It could just be the most important invention I've ever come up with. After all, most of the things I've invented—the ALL BALL, the SIBLING SILENCER, the STINK SPECTACULAR, DISAPPEARING REAPPEARING MAKEUP—make people's lives a little easier or a bit more fun. But this new idea could have a much bigger impact.

I start to imagine people who are struggling with what to do with their lives. They could use this invention and focus on something

that would make them really happy and maybe even help them make the world a better place at the same time.

I'm daydreaming about winning a big prize for my WORLD-CHANGING invention when all of a sudden I'm interrupted by someone at my door.

Knock-Knock!

Emily is standing at my open door. I look

up and see that she has a single braid dangling down the left side of her face. The braid is dyed bright purple. This is apparently the next "thing" Emily has decided to try.

For a while Emily was only wearing black. Then she moved out of that phase and began speaking with a British accent—all the time. Most recently, she started wearing glasses for no apparent reason. She doesn't need glasses, and the ones she had didn't have any lenses in them anyway.

Today, no more glasses, just a purple braid. I've learned that asking Emily "why" about any of these things provokes the same reaction as if I had accused her of making puppies cry, so I've gotten good at ignoring her latest "thing."

And actually, I'm surprised to see her standing in my doorway. She usually keeps her distance, and she almost never comes to my room. So I figure she either wants to: A) give me a hard time about something, or B) she's got a real problem she'd like some advice on.

"I heard about your assembly," she says, unable to hold back a little smile. "Really sorry I missed that."

All right, it's choice A. No big shock there.

"It was different," I say. "But it did show us that the Cat-Dog Translator wasn't really a good idea for Sure Things, Inc."

"So what are you going to do next?" she asks, sounding genuinely interested.

"We've got an idea that we think is really great," I say. "But I'd like to make sure I can invent it before I tell anyone about it."

Emily sighs. "Whatever," she says. "What I really want to know is what you're going to do about Principal Gilamon. You've been his GOLDEN BOY ever since the All Ball. Now, I'll bet you're on his official TROUBLEMAKER list."

Leave it to Emily to remind me of any potential upcoming disasters. Though she does make a good point. I've got to go back to school tomorrow and face

Principal Gilamon after revealing to the world that he farts in his sleep. I don't think I'm going to be his favorite person.

"Avoid him?" I reply, shrugging, knowing full well that is not going to work for very long.

"Good plan," says Emily, raising her eyebrows and running her fingers along her purple braid. Then she turns to head to her room. "Let me know how that works out for you."

Well, that wasn't so bad.

In the meantime I have got to get my homework done. I'll just have to deal with Principal Gilamon the next time I run into him.

"What do *you* think, Philo?" I say, leaning over and looking at him curled up in his soft bed. He stretches his front paws and moans: "URRRRRRaaaa . . ."

I kinda miss knowing what Philo is saying, but I do believe retiring the Cat-Dog Translator is for the best. Most of the time I can read Philo pretty well even without the device. And I do have one stored away in case I ever do need to know what Philo is trying to say.

• • •

The next day at school I walk quickly through the halls with my head down. My goal is to get everywhere as fast as possible and avoid seeing Principal Gilamon—or anyone else, for that matter.

No such luck.

Peter MacHale spots me on my way to lunch. Part of me thinks Peter MacHale must have a tracking device on me, because he *always* spots me first. He was the first one to congratulate me on the successes of the All Ball.

"Hey, Sure, when's your next assembly?" he calls out from down the hall. He cups his hands over his mouth and makes a very loud, very long, very realistic sounding fart noise. **PFFFFT!** Everyone in the hallway is silent, but then I start to hear giggles.

"'Cause that was really fun!" Peter continues, giggling. "When Principal Gilamon—"

"When Principal Gilamon did what, Mr. MacHale?" booms a voice from behind me.

Uh-oh. I'd know that voice anywhere. It's

PRINCIPAL GILAMON! Not only is he about to see me, but also Peter had to remind him—and everyone else in the hallway—about what happened yesterday . . . not that he'd soon forget it.

"Uh, nothing, Principal Gilamon, I mean, I—um," Peter stammers. With that, he rushes down the hall.

"Hello, Billy," Principal Gilamon says coldly. "Any new inventions I should know about?"

"No, sir," I say. "I am sorry for what happened. I had no idea that my invention—"

"—would lead to students calling me Principal Gila-Fart behind my back?" he asks.

Are they really doing that? I wonder, but decide it's probably best not to ask.

"Because I've been told that charming nickname has been spreading around the school ever since the assembly," he explains.

I stare at my shoes, remaining quiet. What can I say that won't make things worse?

"I'm very disappointed in you," he says. "I thought you would be a shining example for everyone at the school. A role model. But now . . ."

Briiiiiing!!!

It's the bell. The lunch bell. The *late* lunch bell.

"Well now, Billy, you're late for lunch," Principal Gilamon says.

Grrr! My stomach grumbles. I've never been late to anything (well, maybe Dad's dinner, but sometimes that's on purpose).

"Sorry, Principal Gilamon," I say, "I really should go—" I turn toward the cafeteria. Everyone is already in there, happily chewing away.

"We don't tolerate tardiness at Fillmore Middle School," Principal Gilamon says, looking at me. "I'm afraid I will have to give you detention."

"Detention?"

"Yes. You will report to detention on Friday and every Friday for the rest of the year until I say you can stop," Principal Gilamon says. "Now, hurry along."

I groan. Did Principal Gilamon just give me, like, a hundred detentions for being late to *lunch*? If it were a class, maybe I could understand, but LUNCH? Is the lunch lady with a hairnet going to give me an F in eating?

I would have never gotten detention for being late to lunch before. Oh no. Maybe Emily is right. Maybe there was something good about being Principal Gilamon's "golden boy" after all. I mean, I never asked to be his golden boy, but I have to admit, it was a nice perk. And now I have detention—every Friday!

• • •

After school I stop at home for a snack and to pick up Philo, who trots alongside my bike as I ride toward Manny's house.

I walk into the office. Philo flops down on his doggy bed. Manny is in the middle of a phone call. Just another day at Sure Things, Inc.

"Yes, it's called the Best Test," Manny says into the phone. "Well, why don't you wait and see what it does before you reject the idea. Great. I'll call you back when we have the prototype." Then he hangs up.

"Who was that?" I ask, settling into my work area, also known as my inventor's lab, or as Manny likes to call it, the MAD SCIEN-TIST division of Sure Things, Inc. In real-ity, it's just a corner of Manny's garage with a workbench, a tool cabinet, a parts cabinet . . . well, you get the picture.

"A counselor at State College," Manny replies. "The guy whose job it is to advise stu-dents on potential careers. I'm talking to him about getting some funding from the college for the Best Test. It will sure make his job easier. Either that or it'll replace him."

"You realize that I have no idea when the prototype will be ready," I say calmly. This is Manny's standard operating procedure—set up the investment, sales, and marketing side of things before my latest invention even exists. I'm kinda used to it by now, but sometimes I do find it a little overwhelming.

"As a matter of fact, I don't even have a rough sketch," I point out. "We only came up with the idea yesterday."

"Uh-huh," mumbles Manny, banging away at his laptop's keyboard, promising potential investors something I'll need to live up to, no doubt.

And I know what Manny's "uh-huh" means. It means: "You are pointing out the obvious, telling me things I already know."

I take a deep breath, grab a pencil and a sketch pad, and I start to lay out what the Best Test will look like when I finally do build it.

"I saw Principal Gilamon at school today," I say, hoping that maybe Manny has an idea to help me.

"Oh yeah? How was that?" he asks without looking up from his keyboard.

"Let's just say that at the moment, he's not my biggest fan," I say. Talk about pointing out the obvious. "Did you know that kids at school are calling him Principal Gila-Fart?"

Manny smiles. "No, but I like it," he says.

"Well, as you might guess, *he* doesn't like it," I say. "He even gave me detention every Friday for being late to lunch today!"

Manny gets quiet. I'm sure he's thinking the same thing I am: If I'm in detention every Friday, I can't invent every Friday. I start adding details to my rough sketch and compiling a list of materials I'll need to build the Best Test prototype.

A couple of minutes later Manny spins his chair around to face me. Philo lifts his head up at this movement, then places his chin back onto his paws.

"I got it!" Manny says enthusiastically.

"Got what?" I ask. "Another investor for the Best Test?"

"Not yet . . . working on it," he says. "No, I have the solution to your Principal Gila-Fart problem."

"Please don't call him that," I say. "It isn't helping anything."

"Okay, but this will," Manny goes on. "What if you started an INVENTORS CLUB for the kids at school? You could be the president of the club and help advise kids who join about how to make their ideas for inventions a reality. Principal Gilamon is always bugging you about being an inspiration to the other kids in the school, right? Well, this would fit right in with that."

"I don't know, Manny," I say. "You know I don't like being the center of attention. We tried the assembly, and look how that turned out."

"But this would put you right back on Principal Gilamon's good side," Manny points out. "You'd be a real hands-on inspiration to the other kids at school who have ideas for inventions. And you could probably run the club on Friday afternoons instead of going to detention."

"I have to think about this," I say, turning back to my sketch. The only sound in the office is the **clack, clack, clack** of Manny typing away.

As uncomfortable as the idea of being in the spotlight makes me, I have to admit, Manny's idea would solve a few problems. Not only would it help me with Principal Gilamon, but it could also help me tie together the two pieces of my life—being a seventh-grade student and being a famous inventor.

"Thanks, Manny," I say. "That's a really good idea. I'll go to Principal Gilamon's office tomorrow morning and see if he'll go for it."

Chapter Three

Inventing a Club

THE NEXT DAY, I ARRIVE AT SCHOOL BEFORE MOST of the other students. Making my way to Principal Gilamon's office, I slip through the door and step up to the desk of Mr. Hairston, the principal's administrative assistant. I've dealt with Mr. Hairston a few times. He's very serious and he loves following the rules about as much as Manny loves sales figures—which means he loves them a lot.

"Good morning, Mr. Hairston," I begin. "I'd like to spea—"

"Number, please," Mr. Hairston says, holding

up his hand while not looking up from the work on his desk.

"Number?" I ask, puzzled.

"Do you have a number?" he asks.

"Um, no, actually," I say.

That does it. Mr. Hairston puts down his pencil and looks up at me. "Do you see that sign?" he asks, pointing to a sign on the wall across from his desk.

I glance over at the sign, which reads: PLEASE TAKE A NUMBER AND WAIT TO BE CALLED.

I look around.

"Um, Mr. Hairston, there's nobody else in the room," I point out.

"Young man, that is entirely beside the point," Mr. Hairston explains. "We have rules in this office, and as you can plainly read, the rules say that you must take a number and wait to be called."

"Okay," I say, reaching into a basket filled with plastic coins, each with a number written on it. My number is five.

"Have a seat, please," says Mr. Hairston.

Then he goes back to scribbling with his pencil.

After about five minutes, he looks up and calls out, "Number four."

I look around the room again. I'm still the only one here.

"Very well," he says, obviously annoyed that no one had number four. "Number five."

I get up, walk to the desk, and place my number five back in the basket.

"May I help you?" asks Mr. Hairston.

"Yes, I'd like to make an appointment to meet with Principal Gilamon after school today, please."

"In reference to what?" he asks.

"I'm interested in starting a school club," I say proudly, figuring that this will speed up the process. After all, it can't be every day that a student wants to start a new club at school.

"I see," says Mr. Hairston. He reaches into his desk, pulls out a form, and hands it to me. "This is form 4351-C, the School Club Start-Up form. Fill this out and return it by three fifteen." Then he turns his attention back to the pile of papers on his desk.

As I slip the form into my backpack and head to the door I hear Mr. Hairston call out: "NUMBER SIX!"

There's no one in the room but him.

As I hurry down the hall, I realize just how lucky I was to have been Principal Gilamon's golden boy. Everyone else who wanted to meet with Principal Gilamon had to go through Mr. "Take a Number" Hairston, like I just had to. As much as it bothered me that Principal Gilamon sought me out and acted like he was my pal—before the whole Principal Gila-Fart fiasco—being a celebrity had its advantages.

The school day itself is pretty uneventful.

Only three kids come up to me making fart noises. I'm feeling pretty good—except for the fact that I have to face Principal Gila-fart, I mean Gilamon, before I can get to the safety of the office.

At three fifteen I march back into Principal Gilamon's office and walk up to Mr. Hairston's desk. Being no fool, I reach into the basket to take a number.

Mr. Hairston looks up from his work.

"And exactly what do you think you're doing, young man?" he asks.

"Following the rules, Mr. Hairston," I say proudly, pointing at the sign on the wall.

"You already took a number—five, if I remember correctly. You are returning for your three fifteen appointment, correct?"

"Correct," I say, hoping that "correct" is the correct word for this situation.

"Then according to the rules, you don't need a number, do you?" Mr. Hairston asks. "Seeing as how you already have an appointment."

"Great," I say, tossing the plastic coin back

into the basket. "Can I just go into Principal Gilamon's office now?"

"I don't know, *can* you?" says Mr. Hairston. He looks at me. I look back at him. I'm not sure what I'm supposed to say. Finally, Mr. Hairston relents. "Fine. You may."

I turn and take one step toward Principal Gilamon's door.

"Provided, of course, that you have filled out the 4351-C form I gave you this morning."

I stop dead in my tracks. I forgot all about the form. Taking a seat, I pull the form and a pen from my backpack and start to fill it out. I'm about halfway done when the door to Principal Gilamon's office swings open.

The principal leans out and says, "Billy, come in, please."

I grab my backpack, my pen, and my half-filled-out form, and stand up. "I'll finish filling this out after my meeting, Mr. Hairston," I say, heading toward the open door. Mr. Hairston just shakes his head and goes back to his work.

"Sit down, Billy," Principal Gilamon says, closing the door.

I take a seat across the desk from him and wait while he settles into his chair.

"I think you know how disappointed I am in you, Billy," he says. "And not just because of your lunchtime tardiness yesterday. After the assembly, I got a few phone calls from concerned parents wondering what exactly we are doing here at Fillmore Middle School. Principals never like getting calls from concerned parents, Billy. NEVER."

I feel the knot in my stomach tighten with each word. Principal Gilamon is not making this any easier.

He pauses, takes a deep breath, and sighs deeply. "Now, what did you want to talk about?"

"Well, sir, I have an idea that I think will more than make up for the . . . um . . . the . . . ah, problems with the Cat-Dog Translator," I begin. "I would like to start an inventors club

504

here at Fillmore Middle School. I could be club president, if that's okay with you, and I would help students who join. I could guide them and show them how to make their ideas for inventions become a reality."

I pause for a few seconds to allow all this to sink in. Principal Gilamon remains silent, his hands clasped together on his desk.

"I know how you have wanted me to be an inspiration to the other kids in the school, sir," I continue, my mind racing for more stuff to say that might convince him that this is a good idea. "I think that this club might be a perfect way to do just that. And, um, if you wouldn't mind, the club could meet every Friday."

Principal Gilamon leans back in his chair and crosses his arms in front of him.

I hold my breath, waiting. If he hates this idea, the remainder of my career here at Fillmore Middle School could be a long, miserable slog.

Principal Gilamon leans forward, placing his elbows onto his desk.

"Billy," he says, a broad smile spreading across his face, "I think that is a TERRIFIC idea!" he says, extending his hand to me.

I'm so relieved that I let out a big sigh. Except my lip gets stuck on my teeth and it almost sounds like I'm making a fart noise. I look up at Principal Gilamon. Thankfully, he doesn't seem to have heard it. The last thing I need now is for him to think I'm making fun of him.

I shake his hand. "Thank you, sir," I say. "I appreciate this chance you are giving me. I won't let you down."

Principal Gilamon leads the way to the outer office.

"Mr. Hairston, please take care of the necessary paperwork to establish the Fillmore Middle School INVENTORS CLUB," Principal Gilamon says. "Well done, Billy. Well done!"

I have one foot out the door when I remember that I still haven't completed the club application form, which I pull from my backpack. "Oh, I haven't finished filling out this—"

"Never mind, Billy," says Principal Gilamon. "We're fast-tracking this project. Consider your application approved. Right, Mr. Hairston?"

"Yes, Principal Gilamon," Mr. Hairston replies through a tightly clenched jaw, staring at me like I have just committed a horrible crime.

Just before I leave the office, I toss the 4351-C application form into the trash.

CRIME: DID NOT COMPLETE FORM!

Chapter Four

Helmets and Hairdos

AFTER MY MEETING I HURRY HOME, GRAB PHILO, AND rush to the office. I'm happy that Manny's idea for an inventors club went over so well with Principal Gilamon, but I'm starting to get the feeling in my stomach that I always get when I have too much to do.

I can't even start to wrap my head around what's involved in running a club. And I haven't started building a prototype for the Best Test. I've got to make some progress on that today.

Bursting through the door to the office, I

see Manny talking on the phone while quickly scrolling through a website on his computer. It looks like he's shopping online.

"No, I don't think the Best Test will put your entire profession out of business," he says. "It can only tell you what you are best at. It can't read you mind, or put you in touch with dead relatives."

I can't wait to find out who *this* is.

Manny hangs up.

"What was that about?" I ask.

"That was the president of PSYCHICS AND MIND READERS OF AMERICA. She's worried that the Best Test will be so good at reading people's minds that it will make psychics obsolete," Manny explains.

"How did she even know that this is in the works?" I ask, amazed at how information somehow leaks out of this place.

"She's a psychic," Manny says. Then he smiles. "Seriously, haven't you checked our website lately?" He looks back at his computer.

"You put something up about an invention

I haven't even started working on yet?" I ask.

"All part of my greater marketing strategy," Manny explains.

"Aren't you worried that someone will steal our idea?"

We've had that happen before. A few months ago Sure Things, Inc.'s biggest rival, Alistair Swiped, pretended to be e-mailing as my mom in order to steal our ideas. Thankfully, Manny and I caught him, and we gave him a terrible idea to steal instead!

"Not this time," Manny says. "Our investors weren't happy with our decision to pull the Cat-Dog Translator, so I'm letting them know what we're working on. It'll bring their confidence up. You know, get the buzz going so they'll invest again."

"Uh-huh," I say. Now I just need to invent the actual thing. No pressure at all!

"So how'd it go with Principal Gilamon?" Manny asks. If I didn't know better, I'd say he was deliberately trying to change the subject.

"He loved the inventors club idea," I report.

"He's going to fast-track the club. We'll have meetings every Friday afternoon starting tomorrow."

Manny nods. He's happy his idea worked, but he's humble enough to not make a big deal about it. Reason #212 why Manny is my best friend.

Pulling out the list of materials I drew up the other day, I start piling stuff on my workbench—a spaghetti colander, an old TV antenna, a handful of lightbulbs in different sizes and shapes, and a big bundle of wires, which I'll need to untangle before they'll be of any use to me. That's when I notice there's *way* more materials in my lab than before. Materials I'd never use—like old cell phone pieces, broken laptop keys, and . . . is that a RAINBOW WIG?

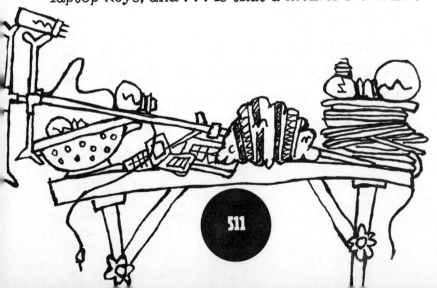

"What's all of this?" I say to Manny. His eyes are glued to his computer.

"Oh, that," Manny says distractedly. He types something on his keyboard and yells, "Yes!"

"Yes what?"

"I just won the auction!" Manny blurts. "Rare number twelve pancake-head metal screws!"

"Pancake-head metal screws?" I ask. "What are they? Why did you buy them?"

Manny twirls his fingers over his keyboard.

"For your lab!" he says. "So that you have more materials to work with. I want to make sure we get the highest quality materials at the most cost-effective prices. Successful products are made with quality materials. I read about it in my journals."

Manny is probably right, but I still don't know what I'm going to do with pancake-head metal screws. Or a rainbow wig.

After about an hour I have turned the colander into the helmet portion of the device, attached the lightbulbs to the sides and top, and screwed on the antenna. I place the helmet onto my head.

"How's it look?" I ask Manny.

He turns away from his desk and bursts into laughter.

"You look like a chef who's been kidnapped by aliens and is being made to reveal his secret recipe for spaghetti," Manny says.

"Great," I mumble. "Well, it's not how it looks that matters, but how it works."

"Okay, Best Test," I say, testing out its voice control commands, "I'm ready." The helmet begins to hum and the lights begin to flash.

A sudden puff of smoke comes from the helmet. If it were anything other than a Sure invention, I'd worry it's unsafe—this is definitely NOT something you should make at home. I yank the thing off of my head and start coughing.

"Well, if it doesn't work as a way to tell people what they're best at, we can always

DO NOT TRY THIS AT HOME!

market it as an instant hair-styling device," Manny says.

"What do you mean?" I ask, waving my hand in front of my face to blow away the remaining smoke. I get up and walk over to a mirror. There, I see that my usually straight hair has been sizzled into curls. "Oh man," I moan. I'm used to early tests failing, but this is a whole other level. Maybe that spare rainbow wig isn't so useless after all.

"No, it's a good look for you, really," Manny says, unable to suppress another giggle.

"I'm going to call it quits for now," I say. "I'll work on this later. I still have homework to do and I've got to start thinking about the club. See you tomorrow."

"Yup," says Manny, without turning around. From the corner of my eye, I see him place a bid on a set of vintage mirrors.

As I pedal my bike home, with Philo happily trotting along beside me, I realize just how exhausted I am. But that doesn't stop the feeling in my stomach from returning. What do I know about running a club? Will anyone even show up? And if they do, will they have any good ideas for inventions? Or *any* ideas, for that matter?

After dinner I settle in at my desk to do some homework, but my mind wanders. I start thinking about my mom. I miss her every day, and sometimes I go weeks without hearing anything from her. I realize that this past couple of weeks has been one of those times.

I'm not getting anywhere with my home-work anyway, so I decide to send Mom an e-mail. She moves around a lot in her job as a research scientist, and for reasons I don't really understand, she can never tell us exactly where in the world she is at any given time.

I write a long e-mail to her, filling her in on the failure of the Cat-Dog Translator, Sure Things, Inc.'s financial troubles, the idea for the Best Test, and the new inventors club. I'm not supposed to e-mail her about my ideas for new inventions, just in case they fall into the wrong hands, but I miss her. And she gives really good advice.

I hit send, take a quick shower to wash the curls and fried pieces out of my hair, and climb into bed. Finally, after a while, my thoughts calm down long enough for me to fall asleep.

I wake up the next morning feeling pretty alert. I must have gotten a good night's sleep. I don't recall waking up at all, which means that it's possible . . .

I jump from bed and hurry to my desk. Sitting there are fully-rendered blueprints for the Best Test! Yes! When I'm working hard on a project, sometimes I sleep-invent. I sleep-write

THE BEST TEST

blueprints for my inventions with my left hand. It's kind of like a SUPERPOWER, but if you asked me what's better, sleep-inventing or flying or being invisible, I'm not sure which I'd choose.

I look over the plans carefully, and they make perfect sense. I can even see what I need to do to make sure that no one else gets an unexpected hair-styling, or worse. After all, the first rule of inventing is BEING SAFE. #1 RULE

I start to feel excited. This just might work. This is going to be Sure Things, Inc.'s Next Big Thing. This will be the invention that gets us out of financial trouble!

My morning is off to a good start. I send a quick text to Manny, telling him that the blueprints for the Best Test are ready. Then I check my e-mail and it gets even better. Waiting for me is a reply from my mom. I eagerly open it.

Hi, honey, I'm so happy to hear from you! I'm sorry I've been out of touch, but I'm into a very intense phase of my research.

I'm sorry to hear about the Cat-Dog Translator. I thought for sure you had a winner with that one. But businesses have their ups and downs, and stuff happens when you least expect it. Hang in there.

Wow, the Best Test sounds fantastic. And I am so proud of you for stepping up and starting a club at school. You'll get to help other kids who, like you, love to invent. Well, work calls again, but I am so glad to hear from you. Love you lots!

Mom

Somehow, when I get an e-mail from Mom, everything else seems okay. I'm in a really good mood.

As usual, I speed through my morning, throw on some clothes, scarf down my breakfast, and run out the door so I'm not late for school. And because the first club meeting is today, I swing by the Sure Things, Inc. office to pick up a few things I'll need. Maybe Manny's online purchases will be useful after all.

Classes go pretty smoothly, but I can't shake this worried feeling about the club. Why does it seem like I'm about to walk into something I have no idea how to handle?

Never in my wildest dreams could I have imagined the sight that greets me when classes end and I arrive at the old science lab where the first meeting of the Fillmore Inventors Club is being held.

A crowd of twelve kids has gathered outside the room. This looks more like a meeting of the BILLY SURE FAN CLUB than of the Fillmore Middle School Inventors Club.

Every kid is wearing a Billy Sure T-shirt! But not just any Billy Sure T-shirt. This one has a horrible picture of me taken in the sixth grade.

It's the photo Principal Gilamon wanted to use on a poster, hoping to inspire kids just

after the All Ball came out. The poster has the words: *You'd Better Believe You're Gonna Achieve!* But the photo makes it appear like all I'm going to achieve is looking like the WORLD'S BIGGEST DORK.

Someone in the crowd spots me.

"Look! Here he comes!" shouts a boy who is not only wearing the Billy Sure T-shirt, but is also waving a copy of the poster, a copy I apparently autographed for him.

"We love you, Billy!" screams a girl who jumps up and down and points at me.

"We want to be great inventors like you, Billy!" calls out a boy holding up what looks like a robot missing its head, with one arm and two legs dangling from its body.

"Will you sign my T-shirt, Billy?" asks a short girl wearing an extra-large T-shirt that hangs down to her knees. I think her name is Samantha. She grabs the bottom of the shirt and stretches it out, hoping to give me a good spot to sign my name.

This is nuts! I mean, I know a bunch of

fan boys and fan girls who love comic books and movies and cool science-fiction stuff. I'm kinda one of them myself. But Billy Sure fan boys and girls? I have no idea how to deal with this. I hate being in the spotlight. That's why Manny always handles the press and publicity. I'll just have to try to change the focus from me to the other students and their inventions.

"Okay," I announce. "I want to thank you all for coming. Why don't we go into the room so the meeting can begin?"

I open the door, and the crowd of kids scrambles past me. I take a deep breath, then walk through the door to somehow start the first meeting of my brand-new club.

Chapter Five

Billy Sure Fans!

"OKAY, EVERYONE PLEASE FIND A SEAT," I SAY FROM behind the teacher's desk at the front of the classroom, realizing that I have never actually looked at a school classroom from the teacher's point of view before.

What I see is a bunch of kids all jockeying to sit in the front row.

"I want to be in front!" says the boy with the signed poster.

"No fair, I was here first and I want to be as close to Billy as possible!" says Samantha.

"It's okay," I say, wondering exactly how

teachers maintain control in a room filled with thirty screaming kids, when I can't seem to get a handle on the twelve in front of me. "Wherever you sit is fine."

The group finally settles into seats.

"I want to welcome you to the first meeting of the Fillmore Middle School Inventors Club."

A hand shoots up from the back of the room. I certainly didn't expect questions after uttering my first sentence.

"Yes?" I say, pointing to the boy whose hand is raised.

"I think we should change the name of the club to the BILLY SURE INVENTORS CLUB."

A low buzz of chatter spreads through the room.

"Actually, what we call the club is not the important thing," I explain.

"How about Billy Sure's Young Inventors?" a girl in the front suggests.

"I think the name is fine just as it is," I

say, wondering how long this will go on. "Let's start."

Another hand shoots up.

"Yes?" I say.

"Mr. Sure, can you fix my robot?" asks the kid with the broken toy.

"Well, first of all, please call me Billy," I say. "And maybe I can take a look at your robot after the meeting is over."

I have to get this meeting started, or we could be here all night!

I lift several boxes of parts and pieces I brought from my workshop onto the desk. I hope Manny doesn't mind how much stuff I took—but knowing Manny, he'll probably just purchase it all again anyway.

"I'd like each of you to come up, one at a time, in an orderly fashion, and take a couple of items from each box," I explain.

I've just barely completed that last sentence when everyone leaps from his or her seats at once and crowds around the desk.

Hands dig into the various boxes. Switches,

wires, metal parts, and unidentified plastic objects are all snatched up. Within a minute, the boxes are empty.

"Okay, now everyone pick a spot at the lab table and bring all the stuff you just picked with you," I say.

One by one the kids find a spot around a long slate lab table. It's got sinks, burners, empty jars, and beakers. The kids pile the pieces they took onto the table.

"Every time we meet, I'll ask you to bring your ideas in for inventions that I, and your fellow club members, will help you with," I explain. "But I thought for this first meeting, I would ask you to help me with an invention I've been having some trouble with."

Again a low buzz spreads through the room along with big smiles and wide eyes.

"We get to help *you*?" asks a girl wearing a baseball cap with the same terrible picture of me on the front. "This is like a dream come true!"

I bring out several bags of spinach, along

with beakers of flavorings, a few formulas I always use for food experiments, and a bunch of paper plates.

"Okay, club members—"

A hand shoots up, interrupting me. "Yes?" I asked.

"Can we call ourselves SURETTES instead of 'club members'?" asks Samantha.

"How about Billy Juniors?" suggests a boy.

"It doesn't really matter what we call ourselves," I explain, growing more and more impressed by the patience my teachers have when dealing with students. "What matters is that we all try our best to invent a way to make spinach taste good. I don't know about you guys, but I really, really, really don't like spinach and my dad is always making me eat it. I want to invent something that will take away the nasty taste of spinach if I'm forced to eat it. Maybe we could even find a way to make spinach taste like candy!"

A silence falls over the room that makes me nervous for a second. Then the whole club

breaks into applause. I can't help but smile.

"What a cool idea!"

"I hate spinach too! We're so alike!"

"This idea is better than the All Ball!"

People cheer. Then a kid in the back of the class raises his hand.

"But, Mr. Sure," he says in a timid voice, "you already invented the Stink Spectacular—the drink that smells terrible but tastes great! Wouldn't the formula for making spinach taste good be similar?"

It's a fair question. The Stink Spectacular is one of Sure Things, Inc.'s best inventions (at least, *I* think so). When I came up with the idea to make spinach and other gross food taste good, I wondered if I could use the same formula for the Stink Spectacular, too.

"The blueprints I came up with are only to make *liquids* taste good," I say. "It's the way that the particles are connected. When they're loose, like in liquids, I can make them taste good, but when they're closely packed in solids, like in spinach, I'm stumped."

There is a murmur around the room.

"So what if you freeze the Stink Spectacular and make it a solid?" asks the girl with the baseball cap.

"I really wouldn't recommend tasting that," I say.

The room explodes into chatter. Making spinach taste great—that could be the Next Big Thing!

"Okay, guys!" I say, raising both hands to get their attention. "This invention doesn't exist yet, and it's baffled me for a long time."

I walk around the lab table, plopping plates full of spinach in front of each student. "I want you to try out different flavorings and formulas to see if you can make spinach taste good. Now put on your thinking caps—"

"I've got mine on!" squeals the girl with the Billy Sure baseball cap.

"That's great," I say. "Okay, guys . . . ready . . . set . . . let's invent!"

The next half hour is filled with the sounds of liquid flavorings splashing and bubbling, edible powders being poured onto plates, and spinach being torn, cut, chopped, and smashed.

"I think I have something!" calls out one boy.

I hurry over to his spot and see a glob of spinach soaked with a pink liquid on the plate.

"I mixed this liquid with that powder, then heated the whole thing and poured it over the spinach," he explains. "Wanna taste it?"

I pick up a small piece of the pink, drippy spinach. Before I can bring it all the way to my mouth, it evaporates into thin air.

"Um . . . back to the drawing board," I say. "But good try."

"Taste mine!" shouts a girl on the other side of the lab table.

I walk over to her workspace and see steam coming off of a piece of spinach.

"I soaked the spinach in this stuff, then heated it," she explained.

I pick up the spinach and it instantly bursts into flames. I toss it into the nearby sink, where it sizzles and smokes.

"A little less heat, I think," I say.

"What about this?" calls out a boy at the far end of the table. He holds up a piece of spinach. It's as stiff as a board.

I take the piece and tap it against the hard granite table. It doesn't bend or break or shatter. It's as hard as a rock.

Briiiiiing!!!

The bell for the end of club period sounds.

"Okay, thank you all for coming," I say. "Good work. We'll continue with this at our next meeting."

As I help clean up, Samantha comes over and hands me a marker. She smiles at me. What can I do? I smile back and sign her T-shirt.

• • •

530

That night, as I try to get a head start on my homework for the weekend, I start dozing at my desk. My head is just about to land on my keyboard when an e-mail arrives from Manny.

> Missing you, Buddy. How's the BT coming?
> M

BT? I wonder. Is that some kind of sandwich or something? It takes me a second to realize that Manny is referring to the Best Test, which, although I sleep-invented the plans, I have yet to build a working prototype for.

I shoot back a quick e-mail telling Manny that the plans are all set and that I'll dive into the prototype first thing tomorrow.

The next afternoon I'm at the office. It feels like I haven't been here for a week, even though I really only missed one day.

"Hey, it's my long lost partner," Manny says, actually turning away from his desk to look at me. "Sorry I couldn't be at your club. I had some calls to make. How'd the first meeting go?"

"You mean the Billy Sure Fan Club?" I reply. "'Cause that's sure what it felt like. They had these T-shirts with that terrible picture from the poster."

"The weird sixth grade picture?" Manny asks.

"Yeah, and one girl asked me to sign hers!" I explain.

Manny laughs, though I fail to see what's so funny.

"Ah, the life of a star," he quips. Then he turns back to his desk.

I get to work revising the helmet I put together the other day—the one that curled my hair. Hopefully the blueprints from my sleep-inventing will fix that little issue.

A couple of hours later I'm done. The base of the helmet is still the spaghetti colander, lightbulbs, and TV antenna, but I've also built in a mechanism that should print out what the test subject is best at on a piece of paper.

It gets late, and I have to be getting home. Philo needs to be fed, and I've got to eat. I slip the prototype into my backpack. Manny hardly notices me leave. He waves good-bye to me and immediately types on his computer. He bids on a set of deflated tires. What could *that* be for?

At home I pull the prototype from my bag. On the way to my room I pass Emily's open door. That's weird. She always keeps her door closed.

Emily looks up from her computer and glances my way.

"What is that weird thing?" she asks in her ever-supportive way.

"It's the prototype for Sure Things, Inc.'s latest invention," I say proudly. "The Best

Test. It can tell people what it is that they are best at in life."

"*REALLY?*" Emily asks. "Does it work?"

"I don't know," I reply. "I haven't tested it yet."

"Well, why don't you test it on me?" she says.

"Really?"

"Sure, why not?"

Fearing this moment of sibling generosity may pass quickly, I hurry into Emily's room for the inaugural test of Sure Things, Inc.'s Next Big Thing!

Chapter Six

The Best Test Is the Best

"THIS ISN'T GOING TO FRY MY BRAINS, IS IT?" Emily asks as I place the helmet onto her head.

"How could you tell if it did?" I shoot back.

"Ha-ha! Very funny, genius," says Emily. "Are you ready, or do we have to wait for a couple of hamsters to show up to run on a wheel to power this thing?"

"Let's find out," I say. "It's voice operated. Just say, 'I'm ready!'"

"I'm ready!" Emily shouts. Immediately a slow hum starts, growing louder and louder. The lights along the helmet start flashing in

How the Best Test ISN'T powered.

sequence. Small sparks sizzle at the ends of the antennas.

"You okay?" I ask.

"Yup."

"Feel anything?"

"My head feels a little warm."

"All right, I'm going to turn the power up," I explain. "That should trigger the result."

Twisting a knob on the back of the helmet, the hum gets louder, the lights flash faster, and bigger sparks fly off the antennas. Uh-oh. This thing might be dangerous. I definitely wouldn't recommend trying it unsupervised. . . .

Ding-ding-ding-ding-ding!!!

When the bell stops ringing, the printer starts spewing out paper . . . and more paper . . . and more paper, until an entire ream of printer paper has covered the floor of Emily's room.

I stare at the paper closest to the helmet. It's blank. Following the long trail of paper, I step backward around Emily's room looking for something, anything written there. Still blank.

Finally, at the very end of the ribbon of paper is a single line of text. I read it aloud: "'Emily Sure is best at pointing out people's flaws.'"

I drop the paper and start laughing. "Well, I could have told you that without this invention!" I say.

"Just because I have deep insight into people is no reason to make fun of me," says Emily, doing her best not to crack up too. She looks around her room and sees the paper covering her floor. "Well, your invention may work as far as telling people what they are best at, but you definitely need to tweak the printout part. We don't need to use half a forest's worth of trees for each person."

"Excellent point," I say as I bend down and gather up the blizzard of paper in my arms.

"Still, it is accurate," Emily says. "For example, some of your flaws include being a know-it-all, always being messy," —she gestures at the paper I'm gathering—"and, of course, not appreciating your sister's brilliance nearly enough."

"Uh-huh," I say when I have finally picked up all the paper. I feel like I'm holding a GIANT SNOWBALL in my arms. I stuff the paper into Emily's recycle bin. It barely fits.

Emily holds the Best Test, turning it to check it out from all sides. "I can't wait to take this to school!" she says.

Oh no! I snatch the device from Emily's hands. "You can't take this to school," I explain. "It's my only prototype, and I need to test it lots more, tweak it, and fine tune it before we can move into the manufacturing and marketing phases."

Emily ignores my comments and sighs.

"But . . . thanks for agreeing to be my first test subject."

"Hmph," is all she says. As I back out of her room I see one side of her mouth lifting into a small smile.

I hurry to my room where I shoot off a quick e-mail to Manny, telling him that the first test of the prototype was a success.

The next day I write to my mom.

I fill her in on the Best Test and the fact that Emily volunteered to be the first test subject. I know Mom always likes it when we get along. *Guess what Emily is best at?* I write. *Telling people their flaws! If that doesn't prove that my invention works, I don't know what will!*

Back at school on Monday I'm swarmed by the members of the inventors club, who are still wearing their Billy Sure shirts (I really hope they washed them) and eager to tell me about their progress.

"Hey, Billy, I covered my spinach in maple syrup!" says one boy. He holds up a plastic bag filled with a combo of dissolving green goo and sticky brown liquid.

"Uh, I would rethink that approach," I say.

"Billy, I put my spinach in the microwave for fifteen minutes!" says the girl with the Billy Sure cap.

The worst of all is Samantha.

"Hey, Billy! I can't figure out how to make spinach taste good, but I bought you these chocolates!" she screeches.

Oh man, all I want to do is get to class. But, still, these kids look up to me. I have to be encouraging. And they really are kind of sweet—just a little enthusiastic (okay, a lot enthusiastic). When I open Samantha's chocolates, I see there's a poem called "BiLLY MAKES MY HEART SiLLY!" tucked in there.

BiLLY makes my heart silly!
The way you invent stuff
makes my heart Fluff!
I love your hair!
And your nice eyes!
My heart is sure
about Billy SurE!

The rest of the day goes pretty well. A few kids that weren't at the first club meeting come up to me in the cafeteria and start to talk about their ideas for inventions. I suggest that they come to the next meeting. They say that they will.

That afternoon at the office, I unveil the fully-working Best Test prototype for Manny.

"Sweet!" he says, looking it over. "And, hey, if it doesn't work, we can always make SPAGHETTI!"

All right, maybe I should have seen that one coming, since the heart of the device is a colander. And I'm always happy when Manny is in a good mood.

"Very funny," I say, powering up the Best Test. "Let's see what you are best at, Mr. Spaghetti. Put it on your head."

Manny places the Best Test onto his head. "I'm ready, Best Test," he says. A loud whirring sound fills the office, followed by flashing and ringing.

And then the printer starts printing . . . and printing . . . and printing. Once again a huge ream of paper spews from the device.

"Gee, I must be good at a lot of things for the Best Test to need so much paper to list all of them!" Manny quips.

"Don't get too excited," I say, gathering up the endless paper. "The same thing happened when I tested it on Emily. My main task for today is to fix the printer part of the device." The Best Test stops. I wend my way to the end of all that paper and find a single sentence printed on the bottom. It reads: *Manny Reyes is best at math and computer science.*

"Well, it works!" Manny says, popping the Best Test off his head and handing it back to me. He looks around at the mountain of paper on the floor. That's my cue to start fixing the printer.

I find an adding machine—an old calculator that prints out numbers—in one of my boxes of goodies and pull out the printer section. Then I pull a roll of thin paper used for printing the fortunes on fortune cookies—seriously, what is Manny buying—and connect the two. After about half an hour, I'm ready to do another test.

"Who should we try it on next?" I ask.

"My parents are both home now," Manny points out. "Why don't we try it on them?"

I grab the device, and we head into Manny's house.

"Mom! Dad! Billy's here!" Manny shouts.

Watson, Manny's big gray cat, greets us, rubbing up against my legs and purring loudly. A few seconds later Manny's mom and dad meet us in the kitchen.

"IT'S THE GREAT INVENTOR!" booms Manny's dad. "What have you cooked up this time, Billy?"

"It's called the Best Test," Manny explains as I set up the device. "You put it on your head and it tells you what you are best at."

I finish making some adjustments to the helmet and hold it up. "Okay, who wants to go first?" I say.

"I will," says Manny's mom. "What do I have to do?"

"Just sit in this chair and I'll place the Best Test onto your head," I explain. "When you're ready, say 'I'm ready.' Don't worry. You won't feel a thing."

I place the helmet onto her head. The device hums to life. The printer starts buzzing, only this time a thin strip of paper comes out about two inches and stops. Looks like the printing problem is fixed! I tear the small strip of paper off and read:

"'Alma Reyes is best at keeping people's feet healthy.'"

Perfect! After all, she's a podiatrist.

"Wow, that's amazing!" she says as I take the helmet off her head. "I cannot stress enough the importance of removing dead skin, of scraping cuticles, and of regular foot maintenance."

"Mom!" Manny whines. "You know how that stuff grosses me out!"

"Your turn, Mr. Reyes," I say to Manny's dad.

I place the helmet onto his head. "I'm ready!" he announces. After a few moments of what has quickly become a smooth routine, the Best Test spits out another small strip of paper.

"'David Reyes is best at telling stories about the past,'" I read aloud.

"Remarkable!" exclaims Mr. Reyes.

I agree, since Mr. Reyes is a history teacher!

"That machine is right on target," Mr. Reyes continues. "Learning from the past may be the most important thing we can do to pave the way for a brighter future."

I had never thought about history that way. It's kinda fun. Manny, on the other hand, rolls his eyes and lifts the helmet from his dad's head.

I start to gather up the Best Test so we can head back to the office and wrap things up for the day.

"Thanks," I say.

"I'd say you boys have another winner on your hands," says Mr. Reyes. A big smile spreads across his broad face.

I'd have to agree.

Chapter Seven

The Club Meets again

I WAKE UP THE NEXT MORNING FEELING ENERGIZED.
I always get this way when a new prototype
is a success. It means that Manny can now
do what *he* does best and turn my idea into a
REALITY.

I check my computer and see that Mom
replied to my e-mail. This day keeps getting
better. I settle at my desk to read her response.

Hi, honey, thanks for your wonderful
e-mail. I am so thrilled that you and Emily
are getting along and even more pleased

that she volunteered to be your first test subject! I'm laughing at how accurate your Best Test is, stating that what Emily is best at is telling people their flaws. Looks like you have another success on your hands, and I couldn't be more proud. I'm also curious. I'd love to try out the Best Test sometime! Gotta run. Love you lots.

Mom

Mom's e-mail gives me an idea. Maybe I'll bring the prototype to the next meeting of the inventors club. The kids in the club are all fans of my inventions. I think they'll get a kick out of having a SNEAK PEEK at Sure Things Inc.'s Next Big Thing. And it might be fun to find out what they are best at.

With the prototype up and running, the next few days are filled with marketing and production discussions at the office. In other words, Manny talks nonstop, showing me charts and spreadsheets, and I nod a lot.

Among the many things I've learned from the whole Sure Things, Inc. experience is just how important it is to trust your partner. Manny and I make such a good team, because we are each best at totally different things. He trusts that I can turn new ideas into actual inventions, and I trust that all those numbers, graphs, and projections actually mean something important.

The day of the second meeting of the Fillmore Middle School Inventors Club arrives. I pack the Best Test prototype into a large cardboard box that Manny got when his latest junk shipped, and label it PAPER TOWELS. I want to keep the prototype a secret until the meeting.

When the last bell rings, I grab the box and scoot to the science lab. This time everyone has taken a seat and is patiently waiting for me. I notice about five people who weren't at the first meeting. The club seems to be catching on, which makes me even more psyched about showing off the Best Test.

"Hi, everyone," I say. "I'm Billy Sure."

The room breaks into spontaneous applause. I thought maybe everyone had gotten over the whole Billy Sure fan club thing, but I guess not.

As the applause dies down, I place the paper towel box onto the desk in the front of the room. "I have something I think you'll all like," I announce. "I brought the prototype for Sure Things, Inc.'s latest invention to the club meeting today, and I'd like to share it with you."

"Did you invent a new kind of paper towel?" one boy asks.

"Can it absorb, like, a whole lake?" asks the girl in the Billy Sure baseball cap.

"Or maybe you've invented psychic paper towels that know when you're going to spill something and roll out to catch spills as they happen!" shouts a boy wearing a T-shirt with a picture of Thomas Edison with a lightbulb over his head.

This is getting out of hand.

"Actually," I say, "this is just the box I used

to carry the invention." I pull the Best Test prototype out of the box and set it on the desk.

"Is it a new way to make spaghetti?" shouts a girl from the back of the room.

Why did I have to use a colander? I think for the hundredth time.

"This is Sure Things, Inc.'s next invention— the Best Test," I say proudly. The room grows very quiet. "What this device does is tell you what you are best at. And, if I can get some volunteers, I'd like to try it out on some of you."

About half the people in the room raise their hands and shout: "Me! Pick me! TEST IT ON ME!" The other half slip their hands under their desks and look down, to be sure that they are not mistaken for someone volunteering.

I randomly pick three kids to try the Best Test. Okay, maybe not so random. I pick the first boy because he is one of the few kids in the class not wearing any Billy Sure apparel.

"What's your name?" I ask.

"Timothy," the boy replies.

"Now, sit right here, Timothy," I say, turning a chair around so it faces the rest of the class. I explain how it works and slip it onto his head. After a few seconds of the now-familiar whirring, humming, flashing, and ringing, a slip of paper prints out what he is best at.

"'Timothy Bu is best at counting steps,'" I read to the class. A murmur of laughter ripples through the room.

"That's true!" Timothy says as I take the helmet off his head. "I've taken four thousand, two hundred and fifty-six steps today."

"Thank you, Timothy," I say as he returns to his desk.

"Four thousand, two hundred and sixty-seven!" he calls out once he sits down.

It's now that I realize the Best Test is not

552

necessarily going to tell everyone what he or she should be doing for the rest of his or her life.

Next up is Samantha. I had to pick her, mostly because when I ask for volunteers, she waves her arms everywhere. She puts the helmet on and giggles. "I'm so, so, *sooooo* ready, new Billy Sure invention!" she squeals. A few seconds later the results come out.

"'Samantha Jenkins is best at watching TV.'"

"Wow!" she says, a big smile spreading across her face. "I can't wait to tell my mom!"

My third test subject is a sixth grader named Clayton. He's actually a random choice. His shirt is buttoned up to his neck and it's tucked tightly into his pants.

Clayton sits down and I slip the helmet onto his head. Out comes the paper:

"'Clayton Harris is best at going to the dentist,'" I read.

Clayton smiles. "I love going to the dentist. My dentist has the best purple lollipops, and I get a new toothbrush each time I go!" he crows.

"Well, I guess someone has to be the best at going to the dentist," I tell Clayton. I try to give him my most encouraging smile. Clayton smiles back up at me. And I can't help but notice that he really does have great teeth.

As I start to pack up the Best Test I hear a grunting sound out in the hall. Looking toward the door, I see two boys—I recognize them from the first club meeting—trying to squeeze a mattress through the doorway.

They finally manage to get it into the room and set it next to my desk.

"Sorry we're late," says one of the boys. "It took a while to get the mattress here."

"Um, what's it for?" I ask.

"We know that you do your best inventing in your sleep," says the other boy. "And since no one has had any luck inventing a way to make spinach taste good, we thought maybe you could fall asleep and invent it for us."

"That's not exactly how it works," I say. "You see, I—"

Cries of: "Please, Billy!" "Come on, Billy!" "Help us, Mr. Sure!" cut me off.

"All right," I say, trying to be open to what the club members want. "I'll give it a try."

I lie down on the mattress. Everyone in the club rushes to the front of the room, forming a circle around me. I close my eyes, but I'm not the least bit tired. It's the middle of the afternoon. Not only that, but THIRTY-FOUR EYEBALLS are staring at me. I open my eyes and they all lean in closer to see if I've solved the spinach problem. They don't really under-stand how the whole sleep-inventing thing works.

I close my eyes again and try to fall asleep, but after a few more minutes I realize how pointless this is. I get up.

"This is not going work," I say. "But thanks for your creativity. Why don't we go around the room and have people share some of their ideas for inventions?" I help the two boys move the mattress over to the side of the room. "Who wants to go first?"

"I do!" says a girl with long red hair. "I want to invent the INSTANT HOMEWORK COMPLETION ROBOT."

A buzz of agreement sweeps through the room.

"I love doing homework," says Clayton, and looks are exchanged.

"That's a nice idea," I say to the red-haired girl. "Who else?"

"I want to invent SPECIAL UNSQUEAKY SHOES that won't make any noise on the floors in my house. Then I won't wake up my little brother when I get up extra early to watch TV on the weekends."

"That one might be possible, but you could also just wear socks," I say. "Does anyone else—"

A knocking on the wooden doorframe cuts me off.

"Do you have room for one more?" says an all-too-familiar voice from the doorway.

"Emily!" I cry. "What are you doing here?" The high school is only just across the campus from the middle school, but most high schoolers never venture over here.

The kids all sit up straight and go silent at the sight of a high school student in a middle school classroom.

"I want to see what your club is all about," Emily says, stepping into the room.

"Everybody, this is my sister, Emily," I say. Samantha's hand shoots up into the air.

"Uh, yes, Samantha?"

"Is Emily also an inventor?" she asks.

"As a matter of fact," Emily begins, stepping up to the front of the classroom, "I'm the vice president in charge of Next Big Thing development at Sure Things, Inc. I'm also pretty good at chemistry. I heard about your club project. And this afternoon I came up with a powder that will make spinach taste good."

A chorus of "Oooohs" sweeps through the room.

Emily opens her backpack. She pulls out a bag filled with spinach and a test tube with green powder inside.

Emily points to Samantha. "Will you come up and help me with this?"

That's my sister. Just walk in and take over the whole meeting, why don't you? But actually, I'm pretty curious to see what she's come up with.

Samantha joins Emily at the front of the room.

"Okay, now, Samantha, I'd like you to take a bite of this spinach," Emily says.

"But I hate spinach," Samantha whines.

"That's exactly the point," Emily says. "Go ahead, just a tiny taste."

Scrunching up her face and holding her nose, Samantha puts a tiny dab of spinach into her mouth.

"Yuck!" she cries. "Gross!"

"All right," says Emily. "Now I'll sprinkle a little of this SPINACH-ENHANCING POWDER onto another piece."

I don't love the name Spinach-Enhancing Powder, and it would never get past Manny, but I am intrigued.

Emily taps a few tiny green crystals from the test tube onto another piece of spinach, then hands it to Samantha, who pops it into her mouth.

Everyone, including Emily and me, leans forward, waiting for Samantha's verdict.

"It tastes a little better," she says. "Not great, but a little better."

Everyone in the room breaks into applause.

"Thanks, Emily," I say.

"No problem," she replies, slipping the spinach and the powder into her backpack. "That's just what we scientific geniuses do."

"Okay, meeting over," I announce. "I'll see everyone next week."

I have to say, the second meeting of the Fillmore Middle School Inventors Club was a rousing success.

As I pack up my stuff, I see the two boys who brought the mattress struggling to get it back out through the door. Maybe I should invent PERSONAL ROBOT MOVERS? I jot the idea down.

Chapter Eight

What Dad Is Best at

THAT NIGHT AT HOME I'M FEELING PRETTY GOOD. THE club seems to be a success. The Best Test prototype is working like a charm. And Emily was actually a great addition to the club meeting this afternoon.

After exchanging a few e-mails with Manny, I head downstairs for dinner.

Dad is hard at work in the kitchen, wearing his "Cooking Is Art" apron and the silly, floppy chef's hat that Mom bought him years ago.

"Okay," Dad says proudly, lifting the cover

off a casserole he's just pulled from the oven. Steam rises from the bubbling dish. Steam that smells like a cross between boiled cabbage and the beach after high tide. "Who's ready for COD AND BRUSSELS SPROUTS SUPREME?"

Emily and I exchange a quick look, but we both remain silent.

Dad inhales the steam deeply. "Yum! Hand me your plates, guys."

We each hold out a plate onto which Dad spoons a big glop of his creation.

I move a forkful slowly toward my mouth, bracing myself for what is about to happen. The stuff tastes fishy and bitter and the sauce is greasy. I smile as I chew. Dad stares at me, wide-eyed, waiting for my review. I nod a bit too enthusiastically and make as close to a positive grunt as I can muster.

Now it's Emily's turn. She takes a teeny, tiny bite of the casserole, moving it around her mouth, trying to find a place on her tongue that might actually make the stuff taste good.

No such luck. I can see that she likes it as much as I do—which is to say not at all. But, as always, we don't want to hurt Dad's feelings.

"Very different, Dad," says Emily. "Surprisingly crunchy, which is kind of . . . new." I can just about see her brain plotting some emergency that would pull her away from having to eat another bite.

"That's my goal," Dad says, smiling. "Whether I'm painting or creating art in the kitchen, I bring a new point of view to whatever I'm working on."

I nod and put another, smaller bite into my mouth.

"Speaking of work," Dad says between shoveling forkfuls of casserole into his mouth, "how are things going at Sure Things, Inc., Billy?"

I fill Dad in on the Best Test, its invention, and recent success. Then it strikes me. I should try it out on him! How much fun would that be!

After dinner, Dad, Emily, and I sit in the living room. I slip the Best Test onto Dad's head. After its symphony of beeps, boops, bells, and flashing lights, it spits out the result.

I look down at the slip of paper and can't believe what I see written there. "'Bryan Sure is best at cooking,'" I read aloud.

BRYAN SURE is best at COOKING

Emily and I stare at each other in stunned silence.

"Well, well, well," says Dad. "I would've guessed that I was best at painting, but, of course, my artistic impulses can express themselves in many ways."

Neither Emily nor I want to be the first one to say anything, so neither of us says a word.

"I mean, I've always considered myself a great cook, but this now inspires me to bring my culinary art to a new level," Dad says, smiling. "And the timing couldn't be better! I just finished my latest series of paintings based on close-ups of Philo's tongue. I can use a little time to cleanse my artistic palette

by indulging in my other great creative skill—
COOKING!"

I smile and nod. Next to me, Emily does
the same.

"It's a win-win for everyone," Dad continues,
his excitement building. "I get to take my
culinary creativity to a whole new level, and
you guys get to eat what I cook!"

Emily finally speaks. "A 'win-win' all
right," she says, forcing a smile and raising her
fist slightly into the air in a mock-triumphant
gesture.

"So, did you guys test out Billy's invention
on yourselves?" Dad asks.

"I tried it," says Emily. "It said that I was
best at pointing out people's flaws."

Dad laughs. "Just remember, Emily, you're

good at lots of other things too. What about you, Billy?"

Up until now, I had never thought about trying the Best Test on myself. I know what I'm best at. After all, I'm the guy who invented the thing in the first place.

"I haven't," I say. "Maybe I will."

For the rest of the weekend, Dad is in his glory. He hardly leaves the kitchen.

For breakfast on Sunday, Dad whips up kale and cinnamon waffles, topped not with maple syrup, but with mustard!

"My creative juices are flowing now!" says Dad as he *thwaps* a glob of mustard onto his waffles.

And, of course, Emily and I have to stand up to this latest assault on our taste buds and stomachs without barfing or hurting Dad's feelings.

"I have to say that these are the greenest waffles I've ever had," I say with as much enthusiasm as I can muster.

"Aren't they?" Dad says proudly, shoving another chunk into his mouth.

For lunch that day Dad whips up a combination hot dog and hamburger. "I can't decide whether to call this a hot burger or a ham dog," he says.

It doesn't really matter to me what Dad calls it. I see him pull out a pack of hot dogs, a lump of ground beef, avocado paste, cottage cheese, and a blender, and my stomach starts to moan.

Dinner that night takes Dad's "creativity" to a whole new level. For starters, he combines mint chocolate chip ice cream with asparagus and then sprays whipped cream over the whole thing.

Words don't even come close to describing how GROSS this mess tastes.

Dad's cooking was always terrible, but now it seems that, spurred on by the results of the Best Test, his culinary choices have gone off the deep end. And there is something else troubling to me about this new development.

For the first time, the Best Test was completely wrong. It took the thing that Dad is *worst* at and said it was the thing that he's *best* at.

I decide it's time. I have to administer the Best Test again, this time on someone who knows exactly what he is best at—me. I ask Emily to join me for the test, and so after dinner we sit in my room.

"This is kind of dumb," Emily says. "I mean, we both know what it's going to say. 'Billy Sure is best at inventing things.' On the other hand, here in your room we're safe from Dad's cooking."

"But that's just what's got me worried," I say. "If the Best Test can be so wrong about Dad, who's to say it can't be wrong about anyone else?"

I slip the helmet onto my head and turn it on. "I'm ready," I say, my voice a little shaky. A few seconds later the paper comes out.

Emily snatches it. Her mouth falls open wide and she starts HOWLING WITH LAUGHTER.

"What?" I ask. "What does it say?"

"Okay, okay," Emily says, trying to compose herself. "It says . . ." Again, Emily roars with laughter.

"Come on!" I shout.

"It says 'Billy Sure is best at spinach farming.'"

"Farmer Billy"

I sneer at my sister. "No it doesn't," I say, grabbing the paper from her hand. I look down and read aloud. "'Billy Sure is best at spinach farming.' What does that even mean?"

"It means you'd look good in overalls and a straw hat, holding a pitchfork," Emily says, bursting into a fit of laughter again.

"Very funny," I say. But not only is this not funny, it's really got me worried. Either my invention doesn't work, or I am really off base about what I'm best at. And Dad, well, there's no way he's best at cooking, right?

"You may think this is all one big joke, but it's not," I say. "This problem has to be solved before we move into mass production. I'm going to have to build another prototype to make sure everything is working properly."

"I still like the idea of BILLY THE FARMER," Emily says, getting up and heading to her room.

Later that night before I go to bed I shoot off another e-mail to Mom. I tell her about the not-so-great results of the Best Test, knowing that she, of all people, will get a kick out the idea of Dad being a great cook and me being a spinach farmer.

So much for things slowing down for me. I now know exactly what I'll be doing at the office tomorrow.

Chapter Nine

Best Test, Take Two

THE FOLLOWING MORNING I GET UP AND CHECK MY computer. As I had hoped, there's an e-mail reply from my mom waiting:

> Hi, honey, I laughed out loud when I read the results of your tests. We all know about your father's culinary skills, though nobody tries harder to be a good cook. And you as a spinach farmer? Spinach is your most hated food!
>
> But seriously, Billy, I hope there isn't a problem with your new invention. I know

how disappointed you were when the Cat-Dog Translator didn't work out like you'd planned. Good luck figuring this out. If anyone can, it's you! Gotta go! Love you lots,

Mom

I lean back in my chair. E-mail is great, and I love hearing from my mom, but it also reminds me of just how much I miss her.

But I don't have time to dwell on that . . . or anything, for that matter. As soon as I walk into school, I start running into members of the inventors club.

First, Timothy runs up to me.

"Hi, Billy!" he says. "Look what I invented all by myself!"

"Hi, Timothy," I say. "You know, now is not the best time. I have an exam, and the next meeting will be here before you—"

Ignoring me, Timothy shoves his invention into my face.

"It's my AUTOMATIC HAIR COMBER," he says proudly. "Watch!"

Timothy's invention is an electric tooth-brush with a plastic comb glued to the spot where the toothbrush normally goes. Timothy flips the switch to turn on his invention.

ZIP! ZIP! ZURRRR!

The toothbrush motor buzzes and whines, sending the comb around and around and around. Timothy lifts the contraption to his head. But his hair isn't automatically combed—instead, he knocks off his glasses and—**smack!**—pokes himself in the eye.

"Looks like it needs a little work," I say, doing my best, as always, to be kind. "Let's look at this at the next club meeting."

I only have a chance to take a couple more steps when Clayton catches up with me in the hall. I notice his shirt isn't buttoned up all the way to his neck anymore.

"Billy, look!" he says. "I made an invention. It's the SPINNING SANDWICH MAKER." He holds up a plastic spinner from a board game. Attached to the spinner are a bunch of metal spatulas. A different sandwich ingredient sits balanced on each spatula—bread, salami, cheese, lettuce, tomato, mustard, ketchup.

"Watch this!" Clayton says.

Just hearing those words makes me nervous.

Clayton spins the game spinner. The spatulas whirl around, sending the sandwich ingredients flying in every direction.

A piece of bread bounces off my head. A slice of salami slams into the wall and slides down, leaving a trail of grease behind it. Chunks of cheese land on the floor. And then . . . you guessed it, the mustard and ketchup sail through the air, splattering all over my shirt. A mixture of red and yellow glop trickles down, dripping onto my shoes.

"Um, I haven't figured out how to make the ingredients land together yet," Clayton admits. "Maybe we can work on that at the next meeting."

"Good idea, Clayton," I say, heading as quickly as I can toward my locker where I have an extra T-shirt for gym class.

After school I race home, pick up Philo, and ZOOM to the office. I have got to nail down another Best Test prototype.

I walk through the door and head to my workbench. Manny, who is on the phone and has his back to me, lifts his hand and wiggles his fingers to say hello.

"No, sir, I think *you're* confused," I hear Manny say. "This invention doesn't tell you what your dog is best at. Well, yes, we had been developing a dog-related device, but our focus has now shifted to learning what people are best at and—what's that? Well. I'm sure if your company invests in Sure Things, Inc.'s Best Test, what *you'll* be best at is counting the return on your investment. No, sir, I'm not trying to be funny. Thank you. I'll get that information right out to you."

"What was that all about?" I ask as I unroll my blueprints and start to gather the parts I'll need to construct another prototype.

"Oh, the usual," Manny replies. "Rounding up investors. Hey, how's the testing going?"

"I'm a little concerned," I explain. Even though it's been a day since I took the Best Test, I've been afraid to admit my result. In my head I practiced what to tell Manny. "I got a couple of weird results. The Best Test said that my dad was best at cooking and that I was best at spinach farming. So today I'm going to work up a new prototype and retest people I've already tried it on."

Manny cracks up. "The thought of you as a spinach farmer," he says. "I can just see you out in the field, in overalls and a—"

"If you say 'STRAW HAT' and 'PITCH-FORK' you may just have to find yourself another partner!" I say, cutting him off.

"Okay, okay, calm down, Spinach Farmer Billy," Manny says, still giggling. "I'd say a new prototype is probably a good idea. After all, I've tasted your dad's cooking."

"Agreed," I say.

"If everything is okay with the new prototype, then I think we can start production by the end of the month," Manny explains. Then he turns back to his desk. I think I hear him mumble something about spinach, but I choose to ignore it.

An hour later I have assembled a second prototype for the Best Test. Building something a second time, especially when I have good blueprints right from the beginning, is generally a pretty quick process.

"Can we bother your parents again to test this new prototype?" I ask Manny.

"No bother," Manny replies. "You know they love seeing you."

I gather up the new device, and we head into Manny's house.

"It's nice to see you again, Billy," says

Manny's mom. "Is this another new invention you've brought over to show us?"

"Actually, it's an updated version of the Best Test," I explain. "Would you and Mr. Reyes mind if I tested it on each of you again?"

"Not at all!" Mr. Reyes booms in a deep voice. "Anything for science! Right, Manny?"

"Yeah, Dad, anything for science," Manny repeats in a tone that tells me that the sooner we head back to the office, the happier he'll be.

Manny's mom goes first. I put the new prototype on her head. A few seconds later it spits out the result: *Alma Reyes is best at keeping people's feet healthy.*

Same exact result as the first time.

Mr. Reyes goes next. Again, the result is the same as the first test: *David Reyes is best at telling stories about the past.*

"Seems to be working just fine," says Mr. Reyes.

While we're testing, I place the helmet onto Manny's head. His result is also the same: *Manny Reyes is best at math and computer science.*

I sigh as I pack up the prototype. I now know that the device works on the people whose result was correct the first time.

"Thanks, everyone," I say. "See you tomorrow, Manny."

I head for home to do the more serious and worrisome tests—the ones on Dad and on me.

At home I run into Emily first. She's in the kitchen, munching on a bag of chips.

"Are you still testing that thing?" Emily asks, spotting the prototype.

"Actually, this is a second prototype," I explain. "After the results for Dad and me, I got worried. Here, let me test it on you and see if the result is the same as the first time."

"Whatever," Emily says, lifting the bag and emptying the chip crumbs into her mouth.

I slip the Best Test onto her head. The result of the test is the same as the first time: *Emily Sure is best at pointing out people's flaws.*

"This is getting boring," Emily whines, lifting the helmet off her head.

"Hey, are you still testing that thing?" asks Dad, walking into the kitchen carrying a bag of groceries he just bought. "Wait until you see what I'm going to cook up for you guys tonight!"

He starts unpacking the bag. Out comes celery, a whole fish with its eyeballs still in place, a jar of hot sauce, and a bag of choco-late chips. My mind reels at the thought of the LATEST HORROR Dad is preparing to unleash on us at the dinner table tonight.

"Would you mind if I tried the Best Test on you again?" I ask.

"Why not?" Dad replies. "I'm sure you'll get the same result. I've never felt more creative or inspired in my cooking than I have in the last few days."

I slip the helmet onto Dad's head. *Here goes!* I think.

Just as with everyone else, the result with the second prototype are exactly the same as with the first one: *Bryan Sure is best at cooking.*

Oh no! I think. *What do I do now?*

"What about you, genius?" says Emily. "Try it on yourself."

This is it, I think. *The big one. Here goes . . .*

I place the Best Test onto my head. A few seconds later the result comes out. I read the piece of paper with great trepidation: *Billy Sure is best at spinach farming.*

I start to wonder if maybe it's time to give up on Sure Things, Inc. and the whole inventing thing and start a new life as a spinach farmer.

Maybe I wouldn't look so bad in overalls, after all.

Chapter Ten

Farmer Billy

THAT NIGHT I HAVE A HARD TIME FALLING ASLEEP. Should I really be a spinach farmer? I know I'm good at inventing things, so why didn't that come out when I used the Best Test on myself? And for the spinach farmer result to come up twice, on two different prototypes . . . that just plain scares me.

Could everything I've done with my life be wrong? How can that be? After all, I'm the guy who invented the device that told me that I shouldn't be an inventor. It doesn't make any sense at all, unless . . .

I don't even want to think about the possibility that the Best Test's basic design is faulty. Sure Things, Inc. simply can't afford two inventions in a row that never make it to the marketplace. No, I do not want to think about that.

When I finally doze off, I dream of fields filled with rows and rows of spinach. In the dream I'm wearing overalls, big boots, and the Best Test on my head as I walk through rows of spinach, yanking plants from the ground and tossing them into a big basket.

In the distance a tractor rumbles toward me, rolling right across the rows of spinach. I see that the tractor is crushing the delicate plants. Shredded green leaves fly everywhere.

At it gets closer I see that Manny is driving the tractor! Just as it is about to run me over, I wake up.

Well, that was really strange, I think as I climb from bed, anything but rested. Maybe I'm crazy, but I have to find out if the Best Test is right.

All week at school I have trouble concentrating. I feel like my entire future is on the line with the next decision I make. After school on Thursday, I decide the time has come to start my new life. If I'm really best at being a SPINACH FARMER, why fight it?

On my way to the office I stop into the local greenhouse. I remember being here with my mom when I was really little, but I've never actually bought anything here myself before today. It makes me feel kinda grown-up . . . and kinda weird at the same time.

The smell in this place is amazing with all the houseplants, veggies, and flowers. I take a deep breath. Maybe this really is what I was meant do.

I step up to the counter. "I'd like to buy some

spinach plants, please," I say to the clerk.

"Certainly," he replies. He places three six-packs of plants onto the counter.

Tiny green shoots poke out of the black soil. It's hard to believe that these little green things will one day grow up to be spinach and cause kids around the world to make excuses not to eat their dinners.

"Would you like the SAVOY, SEMI-SAVOY, or SMOOTH-LEAF?" the clerk asks.

Uh-oh, I didn't realize I'd have to choose a *type* of spinach. I didn't think this would be so hard. Then again, I'm supposed to be the best at this, or so the Best Test thinks, anyway.

"How about one of each?" I ask, smiling to hide the fact that I really have no idea what I'm doing when it comes to growing spinach. I pay for them and hurry from the greenhouse, hoping that that the clerk doesn't ask me any more questions that I can't answer.

I arrive at the office, plants in hand, resigned to tell Manny that I believe the time has come to start my new life as a farmer.

"What's up with those?" Manny asks, snatching up his laptop and heading toward my workbench. I can guess from what's on the screen that he's about to tell me all the things we need to do to get ready for the rollout of the Best Test. "You redecorating the office?"

"Manny, I've decided to follow the advice of the Best Test and become a spinach farmer," I say, trying to sound as serious as I can.

"Uh-huh," says Manny, plopping his laptop down in front of me. "So, back here on planet Earth, we have about a million tiny details to go through."

Speaking of planet Earth, I see Manny's bought a globe for his desk.

"Manny, I'm serious," I say.

Manny lowers his chin and raises his eyebrows. "Okay, first, that's the dumbest thing I've ever heard. And second, time is ticking away, partner. We've got packaging designs to develop, ad copy to refine, investors to make happy, retail chains to—"

"Why is it so dumb?" I ask, not willing to let go of this plan. "The Best Test has been way off twice now. It said that Dad was best at cooking, and I was best at, at . . ." I gesture to the plants sitting on my workbench. "At this!"

"I think 'inaccurate' is the operative word here," says Manny.

"Exactly," I say. "I mean, what if some kid uses the Best Test and it says that he's best at, oh, I don't know, knitting. So then he devotes his life to that, when really he should have studied to be a doctor."

"Knitting?" Manny shoots back, his eyebrows climbing even higher on his forehead. "Billy, knitting is a hobby, and maybe the kid *is* good at it, just like spinach farming can be your hobby. Maybe you're the best at spinach farming out of everyone else you know. But your job is INVENTING, and we've got work to do!"

I realize that trying to convince Manny is pointless, so I turn my attention to the charts and spreadsheets he's worked so hard to put together. As usual I understand about half of what Manny explains, but I trust that he knows what he's doing. A little while later I leave Manny to move full speed ahead on the launch of the Best Test, and head home with my plants.

After feeding Philo, I grab a snack in the

kitchen. I also place my new plants there in a sunny window just above the sink.

"Hey, look!" says Emily when she spots me watering them. "It's Farmer Bill!"

"Very funny," I say. "But I will grow these plants. And with your powder, they will even taste good when we eat them someday."

"Whatever you say, Spinach Boy," Emily says before heading to her room.

I finish watering the spinach and then go to my room. I sit at my computer to whip out another e-mail to Mom:

Hi, Mom, so you're not gonna believe this, but today I bought some spinach plants. I've got to find out if the Best Test is right about me. I'd hate to really have a secret ability to grow great spinach and not follow through on that. Speaking of the Best Test, I now have two prototypes. Were you serious about me sending you one? Let me know. Love you.

Billy

Mom's career has always been something of a mystery to me. I'd love to know what the Best Test says *she* is best at.

As I get into bed that night, my mind is racing. I can feel the stress of trying this new spinach project. I'm worried about letting Manny down. And I'm still wondering if actually releasing the Best Test is a good idea. I mean, I thought the Cat-Dog Translator was a great idea, and we all know how well that turned out.

The last thing that pops into my brain before I finally fall asleep is that tomorrow afternoon is the next meeting of the inventors club.

Just what I need—one more thing to worry about!

Chapter Eleven

The Return of Emily

THE NEXT MORNING I CHECK MY E-MAIL AND SEE that Mom replied.

> Hi, honey, I would love to try out the Best Test. I think we'd both really get a kick out of seeing what it says. When it arrives I'll let you know, and maybe we can set up a video chat, so it would almost be like we are together.

Mom goes on to give me an address in South America. I'm looking forward to seeing what the Best Test says Mom is best at. And I'm kinda excited about having a video chat with her. I have to be extra careful with sending inventions to Mom—again, I don't want any IMPOSTORS to steal my ideas—so when I ship the Best Test out, I ship it in a locked suitcase. I tell Mom that I'll give her the lock code on video chat so that only she can open it.

The school day drags. I fight to keep my eyes open as I move, zombielike, from class to class, all the time wondering how the latest

meeting of the inventors club will go. How can I inspire kids to follow their dreams when now I'm not even certain that *I'm* following my own dream?

After classes I arrive at the room for the meeting, imagining what might be coming next for me—president of the Fillmore Middle School Spinach Farmers Club, perhaps?

I am greeted by a noisy, excited bunch of kids. Luckily for me, many of them have brought in new inventions they have come up with or ones they'd been working on that they have tweaked since the last meeting.

"Hi, everyone," I begin. "Welcome to this meeting of the Fillmore Middle School Inventors Club. Who has something they'd like to share with the rest of the club?"

A whole bunch of hands shoot into the air.

"Me, me!"

"Pick me, Billy!"

"Ooh, ooh!"

I have to admit, the enthusiasm of the club members makes it easy to be the president.

Among the people with hands in the air I spot Clayton.

"Clayton, have you managed to work out the bugs in your Spinning Sandwich Maker?" I ask, pointing to him.

"Yes, sir," Clayton says, standing up quickly and hurrying up to the front of the room, carrying his invention out in front of him with two hands, staring at it to make sure it stays balanced.

"I call this the Spinning Sandwich Maker."

Clayton holds up his contraption for everyone to see. "You put the sandwich ingredients of your choice onto these spatulas. Then they are attached to a spinner I took off of my Climbers and Clingers board game. When you spin the spinner, the sandwich gets put together automatically."

Hoping to avoid another ketchupy, mustardy mess, I stop him.

"Um, Clayton, do you remember the problem you had the first time you showed this to me?"

"Yes, sir," he replies. I really wish he'd stop calling me "sir," but one thing at a time. "I added hinges from my kitchen cabinets to the spatulas so that they flop forward now to build the sandwich. WATCH!"

As Clayton places bread, salami, cheese, lettuce, tomato, mustard, and ketchup onto the various spatulas, I can't help but think about what Clayton's parents will say when they find the hinges from their cabinets missing. It actually makes me think of my early days as an inventor, when I would take apart everything from toasters to TVs to build my inventions. Maybe it's not so bad that Manny buys me supplies now.

"All ready, sir," says Clayton.

"Give it a spin," I say, taking a giant step away from the contraption.

Clayton spins the spinner. The spatulas whirl around and around. As they spin, each spatula flops forward on its hinge, placing in the center of the spinner, in precise order: a slice of bread, a dab of mustard, two slices of salami, two slices of cheese, a piece of lettuce, a slice of tomato, a blob of ketchup, and another piece of bread. A perfectly built sandwich!

The club bursts into applause! Clayton grins the biggest grin I've ever seen.

"Great job, Clayton!" I say as the applause dies down, realizing just how important this club is to some of the kids. Clayton heads back to his seat, getting patted on the back as he goes. It's obvious that he's found something he loves and someplace he belongs. Samantha is so impressed by his invention, she even offers him chocolate. It kinda makes all the worrying and lost sleep worth it.

"All right, who else wants to share their invention?" I ask.

"I do," says a voice from the doorway.

I look over and see Emily standing at the entrance to the room. "Emily?" I say, genuinely surprised to see her here again. "You know that club membership is only open to kids in middle school, right?"

Ignoring me completely, which is something else she's best at, Emily walks into the room. "Yeah, well, in a minute you're going to eat your words," she says, stepping up to a lab table. "As well as anything else you like, because I've been working on *my* Spinach-Enhancing Powder in the high school's chemistry lab, and I think it's a winner!"

I still don't like the name.

Emily opens her backpack and pulls out a bunch of containers filled with all kinds of gross foods. She opens a container and pulls out a piece of liver.

"Who here likes liver?" she asks.

"Yuck!"

"Ew!"

"Gross!"

Only one hand is raised—Clayton's. I have to give it to him—he knows what he likes.

Emily points to Samantha. "Samantha, right?" she says.

Samantha nods her head, smiling, clearly happy that Emily remembers her name.

"Do you like liver, Samantha?" Emily asks.

"No way!" Samantha says. "My mom likes to eat it, but I think it's really gross!"

"Perfect!" says Emily, placing the liver onto a paper plate and pulling out a small container. She sets the plate down in front of Samantha. "This is the latest version of my Spinach-Enhancing Powder. Let's see how it works on liver!"

Emily sprinkles a bit of the powder, now more a blue color than green, onto the liver.

"Go ahead, Samantha. Please take a bite."

Scrunching up her face, bracing herself for the worst, Samantha pops a piece of liver into the mouth. Her face starts to relax, then her eyes open wide. "IT TASTES GREAT!" she cries. "How did you do that?"

Emily smiles. "Okay, who hates lima beans?" she asks, opening the next food container.

Everyone raises a hand . . . even Clayton.

"Okay, and what's your name?" Emily asks, pointing to a boy in the back of the room.

"Robert," he replies.

"All right, Robert, try this," she says, sprinkling some of her powder onto a small pile of lima beans.

Once again Emily has waltzed in to my club and taken over. But I'm glad. The kids in the club really seem to be getting a kick out of her being here. And, if this powder of hers works as well as she says . . . well, one step at a time.

Robert picks up a lima bean and looks at it as if it were radioactive.

"Go ahead," Emily encourages him.

He eats the bean. "Wow!" he says. "This tastes better than candy!"

"Okay, I've saved the best for last," she says, placing some spinach onto a plate. "And Billy, I think you should taste this sample."

She sprinkles some of the powder onto the spinach. It disappears into the folds of the leaves. I catch myself wondering which variety of spinach this might be.

I shove the spinach into my mouth and chew. The entire club leans toward me, waiting to see my reaction. The spinach has a slightly sweet, slightly salty flavor that actually tastes great. It tastes better than before with the Spinach-Enhancing Powder.

"Fantastic!" I say as the room breaks into applause. "And it seems to work on anything."

My mind starts racing, going through a bunch of things all at once. First, I realize that Emily and I might be more similar than we thought—or more than she will ever admit.

Second, maybe the Best Test isn't the greatest idea after all. In reality, maybe it's Emily who's come up with the better invention.

And third, with some fine tuning, Emily's powder could actually turn out to be Sure Things, Inc.'s Next Big Thing!

Briiiiiiing!!!

The bell sounds, interrupting my thoughts and signaling that the meeting is over.

"Thank you all for coming," I say. "I'll see you next week." I turn to Emily.

"Would you maybe come to the Sure Things, Inc. office right now so we can fine tune your powder?" I ask. "I think you may really have something there."

"Okay," Emily says. "But I need a promotion. I'm a vice president now. I'm thinking something along the lines of inventor-in-chief."

Chapter Twelve

Gross to Good!

EMILY CARRIES PHILO OVER TO THE OFFICE IN her arms. I don't tell her that he likes to trot by me—she's too busy petting him, saying things like, "We need to invent some nicer smelling shampoo for you," while simultaneously saying, "You're the best dog in the world!"

"Check out my workbench," I say once we're at the office, "or as we like to call it—the mad scientist division of Sure Things Inc."

Emily walks over to the piles of wires, switches, and tools that cover my workbench.

I notice that Manny's added two mini pitchforks.

"When's the last time you actually saw the surface of the workbench?" Emily asks.

"Probably the day we opened the office," I say.

She looks over at my cabinets, shelves, and peg boards, then pulls open a drawer labeled SMALL SWITCHES, in which she sees a bunch of tiny lightbulbs—and the rainbow wig. "What's up with this?" she asks.

"WHAT'S UP WITH WHAT?" I reply casually.

"So what have you got for us, Emily?" Manny asks, anxious to get on with the business at hand.

She plops her backpack right down into the middle of my workbench, sending parts and tools flying in every direction. Then she unzips it, pulling out a container of her powder and a chemical formula written on a note card.

Now we're getting somewhere. Manny and I look over Emily's shoulder at the formula. It's pretty complex. Sometimes I forget just how smart Emily is.

"That's interesting," Manny says, pointing to a list of ingredients that must be mixed in precise order.

"Hmm . . . ," Manny says. "Have you considered switching the order of these two steps?" he asks, pointing to the paper.

"Interesting," says Emily, intrigued by Manny's question. "I never thought of that, but I can see that making that change might help the rest of these combine more quickly."

"Which should increase the range of food that the powder works on," adds Manny. "It just works on liver, lima beans, and spinach now, right? If we can tweak this formula to work on any food, we may just have a huge hit on our hands."

"Let's try it," I suggest, pulling out a plastic bin and sweeping the debris—otherwise known as my work—from the workbench to give Emily room to play with her formula.

"While you're doing that," Manny says to

Emily, "I'll run into my house and grab the worst-tasting food I can find."

A short while later Emily finishes reworking her formula. The powder that started as green, then morphed to blue, is now plain white. If you didn't know any better, you'd think that you were just sprinkling salt on your food.

Manny places platefuls of Brussels sprouts, horseradish, and chocolate chips on the workbench. "I'm curious," he says, "what the powder will do to food that already tastes good. Well, go ahead," he says, this time looking at Emily. "You're the inventor. You do the honors."

She sprinkles the powder onto all of the food. I pop a Brussels sprout into my mouth. **KERRRR-POW!**

A taste unlike anything I've ever experienced explodes onto my taste buds. I can't even describe it or compare it to any other food. It just tastes *fantastic!*

"This Brussels sprout is the best thing I've ever tasted," I say.

Manny picks up a small dab of horseradish.

Normally even a tiny taste can cause him to choke and tear up. Manny eats it, then grabs more.

"Amazing!" he says.

Finally, we grab handfuls of chocolate chips and each eat some. We all look at each other and smile.

"It's like all the goodness of chocolate, times a million!" Emily cries.

"This is fantastic!" I say, starting to feel better about my doubts with the Best Test. Having a great backup product always makes abandoning the first idea much easier to swallow—so to speak. "This could be a hit for Sure Things, Inc. After all, Emily is a Sure," I say, mostly to Manny.

"I agree," Manny says. I can see the wheels spinning in his brain just from the expression on his face. "But we need to field test it with a bigger sample group before we can think about making it one of our products."

That's when it hits me.

"I've got it!" I announce. "What if we tested

it on the pickiest eaters in the world—middle school kids?!"

"You mean, see if we can make even cafeteria food taste good?" asks Emily.

"We should try it with food that's even more disgusting," I say. "What if Dad cooks a special dinner as a fund-raiser for the inventors club? Principal Gilamon is always encouraging parents to get more involved in school activities. We can invite everyone in the school to try out our new product. Dad will think we're celebrating his great cooking. But we'll make sure to sprinkle a little powder on all the food before the kids eat it—without him knowing of course. If the kids like the food, he'll feel great, and we'll know that powder works on anything!"

"Let's do it!" says Manny, returning to his desk to start working on a marketing plan for Emily's powder, though I see him check the auction website in a new tab.

At dinner that night, Dad serves up something he calls beet surprise.

"What's the surprise?" Emily asks.

"The surprise," Dad says, "is that the beets are stuffed with more beets!"

"Great," Emily says. Then as Dad heads back to the kitchen, she leans over and whispers to me, "I *hate* beets!"

Before Dad returns, Emily sprinkles a little of her powder on each of our servings.

"Well, dig in!" says Dad, joining us at the table.

I cut into my beet, discover the beet stuffing, and munch on a forkful.

KERRRR-POW!

"Wow, this is really delicious," I say. And, thanks to Emily's powder, I'm telling the truth.

"So, Dad, I had an idea about how you could get more people to sample your cooking," I say.

"I'm all ears," Dad says. "Which reminds me. I should pick up some corn—I have a corn and blue cheese soup recipe that I've been dying to try out."

"Mmhmm. So anyway, we're thinking of holding a fund-raiser for the inventors club. How would you like to come out and cook

dinner for everyone?" I ask. "You plan the menu. You cook the food. And Emily, Manny, and I will help serve."

"FANTASTIC!" Dad says. "I'll start planning the menu tonight!"

As I help Dad clean up after dinner, I notice that my spinach plants are thriving. They are twice as big as when I bought them. Hmmm, maybe I really am good at growing spinach. But that doesn't mean that I'm not good at inventing. My enthusiasm for the Best Test is fading the more I think about it.

Manny advertises the fund-raiser dinner so much, we have enough kids to fill the entire cafeteria on the evening of the event! I'm really excited to try Emily's product out on the pickiest eaters.

Dad arrives after school and Emily walks over from the high school. He made all of the food at home because the kitchen can only be used by cafeteria staff. Apparently they're really picky about that. Who knew?

"Can you grab that?" he asks, pointing to a large cooler in the back of his car.

I carry the cooler, Manny takes a tray of food, and Emily picks up a case of juice. We bring everything into the cafeteria.

As each delicacy is unwrapped, Emily, Manny, and I take it and place it out where the kids can help themselves—but not before sprinkling each dish with some of Emily's powder first!

"This is a great idea, Billy!" Samantha says when she spots us setting up the buffet. "You're so smart! I bet your dad is amazing! I mean, he has to be. He's *your dad!*"

Manny looks at me and rolls his eyes. I can tell what he's thinking. *You weren't kidding about the fan club!*

As the rest of the kids line up, Principal Gilamon comes out! I didn't know he would be at the fund-raiser. My last school assembly went so terribly . . . what if this fund-raiser heads in the same direction? His presence just adds to the pressure.

Principal Gilamon addresses the people in the cafeteria.

"Students, we have a very special treat for you this evening," he begins. "The dinner at this fund-raiser has been prepared by seventh grader Billy Sure's father, who is a WORLD-CLASS COOK!"

World-class cook? It takes every ounce of restraint on my part not to shoot Emily a glance or simply crack up.

"Mr. Sure, what have you prepared for us today?" asks Principal Gilamon.

"Thank you, Principal Gilamon, for this great honor and opportunity," says Dad. "On the menu today are: tuna and kale casserole, liverwurst stuffed with sausage, lima bean deluxe, a fish and pickle salad, and burgers using artichokes as buns instead of bread. And for dessert . . . chocolate-covered spinach!"

Cries of "Yuck!" "Gross!" and "I want a hot dog!" fill the cafeteria.

"Now, please," Principal Gilamon say, raising his hands to quiet the room. "Let's give Mr. Sure's cooking a chance, shall we?"

One by one, the kids reluctantly fill their plates. From the expressions on their faces, you'd think they were condemned prisoners on their way to eating their last meals.

But then, as kids sample the various concoctions, their complaints start to change to cries of amazement.

"Wow! This is the best thing I've ever tasted!"

"I thought I hated lima beans, but these are as sweet as candy!"

"My mom is a terrible cook. Can you come to my house tonight, Mr. Sure?"

I smile and breathe a huge sigh of relief. Emily's powder really does work on everything! I glance over at Dad standing in the kitchen with his arms folded across his chest and a huge smile on his face.

This has got to make him feel great. And that's the best part of all.

Later that night, Emily, Manny, and I meet up at the office. "I don't know, Billy, we may have to make room at Sure Things, Inc. for another partner," Manny says.

I think the time has come for me to tell Manny about my concerns for the Best Test. Everyone is in a good mood and we obviously have a great new product to market.

"So, Manny, I've been thinking," I begin.

"Uh-oh . . . that could mean trouble," Manny says.

"The fact that I can be good at inventing *and* growing spinach makes me think that the Best Test might actually limit people," I explain. "And Emily is good at pointing out people's flaws *and* also at being an inventor. I'd hate to have our invention narrow or limit people's focus, especially kids, who have the whole world open to them. Now, I know after what happened with the Cat-Dog Translator, the idea of scrapping another invention is not–"

"Scrap it," says Manny. "Emily's powder is without a doubt our Next Big Thing. It's the product that will get us out of our financial hole. Let's get moving on it ASAP."

Emily screams and jumps up and down with joy.

"EMILY'S FOOD POWDER is going to be the biggest Next Big Thing!" she cries.

"Uh . . . no. Not really," says Manny.

"What do you mean?" asks Emily. She looks like she might shoot lasers out of her eyes at Manny. Leave it to Emily to switch moods so quickly.

Manny backs away from Emily. He knows that look. "I just mean that the name could use a little work. Let's keep it simple and direct. Sure Things, Inc.'s Next Big Thing is the GROSS-TO-GOOD POWDER. What do you think?"

"I like it," I say, feeling relieved that Manny was able to let go of the Best Test so easily. "Emily?"

She shrugs. "Whatever. If you're not calling it Emily's Food Powder, then I don't care what you call it. I'm outta here. See ya later."

Manny turns to his desk. "I'm jumping on

the rollout strategy for the Gross-to-Good Powder."

"Great," I say. "I'm exhausted. I'm heading home. See ya tomorrow. And Manny . . . thanks."

"Uh-huh," he says. He's already so lost in product design ideas and marketing schedules, I don't even see him online auctioning.

Right before bed, Mom e-mails me. She got the Best Test prototype in the mail and wants me to video chat with her as she tries it out. I grab Emily so we can video chat with Mom together.

Ping bong bing! Mom's call blares through my speakers. I hit accept, and she appears on-screen.

"It's so great to see you both!" Mom says.

"Miss you, Mom," says Emily.

"Me too," I add. "Are you ready for the test?"

Mom nods. I give her the lock code I programmed on the suitcase just in case it fell into the wrong hands, and out the Best Test comes! She places it on her head. Immediately, the Best Test flashes and rings, then prints out the result.

"Well, this is weird," says Mom, holding the piece of paper to her webcam so Emily and I can read.

I look at the paper.

Carol Sure is best at keeping secrets.

"Keeping secrets?" Mom says. "Now that's a laugh! In my book club, everyone knows me as the person who spoils the ending! I'm sorry, honey, but maybe you should work on another invention."

"As a matter of fact," I say. "We have already scrapped the Best Test. After all, it said that Dad was best at cooking."

Mom laughs.

"And Emily is responsible for our Next Big Thing—the Gross-to-Good Powder. Whatever you sprinkle it on tastes great—even Dad's concoctions."

"I slipped some into the saltshaker," Emily admits, "so now Dad's meals tastes great, and we don't ever have to hurt his feelings."

"You should see us ask for seconds, Mom!" I say. "Even Philo! Although he's never been the world's pickiest eater."

"Time to sign off, guys," Mom says. "It's so good to see your faces. I love you both and miss you."

"Love you, Mom," says Emily.

"Good night, Mom," I say. "I love you too."

The screen goes blank and I remember just how much I miss her. And as much as I try to ignore the Best Test's result . . . I can't help but wonder about what it said Mom was best at.

If she's best at keeping secrets, what secret is she keeping from me?

DATE	ISSUED TO
1951	Matt Vezza
1977	Jada Reese
1696	Luis Ramirez

TIME MACHINES MAY BE HARD TO INVENT, BUT TIME TRAVEL STORIES AREN'T! GO BACK IN TIME ON HILARIOUS ADVENTURES WITH THE STUDENTS OF SANDS MIDDLE SCHOOL IN

EBOOK EDITIONS ALSO AVAILABLE

PUBLISHED BY SIMON SPOTLIGHT

SIMONANDSCHUSTER.COM/KIDS

Want more Billy Sure?
Sure you do!
Don't miss these other great
Billy Sure, Kid Entrepreneur titles!

LUKE SHARPE is not a millionaire, but he has been trying to invent a machine that can teleport people anywhere in the world since he was eight years old. He has so far been unsuccessful but he has vowed never to give up. When he isn't working, Luke enjoys Hawaiian pizza and skateboarding. He lives near Chicago with his wife and son (named Billy, of course), their gecko, Eddie, and their aquarium full of exotic fish.

GRAHAM ROSS has grand plans for world domination through his illustrated inventions. Right now he's having a "ball" hanging out with Billy Sure, the next sure thing! Graham lives in a little log home in the woods with his inventive family, just outside of Merrickville, Canada.

APR 2018